THE BOOK OF **JONAH**

THE **BOOK** OF

JONAH

a novel

JOSHUA MAX FELDMAN

Dear Kenan —

Thanks so much for coming out
to the reading. Hope you enjoy
it — and looking forward to
good times ahead —

Jo Feld
2/16/15

HENRY HOLT AND COMPANY   NEW YORK

Henry Holt and Company, LLC
Publishers since 1866
175 Fifth Avenue
New York, New York 10010
www.henryholt.com

Henry Holt® and ® are registered trademarks of
Henry Holt and Company, LLC.

"To Live and Die in L.A," words and music by Quincy Jones III, Val Young and Tupac Shakur; Copyright © 1996 by DEEP TECHNOLOGY MUSIC, MUSIC OF WINDSWEPT, UNIVERSAL MUSIC CORP., SONGS OF UNIVERSAL, INC. and VAL YOUNG PUBLISHING; All Rights for DEEP TECHNOLOGY MUSIC and MUSIC OF WINDSWEPT administered by BUG MUSIC INC., A BMG CHRYSALIS COMPANY; all rights reserved. Used by permission. Reprinted by permission of Hal Leonard Corporation.

"There's a certain slant of light" reprinted by permission of the publishers and the Trustees of Amherst College from THE POEMS OF EMILY DICKINSON: VARIORUM EDITION, edited by Ralph W. Franklin, Cambridge, Mass.; The Belknap Press of Harvard University Press, Copyright © 1998 by the President and Fellows of Harvard College. Copyright © 1951, 1955, 1979, 1983 by the President and Fellows of Harvard College.

Library of Congress Cataloging-in-Publication Data
Feldman, Joshua Max.
    The book of Jonah : a novel / Joshua Max Feldman.—First edition.
    pages   cm
    ISBN 978-0-8050-9776-4 (hardcover)—ISBN 978-0-8050-9777-1 (electronic book)
    1. Jewish lawyers—Fiction. 2. Life change events—Fiction. 3. New York (N.Y.)—Fiction. 4. Psychological fiction. I. Title.

PS3606.E3865B66 2014
813'.6—dc23   2013014308

Henry Holt books are available for special promotions and premiums. For details contact: Director, Special Markets.

First Edition 2014

Designed by Kelly S. Too

Printed in the United States of America
10 9 8 7 6 5 4 3 2 1

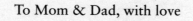
To Mom & Dad, with love

The last of the road sank into the heat shimmer of the horizon behind—and Jonah saw in every direction the unbounded desert—the scrub clinging to its face giving its tracts the look of a vast, sealike rolling. And he lay down with his back on the scorched sand and with his face toward the sun, relentless and colorless—and he unfurled for the Lord his sorrow.

JONAH 5:1

THE BOOK OF **JONAH**

I. NEW YORK
(FORTY DAYS AND FORTY NIGHTS EARLIER)

PROLOGUE. THE SMIDGE

Jonah knew the 59th Street subway station well enough that he did not have to look up from his iPhone as he made his way among its corridors and commuters to the track. He felt lucky as he came down the stairs to the platform to see a train just pulling in—he boarded without breaking his stride, took a seat by the door of the nearly empty car, went on typing. A crowd of people flooded in at the next station, but Jonah felt he'd had a long enough day that he need not give up his seat. But then an older woman—frumpy, blue-haired, with a grandmotherly sweet face and a tiny bell of a nose—ended up standing directly before him, and Jonah decided to do the right thing and he stood.

He was not on the train long, but when he got off he saw that many of those moving past him on the platform were soaking wet: hair matted to foreheads, clothes translucent and sagging. They all bore it well, though, Jonah thought—stoically marched ahead with mouths fixed, eyes straight, as though they got drenched during every evening commute. Then, as he came to the stairwell leading up to the street, he found that a group of twenty, thirty people was standing semicircled around the bottom, not continuing out. Jonah advanced a few steps. Rain cascaded down onto the concrete stairs in an unbroken sheet, making the light shining into the station pale and misty, as if they were all gathered behind a waterfall. Those in the group shrugged to one another at their predicament—tapped away on their smartphones or just stared placidly at the rain, seemingly admiring this temporary transformation of the world outside. Some, having stood there for a few moments, turned up their collars or held out their umbrellas and flung themselves up the steps with a sort of reckless bravery. Those coming into the station—umbrellas bent, hair dripping—looked puzzled at the gathering below, as though finding a crowd of people in the subway unmoving, unshoving—even by and large content to be there—made their surroundings somehow unrecognizable.

Jonah had been running late when he'd left his office, but he knew QUEST events were always well attended; his absence from tonight's cocktail party for another ten or so minutes wouldn't make much difference. He had time, in another words, to stand there and wait out the rain, too—and he found he was glad for this momentary interruption of his day. He had lived in New York for almost a decade now, and was gratified to find, once again, that it could still surprise him.

Jonah Daniel Jacobstein was thirty-two; a lawyer; ambitious, unmarried and dating; never without his iPhone. For all these reasons, his concerns tended to be immediate, tangible, billable. But every now and then such moods of appreciation would wash over him. He would glance out the window of the Q train as it crossed over the Manhattan Bridge and would take in the Chrysler Building, the Empire State Building, the whole of the skyline over the river; he would climb into a taxi on a Friday night with crisp bills from the ATM in his pocket and Sylvia (or Zoey) to meet; he would be drunk at 4:00 A.M. with a great slice of grease-dripping pizza in his hand; and he would count himself incredibly lucky—as he did now, watching the rain in the subway station—to be who he was, when he was, where he was.

But these moods never lasted long, of course, and after a moment he checked his phone again—this having become an almost autonomic response in him, on the order of blinking. He'd gotten a dozen new emails since he'd boarded the train. That afternoon, a case he had spent the better part of a year working on had come to a settlement favorable to his clients. He was pleased to see in his inbox several congratu-latory messages from colleagues—even a few from partners.

He dropped his hand back to his side and saw that a very large Hasidic Jew had appeared beside him: pink-faced, jowly, in black hat, black coat, forelocks dangling gently at his ears, his beard jet-black, wiry and unkempt. The man was only a little older than Jonah, though he was much bigger—an enormous stomach protruding directly out-ward from above his waist. And he stared with peculiar scrutiny at the rain, as though he could recognize some subtle meaning in its drops.

Normally, Jonah was an avid follower of the New York conven-tion of never under any circumstances striking up a conversation on the subway with a stranger. But he was feeling cheerful—and there appeared to have been some temporary reordering of New York con-ventions, anyway. And, too, Jonah, whose own Judaism was charac-terized by deep ambivalence, had always had a certain curiosity regarding those Jews whose Judaism seemed characterized by life-consuming certainty. Recognizing this as one of his few opportunities to talk with such a member of his (ostensible, theoretical) brethren, he turned to the Hasid and said, "Don't you have a number to call when this happens?"

In response, the Hasid pulled the sides of his fleshy face into a grin—sly, knowing—exposing yellowed teeth. He said, "You think I'd be on the train if I could make the rain stop?" Jonah chuckled. "You're on your way to some business meeting, my friend?"

"No, my day's over. I'm just going to, an event . . ." He found he was reluctant to call the cocktail party a charity event, though QUEST was indisputably a charity; describing it that way, however, struck him as somehow disingenuous. But the Hasid gave him a look of being greatly impressed by his answer.

"I could see you were a man of the world. Where would we be without such people?" His voice was rich-toned, Russian-accented, and a little high-pitched, in a decidedly wry sort of way. "You have a business card, my friend?"

This request surprised Jonah, but he didn't see any harm in it—he reached into his jacket pocket and handed the Hasid one of his cards.

"You're Jewish, my friend!" the Hasid said, still more impressed. He studied the card carefully, as if he was taking note of each line, each digit in each of the three phone numbers.

"Well, I was raised Jewish," Jonah answered.

"And you study Torah, my friend?" the Hasid asked, now returning the card. "Do you keep the Sabbath?"

"I feel guilty on Yom Kippur."

The Hasid's grin broadened. "And you know, of course, the story of your namesake, Jonah, son of Amittai?"

Jonah's knowledge of such things had been halfheartedly acquired in the first place, was half remembered at best. "There was a whale . . ." he ventured.

"Oh, my friend, there is much more than the whale!" The Hasid had now moved his massive frame a little closer toward Jonah, whose back was already up against the side of a MetroCard machine. "Jonah was a man of the world, too, just like you. Going about his business, making deals. Then one day *HaShem* came to him and said, 'Jonah, go to the corrupt city of Nineveh and tell them that while they have gold, finery, vast armies, only their body is clothed, but their soul is naked.'" Here the Hasid winked; Jonah nodded uncertainly, not quite sure what to make of this. "But Jonah had other ideas," the Hasid went on. "He tried to flee from the sight of the Lord. And what do you think happened? Storms, whales, disaster.

"*HaShem* sees everything," the Hasid continued, waving a playful finger beneath Jonah's nose. "We think we can hide, but in the end there's no escaping." He inclined his thick-bottomed chin up toward the stairs, where the rain was tapering only slightly. "Look what happens when the Lord sends even a little rain. Everyone runs underground, none can tell his right hand from his left. Won't it be so much more on the Day of Judgment, when calamity rains down from afar?" Again, Jonah could only nod, not sure with how much sincerity the still-grinning Hasid was asking. "One day it's all a big party. Then the angels knock on Lot's door. What will you tell them? Remember, not everyone gets a seat on the ark. America is naked, my friend, as naked as Nineveh. Cell phones, computers, spaceships, yadda yadda yadda. The body is clothed, but the soul is naked."

Jonah believed he was learning all over again why you were supposed to avoid entering into these conversations. "Well, it's all very interesting," he said. "In any case . . ."

This social cue toward ending the encounter was unnoticed or ignored. "You can't hide on the subway from the Lord's outstretched hand," the Hasid went on, "any more than Jonah could hide on the seas. Wouldn't you rather be counted among the righteous when the arrogant are washed away?"

"I don't think the arrogant are going anywhere."

"*Im yirtse HaShem,* we will live to see their destruction!" the Hasid cried.

It was all made the more disconcerting by the persistence of the wry grin on the Hasid's face. Though the rain was still falling heavily, Jonah edged his way around the MetroCard machine toward the stairs. But the Hasid leaned his head and large stomach even closer to Jonah—his breath unpleasantly musty. "Remember, my friend, the Lord seeks out what has gone by. Nineveh, the flood, Sodom and Gomorrah. Don't you know history is full of 9/11s?"

With this, Jonah's patience, which varied in length but not in the consistency of the irritability to which it gave way, was exhausted. Implications that he was damned he could tolerate—because who could take that seriously?—but moralizing about 9/11 was a different story. He had been in the city that day: And no, he had not lost anyone close to him, had not been in any immediate danger—but he felt he had experienced enough of it that he shouldn't have to endure hearing it characterized as some sort of divine punishment. "If you really think God had anything to do with 9/11, you're as ignorant as the people who did it."

The Hasid looked deeply saddened, and shook his head gravely. "Oh, my friend, I'm afraid you've misunderstood everything. It's my fault. I didn't go to Harvard College."

"Neither did I."

"*Nu,* you think it matters to *HaShem* what you think is ignorant?"

And though the Hasid capped the question with a final and more definitive wink—as though the whole conversation were merely a shared joke between them—Jonah decided he had heard enough and walked over to the stairs and mounted them two at a time. "Your bar mitzvah won't save you, my friend!" the Hasid cried—and maybe even guffawed as he said it.

The rain continued to fall steadily, quickly began soaking Jonah's hair, the shoulders of his suit jacket. He saw a few people huddled beneath the overhang in front of a discount shoe store—he ran over and pressed himself against the windows. Jonah didn't think anyone knew what mattered to *HaShem*—or whatever you wanted to call it—but he felt he understood the Hasid's point perfectly: You drew a circle around yourself, and everyone inside the circle was righteous and everyone outside it was not. There wasn't much more to the Hasid's philosophy—such as it was—than that.

He found himself standing beside a scruffy-looking black man—lanky, in a sweat-stained Yankees cap and cargo shorts, with large headphones over his ears, smoking the fingernail-sized remnants of a joint. He was rapping along with the music he was listening to: "Everybody got they own thang—currency chasin'! Worldwide through th'hard time—worryin' faces! Shed tears bury niggas close to the heart, was a friend now a ghost in the dark," the man chanted rhythmlessly, raspingly, then took a hit. Jonah knew he'd heard the song many times, though he couldn't immediately identify it. And it occurred to him how much more comfortable he was standing here beside this man than he was with the Hasid. Then Jonah remembered.

"Tupac," he said aloud.

The man with the headphones turned and looked at him, glanced up and down at his suit suspiciously—and then laughed huskily, smoke pouring from his mouth. "Tupac!" the man cried. "He ain't dead!"

"He ain't dead," Jonah agreed.

This encounter, Jonah felt, was a better answer—a better retort—than any he might have given to the Hasid. Who could ever say who was righteous, and who was not; who was saved, and who was damned? Staying open to the world and its inhabitants—living life—having fun—that was what mattered. If he had a circle, Jonah thought pridefully, this was the compass with which he would draw it.

———

After a few minutes the storm had diminished to the stray drop here and there, and Jonah began walking the last blocks to the QUEST cocktail party. As he made his way down the damp sidewalks of Greenwich Village into SoHo, wet and wary people emerged from doorways and bars, casting mistrustful eyes skyward. At a crosswalk he had to leap—phone clutched tightly—over a massive puddle at a clogged storm drain. Then, going a few blocks farther south, he reached the venue: the unelaborately named 555 Thompson Street, a blue-tinted sign mounted behind glass on the door confirming that this was indeed the location of the 4th Annual QUEST for New York Schools Cocktail Event and Silent Auction.

As he restraightened his tie, neatened his hair by way of running his fingers through it, he tried to recall precisely what QUEST stood for; something like Quantitative Educational Skills and Tools was about right. The organization was a nonprofit started by a dazzlingly charismatic Harvard MBA named Aaron Seyler, who did quantitative analysis consulting on Wall Street. As the narrative on the QUEST website had it, Aaron had decided he wanted to do more with his life than improve annual returns by quarter points: He wanted to make a lasting contribution to the city where he'd become a success (though having met Aaron and seen him schmooze, Jonah suspected he'd have been a success even in a city where they still used shells and beads for currency). The idea of QUEST was to apply the quantitative tools of finance to improving what were called educational outcomes: graduation rates, test scores, college matriculation, and so forth. Aaron's vision, as he was wont to explain, was to harness the energy and insight that daily went into generating billions of dollars for banks and hedge funds toward the betterment of New York City's public schools.

Which was all well and good as far as Jonah—now pushing open the door to 555 Thompson—was concerned. He had been raised in a terrifically liberal household and town—and though his politics had been moderated by exposure to the non-terrifically liberal world outside of Roxwood, Massachusetts (and lately by necessity from working for the sort of megalithic corporations he had been brought up to despise), his politics remained essentially liberal in character. He had yet to hear an argument that made him doubt you should do all you could for the

underserved and underprivileged. More money for schools? That
sounded good to him. But he was not much of a joiner—not really one
for causes, groups, committees. His politics were manifested mainly
in voting Democratic, reading some Paul Krugman, and avoiding
racial/sexual invective. In fact, it was unlikely he would have attended
the QUEST event at all, except Philip Orengo, a friend from law
school, was on the board, and Jonah hadn't seen him in a while; and
he had gotten out of work relatively early; and Sylvia was out of
town and Zoey was with her (nominal) boyfriend; and, not least,
there would be an open bar. All that plus successfully completing a
major case had seemed to him a good reason to have a few drinks. Yet
though he understood it was this combination of convenience and
circumstance that had led him to buy the seventy-five-dollar ticket—as
he emerged from an entry corridor into the venue proper—it still struck
Jonah that his attendance proved some implicit point in his argument
with the Hasid.

The space was massive, square, brick-walled, with mod-industrial
stylings: exposed ducts ran along the three-story ceiling, a catwalk
was suspended above all four sides of a central floor area, where people
mingled and later might dance. The walls were hung with gold-red
bunting and drapery, which made a nice complement to the red brick-
work and the black of the catwalk (and the fact that Jonah recognized
this color coordination made him realize just how much time he was
spending with fashion-conscious young women, between seeing his girlfriend and his not-his-girlfriend). A bar stretched the length of one wall,
and a stage toward the back was set up with a microphone flanked by
placards displaying the QUEST insignia: the dollar-bill eye pyramid,
with a sort of archetypal schoolhouse in its pupil. The space was
nearly filled, as Jonah had guessed it would be. It was a large though
not unpleasantly packed-in crowd of men and women, mostly Jonah's
age or thereabouts—professionals, for the most part, dressed in the
suits and skirts they'd worn to work. As Jonah made his way inward,
he passed several quite attractive young women; everyone had drinks
in their hands, and something in a Cuban jazz mode played as background to the great indistinguishable mix of genial or perfunctory

or flirty conversation. In short—the entire scene looked like a lot of fun.

And in hypothetical continuation of the dispute with the Hasid, Jonah acknowledged to himself the frivolity of all this—and by way of riposte, thought of all the times in which life made frivolity impossible, how frivolity was a sort of collective decision by those engaged in it, how often life conspired against it: So why not drink, flirt, and make merry? There were meetings in the morning, there were breakups down the road, everyone in this room would attend their fair share of funerals. He was not really a fatalist, but his training and experience as a lawyer had taught him that you didn't have to believe in an argument for it to be effective—and so he felt justified in starting his evening of charity by grabbing a beer.

Ten minutes later, this beer was three-quarters gone and he was strolling the path of the catwalk. The silent auction had been set up along its perimeter: Tables were arrayed with paraphernalia representing the various items up for bid—a cluster of La Mer skin-care products for the spa package; a monogrammed plate for dinner with Aaron at Minetta Tavern; a cheese basket for a private tour of the Murray's cheese cave. He was considering making a bid on an aromatherapy massage for Sylvia when he noticed Seth Davis, an acquaintance from law school, standing on the opposite side of the catwalk. Because of Philip Orengo's role in the group, Jonah often saw members of his law school class at QUEST events. Jonah had always liked Seth, though they'd never been friends, exactly. Seth had once explained his decision to get his dual JD/MBA and go into finance rather than law by saying, "If I'm going to spend my twenties working hundred-hour weeks, I'd rather get really rich than a little rich." The financial crisis had probably bent the curve of this accumulation—but Jonah had a feeling Seth was doing just fine.

"Jacobstein!" Seth called when he saw him. He was standing with a group of other men, all in suits like Jonah, all holding beers. Jonah went over and joined them. Introductions were made, hands were shaken. Seth's group was made up of his coworkers at the financial-services firm where he worked and their friends in the industry. (Finance people tended to find one another at parties, Jonah had learned from almost a year of dating Sylvia.) The jocular rowdiness of the conversation suggested that all these men were several drinks ahead of him. An argument was going on over a five-hundred-dollar bid for a Derek Jeter–signed baseball.

"You could get that ball for a hundred fifty bucks on eBay," someone was saying to the man who'd made the five-hundred-dollar bid.

"But why would I want to give a hundred fifty dollars to some fat guy in his underwear, living in his mother's basement?" the bidder replied, and the others laughed.

"You guys aren't factoring in the tax deduction," said another man—and he dramatically wrote a bid for six hundred dollars, to a chorus of "Oh!"'s from the others.

"Yeah, but your deduction is based on what some GED meathead at the IRS decides the ball is worth, right, Jacobstein?" Seth asked Jonah.

"Hey, if you want my counsel, you have to pay my retainer," Jonah replied, and the others laughed again. He didn't usually engage in greedy-lawyer humor—one tended to hear a great deal of it as a lawyer—but he'd found it always played well with the financial crowd.

"Can you even afford six hundred dollars?" someone demanded of the man who'd made the most recent bid. "I saw the ring you bought for Melissa, I know you're overleveraged."

"First of all, that's a CZ," he replied, to more laughter. "Second of all, as long as no one starts buying real estate in the Las Vegas exurbs, my bonus this year will provide all the liquidity I need."

"I'm sure that's a comfort to all the people in Vegas underwater on their mortgages," one of them joked.

"Hey, if you bought a house in the Vegas exurbs in 2005, you deserve to be underwater on your mortgage for at least another decade," Seth said.

They all laughed some more. Yes, they were assholes, Jonah thought, but they seemed to know it, which somehow made it more forgivable. Besides, he suspected there was something to the collective American superstition—enduring despite the events of recent years—that the economy couldn't function without assholes.

At this point, the group was joined by a smiling, gangly man, with flushed cheeks and a long, ovoid face, a puff of disordered blond hair. His name was Patrick Hooper—Jonah had met him through Sylvia— and he was often at events such as this. Some of the others in the group evidently knew him, too, as they exchanged (somewhat) surreptitious eye rolls when he joined them. He looked at the bid list for the baseball and then wrote in a bid of five thousand dollars. He looked up from the page, laughing delightedly.

"The funny part is I don't even like baseball," Patrick said.

"That is funny," Seth muttered.

Patrick Hooper was, by all reports, a financial genius. According to Sylvia, during the financial-products boom years he had devised a series of commodity trades for Goldman of indisputable profitability and at least theoretical legality. Patrick had earned enough from this to retire by the time he was thirty—which he had—*The Wall Street Journal* marking the occasion with the headline A WALL STREET WUNDERKIND TAKES A BOW. Even now, Goldman kept him on retainer, presumably on the chance that he might interrupt a marathon session of World of Warcraft to concoct some new infallible profit-making financial device. What made all the wunderkind talk hard for Jonah to take seriously, though, was the fact that Patrick was among the most socially inept people he had ever met. He wasn't a bad guy, really; he just had an astonishing talent for annoyance. The massive overbid on the baseball—ruining the entire fun of it—was, sadly, typical: Patrick seemed possessed by the very simple and very dumb idea that he could invest his way out of his social awkwardness—discover some trade of assets that would return him genuine affection, or at least popularity. Hence the parties he regularly threw at his massive Tribeca loft; the invitations he sprayed wildly to just-opened restaurants and to exclusive-ish clubs; the outsize donations to next-gen charities like QUEST. And, predictably, the more lavish and transparent these efforts were, the less success they met with.

"I'm impressed you guys came out tonight," Patrick observed. "Y'know, Aaron and I had dinner a couple nights ago," he continued, not knowing, or not wanting, to disguise his pride in this achievement. "We were talking about how important it is to get people to these events who don't actually care about charity." Patrick laughed again, though, again, no one else did.

"Well, if I knew you were coming . . ." one of them said.

"It's really ironic, though," Patrick went on. "Finance is supposed to be so evil, but Goldman does more in terms of corporate citizenship than an organization like this could ever dream of. Even though I retired several years ago, I'm still active in their—"

"Anyway," Seth interrupted, making a show of turning his shoulders away from Patrick. "They're probably going to close the open bar in a few minutes." He turned to Jonah. "You want to come?"

Jonah knew he ought not glance over to see Patrick staring into Seth's shoulder with guileless hope of being invited, too. But he did; and somehow the idea of ditching Patrick struck him as counter to the entire spirit of QUEST—whatever that was supposed to be. "No, I'm gonna make a bid or something," Jonah answered, regretting it even as the words left his mouth.

Seth shrugged, almost sympathetically. "Suit yourself. . . ." And he and the others moved off toward the stairs.

"So, I didn't know you were involved with QUEST," Patrick said as they left.

On top of everything, Jonah's beer was now empty, which only seemed to confirm he'd made a mistake in remaining. "A friend of mine is on the board," he replied.

"Adrian? Jin? Kent? Abbey? Philip?"

It didn't exactly surprise Jonah that Patrick could recite the names of the entire QUEST board from memory; he'd probably been asking them to dinner for months. "Philip and I went to law school together," Jonah explained.

Patrick nodded, a pair of dips of his long head. "And Philip went to undergrad at Princeton with Aaron."

"That's how these things work," Jonah replied.

"So how are things with Sylvia?" Patrick now inquired a little too eagerly. "Things good with you guys?" And he then finished off the glass of champagne in his hand a little too gulpingly.

Of all the irritating aspects of Patrick's personality, this one was the hardest to reconcile with a belief that he was not really a bad guy:

Before Jonah met Sylvia, Patrick had been not-so-subtly courting her—and had never fully stopped courting her, despite the fact that he knew she and Jonah had been dating seriously for months. Granted, Patrick not-so-subtly courted every woman in finance he met; and, in more dispassionate moments, Jonah could even identify a certain integrity in Patrick's attempts to find a romantic partner with her own career and money, rather than just dating a platinum-blond Russian whose greatest aspiration in life was to be spoiled. But even so—how friendly could you be to someone openly hoping to steal your girlfriend?

"Things are great," Jonah lied. "Things are going great."

"We should all have dinner sometime," Patrick said. "She's a rock star, she should be working with my old team at Goldman. Definitely tell her to shoot me an email."

"I definitely will," Jonah lied again. It occurred to him that maybe Patrick deserved to be ditched. "Anyway, I should go downstairs and find Philip."

"I saw you in the West Village the other day," Patrick answered—apparently well accustomed to continuing conversations his interlocutors wanted to end.

"Oh, yeah?" Jonah said, glancing down from the catwalk, searching the crowd for the shaved black pate of Philip Orengo.

"You were in Corner Bistro with some girl."

Jonah's heart immediately launched into sharp, agitated thumping—each beat seeming to clang across his mind with the words, Think of a lie, think of a lie, think of a lie. Unfortunately, this mental activity did not bring him any closer to actually thinking of a lie, and the most he could manage was, "Uh, when?" Fixing on a lie was made still more difficult by the fact that he didn't know whether Patrick attached any significance to what he'd seen: whether he was just making conversation by whatever means necessary or, more ominously, whether he understood there was a connection between the girl he'd seen Jonah with and his own prospects with Sylvia. Who could tell how clueless or calculating Patrick was outside the world of currency derivatives and whateverthefuck?

"Maybe two weeks ago?" Patrick went on, twirling his empty, fingerprint-smudged champagne glass at the stem.

"Oh, yeah, right," Jonah said, as blithely as he could manage. "I was out with some work friends."

"The girl I saw you with was cute." Jonah was tearing through his brain, trying to remember if he'd been stupid (read: drunk) enough to have done any public canoodling that night. "Is she single?"

Was Zoey Rosen single—that, at least, he could answer honestly. "Sorry, man. She has a boyfriend."

Patrick threw back his head in a show of exaggerated disappointment. Then he asked, "Who's she dating? Somebody at your firm?" And again, was he asking because he knew he had Jonah on the hook, knew he was now in a position to get him to acquiesce to any number of dinners, trips to the Hamptons, nights at the club? Or was he—ironically more benignly—just hoping to move in on Zoey now, too? This was what Jonah got for indulging his liberalism.

But he got some sense of deliverance from Patrick's next comment: "Anyway, if they ever break up, give me her number." Still more deliverance came a moment later when Aaron Seyler—six foot four, corn-husk blond, former captain of the Princeton swim team, Rhodes Scholar, MBA, and the person Jonah would have judged most likely to solve (if any one person could solve) the education crisis, or the energy crisis, or whatever crisis caught his attention—stepped to the microphone on the stage. From the catwalk, Jonah could see the ripples of awareness of Aaron's presence spread across the room, as conversations ceased and people adjusted where they stood to get a better view of the stage. Not that Jonah blamed anyone: Aaron stood before the microphone with all the self-assurance and faith in collective approval of an actor who'd just won his third Oscar of the night. But Jonah didn't begrudge Aaron his poise, his charm, his magnetism—he admired it more than he was taken in by it, but he didn't begrudge it. He had the sense that if someone had to be Aaron Seyler, Aaron Seyler was the right man for the job.

"Don't worry, this won't take long," Aaron began. "I know you all have drinks to finish, and, frankly, so do I." This joke got more laughter than it deserved, but Aaron could have been reading selections from *The Tibetan Book of the Dead* and gotten a laugh. "First, I want to thank you for coming tonight. Your donations keep the lights on at

QUEST, and more important than money, I want to thank you for giving what's most precious of all, your time. I also want to direct your attention to the silent auction, which will close at eight, and I want to thank the organizations and individuals who contributed items. I should point out that this year we have two Mets season tickets up for bid, in case anyone is crazy enough to want them." (Laughter.) "I am pretty sure my bid of five dollars is still leading." (More laughter.) "So if anybody wants to buy my tickets for the first Mets game this year . . ." (Sustained laughter.)

At this point Aaron put his right hand in his pocket, moved his face a bit closer to the microphone—getting serious. "We try to have these drinks for the friends of QUEST every year. A lot of you have been with us from the beginning, back when we weren't getting grants and I was giving the spiel you probably all have memorized by now in my living room to small groups of you. We try to do this every year because it's good for the staff and the board and myself to relax and socialize with so many old friends. But we also do it because QUEST, at its heart, is still about those late-night bull sessions in Abbey or Adrian's kitchen, when all we had was an idea of how to fix New York City schools, and the faith that if we gave people a chance to do the right thing, they would.

"Now, our generation gets accused of apathy a lot. And as a member of the MTV generation old enough to have actually watched videos on MTV, I understand why. No, our generation by and large doesn't affiliate with religious institutions. We view politics with deep skepticism. We've seen the limits of what conventional charities can do. But that to me isn't apathy. That's realism. When our generation identifies a problem—and identifying problems is something I think we'd all agree our generation excels at—when we identify a problem in our government, in our society, in our schools, instinctively our first thought is not to turn to some pastor or politician or pundit. We turn to one another. We look to our friends. We go to a friend's kitchen, and we sit down, and we say to one another, How can we make renewable energy affordable? How can we drive social justice in this country? How can we fix New York City's schools and lift up New York City's students?

"Are we that arrogant? Yup. Are we that foolish? Maybe. But we're also that brave and hopeful and confident. And we are not—we are not—apathetic. Yes, we'll do it our way, yes, we'll do it a new way, our own way, but we'll do it. This is year five of QUEST. We're in dozens of schools, we'll double that number in three years, our success metrics are off the charts—whether you want to talk about attendance, exam performance—you name it, we've optimized it. And we did it with cocktail parties, we did it with white-box Chinese food, we did it by trusting each other and believing in each other and that is how we are going to keep on doing it. So please: Make a bid, buy a ticket to the gala this fall, be bold enough to bore your friends and colleagues with our story. And if we do all that, we will be the generation of New Yorkers that saves this generation of students. Have a great night, and thank you for coming." The applause from all corners of 555 Thompson was warm, sustained, heartfelt.

As Aaron's speech began, those on the catwalk had moved toward the railing to see, and in this realignment of bodies Jonah had managed to detach himself from Patrick and their deeply uncomfortable conversation. He'd spotted Philip almost directly below him, standing with other members of the QUEST board. During the speech Jonah noticed that Philip divided his attention between Aaron and the face and figure of a bare-shouldered brunette in a green dress, directly at his two o'clock. As Aaron entered his peroration, Jonah started down the catwalk steps to join Philip, and by the time the applause diminished and the mingling and music resumed, they were greeting each other with a back-pounding hug. "How goes the fight against corporate legal liability?" Philip asked in his lilting Kenyan accent.

"Better than the mayor's plan to turn all of Broadway into a giant bike lane," Jonah answered. Philip was an aide to the mayor, could frequently be seen ("as an advertisement of his honor's diverse administration," as Philip put it) standing back and to the left at press conferences. "Was that your idea?"

Both without drinks, they reflexively started moving toward the bar. "Your attendance tonight is a pleasant surprise," Philip told him. He'd been educated in British boarding schools, and as a consequence tended to speak in these grandiloquent, contractionless sentences.

"We finalized a settlement today, so I got to leave before midnight."

"Congratulations on both counts." As they made their way through the crowd, Philip stopped every so often to shake a hand. Watching him—dressed nattily in a powder-blue suit, smiling with consistent gladness into every face he recognized—Jonah could easily imagine Philip in the role he openly aspired to: mayor of the city. It wasn't impossible, either: He had the intelligence, the résumé, the politician's instinctive cunning (he always won when he and Jonah played chess); he networked relentlessly (though not as effortlessly as Aaron); and, as he often pointed out, there was now a Kenyan in the White House and a bachelor in the mayor's office. The political era redounded favorably on his prospects.

When they reached the bar, Philip ordered a vodka tonic, Jonah a Scotch. As they waited for their drinks, Philip eyed the same brunette in green whom he'd been all-but-ogling during Aaron's speech, now a few feet up the bar from them. "I have observed a strong correlation between QUEST donors and Pilates classes," Philip murmured.

"Quant analysis at work," Jonah laughed. "You going to ask her if she wants to do a quick abs session after this?"

"Unfortunately," Philip sighed melodramatically, "by rule I am no longer permitted to make such invitations. Aaron sent a rather strongly worded email regarding proper conduct at QUEST events. Evidently there is concern that certain members of the board do not display the appropriate motives in attending these gatherings."

"I wonder what that could refer to?" Jonah said.

Philip sighed again. "If I am not for my cock, who am I for?" As their drinks arrived, he added, "I may resign in protest."

"But then what about New York City's schools, right?" Jonah said, and Philip laughed.

This laughter was not surprising—but Jonah had not entirely been joking. He understood that Philip's membership in QUEST was mostly gamesmanship—part of a rivalry that went back to the days when Philip and Aaron were both charismatic freshmen on the same floor at Princeton. Yes, it helped Aaron to have a black mayoral aide on his board, but it also gave Philip access to all of Aaron's contacts; and he could always vent his frustration at being hierarchically beneath

Aaron in the organization by trying to sleep with as many of these contacts as he could (though it seemed Aaron had put a stop to that tactic within their "friendship"). But either as a lingering effect of his conversation with the Hasid, or because of Aaron's speech, or because of what Patrick had seen him doing—or from some combination of all the events across the entire evening—Jonah found he wanted some reassurance that there was more going on that night than an open bar and calculated networking. He took a sip of his Scotch and said to Philip, "Seriously, though. Don't you think QUEST makes those schools better?"

Philip gave him an amused, quizzical frown—and in his imitation of an American accent (which veered sharply toward the Texan), he repeated, "Seriously?"

This skepticism wasn't surprising, either. Seriousness had never figured prominently in their friendship. "Indulge me," Jonah said.

Philip tapped the tip of his broad, somehow regal nose, making a show of thinking. At this point Jonah realized he should not have sought reassurance as to the hopes of saving New York's schools from a man with a career in city politics. "When you consider this notion of applying the tactics of the financial industry to schools, you ought to remember what happened to the financial industry. More fundamentally, I would not rely too heavily on improved standardized test scores as an indicator of improved education. It would seem to me that filling in bubble sheets is a bit of a skill unto itself, maybe not so different from being good at Halo. That hasn't helped New York students much, either." He took a long sip of his drink, put the glass gently on the bar. "White liberal guilt is really all this is in aid of, I am afraid. White liberal guilt and another bullet point on Aaron's résumé. You want to see a school in need? Come to Africa." He shrugged nonchalantly. "But then perhaps I am compromised by my irritation at the founder's sudden bout of Puritanism. Do you, Counselor, believe QUEST does any real good?"

Jonah thought for a moment—and then held his forefinger and thumb apart as if he were presenting an invisible jelly bean. "A smidge," Jonah said. "Even if the tools are imperfect, even if the motives are, let's say, mixed—it's still more effort and attention than these schools usually get. It's better than nothing for your poor black future constituents in Harlem, who deserve something, even if they do have access to clean drinking water."

Philip smiled, and then let out with one of his great, sustained, diaphragm-supported laughs—his most distinctively Kenyan feature, Jonah felt, even beyond his accent. "I concede to the smidge," he declared. "It is a smidge more than we would do otherwise, it is a smidge more than not doing anything at all."

"It's the twenty-five percent tip for the cab driver," said Jonah. "It's holding the door of the elevator for someone crossing the lobby."

"It is helping an elderly lady get her bags from the overhead compartment," said Philip.

They toasted to the smidge. It was an idea coated in irony, of course—but it had a core of comfort, too. As they lowered their glasses, Philip asked, "And where is the lovely Sylvia Quinn this evening?"

"Chicago," he answered. "Work."

"Anything interesting?"

"Interesting enough that she can't tell me anything about it."

"She is an impressive woman," Philip said. "You are a lucky man."

Jonah sighed uneasily. "Patrick Hooper saw me and Zoey out the other night," he told him. He added, "Not doing anything, I don't think, just—out."

Philip gave him a sad sort of smile. "That is still going on, then?"

"The worst part is I told Sylvia I'd move in with her," he said, feeling guiltier than usual at verbalizing this.

"So much for the smidge."

Jonah made small half-turns of his glass on the bar, watched the liquid slosh in tiny waves. These moods came over him, too—guilty, remorseful—but he'd learned that unfortunately, like their antipodes, they never lasted long, eventually gave way to lust, or boredom, or whatever name he might use for the inexplicable attraction that drew him to Zoey—over and over and over. "I guess I did sort of lose my bearings," he confessed.

Philip gave a noncommittal shrug. Jonah was sure Philip thought what any reasonable person would think: that he should end it with one or the other. But along with its lack of seriousness, their friendship did not admit the giving of sincere personal advice, either. It was a limit Jonah had noticed in nearly all his male friendships (maybe it was as much a foundation as a limit). So whatever Philip actually thought, all he said was, "Well, these things do happen."

Aaron Seyler was working the crowd not far away—drawing in all the nearby attention rather in the manner of water flowing to a drain. The brunette Philip had been eyeing was herself now making moon eyes at Aaron. He accepted all the adoration with an affability that approached grace. "Was he always like this?" Jonah asked.

Philip watched Aaron for another moment, weighing, Jonah guessed, all manner of respective advantages and deficiencies in a man who could quite possibly be his rival one day for the Democratic nomination for mayor of New York. Finally he said, "Aaron sees himself as entirely smidge. He makes no distinction. He believes in QUEST, he believes QUEST is improving schools, he believes he is the person best suited to lead such an organization, or any organization, for that matter. In brief, he believes in something. Namely, in Aaron Seyler, which is what makes him so extraordinary, even in this room of rather extraordinary people."

Jonah watched as Aaron went on smiling and accepting congratulations and paying earnest attention to everyone and evidently doing as much—more—than anyone could ask to elevate the underserved and underprivileged. But it occurred to Jonah: If Aaron cared so much about New York City students—if any of them did—why weren't they teachers? "He believes his own bullshit," Jonah said. And somehow it was at this moment that he decided, with full conviction, that he would end things with Zoey. It was, he concluded, the right thing to do.

He sustained this conviction through the rest of the cocktail party, and through the point on his cab ride home when he sent Zoey a text message: "Lunch tomorrow?" Then he immediately felt the uneasiness and preemptive regret that always accompanied his decisions to end relationships with women—but he told himself this was just the inertia and selfishness talking.

Zoey didn't respond for more than an hour, which wasn't surprising, since she'd told him she was spending the evening with Evan, her (quasi-) boyfriend. By the time his phone finally chimed with her reply, he was undressing in his bedroom. "yes but only lunch. Z = busy bee tomorrow."

Jonah smiled and wrote, "Busy tonight?" because the fact that she was texting meant maybe that Evan had left, and with Sylvia in Chicago, they— He resummoned the guilt—he erased the message. In its place, he wrote, "Cool, only lunch. Meet @ 1 @ yr office?"

It was several minutes before the reply came: "i'm too fat for lunchtime quickies now??" Then, in another minute: "i know, i know. don't judge. i have the spoon in my hand. dignified lunch @ 1, schtupping to be scheduled."

He smiled again at the text—and then frowned. Didn't he find all this charming? Didn't he want to schedule schtupping as much as she did? Why exactly was he going to do this again? The answers came to mind: Sylvia, Evan, the momentum he'd built up toward doing it—the guilt now reasserted itself. "See you tomorrow," he wrote—then added, "baby," because he didn't want to worry her (or at least that was why he told himself he did it).

But after he'd hit send and tossed the phone onto the bed, he did feel better: relieved that at least there'd be some resolution—and proud of himself that he had dealt (or anyway was going to deal) with a difficult situation, rather than be tossed back and forth between guilt and self-indulgence. More: He had done the right thing.

And then Jonah caught sight of himself in the full-length mirror on the inside of his closet door. He was naked by now—and for an instant, he saw himself as he would a naked stranger, without the benefit of protective biases, the protective measures he reflexively took. He saw himself with his stomach unflexed, his shoulders slumped, his expression dull—flaccid dick exactly as large as it was. He was confronted with the image of a man closer to full-blown middle age than full-blown youth: He saw flabbiness at the torso, he saw roundness at the thighs and arms, he spotted grayness among the trimmed black hair above his ears. And even more—he saw in the lengths of pink-pale flesh a naked man of jarring vulnerability, of shockingly finite proportions— woefully overmatched for the events of the day, of the life to come. He turned from the mirror uneasily—immediately pulled on the boxers he'd dropped on the floor, flexed his abs and chest, closed the closet door. He picked up his phone, thinking he might call Sylvia—but saw he had an email from Doug Chen, a partner at his firm, requesting a meeting the following day. Jonah had good instincts for these things; he sensed there was something positive in this for him. After he'd replied to the request in the affirmative, he scrolled through some other emails, checked the weather for the following day, checked the Yankees score, added the meeting with Doug Chen to his calendar, added the lunch with Zoey without any attendant emotion, shuffled idly through the phone's collection of names and numbers and apps and games—tools to reach and decipher and shape the entire world if he wanted. The world was so fucking manageable when you looked at it through an iPhone. He turned off the light in his bedroom and got into bed; he wrote Sylvia a text message: "Hope you get out of there before midnight. Love you"; he set the phone's alarm for six the next morning, the glow of its screen on his face the last thing he saw before he closed his eyes—

And Jonah felt much better.

1. THE PRESENCE OF THE LORD

By the next morning the rain had stopped, and any sign that such a thing as rain was even possible had vanished. The sky was immaculately clear—a uniform metallic blue, undisturbed by cloud—and down from this sky, and from a sun that looked like a hole burned out of it to reveal inestimable radiance behind, poured the heat of mid-August. It filled the streets and parks, the doorways and alleys; it infused the concrete and asphalt like water soaking into a sponge; it clung to the windowpanes, it hung in the canyon-walled avenues like great heavy curtains through which pitiable pedestrians had to make their way—mouths open, collars open, sweat at minimum dotting their upper lips in tiny beads, in the most severe cases simply pouring down their faces unimpeded. People moved slowly, they didn't look at one another. If the rain had brought an unusual conviviality to the city, the heat seemed to imprison each New Yorker in his or her own personal lobster pot.

Jonah, however, awoke in the sixty-eight degrees Fahrenheit that his air conditioner made his right. He was apprised of the situation outside by the cheerfully cartoonish sunshine icon on the weather app on his iPhone's screen—the first thing he looked at when he opened his eyes. Drinking his coffee while standing before the windows of his nineteenth-floor apartment, he could even somehow see the heat—as if it enlarged the sidewalks and people, the air itself, with a visible discomfort. But to know about the heat and to feel it were very different things. Jonah was a chronic sweater: dreaded the sensation, to which he was all too prone, of overheating beneath his clothes, feeling the moistening of any fabric touching his skin. Not to be suffering this when such suffering was so manifestly possible added to the peculiar sense of self-satisfaction with which he had awakened. It was as if he'd already put his relationship house in order, thrown off the indecision and guilt over Zoey just by deciding to do so. And as he showered and put on his suit and skipped breakfast, his mind readily turned to thoughts of work.

His job was often stressful and more often exhausting, but he identified an enjoyable gamelike quality to it, both in the adversarial nature of the practice of law and in the competitive culture of his firm. The fact that he knew he was good at this game made him enjoy it all the more. Plus, after three years of law school, two summer associate-ships, five years now as an associate at his firm, he'd found that thoughts about cases and clients had become in some way natural: a relaxation of his mind into its accustomed state, rather than a taking up of a burden.

The walk from the door of his building to the street was enough to confirm his intention to take a cab in to work. It was only seven in the morning, and it must have been ninety degrees outside. Fifteen minutes later he left the air-conditioned cab, crossed another sidewalk, and stepped into the even more aggressively air-conditioned lobby of 813 Lexington Avenue, where the offices of Cunningham Wolf LLP were housed. He noted with satisfaction that he'd been awake for almost an hour and a half, and had spent less than sixty seconds of that time suffering the heat of the sun.

Inside the building's lobby, beyond the security desk and before the elevators, was an enormous tree—the trunk black, deeply twisted, the foliage in every season dense and oviform and a bright, almost neon green. It was an obscure South American species, which could thrive in the seasonally air-conditioned and seasonally heated lobby of a Midtown office building, its maintenance paid for by the investment bank that occupied most of the building's upper floors. Discovering the annual cost of the tree's upkeep had long been something of an obsession for Cunningham Wolf associates. The most common estimate was sixty thousand dollars a year. Pre-crash, pre-bailout, pre-reform, the first-year i-bankers would run naked around the tree on their first bonus day—one circuit for every fifty thousand. This made an enjoyable spectacle for the lawyers who took a break from late-night briefs to watch: There was something pleasantly paganish about it, Jonah had always thought—the clothingless young people with their checks held aloft, shouting and laughing as they circled the massive gnarled trunk. And while 80 percent of these i-bankers were men, there was still that 20 percent. But then came the global crisis, and with it the necessity for demonstrations of austerity, and the tradition ended—though from everything Jonah had heard, the bonuses weren't really much smaller. The tree was still there, too, of course, and maybe because of the memory of the ritual, Jonah felt a mild affection for it whenever he bothered to look up from his phone or coffee on his way in to work.

He rode up to the twenty-ninth floor—went to his office, closed the door, and spent the next two hours before his computer, working. He did not during this time fail to repeatedly check his personal email, and scrutinize baseball box scores, and absorb status updates and photos on other people's Facebook pages (he almost never updated his own), and read parts of about a dozen articles on NYTimes.com. But he integrated these activities as brief respites among the actual work, allowing him never to feel burdened with the tedium of any one task. The morning was productive, he felt, not despite the diversions, but because of them.

He emerged from this digital reverie at around 9:30. His assistant arrived, greeted him perfunctorily. Dolores was twenty years Jonah's senior, African American, perpetually unsmiling, partial to shapeless floral blouses. She performed competently and without any interest in performing any better. Their relationship was basically cordial—occasionally more or less than that—and Jonah tried his best to be patient with her lack of excessive interest in her job, because he realized there had been associates before him, there would be associates after him, and a lot of lawyers were pricks.

"I have to leave early today," Dolores told him once she'd taken off her coat. "My sister is in town. Her husband is allergic to shellfish all of a sudden, so now I can't make shrimp for dinner."

"Okay, Dolores, no problem," he said.

"I need to go to D'Agostino on Second Avenue on the way home."

"Sure, no problem."

He had a second cup of coffee, and this fueled another forty or so minutes of focused work. He was aware that coffee was a necessity in getting him through his days (through his career, really), but he was equally aware of its diminishing returns and so limited himself to four cups a day, unless he was at trial. He was about two-thirds of the way through cup number two when his phone chimed, reminding him that in fifteen minutes he had the meeting with Doug Chen.

The meeting had been at the back of his mind all morning, and though he'd been trying not to fixate on it, he realized it formed another reason for his good mood. Of the thirty Cunningham Wolf partners in the U.S. litigation and arbitration practice, Doug Chen was among the elite, one of the few the senior partners relied on to handle the biggest cases, the most important clients. He was also something of an iconic figure among the associates. He was an intensely—notoriously—well-groomed man: was never seen in the offices without his shoes aglow in black or brown, the Windsor knot of his tie taut in a mathematically precise trapezoid, his jet-black hair parted along a razor-straight line. All this complemented his reputation—deserved, in Jonah's experience—of being one of the best legal minds in the entire firm, if not the city: encyclopedic in his knowledge of precedent, insightful in both legal theory and application, shrewd when shrewdness was required, tirelessly attentive to detail. In fact, he probably would have been a senior partner himself except for one aspect of his character, which at once both crowned his iconic stature and was nearly impossible to reconcile with anything else that was known about him: Doug Chen was addicted to strippers. The most frequently repeated rumor was that he was no longer allowed to hold a firm credit card because, during the course of a monthlong trial in Miami, he had charged over forty thousand dollars at strip clubs. More-dubious gossip involved a three-week disappearance to Puerto Rico and a pregnant nineteen-year-old.

Regardless, he was a very important figure in the firm's hierarchy, and not someone who typically met face-to-face, one-on-one with associates. Even if, as was most likely, he only wanted to talk through the details of a brief Jonah had written or something of that order, it was a promising sign for Jonah that Doug Chen even knew his name.

Having acknowledged to himself how much he was anticipating this meeting, though, Jonah found it hard to concentrate on anything else. He ended up sorting through his Gmail account, deleting old messages, replying to neglected ones: congratulating a high school friend he'd been out of touch with on her birth announcement; writing a few lines to an acquaintance from college who'd relocated to Amsterdam.

At last it was five minutes before the meeting. He stood for the first time since arriving more than three hours earlier—buttoned his jacket, adjusted his hair in the uncertain reflection of himself in the glass of his framed law school diploma (Columbia, '05), left his office, and walked down the hall toward Doug Chen's door. He began to feel unexpectedly nervous as he went—ominously so—and he wondered if he should have spent the preceding hour reviewing the particulars of his case load. But, then, what particular was he not intimately familiar with? Doug Chen might as well ask him how to check email on an iPhone as quiz him on the details of his work, he reassured himself. He reached Doug Chen's office, found the door half open, knocked, and went inside.

The office was suitably large for a partner of this stature, the windows behind the desk displaying a half panorama of Midtown: views south toward the Chrysler Building and the more anonymous high-rises surrounding it. The long sill was bare except for a carved and polished stone—slate-colored, a quarter inch thick, about the size and shape of a magazine subscription card, held in a red wooden base. A seven-foot Mondrian was the only adornment hung on the walls. The desk was similarly bare except for a keyboard and a tabular computer monitor; absent were the broken-spined law books or bursting manila folders or rubber-banded sheaves of paper or even perfunctory family photos that occupied the desk of every other Cunningham Wolf lawyer, including Jonah. Doug Chen himself sat typing noiselessly on the keyboard.

"Please have a seat," Doug Chen said as Jonah came in. When Jonah did, Doug Chen neatly folded his smooth and hairless hands in front of him. His brown bespectacled eyes were, as was typical for him, undiluted in their calm—eerily so, all the associates said. He looked out at everything before him with the same unvarying, unemotive scrutiny. "I understand the Ardis settlement has just been finalized?" he asked.

He seemed to have trained himself to speak at the minimum number of decibels to be comfortably heard across a desk. "That's right, Doug," Jonah answered, trying to duplicate this volume.

"Ryan Parr was pleased with your work."

"I've learned a lot from Ryan."

"In general, it would seem you've demonstrated impressive proficiency in the applications of patent law."

It was such an oddly bland comment, spoken with so little inflection, that for a moment Jonah wondered if he was being sarcastic. But sarcasm was not a tone Doug Chen likely found much use for. "Thank you for saying that, that's good to hear," he answered.

Doug Chen made an ambiguous gesture: lifted one of his hands from the other, lowered it again. He then asked, "You're aware that we represent BBEC?"

Jonah was. And, to his mild embarrassment, his stomach made a little pirouette at the recitation of these letters. BBEC was the largest pharmaceutical company in the United States, and one of Cunningham Wolf's largest and oldest clients. Precisely what Cunningham Wolf did for BBEC was something of a mystery, at least on the associate level.

Special nondisclosure agreements and a quasi-cultlike silence accompanied any BBEC case work. There was apparently a personal connection between Hank Evans, the head of the firm, and the current CEO of BBEC—classmates at Sloan once upon a time, or something like that—and the assumption was that Cunningham Wolf handled only BBEC's most sensitive cases: the class-action suits over birth defects or gender discrimination, the animal-cruelty suits, EU accusations of market collusion, and so forth. What was more immediately relevant for Jonah, though, was that associates who worked on BBEC were, as his fellow associates variously put it, made guys, they were *mishpucha*, they were anointed, they had gotten the nod. There were a lot of metaphors that got tossed around, but, concretely, associates who worked on BBEC cases were made partners within two or three years at the most. These thoughts were enough to distract Jonah from answering, so it was perhaps half a beat too late—and a bit too energetically in the context of a conversation with Doug Chen—that he said, "I'm aware of that, yes."

"We are currently representing BBEC in a dispute with Dyomax, a biotechnology company based in Cambridge."

"Okay," said Jonah.

"In 2006, Dyomax brought a suit alleging that they are the holders of the patent to a molecule that is the basis for BBEC's drug Lumine. Relatively amicable discussions over the last four years have not resulted in a settlement. We now feel trial represents the best course toward achieving a favorable outcome for our clients."

Jonah nodded. "How large a company is Dyomax?"

Doug Chen lifted and lowered one hand again. "Suffice it to say, the molecule in dispute is currently their chief asset."

"I see," said Jonah, and he did see—saw, or imagined he saw, that this sketch of the case had been a form of a test: as to whether he could understand the meaning embedded in a few brief sentences. Dyomax was a small company; BBEC was a giant company. A settlement hadn't been reached after four years because settlement was never the plan. Cunningham Wolf was—to use more hallway billingsgate—bleeding the goat: deploying a floor's worth of attorneys to ensure that the case dragged on with the speed and apparent progress of a World

War I trench battle, all the time (and not incidentally) costing Dyomax and BBEC more and more in legal fees. The difference was that BBEC could afford it. The fact that they were going to trial meant they believed Dyomax was now on the cusp of going under. The point when the opposition could least afford a trial: that was the time to walk into court. Jonah had to admire, if not the elegance, the passionlessness and proficiency of it all. They were using the law not so much to adjudicate the dispute as to choke the adversarial party to death. "We'll go to trial soon, then?" Jonah asked.

"Based on reasonable assumption, the case will be tried next month," Doug Chen answered. He turned to his computer monitor, typed something for a moment—and Jonah noticed there was a waxiness to Doug Chen's face, a sort of even gloss to his forehead and cheeks and chin, to the skin of his throat above his bright white collar. He returned his impassive gaze to Jonah. "I would like your assistance on this case," he resumed. "You should anticipate working much of the remainder of the year from our offices in Boston. Aja Puvvada and I have already discussed this."

Jonah had the self-control to nod with equanimity. "I'm eager to get started," he said.

"Confidentiality in this matter will be of the utmost importance."

"Of course."

"No documents pertaining to this case can ever leave our offices. No documents should ever be photocopied or otherwise reproduced. To that end, sensitive documents have been uniquely watermarked, such that copies that are made can, if necessary, be traced back to the original document. Further, please keep digital correspondence related to this matter to an absolute minimum."

Fuck, Jonah thought. They actually stole it.

"Also, you will be asked to sign additional NDAs, beyond whatever NDAs you may have already signed."

"That all sounds reasonable to me," Jonah said. But really, Doug Chen could have asked him to draw a pentagram in his own blood on BBEC letterhead, and he would have said it sounded reasonable.

Doug Chen looked at him, blinked metronomically for several seconds. "I would like to add a more personal note." Jonah could only assume he was going to make some comment about the strip clubs in Boston—this affinity being the only trace of personality Doug Chen was known to have—and he tried to stiffen his poker face against a discussion of tipping in champagne rooms. But Doug Chen said, "I am an adherent to the principle of perfection. Associates of your generation seem taken with the deleterious notion that their duties extend no further than the execution of 'their best.' Logically, however, one's best is only good enough up to the point at which it is not good enough. Perfection, on the other hand, is the demand and offer not of one's best, but rather of the objective best.

"Further," he went on, "it is my strong belief that the practice of the law itself is predicated on the principle of perfection. To wit, the law is followed only to the extent that it is interpreted and executed accurately. All else is a distortion of the law and its intent. Hence, we as lawyers are doing our job correctly only if we do it perfectly. And if in achieving perfection we do not achieve a favorable resolution for our clients, I am willing to abide that outcome. We can be perfect, even where the facts may not be."

Jonah found it hard to take this seriously—in the same way he found it hard to take seriously the fanatics who wandered around Times Square on New Year's, screaming about the End of Days. It was not that he didn't think Doug Chen meant what he said; it was just incredible to Jonah that anyone could mean it. He doubted anyone else he had ever met could have given this little speech without introducing at least the barest trace of irony. He only wished Philip Orengo could have been there to hear it, too. It was clear, though: Doug Chen believed in perfection. And this actually helped explain for Jonah the obsession with strippers. There was, after all, a tidiness to the transactional nature of the encounters in a strip club: They smoothed away all the ambiguities, all the mystery and bodily unpredictability associated with sex. This really might appeal to a mind so resistant to the idea of error and imprecision.

"Well, I'll be honest with you, Doug," Jonah said in his "I'm being frank" voice, which he'd perfected while speaking in his law school classes and which had served him well in his career ever since. "I understand the opportunity that working on a BBEC case represents, and what that client means to our firm. If perfection is what you want, perfection is what you'll get." But as he said this, for the first time he felt a twinge of anxiety over this new assignment. After all, hadn't he just promised to do something that was, by definition, impossible?

Doug Chen repeated his gesture of lifting a single hand. "I have no reason to believe you will not be an asset in the successful execution of this case."

It was not exactly a pat on the back, but Jonah tried to take it as a vote of confidence. "Thank you, Doug."

"The files will be delivered to your office this afternoon. Review everything. We'll speak again Monday morning."

"That's fine." Jonah stood up and they shook hands. Doug Chen's hand was cool, and, like his face, somehow surfaceless—as if there were no folds or creases in his palm. He resumed typing, and Jonah walked out the door, leaving it half open, as he had found it.

He went halfway down the hall, then couldn't suppress a muted fist pump. "BBEC," he said under his breath. "Fuck yes."

Walking down the hall from Doug Chen's office would form the peak of the sense of satisfaction with which Jonah had begun the day. By the time he had stood waiting for more than half an hour on the paved plaza outside Zoey's building, it had all but vanished. There was no shade anywhere on the plaza—if anything, its brick seemed to recirculate the blasting midday heat back up from below. He had already removed his jacket, loosened his tie, unbuttoned the button at his throat, was now engaged in the self-defeating activity of concentrating as hard as he could on not sweating. But despite (or because of) these measures, he could feel a pool of moisture forming at his lower back, on his torso beneath his chest; he had to continually wipe perspiration from his face with the back of his right hand, in which he held his phone.

In the heat, it was becoming wearying even to look for Zoey: to follow with his eyes any female who appeared from the elevators at the back of the glass-fronted lobby and walked out the revolving door at the mouth of the building. He found that the more people he stared at, the more the boundary between Zoey and not-Zoey seemed to smudge—as if he were trying to trick himself as to whom he was seeing in order to effect an immediate departure to anywhere thirty degrees cooler. At one point he went so far as to raise a hand in greeting to someone who turned out to be an Indian woman thirty years Zoey's senior, having momentarily convinced himself she might have gotten a new haircut and a spray tan since he'd last seen her.

He glanced at his phone again. Another two minutes had gone by since he'd last checked. He couldn't wait much longer: He'd been gone from his office for nearly an hour now, and even if he and Zoey didn't actually sit down to lunch, it would be difficult to get back in time for the 1:30 meeting he had on his calendar. He would need time before this meeting, as well—not so much to review the materials that would be discussed, but rather to sit unmoving in his air-conditioned office for the ten or so minutes it would take him to stop sweating.

He considered calling Zoey again, texting her again, but she hadn't answered the first four rounds of calls and texts; he doubted she would respond to the fifth. Besides, he felt he could in good conscience hurry her only so much, given what he had come to do.

At some point, the heat had reawakened the doubts he still held about this conversation: exacerbated them, merged with them, become indistinguishable from them. The temptation was growing simply to abandon ship. He could text Zoey that he hadn't been able to wait any longer, could go back to his office—not mention anything about a breakup to her. After all, if he'd known he was going to have a BBEC case to celebrate, he might have waited until after the weekend to end things, anyway.

He reminded himself, however, that there were not merely moral arguments (the force of which seemed to have faded considerably over the course of the morning) in support of the breakup. There was also what might called the weight of precedent. To wit, he and Zoey had been breaking up and getting back together for going on ten years now: ending things by mutual accord, or not; not talking for weeks or months; and then emailing each other out of the blue, or texting from a bar or a party; hooking up again, dating again, and then—seemingly by force of the same gravity that had brought them back together in the first place—breaking up again, vowing never to speak again, and starting the whole process over—over and over and over. In all their incarnations over the last ten years—hooking up, or dating casually, or dating exclusively, or cheating with each other, or cheating on each other—they'd never managed to achieve anything sustainable, never managed to recover the jarring and perspectiveless love of their first few months. That love had given way to reality, Jonah told himself, and reality turned out to be an environment to which their relationship was ill-suited, regardless of form. There certainly wasn't any reason to think their latest iteration would be any different, given that he was moving in with Sylvia and she was seeing Evan, the intermittently employed actor she'd been intermittently dating for close to a year now. If he didn't end it today, it would just end some other day.

He found this case he'd made to himself fairly convincing—but felt it contradicted almost instantly when he saw a young woman of medium height, brunette and narrow-shouldered, with a distinctive gait of short, choppy steps that were at once both hurried and measured—as if she were resisting an urge to run—and recognized her immediately as Zoey.

She had a phone pressed against her ear. When he approached, she smiled—momentarily, apologetically—then returned her attention to whomever she was talking to. "Then we want to link to it on their site?" she said into her cell, her toe tapping agitatedly, her thumb at her mouth, her expression one of brow-furrowed concentration as she stared off into the middle distance. She was dressed in a black-and-white Rorschach-patterned dress and black high heels, and Jonah could see in silhouette created by the sunlight pouring onto the plaza the shape of her slender figure under her dress, the darker outlines of her bra and panties. He found he couldn't stop staring at this sight, despite his intentions here—and despite having seen her entirely naked maybe a thousand times before. Finally he feigned interest in his own phone, reminded himself that Sylvia had a pretty great body, too, though in an entirely different mode.

"Then we can just post the whole thing, right?" Zoey was saying. "And I could definitely get a quote from his publicist. . . ." She was, to use a term she had coined herself, a B-girl: a writer for the blog *Glossified,* a culture-cum-gossip website popular among young urban women. It was a job many envied her for—many young urban women, at least—but, characteristically, Zoey managed to hate it. Her career was a source of deep, persistent anxiety for her—as were her vast credit-card debt, her recurring ulcer, her smallish cup size, her nose: long and tall from her face, with a slight bump at the center that she referred to as "the mogul." Despite Zoey's loathing of it, though, Jonah considered this nose her sexiest feature—the one that gave her face the distinctive character that, for whatever reason, he always associated with the letter Z.

Indeed, nothing that bothered her so much about herself bothered him at all; he even found the persistence of all the (to him baseless) anxieties charming. And as he watched her frowning at whatever she was hearing on the phone, still chewing her thumbnail (a habit she had been trying to break for as long as he'd known her), it became difficult for him to distinguish between his reluctance over the breakup and his affection for her, because there really was so much about her that he found charming: the inchoate worries; her candor, her wit; her idiosyncratic habit of swearing only in languages other than English; the drama of her facial expressions—she being a woman whose brow furrowed, whose laughter was loud and openmouthed, whose nervousness brought tautness from her forehead to her chin, whose almond-shaped brown eyes narrowed and darted, and whose head tilted just so when she was flirting.

"Five hundred words? Two fifty?" she continued. "Sure . . . And then you saw the emails? Okay. Call me on my cell when you hear from Anika, all right? Okay, thanks, *ciao*." She hung up, dropped her phone into her voluminous purse, and, with the same hand, immediately began digging around in it. "You have no idea, Yonsi"—this being her nickname for him—"I have been on the phone nonstop since I walked in this morning. I haven't even had the chance to do something terrible for my body." She pulled out a lighter and a pack of cigarettes, by smooth rote motions put one in her mouth and lit it. As she took a deep drag, she looked at him from feet to moist forehead. "Remember, it's good for your pores," she said consolingly. "Do you want a tissue?"

"No, it's okay . . ." he said, wiping his face again, guilt now taking a place among the doubts. She was so complicated and contradictory in so many ways that he was often caught off guard by how plainly nice she was to him. She was the closest thing to a Jewish mother he had ever had.

She took another tug on her cigarette. "The star of one show you never watch is writing a memoir about his gay escapades with the star of another show you never watch. And Darla's old roommate is an assistant to some agent in L.A., and she sent us the proposal. It's mass hysteria up there, Yonsi, really, B-girls gone wild. I had zero time to answer your calls. The details are absolute pornography, and guess who has to write about it? That's what I get for graduating magna from NYU. Tell me I have the most soulless job of anyone you know."

He glanced at his phone—he had only about five minutes left. Again he pondered reversing course. But he knew himself, knew that if he failed to do it now, it would be weeks before he put himself in a position to do it again. It was still the right thing to do, he reminded himself. So he took a decidedly calm breath and said, "Look, Zoey . . ."

Her eyes immediately narrowed, she scrutinized his face suspiciously. Then she let out a disgusted sigh. "*Scheisse,* Yonsi . . ."

"Zoey . . ."

"Please stop saying my name like you heard my cat died."

"I just think that we—"

"You're doing this to me again?"

"How often has it been you doing it to me?"

"Yeah, but I always had good reasons."

"Sylvia and I . . ."

She rolled her eyes preemptively. "She does not qualify as a good reason."

"We're moving in together."

He had meant to deliver this piece of news more gently, but had found himself feeling immediately on the defensive, and so the most compelling rationale had come tumbling out. There had, of course, been many such revelations over the last ten years: new significant others, new seriousness with those others, new intentions of exclusivity.

Only three months previously, Zoey had mentioned—with a certain grimness—that Evan had started making veiled references to possibly getting engaged at some point. But actually living with another person was something new to them—and maybe because it was new, Zoey looked puzzled when she first heard it, and her first response was, "But you said she didn't even vote for Obama."

"I said I didn't think she voted for Obama," he answered, though the only reason he wasn't certain was that he hadn't wanted to ask and know for sure.

She asked skeptically, "You really want to live with *Schlampe*?"—this her nickname for Sylvia.

"I don't know," he answered—more honestly, he realized, than he probably should have. "I can really see a future with her," he added quickly. "And with us," he went on, "it just isn't meant to be."

This point seemed fairly obvious to him—self-evident, really. But as he watched, tiny tremors began in her lips and her forehead, a reliable harbinger of tears. Though her cigarette was only half smoked, she dropped it to the pavement, stamped it out with her toe as her hands began digging into her vast purse for another. "You have such a talent for saying the most hurtful things."

"Zoey . . ." he began.

"There's that word again," she said into her purse.

"You know I never wanted to hurt you," he mumbled.

"That must make you feel much better about all of this." She didn't look up until she had another cigarette between her lips. As she clicked her lighter before it, she said, "Would it never work out because of my A cups? Or because I didn't go Hah-vahd like *Schlampe*?"

"C'mon, Zoey, we aren't even dating," he said, guilt giving way a little to irritation.

"Therefore I shouldn't mind that you're dumping me to live with another woman?"

"I'm not dumping you—we aren't dating!"

"I guess I'm not aware of the legal definition of getting dumped. But then again, we didn't all go to Columbia Law School—"

"You have a boyfriend! You're talking about getting married!"

She lifted the hand holding the cigarette, flapped her bare ring finger. "You were the one who said it didn't mean anything until he got me a ring."

"I never said that," though he knew he had.

"No really, it's fine," she said, with mock breeziness. "I was looking forward to a joyless marriage with a man who can't support me. Maybe I'll see *Schlampe* pushing one of your blond babies around Prospect Park someday."

She turned away, stared off toward the traffic on Seventh Avenue, her forehead still trembling a little, but her mouth now set in a hard, tight frown. Jonah glanced at his phone—a bead of sweat dropped from his forehead onto its face. If he didn't get in a cab in the next three minutes, he would be late. And there was, he told himself, no point to this conversation anymore. He'd learned from his past breakups—with her, with anyone—that everything beyond the delivery of the hard, essential message was only a sort of ritualistic airing of grievances: kabuki theater in which the aggrieved party tried to elicit as much guilt as possible, while the person doing the aggrieving made parrying attempts to end the conversation without giving any new cause for being thought an asshole, or at minimum, to escape before the crying started.

"Zoey, you were late, I've got to go. . . ."

"My therapist says I have a problem with patterns," she responded, taking another drag on her cigarette and exhaling smoke from the corner of her mouth. "Dr. Popper explains that my anxiety makes me do what's familiar, even when it's bad for me. Your name came up. Shocking, I know. Thanks for making her look so smart." She punched him—hard—on the arm.

"Jesus," he said. But he knew the punch was, if not exactly affectionate, then at least not entirely hostile, either. If nothing else, it was an acknowledgment of something. "Look, I feel really shitty about this," he told her.

"That's nice of you to say." She was standing perpendicular to him now, and this lessened the translucence of her dress—which was a relief—but allowed him the full profile of her nose—which was not. It was not that Zoey was prettier than Sylvia; by conventional reckoning she wasn't. There was simply a lot more going on in Zoey's face than in Sylvia's neat, all-American-by-way-of-Ireland features. Zoey glanced over at him, her brown iris filling the corner of her right eye. "Tell me the truth. Does it mean anything if there's no ring?"

Jonah rubbed some sweat from the back of his neck. "I was being a dick. Of course it means something."

Whether she was comforted by this or further distressed, he couldn't tell. She couldn't tell, either, was his guess. Profound ambivalence had always been a hallmark of her feelings toward Evan. "But she'll see a ring from you, is that the idea?" Zoey asked. "It'll be you and *Schlampe*?"

He didn't answer. He didn't know the answer—and he wouldn't have known how to phrase any answer, given who was asking. But his best guess was yes—him and *Schlampe*. Wasn't that the whole point of doing this?

"I got a BBEC case," he told her. "I'll be working with Doug Chen—y'know, the one with the strippers. It puts me in good shape for partner." He realized it was unfair to tell her—to dump her and in the same breath mention how great his life was going. But it was important to him that she know, for some reason.

She turned to him, and smiled in a way that was not entirely convincing, but strived for sincerity. "I'm happy for you, Yonsi. You've worked really hard for that." She moved the cigarette toward her mouth, then stopped. "The thing is," she said, "I get it. She does seem like the kind of girl a partner in a law firm would want to marry. And no, that is not entirely a compliment, but it's a much nicer thing than you've ever said about Evan. And yes, he is kind of my boyfriend, and I suppose there's even a chance he'll ask to marry me. It's just that . . ." She returned the cigarette to her mouth, expelled its smoke in a sigh. Her expression was tired now—forlorn. "I thought things were going really good this time."

"They were, they were, it's . . ."

"How come you never wanted to live with me?"

He was grappled with a powerful tenderness toward her—an urge to take her in his arms, tell her he hadn't meant any of it. And whether it was fueled by guilt or nostalgia or pain avoidance or genuine affection: It was still tenderness. "It's not that, y'know, I at any point rejected the idea of us living together."

"You sound so lawyerly these days," she muttered.

Luckily, or so he would think later, at this moment his phone chimed with a reminder for his meeting. "I'm sorry, Zoey. I have to go."

"Yeah, yeah, yeah," she said. "Don't think I don't have five hundred words to write about two closeted TV stars groping each other. Meanwhile you and *Schlampe* ride off into the sunset." She flicked her cigarette in the general direction of his shoes. "In the past when you've done this to me, my phone rings at one in the morning, you're a little slurry, and *Schlampe* or whoever it is isn't around, and you're wondering if I maybe want to re-create that time at the W."

"That won't happen this time." She pursed her lips dubiously, as though she'd heard it all before—which she probably had. In an effort to convince her of his seriousness, he added, "It was really wrong what we were doing, Zoey."

She studied his face very carefully for a moment. "*Vai all'inferno e restaci*, Yonsi," she said.

"I'm assuming that wasn't very nice."

"What do you care? I'm just the girl you were cheating with, right?" She pulled her purse up onto her shoulder. "I look forward to not hearing from you." And she walked away and into the building.

He watched her as she crossed the lobby, disappeared into an elevator. For another moment he stood in the heat—wishing he'd somehow been able to communicate that, while he did in fact intend to never see her again, he nevertheless cared about her very much. The longer he thought about this, though, the more frustrated it made him—and he finally concluded that any attempt to communicate such a plainly self-contradictory idea was doomed from the start. He wiped the sweat from his face once more, annoyed at the heat, at how the conversation had gone, and most of all annoyed that he'd run into her six months earlier on St. Mark's Place outside a theater where Evan was performing, which was the only reason they'd started talking again and having sex again and any of this had ever happened again—and he mumbled a "damn it" in the direction of this unlucky happenstance. But then he

was on the move, mercifully departing the plaza, heading toward the
street, where several open cabs were stopped at a light. It had been
shitty, but not as shitty as it could have been. And, more important, it
was done.

To become a partner at Cunningham Wolf—and that had been Jonah's
goal from his first day as a summer associate at the firm—you had to
bill an average of 3,000 hours a year. The rule wasn't written down
anywhere, and for that was all the more reliable. Billing 3,000 hours a
year generally meant working at least 3,500. That was an average of
9.5 hours a day, 365 days a year. Practically speaking, though—
because even ambitious associates took off the occasional holiday,
birthday, hungover Monday—that meant most days were twelve or
fourteen hours long, not excepting Saturdays, plus a half day most
Sundays. All told, Jonah figured he had worked at least 17,500 hours
since graduating from law school five years before. That was more
than two continuous years of briefs, memos, depositions, filings, emails,
meetings, takeout, two-faced colleagues, abusive partners, hysterical
clients, incompetent assistants, flame-out first-years, senile judges, gossip,
rumors, motions, dismissals, settlements, conference calls, and four (or
more) cups of coffee a day. And now partnership was just one more
case away.

So, back in his apartment, Jonah had opened a three-hundred-
dollar bottle of Scotch he'd bought on a trip with some law school
friends to the Scottish Highlands. The man who'd sold it to him—
rich-brogued, bronze-sideburned, stereotypically Scottish in every way
but for lack of a kilt—had put three bottles on the table before him
and his friends and, passing his hand over each one, said, "This is
what y'drink with the father of your wife on your wedding day. This
is what y'drink when your first child is born. And lads, this is what
y'drink when your first son is born." It was a good line, got a good
laugh from the group of American law school students on what would
likely be the last summer vacation of their lives. Of course, they all
bought.

He poured the golden-amber liquid into a glass from the dishwasher.

He'd never intended to wait for the birth of a son; fatherhood wasn't something he thought much about. He figured he'd eventually open the bottle in celebration of something in his career, and over the years that something had naturally become fixed as Cunningham Wolf partnership. True, he was not a partner yet, it could still all go wrong. He could fuck up his work with BBEC, an asteroid could strike 813 Lexington. But neither event was very likely. Indeed, the asteroid seemed the more probable. He'd learned what it took to succeed as a lawyer: It took intelligence, which he'd been born with; it took diligence, which, ultimately, was really just a question of deciding to be diligent; it took a modicum of interpersonal skills, a high tolerance for bullshit, a passion for being proven right—he had it, he'd acquired it, he seemed to find more of it every day. So leaving aside the possibility that BBEC operated differently from any other Fortune 100 company with turf to protect (and he knew it didn't), and barring the asteroid or whatever—he would within a few years be a partner at one of the oldest, most prestigious law firms in the city.

He carried the glass from his kitchenette into his living room. He had lived in this apartment for three years and somehow had managed not to have completely unpacked yet; bulging cardboard boxes were still stacked behind the couch. Pre-Sylvia, it had been even worse: Boxes had functioned as the dresser in his bedroom, as an impromptu entryway table by his door. She'd imposed some order, as was her way, and as for these last few behind the couch, they both felt there was no point bothering. He would soon be moving again.

Outside the living room windows, a purplish dusk was descending over the city—windows on the faces of buildings brightening into little squares of gold. It looked as if the city were putting on its showier, colorful clothing, too, for the Friday night ahead. The bars would be filling up, the lines at restaurants forming, opening acts starting their sets. Ordinarily he didn't mind spending Friday nights at home, alone. He was usually more than content to order in and get drunk on his couch, watching whatever on TV—unwinding. But tonight he could sense on the other side of his windows the great inhalation of breath before the city dove into the night ahead. He took his first sip of the three-hundred-dollar Scotch. During the Highlands trip, he'd become adept at the jargon of Scotch: malty, peaty, finish, nose. He'd forgotten all that by now; the best he could come up with by way of description was that this Scotch tasted really fucking great.

He took out his phone and called Sylvia. She was a senior analyst for Ellis–Michaels, and for the last two months had spent her weeks and the majority of her weekends in Chicago working on a deal, the details of which she couldn't divulge. It was only 7:00 there, she would almost certainly still be working, but he hadn't talked to her all day— hadn't told her the good news.

After several rings she answered. "Hey, we're still at it. Can I call you back in three hours?"

"Maybe," he said. "I think I might go out."

"I'll call you while you're out," she replied.

"It won't be late, though. I might go in before we meet the broker tomorrow."

"This could take until midnight."

They both agreed her frequent travel to Chicago had put stress on their relationship. Already he could sense the implicit competition in their words: Who worked more? Who had less time for whom? Who put unfair demands on the other? Tonight he wasn't in a position to ask for much: She was flying back the next morning to look at apartments with him; they would have dinner, and then she would fly back to Chicago that night to be in the office Sunday morning. Of course, he hadn't asked her to, but she had made no secret of the inconvenience of it all, of the effort she was putting in, for their sake.

"Look, do you have thirty seconds?" he asked. "There's something I want to tell you."

He heard some shuffling, a closing door. "What's going on?"

"I got a BBEC case. We're going to trial maybe next month."

"Really?" she said. "So that means partner?"

"In a couple more years, but, yeah—that's what it means."

"That is fantastic news. Congratulations, Jonah."

"A lot of work went into it, so."

Then there was a pause, and she said—with a kind of determined enthusiasm—"I really am happy for you." And he guessed—knew— she was thinking about her own (ostensibly) stalled career. The next rung on the Ellis–Michaels ladder for her was vice president, and the company was notorious for its lack of female vice presidents—for its lack of females in any roles, in fact. As Sylvia explained it, they didn't want to pay someone $500,000 a year to get pregnant.

He had another sip of the wonderful Scotch. It wasn't that he was unsympathetic, but: "Is it impossible for you to be happy for me?"

"I just said I was happy for you."

"Did you mean it?" She didn't answer.

He could picture her: standing in some hallway—carpeted, fluorescently lit, all the cubicles around her empty for the night—wearing a suit with a sports bra underneath (otherwise, she said, the suits never fit right, her large breasts as much a burden to her as small breasts were to Zoey), her bobbed blond hair parted neatly across the top, the facile frown on her face that she always wore when they disagreed—as if she were neither angry nor culpable, simply tolerating the unpleasantness—her small, symmetrical nose ever so slightly flared at the nostrils. When they argued, it was easy for him to understand her success in a male-dominated industry. She could project formidable intensity in her face, in her five-foot-five frame. He guessed she'd developed this visible toughness from a lifetime of dealings with her father, but that relationship and its consequences she didn't like to talk about. "I am truly happy for you, Jonah," she finally said. "I am in the middle of a thousand things, but yes, I am truly happy for you. I'll have Linda make us a reservation at Le Bernardin tomorrow night to celebrate."

The last thing he'd wanted when he called had been to argue, and so he accepted her offer to move the conversation in a more amicable direction. "That sounds great," he said. "I just wish you were here to celebrate with me tonight." And before she could start to answer, he added, "And I know it's not by choice. It's only, y'know, too bad."

"You are an excellent lawyer. You deserve this."

"We can tell the broker we can look at six-thousand-dollar places."

"That's true," she said. "There was the loft on Bond Street, remember? I emailed you?"

Lofts weren't his preference; he had an affinity for closing doors. But he said, "Yeah, I remember. That place was great."

"It's exciting, Jonah."

"I'm going to be in Boston a lot."

"Well," she said, "it's an hour on the shuttle from LaGuardia." And this reminded him of something he loved about her: how undaunted she was by circumstance, how adaptive and capable, in such contrast to—well, other people.

"Look, Syl, I know things haven't been perfect lately," he said.

"I can't talk about that now," she answered quickly.

"I know, I know, I just. I think we're going to have a great future together."

She didn't answer for a moment. Then she said, in a hushed, measured tone, "That means a lot to me, Jonah." Then, more loudly, "Anyway, I should get back."

"Were you in early, too?"

"On the treadmill at four-thirty, in the conference room at six."

"Jesus. Hang in there, Syl."

"I'll see you tomorrow morning."

"I love you."

"Ditto. See you tomorrow."

He hung up—reaffirmed, he felt, in his decision to end things with Zoey. He didn't deny that an affection for her that had lasted nearly a decade would likely always be with him, in some form. But did she have any idea what it took to become a partner at a major New York law firm? Sure, B-girls worked long hours. But there were long hours, and then there were 17,500 hours. Sylvia could tell him he deserved to make partner and it meant something. She worked brutal hours in a brutal industry, too. She was a peer in that sense.

The bottom line was that it really wasn't meant to be with Zoey and him. Maybe it could have been, once—but there were things you couldn't control. For ten years they had been going nowhere, circling around the inescapable fact of their ultimate incompatibility. He and Sylvia, on the other hand, continued to steadily reach recognizable markers of relationship progress: from blind date to weekly dates; from weekly dates to thrice weekly; to (professed) monogamy and exclusivity; and now they were moving in together. No, things between them hadn't been great lately, but they both concluded that that was because they didn't see each other enough, and living together would help.

And yes, he had fucked up with Zoey over the last several months. But he could call that the last reflexive twitches of an old habit—fading penile muscle memory, he thought with a smile. He could focus now—fully, and in full sincerity—on Sylvia. He swallowed the last of the Scotch, and in its satisfaction imagined he tasted a satisfaction with life in general. He went into the kitchenette and poured himself another glass.

He leaned against the stovetop (he might have checked if it was on, if he had ever turned it on) and scrolled through the numbers on his phone, eager to share his good news, his good mood. His father, a fund-raiser of indeterminate title with the Democratic Party, was in London on business that week, and it was two in the morning there. He would be in bed at this hour, likely, Jonah guessed, having eaten a lavish dinner with *consiglieri* of the Labour Party, likely with a woman lying beside him, either brought to London, or met in London, or, for all Jonah knew, the London girlfriend. Ever since his divorce from Jonah's mother decades earlier, Jonah's father had had many romantic partners, and they were not easily kept track of. Jonah briefly considered calling his mother, but only briefly. She ran a catering business, which, to hear her tell it, had been only one canceled wedding away from bankruptcy for the last decade. She tended to take news about his career as an opportunity to describe the trials and tribulations of her own. She acted as though he didn't respect what she did, which had never made any sense to him until he realized that his father didn't respect what she did. Jonah's parents had a habit of making him a proxy for their complaints about each other.

His landing a major case that put him on a partner track was also not the sort of news he felt he could share with his law school friends, not without sounding arrogant: Most of them were at competing firms and had exactly this goal for themselves. Philip Orengo might be truly happy for him—but he would express this by telling him that BBEC was a corrupt multinational responsible for countless abuses in the developing world and Cunningham Wolf had now gobbled up the last of his immortal soul.

Eventually he came to the number of his cousin Becky. She was a cousin on his father's side, was in her early twenties, had moved to

New York a couple of years previously to take a job as an assistant at a record label. He didn't see her as much as he should have, but he liked her, had always gotten along with her when their families gathered for holidays or weddings. She showed some of the free-spiritedness of his father's side of his family. He called her.

"Jonah!" she cried enthusiastically when she answered.

"How's it going?" he said.

"I can't believe you called!"

"No, I know, work has been . . ."

"I was positive you'd forget my birthday."

"Come on, we're family," he said, improvising. "Happy birthday, Becky."

"Aw, thank you, Jonah! You're coming over tonight?"

He stared at the black face of his microwave, as if some recollection could be summoned there. Had he seen an Evite to a birthday party? "Yeah, I was thinking about it. What's the address again?"

"Three ninety-one East Fifty-third Street, between First and Second Avenues. Just call me when you get here, we might be up on the roof."

"Three ninety-one East Fifty-third, between First and Second. I'll bring champagne."

"That'd be perfect," she said. "I know everyone's going to show up with beer, but one of Aimee's friends is bringing a keg." He thought it was possible he'd heard this Aimee mentioned before, but wasn't sure. "We already started pregaming, so come over whenever you want. I'm already so drunk, Jonah." He heard someone shout her name. "I'll see you," she said, and hung up.

He carried his glass of Scotch into his bedroom, changed into jeans and a T-shirt, then carried the glass into the bathroom. He pissed, reached under his shirt to put on deodorant, examined his face in the mirror: high forehead, deep-set brown eyes, dark hair retreating toward the crown of his head but still thick, his nose an ambiguous feature, he had always thought, appearing at some angles large and hooked in a stereotypically Jewish way; at others more classically Roman, like something off a bust of Caesar at the Met; and, when he looked at it straight on, as he did now, even a little narrow—an almost inconsequential part of his face. It was a handsome face, in some ways getting more handsome with age—and it occurred to him that realizing you had a handsome face was really all you needed to flirt effectively (but innocently!) with the girls in their early twenties who would be at Becky's party. He drank down the remaining Scotch, sloshed green mouthwash around his mouth.

Going back into the living room, he put his wallet and keys in his pockets, checked his phone, and saw he had a text message from Sylvia: "7PM Le Bern confirmed. Looking forward."

He wrote back: "Will it be a leisurely meal?"

After a moment she replied: "Not now! ;-)"

His text had referred to certain escapades that had occurred during certain of their dinners. Sylvia was, generally speaking, a little stiff, a little restrained, when it came to sex. He blamed this on the Connecticut all-girls boarding school she'd attended, and on the fact that she'd never smoked pot. But she also had a transgressive streak, and after a few glasses of wine she sometimes gave him blow jobs in the bathrooms of fancy restaurants. It seemed there was at least a possibility they would add Le Bernardin to the list tomorrow. It was a pretty good quality to find in a girlfriend, he thought—and Zoey, for sometimes better but more often worse, was practically schizophrenic when it came to sex.

And so, with visions of dancing twenty-two-year-olds, excellent food and bathroom head, of professional success and a million-dollar salary and the whole cacophony of opportunity with which New York announced itself now filling Jonah's head, he opened his apartment door and headed out for his Friday night.

Becky's apartment building had all the character of a place a father wouldn't mind paying the security deposit for his daughter to live in when she first moved to New York: new construction, doorman, garbage chute, double-dead-bolted doors, a plaster wall across the living room making of a reasonably livable one-bedroom apartment an only-just-livable two-bedroom. Not that Jonah was in any position to judge. His building had all the character of a place a lawyer who would never be home would choose to live.

Becky had certainly done more to personalize her living space than he had, as well. The walls had been painted a cheerful shade of yellow, there were framed photographs and posters from art exhibits on the walls, and for the occasion a HAPPY BIRTHDAY sign was strung above Becky's bedroom doorway. Folding tables had been set up in the back of the living room, and these were arrayed with plastic bottles of booze, mixers and plastic cups, bowls of chips, cupcakes frosted in various pastel colors—these baked by Aimee, who, it turned out, was Becky's roommate, and someone Jonah had been told about on several occasions. The promised keg was in the kitchen, sitting in a great plastic tub of ice; music Jonah recognized from Duane Reade played from an iPod plugged into portable speakers. The girl-to-guy ratio of the guests who mingled in pairs or in small groups was about 2:1— and Jonah couldn't help but feel some sympathy for the packs of guys poking their heads into bars all across the city and finding the opposite ratio or worse, when what they were really looking for was this party. Indeed, when he'd come into the apartment and seen that Becky's coworkers and friends-from-college had responded to the relative lack of available males by (as he'd often observed women do) getting especially drunk, he almost had some sympathy for himself—now firmly, firmly embedded in his relationship.

Relationship or not, though, he could still party with those present, could still celebrate BBEC by getting drunk. He'd followed the Scotches at his apartment with a couple celebratory birthday shots with Becky when he'd first arrived, then had a few beers from the keg, and now he was working on a vodka tonic prepared by Aimee, the alcohol-to-mixer ratio of which also happened to be 2:1. She and Jonah were talking in her room—she was seated at her desk, showing him on her computer the food blog she wrote, trying to convince him to read it as he stood over her shoulder.

"See?" she said as the screen filled with a photograph of streaked crimson ice cream in a small paper cup. "This is from Wednesday. The rhubarb-and-anise ice cream from the Emilia's truck in SoHo is the best in the city. You'd know that if you read my blog!"

"I dunno, Aimee," Jonah said mildly. "The McDonald's on Forty-fifth Street makes a pretty good McFlurry. Maybe I should write a food blog."

"Oh, come on," she laughed, and tapped him gently on the leg from her chair—something she had been doing with increasing frequency, he'd noted. Though she was undeniably cute—Korean, pretty-faced, dressed insouciantly in a fedora and skirt—he concluded this touching was a permissible indulgence: maybe *malum in se* with regard to monogamy, but not necessarily *malum prohibitum*. "If you like fast food, you should at least stick to Shake Shack," she continued. "I heard they're going to open a new one near the new World Trade Center, or, like, whatever they're going to call that now." She started to type on the keyboard. "Here, let me show you something else." He took another sip of his drink, drifted over to the photographs on her bookcase as she typed. "I'm actually really committed to all this," she went on, in a slightly more serious tone. "A girl from my year at Barnard already has a book deal for her blog. Like, you can really make it happen."

"All it takes is a blog and a dream," he said, and she laughed.

"I never knew lawyers were so funny!" she said.

"You should see me in court," he answered, but now one of the photographs had caught his attention. It appeared to have been taken at a restaurant, as Aimee and the two other women in the image were seated at a white-clothed table. The woman to Aimee's right was also Korean, resembled her, though she had a rounder face, wore glasses—Jonah figured this was her sister. But it was the third woman in the photo who interested him: thin, long-necked, and very pale, with a mass of jet-black hair. And though she smiled thinly, there was a certain eeriness, he thought, to her look.

"There's this little organic place on Allen Street I'm doing a post on . . ." Aimee was saying.

"Who's this?" Jonah asked her, still looking at the picture.

Aimee turned around in her chair. "Oh, that's my sister, Milim. That's randomly the only picture I have of us together. She's a doctor now. My dad is obsessed with her, of course."

"No," Jonah said, and tapped the glass beside the face of the pale woman. "Who's she?" He could not quite identify what he found so strange about her—which had the effect of making her appear all the stranger. Her nose was unusually large, she had a black mole that dotted the top of a cheekbone, but it was the look in her eyes, he eventually decided, that was so odd: hollow—ghostly—as if she stared at the camera from a great distance, though it could have only been a few feet away.

"That's Milim's roommate at Yale. Judith."

And then he remembered where he had seen this look before. "Judith looks like you just liberated her from a death camp."

"Oh, don't!" Aimee said, laughing. "It's the only picture I have of us. Besides, that girl has a really sad story."

He looked at this girl, Judith, for another moment—then shrugged and turned away. "Eh, some people's lives don't turn out the way they want," he said with exaggerated insensitivity. He returned to the computer, which now displayed a picture of a (he had to admit very appetizing-looking) spinach quesadilla. "Y'know, I've been to Taco Bell a hundred times, and I've never ordered that," he joked, and had every expectation of never thinking about Judith again.

"Those places are terrible for you!" Aimee said, tapping his leg again. "Seriously, you will drop dead of a heart attack, I am predicting that now."

"Hey guys," Becky said, coming into the room accompanied by a tall, square-shouldered man Jonah thought he maybe recognized. "What are you talking about?"

"Taco Bell," Jonah said.

"Becks, you didn't tell me your cousin looked like Jake Gyllenhaal," Aimee said to her playfully.

"Right, he wishes," Becky answered, giving Jonah a knowing glance. "Can you help Jasmine with the sangria? I think they're messing it up."

"Yeah, cool," Aimee said, standing. "Jonah, promise me you'll check out the blog, okay? It's bigcitysmalltables.com. Leave me a comment and maybe we can try that ice cream sometime." She winked at him and left.

"Sorry," Becky said. "I swear I told her you had a girlfriend." Becky was no more than five-foot-one, *zaftig* (as her mother, Jonah's aunt Sheila, relentlessly put it), had long and curly brown hair, a mouth that smiled easily, a nose that was more overtly hooked than Jonah's. She wore a bright red dress, over that a black jacket with the sleeves rolled up, and had a tiara in her hair, for her birthday.

"There are worse things than being hit on by a food blogger," he answered. "Should I actually read it?"

"I dunno," Becky said. "How interested are you in desserts made with vegetables?" And they both laughed. Jonah was an only child, wasn't used to the easy rapport possible among family members of the same age. It surprised him how similar they were, having seen each other only for a few hours here and there over the years—similar not even in personality, but in outlook. "Anyway, you remember my boyfriend, Danny, right?" she said, now gesturing to the man standing beside her.

"Good to see you, Jonah," Danny said, shaking Jonah's hand firmly. Jonah did remember meeting him now, and remembered, too, that he was an accountant—reminded of this because, with his neat, 1950s-vintage crew cut, his starched blue button-down shirt, his wrinkle-less khakis, Danny made such a strong impression of accountancy, of being an accountant-in-full. There was even something accountant-like in the robotic way he slung his arm around Becky's shoulder: as if he had this arm around his girlfriend only because that was where he knew his arm was supposed to go, in the same way he might put another depreciated asset in the debits column of a spreadsheet. "We were so glad you could come," he said to Jonah.

"I was so surprised," said Becky. "I mean, in a good way. I didn't even know if you got the Evite."

"Well, y'know, family first," Jonah said. From the many expressions of unexpected pleasure at his being there, it had become clear to him that his presence tonight was a very large surprise; not that anyone was wrong to be surprised, of course, as his attendance was basically accidental. He decided to change the subject, taking the only course that presented itself: "Danny, you're an accountant, right? How's work been for you?"

"Terrific, as a matter of fact," Danny answered. "Everybody wants

an expert handling their money in this economy. Fear is the best sales-
man for CPAs," he said pleasantly. It was such an oddly tin-eared
comment that Jonah could only think to nod, as if in agreement. "Are
you invested?" Danny asked him.

He wasn't, not in any meaningful way, but Sylvia had hinted that,
in the not too distant future, she would be handling all of that. "I play
some online poker," he said.

"Jonah, I actually wanted to ask you about your job," Becky said.
"I'm thinking about taking an LSAT class this fall."

"Really?" he said. "I thought you wanted to be in the music
industry."

"Yeah, well," she said with a shrug. "The music business isn't quite
what I thought it would be. You like being a lawyer?"

He looked at Becky, with her tiara; he looked at Danny, with his
strangely wooden grin. He really didn't know what to say—felt as if
he'd been asked whether he liked being named Jonah. But then he
decided—yes, he did like being named Jonah. He did like being a lawyer. "It's a lot of fun," he laughed. "It's a lot of fun."

"Oh God, you're totally drunk," Becky moaned.

"Not totally." Then, with a long swig, he finished off the drink
Aimee had made him. "I'm working on it, though," he said, feeling that
this was all he had been trying to do for the last twenty-four hours:
have some fun.

The project of intoxication was accelerated considerably when, a
few minutes later, it was decided to move the party to the roof. The
keg was lugged to the elevator; everyone grabbed bottles of liquor and
beers from the refrigerator. The elevator let out in a glass vestibule,
beyond which was a roof deck that traced the edge of the building. The
heat of the day had faded now. Three hundred feet up, the night air
was mild, comfortable, conducive to partying all night. Jonah shared a
joint with a coworker of Becky's, a hipster in full regalia: sub-30-waist
jeans, elaborately manicured facial hair, ironic watch fob. They talked
about music, a topic Jonah had once flattered himself to think he
knew a lot about—once upon a time he'd attended dozens of Phish
shows—but he found that after several years away from the scene, he
didn't recognize most of the bands his smoking companion named.

They agreed to exchange mixes through Becky. Now both drunk and high, Jonah played some beer pong, then assisted in some keg stands, then did one himself. He flirted a little more shamelessly with Aimee, even went so far as to dance with her, which was a sign of just how wasted he was, because as a rule he had to be very wasted indeed to do any dancing at all. But he was proud of himself for not letting either their joking or the her-back-to-his-front dancing get out of hand.

It got to be past one. He'd intended to be home an hour earlier—but you can't always do what you intend, he reminded himself happily, nor did you have to. He went to the edge of the roof deck and took out his phone and wrote a text to Sylvia that he knew she wouldn't receive until the morning: "Thnking about how much I love you." He hit send and then leaned his elbows on the railing. Becky's building was about thirty stories—nothing so soaring by Manhattan standards, but to the human eye it was still enough to create of the city a great, spangled sea of bright windows on heaves of buildings, densely illuminated rivulets of headlights, taillights, flowing through the streets below. A little farther down the railing, Becky was writing a text message of her own, frowning into her phone. Jonah went over and gave her an affectionate squeeze.

"It's really great to see you," he said to her.

"It's great to see you, too," she answered. "You think it's okay if my friend brings a few other friends, right? We're not too loud?"

"Don't worry about it," Jonah assured her.

"Hey, did you tell Aimee you'd take her to Nobu?"

Maybe he hadn't cleaved as closely to the innocent as he'd imagined. "Mmm, yeah, well—I'm not actually going to do it."

"How nice for her," Becky laughed. "Y'know, I've been wanting to tell you something." She leaned a little closer toward him, spoke a little more quietly. "Danny and I are talking about . . ." And her smile seemed to broaden and brighten past the point where she could continue. "Engaged," she mouthed.

"No shit?" said Jonah. "Didn't you guys just get together?"

"Two years ago, Jonah."

"Fuck. Time moves pretty fast when you live inside a law firm," he muttered.

"You think he's a good guy, though, right?"

He recognized he hadn't been appropriately enthused in his initial reaction. "Of course he's a good guy," he told her. And, as he thought about it, he decided he had been too hard on Danny—that he was definitely a good guy. After all, wasn't it better to have your cousin marrying a guy who was a little too much an accountant as opposed to, say, a little too much a pot dealer? Plus, anyone could tell from the way she beamed just talking about marrying him that she was in love—that she was happy. And in that moment his cousin's happiness was very important to him. "He's a really good guy," Jonah told her.

"We walked by Harry Winston the other day and he randomly wanted to go in," she said. "That's a good sign, isn't it?"

He thought about Zoey, about Evan and the ring he hadn't offered. "Yes," he told Becky. "That is a very good sign."

"Don't tell your dad, though, okay? I want to surprise my parents."

"Lips are sealed."

"I am ninety percent certain he was ring shopping the other day. He was gone the whole afternoon and wouldn't say where. So, I don't know, maybe it'll happen soon."

As he looked into her earnest and hopeful face, Jonah saw that she was changing. He remembered her, as a teenager and even in college, having a decided hippie streak: wearing her hair long and unwashed, playing acoustic guitar at open mics, bringing an olive branch to Passover one year "in honor of Palestine bondage." Now she was going to get engaged to a CPA and wear a Harry Winston diamond and probably take the LSAT. But then, relationships changed people. Thanks to Sylvia, he had belts in three different colors and no longer drank soda. Maybe a progression away from hippie values was simply a natural consequence of maturity—or anyway, of a further entrance into adult life. Besides, he was the one who, after all those Phish shows, didn't know if that band was even together anymore. "I'm really happy for you, Becky," he said with sincerity. "It's going to work out, I can tell."

She rubbed his shoulder. "Thanks, Jonah. Anyway, come over to the other side with me, 'cause I want to start flip cup."

"I have to piss first. Is it okay if I go over the edge?"

"You're forgetting I didn't have brothers," she said. "There's a bathroom by the elevators. Come soon!" And she hurried away.

It was going to work out, he thought, as he walked around the deck—a little stumblingly—pushed open the door to the vestibule, where there were the elevators, a door to the stairwell, and, yes, a door to a small bathroom off to the left. Everything was going to work out, he thought, as he went inside, flicked on the light, latched the door behind him. He liked bathrooms—or rather, he liked taking refuge in bathrooms—bathrooms with one toilet, one sink and a mirror, where you could lock the door and be by yourself and—take stock of things. Sometimes even during dinners with clients or colleagues he would do this—feign the need for the toilet, go inside and lean against the door, check his phone and just enjoy the respite from needing to be yourself. Often, as he did now, he looked in the mirror—and thought again how all, everything, was going to work out—because Danny was a good guy—reliable and dependable and kind, and what else would he want in a husband for a family member? Because Sylvia in her relentless way was absolutely in love with him, and he was in love with her, too—maybe not with the fervor of his first months with Zoey, but that had been an aberration, fleeting; his love with Sylvia was tougher, more mature—they would make it work. All of them—he and Sylvia and Philip and Doug Chen, and the Aaron Seylers of the world, his parents, Zoey and Evan—they'd all make it work, it was all moving toward a common good end, a final good end. Maybe, just maybe, the whole world was entirely perfectible—and it was around then that he noticed something very bright and glowing on the very tip of his nose.

He thought maybe it was a pimple but immediately understood something very strange and probably very unfortunate was happening to him—a seizure at best—because the light on the tip of his nose expanded, rapidly whiting out his entire field of vision and revealed itself as the all-encompassing white to which all colors combine in nega-tion—a blankness oceanic in depth—encompassing all things seeable and not in a single uniform absence the way inky darkness did—and the first thing he saw looking through this whiteness into the mirror behind was his own aged, ragged face—its wrinkles and weakness and discoloration apprehended as the common end of all things—because it was only a matter of time—and in the lines of this face he could see the avenues of the city he flattered himself to think of as permanent but had no more permanence than any single resident of it or day on its calendar—the Empire State Building collapsed and Grand Central Station collapsed and the subway tunnels flooded with water and then water rising to the streets through the concrete so that what had been the city, this city, became an island again interlaced with rivers and buried in the rubble of things collapsed or burned or bombed or pulled apart like the shining marble pulled from the pyramids and the city that had surrounded them because really—it was only a matter of time—before all, everything—every name, street, partner, marquee, gigabyte of memory, scrap of paper, cupcake, T-shirt, actress, taxi-cab, chai, beer bottle, mouse, MetroCard, friend, colleague, book, bill, exhibit, bench—every person loved and unknown—and Jonah Daniel Jacobstein—would vanish like a closed eye—and against this empty white he saw now as if inscribed in fire upon it, small and still and unmistakable: יונה הנני

And then it was just a five-by-five bathroom, with the distinct odor of natural mildew comingling with synthetic evergreen. And it was just his face—though he saw it as he had never seen it before: insepa-rable from its mortality—as Judith's had been. His heart was pound-ing, his clothes were soaked in cold sweat. He gripped the sides of the sink, worried he might pass out, and was immediately relieved to feel its solidity—the cold, dull, porcelain banality—but the relief was tem-porary because, as he leaned forward, he cracked the sink from out of the wall and was hit with a jagged stream of water from the pipes behind.

He fled. He rushed from the bathroom, punched the down button on the elevator with the palm of his hand, waited about three seconds, then shoved open the door to the stairs and started bounding down them, two at a time. At the first landing, he came upon another vision: two men wrestling. Then he realized the two men were not in fact wrestling but rather were involved in a passionate make-out session—arms wrapped around each other, mouths pressed tightly together. Jonah hurried past them, saw that one of the men was the hipster he'd smoked with—and then, as he brushed by, that the other was Danny.

At just that moment Danny opened his eyes—their eyes met, and Jonah continued his run down the stairs.

For several floors he thought he was caught in an endless Escher staircase, that the vision had exploded the physics of reality altogether—but then some less hysterical part of him noted that this was how it felt to try to run down thirty flights of stairs. His heart was still thumping wildly; to stop himself, he grabbed at the railing, spun to the floor, and crashed onto his knees. He was so covered in sweat, both cold and warm, with water from the broken sink, that he felt as if he had been plunged into the ocean. He heard a painful heaving sound. It took him a full minute to understand this was his own labored breath. He wondered if he was indeed having a heart attack—but after several minutes the panting had ebbed a little, and he was still alive. He pulled himself to his feet. He forced himself to walk slowly down to the next landing, where he exited the stairwell and pushed the down button on the elevator. When it came, it was empty: There were no shining angels or horrifying demons. He rode down to the lobby—and then, eyes on the black polished floor, he walked to and through the revolving door and out of the building. Eyes now on the sidewalk, he raised his arm for a cab, and when it pulled up he got in and told the driver where he lived. He squeezed his eyes shut for the ride home—and it was only as the cab jerked forward that he realized he'd pissed his pants on top of everything else.

2. JUDITH, OR THE GOOD STUDENT

Judith had one of those happy, complete-unto-itself childhoods that seem to exist as a sort of aspirational fairy tale in the American mind.

Her parents were upper middle class, steadily employed, stable people, in love with each other and in love with their only daughter, committed to giving Judith as perfect a girlhood as possible. The family took ski trips to Colorado, beach trips to Hawaii, culturally edifying trips to Paris and London and Athens and Israel; they went on safari in South Africa when Judith graduated junior high. Her birthdays were always resoundingly celebrated, she received a present on each of the eight nights of Hanukkah. As far back as she could remember, she was encouraged, she was supported, she was continually reassured as to how special and brilliant and beautiful she was.

And somehow in response to all this, Judith worked nonstop. She was one of those kindergartners who was thrilled the day she got her first piece of homework: happy to get it, proud to do it. On the bulletin board in the classroom recording the number of books each student had read, the line of cutout stars tacked beside Judith's name was always several inches longer than any other child's. She would put herself to sleep reciting the multiplication tables, one through twelve; she prepared for science or history tests by creating fat stacks of note cards that she would study one by one, over and over, with monkish concentration. Her greatest disciplinary problem as a child was reading ahead in her books against her teachers' instructions.

She was the one who, at twelve, had requested an SAT tutor, knowing full well it was a test she would not have to take for more than four years. But she was hardly the sort of girl who shied away from the extremes of preparation. Once, when she and her parents had gone over to a neighbor's for Passover, she spent the pre-Seder mingling time sitting on the rug and working on her Latin homework on the coffee table. Observing this, the mother of the hostess—a compact old woman with brilliantly silver hair and the weathered skin of someone who had spent the greater part of her adult life either over a stove or on the beach in Florida—said of her, "She's like a dog with a bone, that one." *Os, ossis,* thought Judith.

Her labors were not limited to schoolwork, either. There were also the many activities—in theory recreational but, as she got older, intended more and more to enhance what her father called "the old college application." In elementary school she took piano and private French lessons and pottery. By high school, to these had been added model UN, debate, various honor societies, B'nai B'rith Girls (local and regional), monthly volunteering at the local soup kitchen, and running cross-country.

This last area was the one in which Judith distinguished herself least. Though she was theoretically built like a distance runner—unusually

long-limbed and tall since girlhood—she was not athletic, and the rituals of team sports (the whooping after victories, the sobbing after losses)
did not come naturally to her. The dynamics of the sport were intuitive
enough, familiar enough, though: Just go. And the greater purpose, as
her father only occasionally had to remind her, was to demonstrate that
she was a well-rounded young woman.

By the end of her sophomore year, it was clear Judith would have
enough credits to graduate from high school a year early. This situation
was deemed worthy of an official family meeting, so Judith and her
parents gathered in the living room, sat on the couch underneath the
portrait of Judith's father's grandfather—ancient, white-bearded, dour
in black coat and black skullcap—looking, Judith always thought, as
though he'd stepped into the painting directly from some authentic
Jewish *shtetl* past.

"I'll be honest, I'm selfish," her father, David, said, in his jokey, half-
ironic way. He was a professor of literature, who had at the time recently
completed a highly praised translation of *The Canterbury Tales*. "I
don't want to lose my favorite person in the world a year early."

"We don't need to frame it that way, David," her mother, Hannah,
corrected him. She was a prizewinning poet and novelist and an artist-
in-residence-cum-professor at the same college where Judith's father
taught. "Sweetheart," Judith's mother said to her, "you can have our
advice if you want it, but ultimately this is your decision. And we'll
support you regardless. But," she added delicately, "I think it's important to remember, you have your whole life to be an adult."

"Very true," her father assented quickly, winkingly.

"Your days as a child are fleeting," her mother said, and snapped in
the air—a flourish typical of her mother.

The three of them discussed the issue at length—weighed the advantages and disadvantages with regard to college applications; considered
the possibility of a gap year and how it might be spent; speculated on
the social implications of starting college at seventeen. And, in the end,
Judith decided she would not graduate high school early, but would
instead spend her senior year compiling AP credits that could be used
to graduate from college early. Her logic—for which David and Hannah commended her—was that she could still put herself a year ahead

in her education, but without sacrificing her last year of high school with her friends and without having to enter college as the youngest person on her freshman floor. Plus, it was the financially prudent decision: a fourth year at her private high school, Gustav Girls' Academy, though not cheap, would be cheaper than a fourth year at whatever private college she ended up attending. Of course, her parents told her that financial considerations shouldn't matter to her. But really, none of the logic mattered to Judith at all. She made her decision because she agreed with her father: She didn't want to lose a year with her favorite people, either. She didn't want to miss any family meetings.

It was not as if Judith was in any hurry to be done with the work of high school, either. True, she was often stressed, nearly always sleep-deprived. But these were not conditions she minded. In fact, she took a certain pride in her fatigue—as though it were a state to be aspired to. From this perspective, she could appreciate better the notions of athletics: When she and her teammates were sweating and staggering up the hill on Triangle Street, she felt a particular form of communion with them—the same she felt walking into the library at Gustav Girls' Academy on a Saturday to see it crowded with her classmates, her mammoth backpack heavy on her shoulders with books and binders.

Later in her life—when she would occupy long hours at galleries and auctions, staring at works of art she might buy to decorate the walls of the Colonel's casinos—she wondered quite what had impelled young Judith to work quite so hard. She had been, if anyone was, a child of the leisure class. Why, then, had there been so little leisure?

Some of it, she understood, was just the twists of her DNA—"who she was." She had classmates at Gustav's who smoked pot between classes, went to Ani DiFranco shows on the weekends. But the majority—even the vast majority—had been little terrors of self-discipline, like her. The differences between most of her classmates and her were the differences in degrees between fervor and fanaticism.

The work, Judith came to believe, was somehow intrinsic to the proposition of being a daughter of the upper middle class. On the most basic level, Judith and most of those she went to school with were raised to believe that the key to success in life was hard work: to have the life and career you wanted, you had to go to a good college; to get into a good college, you had to do well in high school and in everything else; and to do well in everything required hard work. It was the fundamental proposition—the promise—of American achievement. Yet the intensity of the effort, she understood later, was out of proportion to this logic. The 5:00 A.M. wake-ups, the summers at SAT-prep camps, the time spent studying in class, outside class, in the car on the way to National Honor Society meetings: It was as if they felt they owed it to themselves, to their parents, to the big bedrooms in which they slept and to the new cars in which they were driven and to the backyard pools in which they swam. It was as if the work, finally, made them not rich, but deserving.

There was also for Judith—as for many of them—another element to her diligence, though it was one she tended not to dwell on in her adult life: She was Jewish. Her family was not observant in the Orthodox sense of the word—they didn't keep kosher, didn't refrain from watching television or handling money on Friday night. But Judaism was important to them. They belonged to a Reform synagogue, went once a month for Shabbat and on many of the (major) holidays. They participated in any food drives the synagogue held and made regular donations to MAZON and to the ADL, understanding such giving to be as much a practice of their religion as eating matzo on Passover. There was Judaic artwork throughout the house, a *mezuzah* on the front door. Hannah, whose own mother was a survivor of Buchenwald, always set her novels among the highly Jewish milieu in Philadelphia in which she'd been raised; she won a Brochstein Medal for her translations of Yiddish poetry. And perhaps most powerfully—there was among the family a collective reverence for thought, for academics, for scholarship. For Judith, the obligation to study had been inextricable from her idea of what it meant to be a Jew. The Jews, she was taught, were the Chosen People—and this was not a guarantee of exceptionalism but instead an obligation to carry on a tradition that included the articulation of monotheism, the founding of many of the world's great philosophies, the invention of psychotherapy, and the discovery of relative physics. Her most profound moments of religious feeling came not in temple, but rather when she would be in her bedroom working on a paper or problem set, and hear her father typing away in his study; hear her mother gently, quietly reciting verse. Then Judith would feel—would feel she knew—that God was real, imminently real, and they were all a part of something much larger than themselves.

But again, as an adult, Judith didn't think much about such memories—and if she did, her attention soon returned to the Hirst or Koons she had been charged with buying at auction; she would maybe hold before the work a fabric swatch from a curtain—try to envision it all.

By the time Judith began high school, her parents—despite being so strictly proud of her—sometimes did worry about their daughter, who appeared to them so profoundly studious, maybe to the exclusion of other things she might have been. She had a couple of friends going back to elementary school but could not be called popular; there was a boyfriend for a few months during her junior year, but they had immediately recognized that he was hopelessly overmatched beside their daughter (indeed, literally so, as Judith was three inches taller). And while they were not lying when they told her how beautiful they thought she was—inside and out—neither did they claim that this beauty was of a conventional kind.

Judith herself recognized she had pulled a few of the least desirable cards from her parents' combined genetic deck. She had her father's long, lanky frame, but without the unexpected grace that made him a good dancer at weddings. She had her mother's proud beak of a nose, but without the delicacy of eyes and mouth that had once induced Hunter S. Thompson to drunkenly proposition her at a party in the early seventies. (She declined, or so she said.) Least fortunately of all, Judith had inherited the hair of David's mother—what the girls in B'nai B'rith Girls cheerfully referred to as her Jewfro: jet-black, Brillo coarse, antigravitational in its growth. Judith and Hannah tried innumerable strategies over the years to tame it—involving the use of dozens of different conditioners, wide-toothed combs of various compositions, mornings of flat ironing, an entire summer of professional straightening—but ultimately concluded there was simply nothing to be done. For all of high school and college and for her year of graduate school, Judith wore her hair in two slablike waves, separated by a side part.

But Judith was not an overly self-conscious teenager. She did have uncomfortable moments of visualizing herself as she walked down the hall at school: the tallest in her class, with a gangling gait, elbows and knees more prominent than breasts. But she tempered her awareness that she was a somewhat odd-looking young woman with the confidence that there was something compelling in this oddness—in the stark contrast of her pale skin and her black hair, in the small round mole just below her left eye. If this unconventional look was not to be appreciated now, she had faith it would be someday. Besides, half the indisputably beautiful girls at Gustav's were anorexic. Literally none of the teenage girls she knew seemed entirely happy with their appearance.

And she could not help but derive at least some added bodily satisfaction from having lost her virginity to a twenty-five-year-old.

Judith's parents would have worried less about their daughter's social life if they'd known that while she was indeed profoundly studious, she was not merely so. Indeed, she prided herself on this broadness of character. But if her parents had had a fuller picture of their daughter's life—interior and exterior—they would have only worried more, and with better reason.

The intensity Judith showed in her schoolwork was only one manifestation of a general intensity she was aware of in her character—a kind of insatiable avidity that at times got out of her control. When she was eight, her Hebrew school teacher explained that the *yad* in the glass case on the principal's desk had been saved from a Lithuanian synagogue burned during World War II. Judith stole this—and for two weeks she would lock the door of her room and secretly admire the beauty of the *yad*'s weathered bronze, the elegantly articulated fingers; would sleep with it under her pillow, as though trying to absorb the potency of loss and survival and holiness the object seemed to her to emanate. Then the rabbi gathered all the students of the Hebrew school into the *shul* and talked for forty impassioned minutes about the legacy of the Shoah, the necessity of its remembrance in object and thought, the inestimable value of artifacts like the *yad*—and about ten words into this, Judith realized, with the suddenness of being shaken awake, that despite the sense of piousness she'd perceived around the whole project, she had done something very, very wrong. Fortunately (or so she judged at the time), she managed to secretly return the *yad*, and her guilt was never discovered.

Judith's zeal had an indiscriminate, free-floating quality, fixing on objects ranging from the somewhat predictable, such as her religion, to the ostensibly random, such as ancient Egypt—which her fifth grade class spent three months studying, during which time Judith memorized the names of every pharaoh of the Middle Kingdom and taught herself dozens of hieroglyphs. Growing up, Judith simply had a zeal for zeal: a passion for levels or acts of greater vehemence and sharpness than those around her appeared satisfied with.

This zeal found a new outlet when she discovered masturbation—creating a link between a penchant for extremism and sex that, she would realize later in life, was not altogether beneficial. Like most of the girls with whom she swapped stories when she got older, she had basically no idea what she was doing at first. She would be watching a PG-13 bedroom scene or even just looking at photographs of Greek statuary, and an unfamiliar mood would come over her. She would retreat to her bedroom, lock the door, and, through some clutching and unclutching of her legs around the corner of her mattress, effect waves of sensation that seemed to issue from the source of the unfamiliarity. Practice led to more sophisticated methods—until she could spend hours engrossed in a secret world whose dimensions and sensations could not be articulated. She realized, of course, that other people masturbated, too; she'd had the Conversation with her mother well ahead of her first period, she'd endured a sixth-grade sex-ed class. But with her eyes clenched tight and the windows of her bedroom thrown open—she believed no one masturbated quite like this.

Such points of differentiation were important to her. Like many high-achieving teenage girls (like many high achievers of any age), she had an instinctive anxiety around being "normal": being like anyone else, not special, just another Gustav's girl. This concern, she believed, was at least part of why anorexia was so rampant among her peers: It gave you a secret—a secret suffering.

But if by the start of her sophomore year she regarded masturbation as a mark of distinction from her classmates, she was also aware
that in most sexual endeavors she had yet to distinguish herself. Girls
in her class had gone to second base, third base, even had sex with
boys from other schools in town. Aside, though, from a few awkward
smooches during a single game of spin-the-bottle at a friend's bat
mitzvah reception, until the fall of her second year of high school,
Judith's sex life had remained a strictly one-woman affair. She simply
did not know how to flirt with boys, how to make herself attractive to
boys, how to transform the friendships she did have with boys into
anything physical. The gap between stilted coed hangouts at the
movies and the aching joys of an orgasm seemed to her more or less
impossible to bridge. And this frustrated Judith, not so much because
she thought she'd actually get much pleasure from having a boy "feel
her up" (the slang here all too accurate, given her height) but rather
because not knowing something was antithetical to her disposition—
really, to her entire way of life. The fact that she couldn't find a boyfriend made Judith feel stupid. As a fifteen-year-old, Judith did not
think of herself as lonely; she had several friends at school, and she
had two best friends she lived with, Mom and Dad. Yet she understood that there were forms of companionship she was missing. She
was, after all, a young woman who strove to be well rounded.

And then she fell in love with her English teacher.

The class was called Nineteenth-Century Writers and the Invention
of America. Judith and the two other girls in the class, Amanda Veen
and Stacy Barashkov, gathered on the first day in Room 13—sat around
a circular wooden table by a picture window overlooking the commons
in the back of the school. Gabe came in wearing an outfit she would
come to know as typical for him: button-down shirt and tie, jeans and
no jacket. He was really (really!) not much older than her, only a few
years out of college; had been a creative writing and English major at
Berkeley, the previous summer had completed two years of teaching
in Uganda for the Peace Corps, had a short story published in *The
Kenyon Review* and a half-finished novel on his desk in his apartment. But she would learn all that only later. When he walked to the
table that day—with an insouciant, self-assured gait that struck her as

distinctively masculine—all she knew about him was that he was new to the school, that he was very tall (six foot four), dark-haired, Grecian-nosed—and he pulled a dog-eared, jacketless book from the messenger bag slung across his chest, and read, " 'The atmosphere is not a perfume, it has no taste of the distillation, it is odorless, / It is for my mouth forever, I am in love with it, / I will go to the bank by the wood and become undisguised and naked, / I am mad for it to be in contact with me.' " Then, closing the book and dropping it on the table as he pulled the messenger bag off his shoulder, he asked them, "So, ladies. What is Walt Whitman talking about?"

So that's how this feels, Judith thought.

In truth, they were all in love with him. Amanda Veen responded by encasing herself in a stunned silence that lasted the entire semester, Stacy Barashkov by answering questions in class with anxious, rehearsed monologues, her hands flailing chaotically before her. Judith—in whom the most powerful of internal emotions tended to produce a useful if eerie (even to her) sort of calm—concluded that her best course to winning his affection was to show him that she was brilliant, too.

Her mother, reading over her first paper on *Leaves of Grass*, said with sincerity that she would have given it an A if one the students in her Poetry for Poets course had handed it in—this one of those times when she was even a bit awed by her daughter's intellect. Gustav's had a principled stance against letter grades, but Gabe was effusive in the praise he wrote at the bottom of the page beneath her conclusion. For her next paper, on Emily Dickinson, Judith did hours of research in the library, tracing connections between the poet's life in Amherst and the "psychological themes" of her verse. This time Gabe was a little awed, too. Judith was careful not to make her papers too fusty or schoolgirl pedantic: She wanted to demonstrate that she grasped the beauty and expansiveness of this writing, that she shared Gabe's evident passion for it, saw the same sparks of the world it promised—sparks that she believed formed the twinkle in his eye when he read aloud to her and Amanda and Stacy (though she liked to think just to her), " 'Heavenly Hurt, it gives us— / We can find no scar, / But internal difference, / Where the Meanings, are—' " Most of all she wanted to imply that she ached with the same longings that animated the writing itself. "The garden behind her home became for the young Emily Dickinson the imaginative landscape in which dramas played out that she both craved and feared to experience in her actual life," she wrote. She was aware that she was maybe falling love with nineteenth-century American literature as much as she was with Gabe—but, in an interpretation of events that was maybe a bit too imaginative for anyone's actual life, she concluded that there really didn't have to be much difference.

Either way, the papers had the desired effect, and at the bottom of her creative-writing exercise exploring Transcendental themes in her daily life, Gabe wrote, "Judith, you are an exceptional young woman. Let's find some time to get together to discuss your writing face-to-face." This comment—which, in an exceedingly rare occurrence, made her alabaster cheeks darken with color—would remain the highlight of a distinguished academic career.

They met after school for coffee in the café in the lobby of Gustav's. In his usual amiable, relaxed way, he told her about going to college at Berkeley, about teaching in Uganda; he asked her about her family, her friends, her plans for college and after. It surprised her how easy it was to talk to him—or, rather, how easy it seemed for him to listen to her, have a conversation with her. She was used to boys being a little perplexed or put off by her demeanor, which, unlike that of many girls her age, was not bright and giggly, but contemplative, muted. She did not think of herself as shy, exactly—more reserved, though this was a distinction few adolescent males bothered to notice. But as she talked to Gabe in her measured, somewhat low voice, he nodded, he watched her face, he responded—all with an interest and evident appreciation she had never seen from a man who was not her father. And why should he react to her the way boys did? she asked herself at one point: He was not a boy. And Gabe would tell her—much later—that he found the calm way she talked, the watchfulness of her eyes intriguing, even sexy.

At the end of the coffee, they exchanged email addresses. He began to send her poems—Philip Larkin, W. H. Auden at first; later Pablo

Neruda, e. e. cummings. Sometimes he would send her a message consisting of only a single sentence or phrase in the subject line: "There's nothing so spiritual about being happy but you can't miss a day of it." "Glamorous nymph, with an arrow and bow." She would track down the fragments of poems or song lyrics, buy the poets' books, buy the albums, send poems and song lyrics back, saving, printing every email, and keeping them all hidden under her bed in a worn leather case that she'd pulled from her mother's closet, and which she would sometimes take out at night—tracing the creases in the leather with her fingers, as though reading some private mystic Braille.

They started meeting for coffee once or twice a week. He kept the mood casual and the topics generally teacher–student appropriate, but soon she began to notice that his leg would be shaking when she sat down, or that his finger would silently tap the side of his coffee mug as he watched her speak. He started telling her about his own writing, his novel (a bildungsroman about a man trying to model his life after the young James Joyce), his own plans for the future. "You're an old soul," he told her as they stood from one of their coffees. "Sometimes I think older than I am." It was at that moment that she recognized he had lowered a barrier she had been trying with all her intellectual might to get him to lower: that she had succeeded in expanding the way he perceived her.

Looking back on it as an adult, she sensed a certain inevitability to how events transpired after that—though maybe it had been inevitable from the first coffee, the first email. Regardless, at some point it had gotten to be that they both wanted the same thing, and then it was just a matter of time, until he offered to drive her home one afternoon; and they managed to collectively have the idea of taking a brief hike before he dropped her off; and this hike led them through a sparse woods to the side of a creek, afternoon sunlight glinting off its face, the two of them sitting side by side on a log so conveniently placed along its banks it seemed to have been put there just for them.

"You are so extraordinary," Gabe told her, almost sadly. Something in his tone caused her heart to start slamming itself against her rib cage; she had to breathe through her nose in order to hide the quickening of her breath. These were sensations familiar only from the end of her longer cross-country runs, but somehow here this was not really an unpleasant condition. "I feel such a connection with you," he went on. "You must sense that. Judith," he said, turning to her—his soft brown eyes only escalating the riot of nervousness and arousal inside her. "Let's cut the bullshit. We are in very, very dangerous territory." She managed to nod with equanimity. "You should know, I have a girlfriend. In California. Emma." *We have a new enemy* was the phrase that popped into her head—a quote, she realized immediately, from *The Empire Strikes Back*, a movie she had seen an embarrassing number of times with her father. This might have alerted her to the fact that she really was too young to be doing this, but—her mind was occupied with a different set of concerns at the moment. "I have to take you home now," he told her. Neither of them moved, of course. "I'll still be your teacher. We can stay friends."

"I want more," Judith said.

Maybe she realized there was a line he would not let himself cross with her—maybe this impelled her even more powerfully to cross it, answering again the insatiable zeal that had induced her to steal the *yad* from off the principal's desk. She reached up and took his head in her hands, pulled his face to hers. These first touches were searing in their intensity, and for a fifteen-year-old enamored of nineteenth-century American literature—enamored of the idea of it, enamored of its passions, and of passions she'd been seeking her entire life—to lose her virginity on the banks of a creek, her skin imprinted with twigs, her hair tangled in the grass: It was all about as much as Judith Klein Bulbrook could ask for. When he lifted himself off her and went to look in the grass for the underwear that had been tossed aside, she lay there watching the sky, the path of clouds between the branches at the tops of the trees, her fingers dangling against the cold surface of the creek. She thought of what she had just done, the home she had to go home to, the future that now offered itself before her—and she sensed a perfect wholeness across her entire life. It was the happiest moment of her life, she realized—and she thanked God for it.

The moment didn't last, of course. When Gabe returned, holding her sun-yellow panties dotted with little flowers (she hadn't guessed today would be the day), she burst into tears—the blunt facts of what had happened suddenly, jarringly apparent. She was fifteen and she'd lost her virginity to her English teacher; she was lying half naked beside a creek; a man was standing over her with her underwear in his hand. But she would always judge him to be a good man for what he did next: knelt down beside her, stroked her coarse hair, promised her it would be okay.

The affair did not last long. Really, it was all too, too intense for both of them, and maybe even more so for him. He felt a great deal of guilt: first for cheating on Emma, the California girlfriend; and more, he could never rid himself of the worry that he was "taking advantage" of her, no matter what she said or did to reassure him. The risks weighed on him, too, risks that only began with his relationship, his teaching career. Judith didn't think her parents would go so far as to have him arrested for statutory rape if they found out—but she couldn't be sure, either. She'd never had a serious disagreement with them. During the month Gabe and she were together, he lost weight, told her he didn't sleep well, couldn't work on his novel. Some mornings he looked so ashen in class she actually felt sorry for him.

For her part, Judith was aware that her zealotry had gotten her in way over her head. She enjoyed the sex—this, a radical understatement—but indeed, that was the problem. It was shocking to her—it was frightening, almost—the way her body ran away from her as it neared an orgasm with him, to say nothing of what it did when it actually had one. She found it was hard on her to go in a single afternoon from a girl whose bra had never been unclasped by hands other than hers to a full-fledged sexual being. She started to wish she had been felt up at some point. And it all made her feel a little alien within her own life— alienated, if to a minor degree, even from her parents, to whom she now had to lie for the first time. She was by turns blithe and regretful; euphoric and then fearful, conscience-stricken. Such mood swings were so unlike what she knew of herself—seemed to her so teenager. It was at a diner twenty minutes outside town, as they were weighing whether he should spend a night at her house while her parents were out of town for the weekend, and she noticed she'd bent the cheap metal fork on the table into a figure eight, that they decided, without much discussion, that it needed to end.

That night she reread all the emails and poems, as though reliving their former elation as present sorrow, sobbed herself to sleep. But when she woke up the next day, she discovered she was relieved. And as she walked down the halls of Gustav's that morning, she realized that she now had a secret that would surpass that of any other girl in the school. She imagined as she went from class to class, her books clutched to her chest, her nimbus of black hair floating above her pale brow, that if anyone looked closely enough, they would see that the twinkle she had first seen in Gabe's eye was now made permanent in her own. (At the time, she didn't think this was why she had had the affair—but by the time she was in Las Vegas, she was not so sure.)

There was an unhappy coda to the relationship, however. Judith had been taking the pill since she was thirteen, in order to keep her periods regular—but no one gets A's in everything. And Judith—being an extremely busy high school student with umpteen thoughts, assignments, activities on her mind at any one time—was less than perfect about remembering to take her birth control. She gave it a lot more attention after she started having sex, of course—but as she'd learned in her sixth-grade sex-ed class, after you start having sex can be too late.

After the fifth day without her period, she told him. They were sitting in the car at the trailhead, near where they'd first had sex. A pea soup greenness crept across his face, his expression not so much panicked as progressively catatonic. Then he burst into tears. "The last thing I ever wanted was to ruin your life," he said.

This time, she comforted him. As emergency appeared increasingly likely, one of her calms had come over her. She had thought it through: She would tell her mother but not her father; she would refrain from revealing Gabe's identity and believed her mother would respect this choice; she would go to the college health center, where she had been taken her whole life for colds and strep, and she would have an abortion. And that would be terrible, she told herself, but it was the logical course of action—and in the end she would be okay. She would be able to live with it, and she would still get to go to whichever Ivy she chose, still become renowned in whatever field of study she picked. Her life, in short, would not be ruined: It would still play out just as it would have.

When he'd stopped crying, he tried to rally himself—for some reason this involved him pulling off his tie—and he said, "Okay, well, let's go get you a pregnancy test."

They drove to a Walmart forty minutes down the highway. When they got there, though, Gabe lost heart again. With shoulders slumped forward, his hands gripping the steering wheel, his eyes on the dormant speedometer, he told her, "I can't go in with you." Then he added, "You might as well just take it in the bathroom. We might as well find out now." That he would make this suggestion stunned her—but, collecting herself, she tried not to blame him. After all, she reminded herself: He had prison to think about.

She maintained her composure while walking across the parking lot. As she entered the cavernous store, alone, however, craning her neck to read the signs ten feet over the aisles—camping supplies, cookware, appliances, groceries—her sangfroid began to crack. She searched among endless shelves of vitamins and creams and tampons, finally found the pregnancy tests—dozens of them, on a rack rising from her ankles to her forehead; and, as she stared at all these boxes, she realized how badly she did not want to have to do this: take a pregnancy test in a Walmart bathroom—have an abortion at fifteen. "Oh, God," she said under her breath. "Please don't do this to me. I'll be smarter now, I swear."

She selected the most expensive test, concluding that a flawed rationale for choosing one was better than none. She took it to the front of the store, placed it on the belt at the checkout line, then for cosmetic purposes piled two magazines and a pack of gum on top of it. The woman at the register was only a little older than her, African American, wore gold hoop earrings and had long, elaborately decorated fingernails. She ran the gum and the magazines over the scanner, then came to the pregnancy test—gave Judith a quizzical, up-and-down look.

"You know what this is?" she asked. Judith stared back at her blankly. This was a conversation she deeply, deeply did not want to have. "What are you, thirteen?" Reason was abandoning Judith—a sensation all the more disconcerting as she'd never felt it before. She was terrified this woman was about to call her parents. But then the woman just shook her head, scanned the pregnancy test. "Thirteen year-old girl and you in here alone," she said as the scanner beeped. "They always let you down, don't they?"

Judith grabbed the pregnancy test, left the magazines, hurried to the bathroom, managed to slam the door and lock it ahead of the tears. The reality of all this was encroaching further and further from the imagined landscape and into her actual life. "Oh, please, God," she said. "Please, please, please."

The bathroom was, mercifully, a single-person unit—just her and the sink and the mirror and the toilet. She pulled the pregnancy test from the box, read the instructions from start to finish (though the gist was clear from looking at the device: Piss here), pulled down her pants, and sat on the toilet. She took one last, pleading breath—looked down at her underwear and saw she had gotten her period. "Thank God," she whispered. "Oh, thank you, God, oh, God, thank you."

After this trauma, Judith and Gabe restricted their interactions to the classroom. Even emails now seemed too emotionally fraught and risky. Occasionally when he read aloud in class, he did seem to be looking at her with special attention, but this aside, there was never again any outward indication from either of them that they had ever been more than exceptional student and favorite teacher. It was a somewhat sad way for their affair to end, Judith thought—though it was a kind of sadness she found she could enjoy. In any case, far worse endings had been possible.

That summer she went on a youth trip to Israel, and by the time she returned, Gabe had moved back to California—had resigned from Gustav's and taken a job teaching at a private school in Santa Barbara. She presumed he was living with Emma, but he didn't specify in the brief, quietly heartfelt email he wrote her, the last one she put in the leather case underneath her bed. "Judith, you are a woman of tremendous promise," he wrote. "I can't wait to see all that you accomplish."

For a while she kept an eye out for his accomplishments, too—though the novel she expected to see never appeared.

She didn't date much, or try to, for the rest of high school. She did have the boyfriend her parents judged overmatched during her junior year, but overmatched was pretty much her assessment, too. He was the captain of a debate team Gustav's had beat in a regional competition: She found him sweet but ultimately uninteresting, handsome but impatient and inexpert when it came to anything below her waist. Overall, there was no comparison to Gabe—and Judith was content to wait until later in life to find worthy romantic companionship. Really, she was content to be simply another Gustav's girl for a while. She would never forget how lucky, how blessed—how watched over—she had felt in that bathroom to find that she had retained the privilege of this status; to find that her world, which for an instant had seemed so fragile, was in fact so durable.

But by the time she was in Las Vegas, these were only memories—the sentiments enviable, and vain.

3. BUT JONAH SET OUT TO FLEE

Jonah had quit smoking during his first year of law school, but in the wake of what he'd seen in the bathroom at Becky's party, it struck him that, lung cancer or not, if he was going to stop his hands from shaking and his mind from racing frantically over the details of what he'd witnessed, nicotine's sedative powers were going to be essential. It was all hands on deck, in other words, and so he told the cab driver taking him home to stop at a bodega, and he bought three packs of American Spirits.

The queasiness of smoking his first cigarette in eight years, though, only added to the helpless feeling he'd had on opening the door of his apartment, taking in the bare floors, the cardboard boxes behind the couch, the forty-six-inch television—and realizing this was all he had to come home to. He'd felt an instinct to call Zoey; whatever else she was, she was among the most genuinely caring people in his life, and she knew him in a way, with a depth, that even Sylvia did not. (He recognized this was a bad sign for the relationship he'd chosen to pursue, but figured he had enough to worry about at the moment.) By the time he'd peeled off his sopping wet clothes and changed into dry ones, however, he'd concluded that Zoey wouldn't believe him—nor would Sylvia, nor either parent, nor any friend. The most they would do would be to try to convince him of their own doubts—and one of the most remarkable aspects of what he'd seen was how pitiably inadequate it had made doubt appear to be.

As this thought occurred to him, the silence in his apartment became perceptible—as though he could apprehend the vacuum all around him, where doubt had been. He immediately turned on the television, cranked up the AC to full blast, began blaring a Rolling Stones album from his stereo, lit another cigarette, took a few swigs of three-hundred-dollar Scotch. This cacophony of sound, video, cigarettes, and alcohol succeeded in crowding away enough of the fear and agitation to allow him space to think, and he'd grabbed a pen and an unopened letter from the Vassar Alumni Association, sat down at his coffee table, and begun a list he titled "Logical Explanations." (He understood now that this list, currently crumpled in a ball on the floor, had in fact been his desperate attempt at the reassertion of doubt.)

The first item written on the list was: "1) Smoked bad weed." Theoretically, there was a great deal to recommend this explanation: circumstance, as he'd smoked the joint with the hipster only an hour or so before going into the bathroom; and convention, too, as the majority of modern hallucinations were attributed to hallucinogenics. The problem, though, was that he had smoked bad weed before—or anyway, weed that had been laced with angel dust. It had happened at an outdoor music festival he'd attended during college. There were no hallucinations, he'd only felt very, very high, then lost sensation in his arms and legs, and then had to spend the rest of the afternoon eating orange slices in the chill-out tent. He'd done mushrooms a couple of times, too, and dropped acid once. The former had only made him giggly and awed at everything he saw, and while the latter did produce some pretty intense delusions (most notably the notes from Trey Anastasio's guitar appearing as orange butterflies that floated into the sky before merging with the sun), there had always been to these images an unmistakable tinge of the unreal, of the chemical. In other words, he'd known the whole time he was tripping that he was tripping. Whereas in the bathroom, what he'd seen had not struck him as a distortion of reality, but rather as a sudden and jarringly clear exposure of reality. Plus, more concretely, when you were tripping you didn't take something, see some crazy shit, and then stop tripping. There was a rapid crescendo into the trip and then a long, slow decrescendo out of it, for better or worse the whole experience lasting at least four or five hours. And he'd never felt more hopelessly sober than when he'd been running down those stairs.

Next on the list: "2) Seeing things bc exhausted, stressed, hungry." If the delusion was not the work of some foreign pharmacological agent, maybe it was simply the predictable malfunctioning of a brain under siege: the misfirings of his beleaguered neurons. He had been up since six that morning. He had ingested nothing all day but a turkey sandwich at his desk, a slice of birthday cake, plus four cups of coffee, countless units of alcohol in various forms, and half a joint's worth of weed. But none of this was exactly atypical. In truth, he spent most days exhausted, stressed, and hungry. The most it had ever produced before were the spots and stars of a migraine headache. Besides, he'd been feeling good at the party—had been having a great time, as a matter of fact, until he'd witnessed the downfall of New York City in the wrinkles of his elderly face.

This left "3) Schizophrenia?"—and staring at the word after he'd written it, he'd been troubled enough to add the question mark. He had to admit, it seemed a plausible explanation. He searched for definitions of the disorder on WebMD and MayoClinic.com, but even this cursory research revealed that the condition was more complicated, in ways both reassuring and not, than its portrayal on television and in movies suggested. But wasn't it obvious? he'd demanded of himself. He'd seen things that, objectively speaking, could not have been there. Didn't that make him, QED, crazy? Didn't madness provide a comprehensive explanation for everything that had occurred? Wasn't he obligated, by dint of *lex parsimoniae,* to reject all other hypotheses? Wasn't madness the only sane conclusion?—and at some point he'd

realized these questions were no longer the products of reasoned thought, but were in fact merely another expression of fear and agitation, and he'd crumpled the envelope in frustration and tossed it to the ground.

Now two of the three packs of cigarettes were empty, the third only half full. The neck of the three-hundred-dollar bottle of Scotch poked out from the under the couch at his feet; the Rolling Stones album was beginning to repeat for the fifth time. He didn't want to think he was crazy, of course—but his dissatisfaction with the explanation went beyond that: It was visceral, instinctive. An explanation of insanity felt insufficient to him—in some strange way, too easy. You could, he thought, assert that seeing things was a symptom of madness, just as you could assert that sneezing was a symptom of the flu. But in both cases you had to allow that the symptom—the vision, the sneeze— might actually be attributable to something else.

But, then, what else?

Omitting drugs and stress and insanity—what did that leave?

Abruptly he thought of his conversation with the Hasid in the subway. What if this man had cursed him? Doomed him to repeat the experiences of the biblical prophet he'd been named after? He grabbed his laptop from where it was sitting underneath the coffee table, did some searching, and found the text of the King James Version of Jonah online. What he read wasn't very enlightening, though: There were "mariners" and a place called Joppa and a ship heading to someplace called Tarshish, plus the whale, which didn't actually do much besides provide the setting for a somewhat tedious prayer. Little of the story seemed to correspond to the one he'd been told by the Hasid, let alone what he'd seen. This Jonah had been instructed to "cry against" the city of Nineveh. He hadn't been instructed to do anything, not in any way he could understand, at least. He hardly thought he was in any position to "cry against" New York, either. Crowded subways and inflated cost of living aside, he loved the city enough that it had been heartbreaking for him to see it destroyed. Plus, in the end, Nineveh was specifically not destroyed, which suggested the biblical story had the opposite message of what he'd witnessed.

He slapped the computer shut in frustration. Strictly speaking, he was not even named after the biblical Jonah. He had been named after an uncle on his father's side who'd lived his whole life in Newark and who'd been dead for forty years. The most remarkable thing he'd ever heard said about that Jonah Jacobstein was that he'd invented a prototype for the front-loading washing machine. And as he began to speculate on ways he might lift the Hasid's curse, the whole idea seemed increasingly asinine, sitcom-farcical—utterly incommensurate as a cause with the effects with which he'd been afflicted.

What about the Hebrew, then? Could there be some clue to something there? He picked up the envelope from the floor and smoothed it out on the coffee table, took the pen and tried to re-create the characters he had seen. He made a few curved lines, a squiggle; his knowledge that Hebrew was written right to left only hampered his efforts. And even if he could re-create the words, he'd be no more able to understand them now than he'd been when he'd first seen them. He tossed the pen across the coffee table. He should have paid more attention in Hebrew school, he thought—with more grimness than irony.

But Hebrew school had at the time seemed a form of sanctioned abuse. Every Sunday and every Wednesday after school, he would be driven by his father to the Jewish Community of Roxwood, the local Reconstructionist synagogue. He'd go down into the finished basement, where the four classrooms constituting the religious school were located, and suffer through two hours' worth of Hebrew vocabulary lessons, Israeli history lessons, Torah lessons, prayer lessons. These would be doled out by Jewish studies or Hebrew majors from one of the local colleges, many of whom showed only marginally greater interest in being there than he did. The whole experience was given the particular piquancy of injustice, as well, due to the fact that Jonah's non-Jewish friends didn't have to endure anything like it.

His early experiences of synagogue were similar in that they were characterized chiefly by boredom. Services included interminable stretches of Hebrew, which he, along with 90 percent of the congregation, couldn't understand. Seemingly every other prayer required everyone to Rise, and then thirty seconds later to Be Seated, making escape into daydreaming impossible. On the other hand, the more closely

Jonah paid attention to the service, the more repetition he noticed. Even a basic Friday night Shabbat service lasted more than ninety minutes; a Saturday morning Torah service took two and a half hours. And the High Holiday services—attendance at which was categorically unavoidable—took all day. His father never made them stay the entire time, of course—his own participation having more to do with guilt than conviction—but every Rosh Hashanah and Yom Kippur, Jonah could count on being in synagogue for something like three hours in the evening and then five hours the following day—which, to a ten-year-old accustomed to thirty-minute cartoons and Game Boy, felt as if it stretched toward eternity.

When he got older, Jonah was at least permitted to sit in the balcony with his friends. The rabbi would glare up at them from the pulpit as they laughed at jokes about the cantor or any other congregant they noticed worth lampooning, passed between them copies of *Sports Illustrated* or *Uncanny X-Men*. Those moments of camaraderie and mild defiance were probably his best memories of being in temple—though eventually, inevitably, an usher would appear and scold them with the shame of five thousand years of disrespected tradition, and the clutch would be forced into silence or broken up altogether.

Like almost all the Jews in his grade—of his generation—he'd had a bar mitzvah. For six months to the burden of Hebrew school was added the burden of weekly *haftorah* lessons, followed by the abject terror of the moment itself—his hand trembling as he traced the *yad* across the parchment of the Torah. But after his bar mitzvah he was finally allowed to stop going to Hebrew school, and soon after that his parents got divorced. Jonah's compulsory participation in Jewish ritual ended along with his parents' marriage.

Occasionally during college he would go to services, but it was always done from some nebulous feeling of guilt—the same feeling, Jonah imagined, that had prompted his father to force his attendance as a child. By hour two, the guilt was always more than assuaged, and Jonah would find himself eyeing the young women in attendance, identifying something undeniably erotic in their shows of piety: the calm faces, the hair combed to sedate luster. Then he would feel guilty all over again, for entirely new reasons, and soon leave.

After college he basically stopped formally practicing Judaism altogether. Zoey, in the midst of a brief period of Judaic fervor following the death of her grandmother, had insisted one year he go with her to evening Yom Kippur services at a Reform congregation on the Upper West Side (this death and the subsequent necessity of going to *shul* being her excuse for contacting him again after six months). But the lack of Hebrew in the Reform service bothered Jonah for some reason—as if the service didn't count if he could understand it—and Zoey was by turns bored and teary-eyed with grief. They decided it would be more spiritually edifying to spend the following day strolling Central Park in unstructured contemplation—and predictably they ended up fucking.

Jonah's relationship to Judaism was additionally complicated by the fact that, while his father was Jewish, his mother was not, so he was really only half Jewish—or not Jewish at all, as far as the Orthodox were concerned. He'd once mentioned this issue of matrilineal descent to his father on a car ride to Hebrew school, citing it as a rather compelling reason why he shouldn't have to attend. His father only shrugged nonchalantly and and said, "If we'd been in Germany, they would have killed you. That makes you a Jew."

But none of this—his status as a half-Jew, or a quasi-Jew or whatever he was, or the fact that he found the actual practice of Judaism so tedious—stopped Jonah from identifying himself as Jewish, or from enjoying being Jewish. Passovers and Hanukkahs—holidays celebrated outside of the synagogue—were, he thought, a lot of fun. He liked seeing his father's side of the family: Becky and his other cousins, his grandparents (when they were alive), his aunts and uncles; he liked the food-driven narrative of the Passover celebration, he liked that Hanukkah involved a two-minute menorah lighting followed by an evening of presents, latkes, and dreidel. He definitely enjoyed playing Seven Minutes in Heaven with Lisa Zuckerman at his bar mitzvah reception; it was during B'nai B'rith Youth Organization sleepovers that he'd gotten high for the first time, gotten past second base for the first time. More generally, he liked the community of Judaism: the instant bond he felt toward any -berg, -man, or -stein he encountered, the connection he could claim to Albert Einstein, Sigmund Freud, Sandy Koufax, the Coen brothers, Bob Dylan, and everyone else in the familiar litany of distinguished Jews.

As Jonah sat on his couch, conducting this review of his spiritual biography—now lighting a fresh cigarette with the remnants of the previous one—he thought how somewhere in all these experiences and associations, good and bad, was or ought to have been an experience of the holy, the eternal, the sacred, the Prime Mover—the above, the beyond, the whatever. (The Jewish Community of Roxwood had never been very picky about notions of divinity, it being one of the more liberal institutions in a very liberal town.) But Jonah—now standing, starting to pace his apartment from couch to windows—had never considered himself a spiritual person, and certainly never during any of his mind-numbing hours in synagogue, or while singing *"Dayenu"* at his aunt Sheila's house, or while fumbling to unclip Suzie Meister's bra under the bleachers at a BBYO picnic, had he ever felt anything like the presence of the Lord. When the whole congregation sang the prayers the whole congregation knew, he felt a sense of beauty and community; when he and his father both cried during *Schindler's List,* it was moving and unsettling because it was the only time he'd ever cried with his father; he felt a unique bond with his Jewish friends. There was never in any of that a sense of elevation, however: He never for a moment thought the prayers he joined in saying were actually going anywhere; he never felt himself in contact with something greater, or believed that anyone else was, either.

If he'd thought about it—and he rarely had—he would have allowed the possibility of something Almighty-ish: some sort of vague and unfathomable field of enormous but inscrutable power. He thus understood divinity the way most people understand Wi-Fi. But he certainly didn't believe this meta-field, whatever it might be, had any role in human life. It certainly didn't have any role in his life.

Until now, it seemed.

He stopped pacing. He looked over at the wrinkled envelope on the coffee table, his chicken-scratch attempts at Hebrew visible across a creased corner.

He remembered how, in elementary school, he'd once told a teacher he wanted to be attorney general. He'd had no idea what the attorney general did, of course; he'd only understood it was an important and highly respected position—someone who appeared on TV a lot. He remembered, too, when he was in high school, coming home from a girlfriend's house or a party, how he would sometimes go into the living room of his sleeping house and stand before the floor-to-ceiling windows, with their views of dark Massachusetts hills. He would stand there in the silence, and with a kind of stillness of mind feel as if he were announcing himself to some great mystery—feel, very clearly, that he was only at the start of something vast, and profound.

Jonah had always understood himself, in other words, as having some great destiny. He had always believed in something More: something more for himself, something more attainable. He had never known what this More was—had certainly never thought of it as having any connection to Judaism or to spirituality. But it occurred to him now that it was a notion in which he had always had a certain faith. Even through college and in the years immediately following—when his life had been made up mostly of drinking and getting high and going to Phish shows and reducing as much as possible the impact of the hours he spent at his job as a paralegal—he would see himself as pursuing this Moreness.

Nebulous fourth-grade aspirations notwithstanding, he'd never really wanted to be a lawyer. But he'd understood that law school was always an option for him: a rip cord he could pull that would deliver him into an adult life of remuneration, of parental and societal approval. Eventually he'd decided to pull this cord, and, characteristically, once he'd settled on becoming a lawyer, he dedicated himself to becoming the most skilled, the most successful—the most More—lawyer he could be. Jonah had never lacked for ambition, and it had struck him more than once that what he liked most about his job was that it gave his ambition, his aspirations, such a clearly defined channel. He wondered now, though, if in following this channel he'd lost the essential quality of the More he believed in. Because what was most remarkable about what he'd seen—more remarkable than the clarity, more remarkable than the instant sobriety, more remarkable than the humbling of doubt—was that the vision hadn't surprised him. It was as if he had been waiting to see the total whiteness, his own aged face, the collapse of the Empire State Building—perhaps not waiting to see these specifically, but waiting to see something of that magnitude. It was the lack of surprise, the sense of unconscious expectation realized—like finding yourself there when you wake up in the morning—that finally made every Logical Explanation inadequate. The problem was, he knew the explanation. Somehow, without even knowing it, Jonah had always been a believer.

So, he concluded, he was fucked. He sensed something fundamentally irreconcilable between this vision and his life as he had known it. In the crudest terms: Cunningham Wolf partners didn't have visions. This realization now led to an immediate, panicky mourning for his old life (so much for the blow job in Le Bernardin!) as well as a deep anxiety about what his life would now become. He imagined himself in a hair shirt, shouting at people in Central Park, in and out of Bellevue until he was inevitably loaded up with so many meds that his greatest cognitive exercise would be drooling. At best he would end up like that Hasid: wearing a heavy coat all summer, living in Borough Park, endlessly walking to and from synagogue with his bald wife and nineteen children in tow. Or he would simply become one of those sad, shabby figures on the subway, thumbing through a tattered Bible, making anyone who sat next to him uncomfortable with the murmurs of his praying lips.

"I'm so fucked," he groaned, lighting another cigarette. He was feeling nauseous from all the smoking—but at least nausea was familiar. He picked up the Scotch from under the couch, drank the last, vaporous drops, tossed the empty bottle onto the cushions.

Then his phone chimed: the sound so innocent and unchanged that he was almost touched—the synthesized *tink* like the cry of nostalgia itself. He picked it up off the coffee table. He had a text message from Sylvia: "Just landed. Cu @ Corcoran offices @ 8. xo." He reread the message several times before he could comprehend it. He looked at the row of windows running across his living room wall: a grayish light, more a thinning of night than dawn, filled the sky. He looked at his phone again. It was 7 in the morning.

He moved closer to the windows. As on the previous day, tiny figures, tiny cars, were bustling about the sidewalks, the streets. Only today he saw something so gentle and toylike about it all. He envied everything uniformly for the privilege of not being him.

He had a sudden urge to tell Sylvia—about Zoey, about the cheating. This would be, he felt, a great relief—the true relief he'd sought, it seemed now, when he'd broken up with Zoey. He had never cheated before—at least, never so pathologically. And he'd felt guilty from the first lie, the first shower before seeing her. But the guilt was intermittent; it could be ignored, or suppressed. Guilt, it turned out, was really no more powerful than doubt: The trick was to commit oneself to a truth even though you knew it was false—hold the hand, get under the covers, brush away the eyelash as if there were only one woman with whom you shared these intimacies. He'd been surprised to find how easy it was to exist in a reality to which his feelings did not subscribe.

He understood clearly now the daily cruelty of this, and wanted very badly to apologize. But it was as he found Sylvia's number in his contacts—as he was about to press his thumb against the button to call—that it occurred to him: He didn't have to. He didn't have to tell her, didn't have to break their plans to meet this morning—didn't have to give up his life. He could still move in with her, still become a partner, still get his blow job at Le Bernardin—each of these prospects now breaking forth in his mind like an individual gulp of air after surfacing from the water. He actually started to laugh.

He had been grappling all night with his vision—forgetting that he could simply not grapple with it at all. He could ignore it: ignore what he'd seen, ignore its consequences, ignore whatever explanation it might have. He was free—he specifically remembered from Hebrew school that in Judaism humans had free will! He was free to ignore whatever he wanted.

He was even giddy as he wrote back to Sylvia: "Ok, cu. Bagel?" He hurried into the kitchenette, still clutching his phone, and turned on the tap at the sink, filled his coffeepot, turned on the coffeemaker, watched as it buzzed and gurgled to life. He would have to hurry—hurry to shower and shave and drink coffee in order to make it on time and in the guise of someone who had slept for at least an hour or two. But he knew how to hurry. Didn't he always make it when he hurried?

His phone chimed again: "No thx," Sylvia had written. Here it was, he thought, as the kitchenette now filled with the pleasing odor of steaming fair-trade Ethiopian coffee: his life, right where he had left it—a weekend morning of coffee and Sylvia and apartment hunting—and he could still make of it whatever he chose to make of it. It was a tremendously joyous thought—tremendously powerful, too—in that it achieved the reverse-alchemical miracle of reducing the world back to what could be known and comprehended.

4. A MIGHTY STORM CAME UPON THE SEA

Jonah didn't have to dodge any lightning bolts as he walked to the deli a few avenues from his apartment; the aproned Hispanic man who sliced and smeared cream cheese onto his bagel didn't gape in fear and yank out a rosary upon seeing him; the bagel itself didn't turn to dust and ashes in his mouth. It was the purest and simplest vanity, Jonah thought, to have imagined some change in his place in the world. Greater men had surely ignored more profound revelations—and the earth had kept on spinning.

He was almost cheerful as he boarded the taxi for the Corcoran offices—would have been but for the lack of sleep, the assorted physical consequences of all he had drunk and smoked the night before. His head felt as if the skin were stretched too tightly across his forehead; his mouth—even after the coffee and bagel—tasted of a dry and tongue-swollen sootiness, like he had chewed up and swallowed the three packs of cigarettes. But the rush of air from the open taxi window helped keep the nausea at bay—allowed him the benefit of the bright August morning, the temperature today much cooler.

As the cab pulled up, Sylvia was standing beside the entrance to Corcoran, sipping an iced coffee. She looked, as she always took care to look, well put together, despite the fact that she had probably been up since four: dressed in gray chinos and a tank top that showed off toned arms, her short blond hair parted neatly with a bobby pin, the natural prettiness of her features accentuated with makeup applied just so. She carried a large beige shoulder bag that would have her laptop and phone and charger and book for the plane and whatever else she would need for twelve hours in New York. Jonah found something greatly reassuring in the sight of this bag on her shoulder—physical confirmation that life as he'd known it still went on. As they met on the sidewalk, they kissed on the lips—briefly, but not unaffectionately. Observing his face, she ran her finger across the thick, dark line of his left eyebrow. "Babe, you have to remember to trim these," she said.

And he told her with sincerity, "It's really good to see you."

She smiled suspiciously at his tone. "How much sleep did you get?"

"Let's just leave it at less than eight hours. But I'm okay." She nodded, a bit uneasily. "I just got a little carried away celebrating BBEC," he told her. "Really, I'm fine."

It was reflexive discomfort—a learned instinct that had nothing to do with him, she'd explained. Her father had created all manner of negative associations with heavy drinking in her mind. He knew she trusted him—and she knew it, too—and now she gave him the half-amused half smile she often did when she judged him to have done something boyishly foolish but maybe for that also charming. "Why am I not surprised?" she said. "I guess celebration was in order." She kissed him again. "I'm so proud of you, Jonah." And he was so grateful that he had not ruined this happiness—their happiness—by telling her—anything. They went into the Corcoran offices to meet their broker.

Jonah had expected the broker to have the skittish-eyed, harried look he'd found in every broker he'd worked with—whatever bravado they evinced edged, like the eyes of abused dogs in ASPCA commercials, in a persistent anxiety that someone was about to beat them with a stick. But, to his surprise, the broker greeted them with seemingly genuine pleasure, happily sat at his desk and chitchatted with them for ten minutes about topics other than apartment listings. His name was Brett, he was about Jonah's age, he was dressed casually in khakis and a polo.

"I was at Lehman for six years," Brett told them amiably. "I loved my bonus but hated everything else about my life. Whole weeks would go by and I'd never see the sun—at my desk before five, home in a cab at night. I was pretty depressed when it all fell apart, but really, it was the best thing that ever happened to me. I don't make as much, but I do yoga four times a week and have a dog. A buddy called me the other day and asked if I wanted to come over with him to work at B of A. Fifteen-hour days, plus everyone who knows what you do looks at you like a child molester? Honestly, I'd rather work on commission."

Jonah found this story enormously pleasing for some reason, though Sylvia told him later she thought it both highly implausible and somewhat insulting. Regardless, they both liked Brett well enough—and, again in contrast to the other brokers Jonah had worked with, he was actually competent when it came to the business of showing apartments to rent: The interiors of the spaces matched his descriptions; he didn't unlock doors to residents reading the *Times* in their underwear; and nothing he showed them was patently unlivable on first sight. Jonah sustained himself with Advil and multiple trips to Starbucks; Sylvia was patient with this, sympathetic. And while he knew that on the other side of all the gel caps and caffeine was a severe physical crash, he figured he could delay it until Sylvia headed to the airport after dinner, and then it wouldn't matter if he collapsed facedown on his couch and fell back asleep until noon. He would still have time the next day, Sunday, to read enough of the BBEC files to be prepared for Monday morning. In short, all things considered (or, more precisely, not considered), the day was going great.

They saved the best for last: the listing Sylvia was most excited about, the loft on Bond Street. The building was five stories, white brick, faced in arched windows bordered with columns in bas-relief, elaborate molding on the roof completing the neoclassical motif. Brett entered a security code at the door—from memory, Jonah noted—and led them down a narrow entry corridor to a freight elevator. "There are probably less than a dozen successfully gut-renovated buildings in this neighborhood," he said, pulling the elevator's folding metal door closed. "And you'll see what I mean by successfully when we get inside." He pushed a fat black 5 button—the car trembled gently and began to rise. "This building is landmarked," he went on, "which always makes things tricky in terms of renovation. The developer wanted to replace this freight elevator, for instance, but that violated code. But just listen." He held a finger aloft. "You notice how you don't hear any clanking or grinding? What he was able to do was replace the motor and cables of the original with hydraulics. So you get industrial character without industrial noise. Pretty ingenious, right? That's the kind of work-around you need to create luxury amenities in this area.

"I actually learned something very interesting the other day," Brett continued. "Do you know why there are so many townhouses and low-rise apartment buildings down here? How before 9/11 you could stand on Lafayette and see all the way to the Twin Towers? Do you know why that is?" He paused for a beat. "Shallow bedrock," he revealed with a satisfied smile. "You just can't build tall down here. That's what allows the neighborhood to keep its charm—the cobbled streets and brownstones and everything else we all love about it. Now," he said, as the elevator came to a noiseless halt. "Here we are." He took hold of a brass-handled lever and pulled the folding door aside, let Jonah and Sylvia walk out first.

The loft was vast, spacious and spare, buffed and shining hardwood floors stretching off toward newly painted white walls topped by a high white ceiling. Three exposed beams stood roughly a third of the way from the entrance, giving the space an expansiveness that was almost forestlike. Opposite a kitchenette recessed into the wall were double-height windows, the glass at the arched top faintly blue-hued, the sunlight coming in reflecting in lustrous yellow off the floors.

"Fifteen hundred square feet, Australian cypress flooring, eighteen-foot ceilings," Brett said as Jonah and Sylvia wandered around the room, their heads slightly raised, as if in continuous disbelief at the height of the ceiling. "Kohler in the bathroom, Bulthaup in the kitchen, satellite on the roof serves the whole building. You've got central air and a washer/dryer hookup, all the usual utilities included, a storage unit in the basement, and they're giving you free Equinox membership. And, obviously, quiet, tree-lined street, landmarked building with southern exposures giving natural light all year." Brett recited this litany of virtues without referencing any notes, and as if each trait had not only aesthetic but even moral resonance. Whatever Brett had done in his past life, Jonah imagined he had been very good at it.

"Oh my God," said Sylvia. She had disappeared through a closet door and now reappeared again from the bathroom. "Jonah, come look." He walked over to her and she led him by the hand through the door: They entered a walk-in closet, with shelves to the right, three levels of closet rods to the left, and then she led him out an opposite door into the bathroom. She looked into his face with delight and laughed, in an uncharacteristically childlike way.

As they came out of the bathroom, Brett, leaning against the wall by the elevator, said, "Sylvia, you think you can find a way to fill that?"

"I'm not even clothes-obsessed," she said. "But that is . . ."

"A true walk-through closet, put in in 2008. Frankly, this apartment has a lot of wow features. Now," he said, "what they'll do if you want is put up a wall extending from the closet east." He drew a line in the air with his finger. "So then you've got a true one-bedroom, with the walk-through connecting the bathroom and the bedroom, which is optimal. Now, also, when or if you start to think about children, or even just a second bedroom or study, you extend another wall through the back of the bedroom"—he drew another line in the air—"and you get the nursery or guest room or office. Simple."

Sylvia glanced at Jonah—and he shrugged. Generally they restricted discussions of children to the realm of hypothetical possibilities for an undefined time in the future. But considering how well everything was going, why not affirm it as a more concrete prospect? He could always say he thought she'd been alluding to a guest bedroom.

In any event, it was clear to him that she had been entirely seduced by the loft: Her smile was in full bloom, the lower lip extending away from the upper as if to swallow up joy floating in the air. Apparently the seduction was clear to Brett, too. He made a show of looking at his phone and said, "I'm going to go downstairs and call the owner just to confirm everything in terms of deposit. But look around, turn on all the burners, flush the toilet, check the water pressure in the shower, and call me if you have any questions. I'll be right back up." He walked into the elevator—it descended with no more clanking or grinding than seemed to exist in his personality.

When Brett was gone, Sylvia gave Jonah a kiss—lips parted, lascivious and lingering—and then she drew away, skipped across the floorboards to the center of the room. "I love it," she said, spinning and swinging her bag.

"I do, too," he answered—though this love was more theoretical than felt. He could recognize the New York–real-estate-porn characteristics of the place: the high-end appliances, the exposed beams, the double-height windows, and the rest. But he couldn't quite gather these features together to form a coherent reaction to them. What he really loved was how happy Sylvia was.

"We could put those walls up," she said, this time leaving no room for doubt about what she alluded to. "Jonah," she said to him. "Can't you picture our life here?"

She had settled beside one of the beams, her bag hanging from the bend in her elbow, one foot in a black ballet flat tucked behind the other, was staring toward the back wall, the longest in the loft, with her index finger resting lightly on her nose—silent and smiling, as though even the bare wall was a source of delight. She rarely assumed such moods, such poses. Her job required seriousness: She worked on deals involving billions of dollars, thousands of jobs, international parties. That seriousness—the hours and the effort of it—inevitably bled into the rest of her life, made the moments such as these, when her whole attention was captured by a seemingly undisturbed happiness, fewer, and harder to sustain. He recognized the same in himself.

He was struck now by an entirely new feeling toward her: compassion. He felt, so strongly, that she deserved ease, contentment, glee— wow features and children and whatever else she imagined of an orgiastic future she could see as if projected on the long blank wall she stared at. He loved her. He felt the truth of this with such simple and perfect clarity. And in the same moment of inarguable lucidity, he understood that they had no future—here or anywhere—together.

They had been set up by mutual friends on a blind date: strolled through an exhibition at the Whitney called "Metaphysics and the Modern," and then ate dinner at a Middle Eastern fusion restaurant. It had surprised both of them how well it went: to find the other attractive, and successful career-wise, and intelligent, and funny at times, and not possessed of any ruinous quality that torpedoed most blind dates. Maybe merely that surprise had been enough to inspire a second date, and then a few more—and then the ball was rolling and here they were.

It seemed to him now, though, that each time they increased the seriousness of their relationship, it had been done with the expectation that at this point—at last—things would be truly good between them. Because from the start there had been fights: the petty squabbles and skirmishes of their early days evolving into the open brawling of recent months. And, of course, up until the day before, he had been cheating. They weren't stupid, they both knew something was wrong. But it was as if they believed they could find a solution if only they burrowed deeply enough within their relationship: if they only saw more of each other; saw only each other; if they lived together.

Jonah now understood that this was false hope—a sustaining myth between them. They didn't struggle on account of a failure to find the solution to their problems: There was not some mode of togetherness that would make her feel secure in his respect for her upbringing (rich and Republican), properly supported in her career; would make him feel that her love had depth and warmth, that she wanted to be with him and not a version of him she might fashion. Their problems were a fact of their togetherness itself.

It made him nauseous again, to understand—with the sudden force of revelation—that for all the fighting, for all the relationship work, for all the efforts of two very capable people, for whatever they might ignore, tolerate, learn to live with, for all the nights on the couch, the takeout and delivery and movies and restaurants and exhibits and cocktails and mornings shopping in SoHo and afternoons lazing in Central Park, for all the thoughtful gifts, vacations, orgasms—for the time in Cape Cod when she had emerged from the water in her red bikini and flopped beside him on the sand and in that moment his heart had almost overflowed with a sense of undiluted contentment—for all the luxuries of any loft they might share: Something would always be missing.

"This would be our home," she said.

Now was the time to tell her: about Zoey, about what he'd seen, all of it. Didn't he owe her the truth when he recognized it? "Sylvia," he said.

She had her hands behind her head, elbows in the air, adjusting the bobby pin in her hair—she twisted at the waist and their eyes met. She had caught something in his tone—already there was a tension, the anticipation of disappointment, in her face. But hadn't he decided—that he would ignore— The thought seemed to stumble into pieces as it formed. What, exactly, did this have to do with God?

"You don't like it," she said, her hands dropping, her smile closing.

The nausea was growing. "No," Jonah said defiantly. "No, I love it. And I love you. And I want it—I want to live here with you." He was hurrying toward the elevator as he said this, pushed the button. "I'm going to tell him."

"You—really?"

Still not looking at her—wanting to avoid the dubious look he knew she was giving him, wanting to avoid the doubts of his own—he pulled open the elevator door as it arrived, said, "Just need some air, but I'll—security deposit."

He made it to the ground floor and out of the building. Unfortunately, the humidity had thickened as the morning continued, and he managed only a few steps toward his intended target—the metal-caged base of a tree—before he vomited an incompletely digested bagel onto the sidewalk. After that, he dry-heaved for several minutes, beads of sweat dripping from his forehead onto the ground. Maybe there were worse things than the lightning bolt.

A paper napkin appeared at the corner of his eye. He looked up from his doubled-over position. Brett was offering him the napkin, smiling sympathetically. Jonah took it, wiped his mouth. "I have breath mints when you're ready," he said.

"Thanks," muttered Jonah, still doubled over.

"Few too many last night?"

"Something like that."

Brett nodded with understanding. He held out another, clean napkin, with this took the dirty one from Jonah, walked to a trash can, and threw them away. When he returned, Jonah straightened, and Brett gave him a breath mint.

"I think we want the place," Jonah said. "Don't hold this against us, okay?"

Brett laughed. "When I was at Lehman I used to do that every morning. I used to spend twenty dollars at dinner, tip the waiter a hundred so he'd charge me three, expense the whole thing, and then use the other two hundred to buy coke. EAB, we called it: expense account blow. And you know what I worked on? Sure, I'll say it. Mortgage-backed securities. Jonah, I've learned not to hold anything against anyone."

The nausea returned and Jonah was doubled over with dry heaving again. Brett continued, "I've learned that nothing matters in this world except happiness. That's an incredibly liberating idea. Look at this magnificent, sunny day!" The muscles of Jonah's torso felt as if they were trying to yank themselves free of the bones of his rib cage; he was physically incapable of moving his head to look at anything but the puddle of vomit on the sidewalk directly beneath him. "When I worked at Lehman, do you think I ever took a moment to appreciate this?" He sighed with satisfaction. "Forget the past. Forget the future. How are you doing right now? Right this second?" Jonah's stomach spasmed violently, and a guttural anti-chortle shook out of his windpipe. "Jonah, maybe you'd be interested in meeting my guru."

Finally, Jonah collapsed back into a seated position, his face dripping, his arms limp at his sides. Brett was holding out a business card—Jonah reached up and took it. It had a picture of a sage white man with a long gray beard; phone numbers and a URL and a Twitter handle appeared beneath the words "Guru Phil," written in a mustard-yellow Oriental font.

"This is some kind of . . . Eastern thing?"

"Not exclusively," Brett said. "Guru Phil teaches the best of Christianity, Judaism, Islam, Buddhism, and Hinduism. His message is one of universal love, acceptance, and self-esteem. Jonah, I think he could help you. Guru Phil will show you that whatever your drinking is about, it's really not that important."

"I'm not an alcoholic," Jonah answered, offering the card back.

Brett chuckled knowingly. "You know how I knew I wasn't an alcoholic? Because I took a quiz online. The guru teaches that it doesn't matter what's on the Internet. True knowledge can only be found on the inner-net."

Jonah found this unspeakably corny—but it was clear Brett wasn't going to relent and take the card back, so he put it in his pocket. Brett looked pleased. He helped Jonah to his feet and gave him another two breath mints.

"Can we not make a point of mentioning this to Sylvia?" Jonah said—ashamed enough at having to ask this that he felt his cheeks redden.

"No problem," Brett said. "Just make me one promise. The next time you think about having a drink—"

"I'm really not an alcoholic."

"Remind yourself that God loves you, and Jesus loves you, and the Buddha loves you, and the Prophet Muhammad loves you, and all these faces of God love you for one simple reason: Because. You. Exist." He put his hand on Jonah's shoulder. "I exist. You exist. You exist, Jonah."

"I know."

"You exist," Brett repeated, nodding.

"How much is the security deposit?"

"It's eighteen thousand dollars. Plus the broker's fee. You exist, Jonah."

"Let's go upstairs now, Brett."

Sylvia and Jonah ate lunch (Jonah had a salad, for which Sylvia praised him, but really there was nothing else on the menu he could stomach), and then they got on the subway to go to his apartment. She had a couple of hours of work to do before dinner; he would begin filling out the paperwork for the loft so they could submit their application on Monday morning. Sylvia held Jonah's arm as they descended the subway steps, discussing possible furniture configurations for the loft. He still felt physically overwrought, emotionally overwhelmed, and on top of that was enduring the itch of a nicotine craving—entirely familiar, even after all these years. But he was thinking he could at least take a nap before dinner, which would help on all fronts.

"What if we ask my friend Maya to help us decorate?" Sylvia said as they swiped their MetroCards at the turnstile. "Do you know who Patrick Robinson and Virginia Smith are?" She knew she didn't need to bother to wait for his response. "She did their townhouse in Tribeca."

"I dunno," Jonah said, pushing through the turnstile behind her. "Wouldn't it be better if we did it ourselves?"

"This from a man who didn't even own a bath mat when we met," Sylvia laughed, taking his arm again as they descended another set of stairs to the platform. "It's not like either of us has the time over the next few months to go hunting around for furniture. Besides, I'd only ask Maya where to go. Why not have her go there for us?"

"Yeah, but hiring a decorator, doesn't that seem a little . . ." He wiped his forehead with his hand; it was fifteen degrees hotter on the subway platform than it was outside. "I just think it's a little bourgie," he told her.

She drew in her lips briefly, let go of his arm, took out her phone. Scrolling through emails, she said, "It's going to take a lot longer to do it ourselves."

"That's okay with me."

She held down the button to lock the phone, dropped it back in her bag. She hadn't taken off her sunglasses when they headed down into the subway, was facing across the platform to the tracks—a view that, with or without sunglasses, was a barely differentiated field of sooty grays and dust-blackened rusts and browns. "You realize that this is something I'll have to do, right? If we don't hire a decorator, it's going to fall on me to furnish and decorate our apartment?"

"I'll help."

"You'll veto."

She was right, of course—and by way of acknowledging this, he rested a clammy hand on her lower back. "Can I at least talk to Maya before we hire her? I mean, I feel like if it's your friend, it will skew toward your style, and okay, maybe that's inevitable, but I just want it to be clear when you walk in that a guy lives there, too."

She was looking into his face, he could see her eyes darting to watch his behind the honey-colored lenses of the sunglasses. "Why are we fighting about this?" she asked.

He hadn't even noticed that they were fighting—or rather, hadn't noticed any difference between it and not fighting. He said—to reassure himself as much as her—"Apartment hunting is stressful. But that doesn't mean we aren't making the right decision."

She leaned her head forward and rested it on his chest, wrapped her arms around his back. "Jesus, you're sweaty," she laughed.

"It's fucking eight thousand degrees down here." And she laughed again. He kissed her on the top of her head. It wasn't easy—to love her so much and to end up fighting so often. Then with a tremendous Doppler roar and grinding of hundred-year-old metal against metal and the labored moan of air brakes and brake pads and the cataclysm of thousands of pounds of subway train redistributing its weight from speed to stillness as it foreshortened madly toward them—the train was in the station.

The subway wasn't crowded; they took two seats toward the middle of the car. "I wish you could stay tonight," he said to Sylvia. He'd immediately felt better entering the hyperactively air-conditioned train—believed he could spend the rest of the afternoon sitting there.

"I'll bet you do," she said.

"No, I mean it. It'd just be nice if we could, y'know—have a few more hours together."

"Believe me, if it were up to me . . ." she muttered. "I don't exactly love spending my weekends in a hotel. Did I tell you what happened with the bedspread? I came back to my room last night and—"

"I'm sorry ladies and gentlemen," a woman's voice cried out. She stood by the door at the back of the car: dark-skinned, scrawny, hair a kind of tangled explosion from the top of her head, dressed in flip-flops, jeans torn above scabby knees, a T-shirt that dangled loosely at her neck—so filthy it looked like she had been rolled in ash. "I'm sorry," she bellowed again, and then stopped—mouth open, eyes haggard—as if not knowing or not remembering or simply too strung out to know what to say next. She just stood by the door, wavering slightly on her feet.

"Jesus," Sylvia muttered. She went on. "I put the bedspread in the closet every day when they put it on the bed, and every night I come back and the housekeeper has put it on again. So this time—"

"Ladies and gentlemen can you help me?" the woman called in a hurried tumble of syllables—as though suddenly remembering her lines.

"So this time I wrote her a note, and I left it on the bed."

"Can anyone . . . Can anyone please help me out?"

"And it said, 'Please do not make up the bed with the bedspread on it.' "

"Ladies and gentlemen!"

Jonah glanced around the car. There was a narrow-faced young man in horned-rimmed glasses and headphones with a soul patch on his chin; a black teenage girl reading from a biology textbook; a dour man whose brown and baggy hooded sweatshirt gave him an oddly monklike appearance; two large Hispanic men in matching orange construction vests, their faces torpid and eyelids drooping. Closest to the woman sat a balding man in a tuxedo shirt and bow tie with a violin case across his lap. Though the woman was directly in front of him, he stared ahead with a sort of willed vacancy.

"And that night she'd put the bedspread back onto the bed—and left the note on top of it."

"Please, please." The woman took a step forward. There was no movement for purses, for wallets. The woman dropped to her knees. "Please . . ." she whimpered—mewled—as if now overcome by a still deeper sorrow, her eyes closed, hands clasped before her chest. "Please help me!" All on the train avoided looking at her, at one another.

Jonah had seen this before: The most dramatic, the most humiliating pleas from panhandlers were almost always ignored. The song, the joke, the tidy request for a dollar or a quarter for something specific like a sandwich: This was what people responded to. The greater shows of desperation seemed to violate somehow the social contract between the beggars and those from whom they begged.

"I mean, can you believe that? Now, I know it's possible she couldn't read it. But I've mentioned it to the concierge and I've called housekeeping about it."

The woman was still on her knees—head down, eyes closed, lips moving soundlessly. Her body was tilting to one side, threatening to topple over onto the man with the violin. He was pressing himself into the corner at the end of his bank of seats—seemed to be weighing whether he could stand and move away without brushing against her.

"For what it's worth, I am Starwood platinum."

Jonah took out his wallet; he had only twenties. "Jesus," Sylvia whispered sharply.

He didn't, as a rule, give to people on the subway. The musical performances annoyed him, he simply didn't credit the requests for shelter money or bite-to-eat money; was sure his spare change would end up going for drugs and or alcohol. What prompted him now was not the woman, not even the reactions to the woman from the others on the train: It was noticing it—it was that he couldn't ignore it.

"Look, do you have any singles?" he asked Sylvia.

"No," she said—her sunglasses-covered face inclined toward her knees, her purse now clutched between her arms against her chest. The woman was shuffling toward them, supporting herself by grasping the metal bar fastened to the roof of the train. From under her arm a great tuft of black hair was visible, flecked with beads of moisture and dandruff. Jonah could smell her from ten feet away—urine, sweat, and a thick, indistinguishable commingling of other bodily odors. She now dangled above him from the subway bar, her face still distorted in folds of anguish. He could see a strange whitening at the corners of her eyes and mouth, dark purple bruises on her forearms and legs. He took out forty dollars. Her fingertips were as if charred black, her palm was ashy. He tried to hand the money to her so that the bills stayed between their skin, but as she clasped them, her coarse fingertips dragged over his palm, and something in his stomach and his balls clenched reflexively.

The woman stared at the money in her hand for a moment like she saw in it only another object of grief—and then she closed her hand around the bills and shoved her fist into the pocket of her jeans. She looked very agitated, very frightened now, and, hand still balled in a fist in her pants, she took awkward and clumsy steps to the end of the car, and pulled open the door, was gone.

"And now she's doing the exact same thing in there," Sylvia muttered without looking at him. They rode in silence to their stop.

Sylvia didn't speak again until they had surfaced, a few blocks from Jonah's building. When she did, she said, "You are such an asshole, you realize that?" He felt too worn out to disagree. He waited for her to elaborate, which she did. "You realize that woman was an addict, right? Those people are dangerous. Did you ever think about that? Do you know what addicts will do for a fix?"

She was saying "addict" the way commentators on CNN said "satanist," he thought. "Nothing was going to happen," he muttered.

"Of course, you're so worldly about these things," Sylvia shot back. "Sorry if it offends your liberal sensibilities, but you can't just go around throwing twenties at every homeless person you see." She shook her head. "This all goes back to the warped values of your Roxwood upbringing."

With this she had succeeded in irritating him—which, he guessed, was her intention. "Right, I should have told her to write her congressman about lowering the capital gains tax."

"Make fun of me all you want, but those of us who understand how the economy actually works—"

"Jesus Christ, Sylvia."

"It's not like forty dollars will change anything for her. In fact, it will probably only make things worse. You probably gave her enough to OD on." These words were shot out with a rapid, staccato wrath, as if she were trying to pelt him with stones.

"What the fuck is your problem?" Jonah shouted, a day's worth of hangover and seemingly unbroken and unbreakable frustration now finding shape in anger. He understood that this anger involved Sylvia only tangentially—but none of its other sources were around to be yelled at. "Okay, I gave money to a crack addict because I'm some naïve tree-hugging socialist. What the fuck does it matter to you?"

"Because you did it just to insult me!" There was another tone ·

entering her voice—something more tremulous and wounded. He knew that when he yelled it brought back all the bad old memories of her shitty father. But he felt justified in ignoring this. She'd wanted to fight—so here they were.

"That's right, Sylvia, no one gives money to a homeless person without thinking about how it will affect you."

"You're so hung up on class issues and the way I was raised!"

"Giving that woman money has nothing to do with your fucking house in Nantucket!"

"Then why did you say it would be bourgie for us to use a decorator?"

"Because it would be bourgie to use a decorator!" He couldn't believe the argument, by its own ineluctable gravity, had reached such an absurd point—but of course, neither was he willing to let any of it go. Evidently, neither was she.

"Forgive me for wanting more in my apartment than a couch and a giant television!" she shouted. "Forgive me for wanting to live in a place that actually feels like a home!"

"The ABC Carpet showroom is not a fucking home!"

"So to prove to me what a, a, a man of the people you are, you put me in danger and probably—"

"I just wanted to give that fucking crack addict some fucking money! And if you're too much of a spoiled, conservative snob to accept that . . ." The bottom of her face was bent in a sorrowful frown; he felt entitled to ignore this, too. "You've never given a shit about anyone but yourself," he finished.

"Fuck you, Jonah." Tears were sliding from behind the lenses of her sunglasses. Of course they were, he thought. Hadn't she wanted that, too? Maybe they both had wanted it, all of it: Maybe this was all they had to offer each other.

When they got back to his apartment, she went directly to the small table adjacent to the kitchenette—the one they'd gotten so they could eat breakfasts together. She took out her laptop and began silently to adjust some mammoth flowchart. After an hour or so, he started to feel regretful, guilty—but any attempts he made to talk to her, to touch her, were ignored or shaken off. He stoically filled out the apartment paperwork: the salaries, the employers' addresses, the names and numbers of references.

As the afternoon light ebbed toward dusk, she abruptly closed her computer, stood. He was seated on the couch—for some reason he stood, too. "I changed my flight," she announced matter-of-factly. "I'm going to the airport now."

"Come on, Sylvia, don't do that . . ." She didn't answer—her eyes as sheerly unemotional as the lenses of the sunglasses she'd worn. "I'm sorry," he told her. She began to gather her power cord and other things into her bag. "Don't say goodbye like this." She let out a sharp, sarcastic scoff. He knew, he ought to let her go. But in some way it was easier to say, "I need your signature. For the credit check and shit."

She stopped, her face still down toward the open mouth of her bag. "It surprises me you want to live with a spoiled conservative snob."

"But you're my favorite conservative snob." She showed no trace of amusement, and the joke had been halfhearted at best. "I got angry—I didn't sleep, I . . . I didn't give that woman money to insult you."

She shook her head—either at him, or herself. She looked at him assessingly for a moment—then took the papers and signed them. "You gave that woman forty dollars, and you made me feel like shit. I hope you understand what that means."

He was sure he didn't, but he said, "I get it, I'm sorry."

She let out a slow, irritated sigh—the sigh of a claim to infinite patience. "If this is going to work . . . Do you want this to work, Jonah?"

He knew there was a truthful answer to this question in some far-off corner of his mind—but it appeared so distant, he felt so tired, that retrieving it seemed impossible. "Of course," he said.

"Then it will," she said with determination—determination that he realized was as necessary a condition of their relationship as any quality each found attractive in the other. "We can decide to make it work."

As she looked at him, her face softened—if slightly, if only for the sake of appearing to soften. She gave his hand a token squeeze; he leaned forward to kiss her, but she drew away. The hand squeeze was going to be the extent of it. She picked up her oversize bag and slung it over her shoulder and went out the door. His relief as it closed was inestimable, as was the strangeness of how much he immediately missed her.

Within five minutes he had the shades down, had dug the noise-canceling headphones he used on long-haul flights out of a drawer, had kicked off his shoes and lain down in bed. The blackness flooded and churned behind his eyes—but he didn't sleep. He felt too adrift in the space of his own head to sleep.

They were, empirically, so compatible: They were about as attractive as each other, they made about the same amount of money, they were both white New Englanders from divorced homes, they shared (well, had shared) a basic disinterest in organized religion, they were the same age, had the same build. They made each other laugh, they liked a lot of the same movies; he wasn't intimidated by her success or ambition, she gave him blow jobs in restaurants. In sum, they made a lot of sense. One could even say there was no rational reason why they should not be together. And this, Jonah finally understood, was the only reason they were together at all—the only reason they'd progressed beyond a first date, the only reason they might progress any further.

They liked each other—they loved each other. They could probably convince themselves to spend the rest of their lives together. But there was some form of trust or belief or blind affection they simply had no capacity to feel for each other. Ultimately—they had no faith in each other.

His wallet and phone formed an awkward bulge in his pocket. He pulled them out and, as he did, he found a card stuck to the wallet. He saw Guru Phil—whose serenity was ensured because it was based merely on existence. Which was all well and good, Jonah thought, except for the times when existence sucked—when it was contradictory and answerless—when you were assaulted by— He crumpled up the card and tossed it to the floor. It settled among the massive dust clusters and half-consumed bottles of water that lived like the relics of some lost civilization beneath his bed. He didn't so much fall into sleep as he was swallowed up by it.

5. THE SHIP WAS IN
DANGER OF BREAKING UP

Jonah awoke feeling greatly refreshed, greatly relieved that his sleep had been dreamless. He looked at his phone, laying on the bed beside him: It was ten in the morning. He felt better still as he scrolled through his emails, considered the day ahead of him—a Sunday ensconced in his office, reading through the boxes of BBEC files. He had his job to do: his rationally defined, entirely predictable, emotionally characterless, utterly secular job.

He took his time showering, and, finding himself unusually hungry for this hour of the day—his first meal typically not eaten until about one—he detoured on his trip to the subway to a bodega, bought two egg-and-cheese sandwiches and a pack of cigarettes. He ate one of the former and smoked two of the latter on his way to the train. The station was a little more crowded than he would have expected for a Sunday morning, but by then it was almost eleven; he figured people were heading out to brunch.

813 Lexington was surprisingly busy, as well. The lobby, with its familiar tree—which he was particularly glad to see today—was filled with suited men and women engaged in intent-faced, jargon-laden conversations, just as it would have been during the week. Jonah even felt a little underdressed, in his jeans and polo. The bankers must have had some Chinese or Saudi oligarch in today, he concluded as he boarded the elevator. As he rode up, he returned to the emails on his phone. New messages had poured in overnight, were still accumulating now. He was looking over these messages as he made his way down the hall—and was surprised to find Dolores at her desk outside his office.

"You came in today?" he said to her.

She seemed not to know how to respond. "There are several messages," she said.

"There are?" He frowned—glanced down the hallway: full of lawyers, paralegals, assistants. The nickel was dropping by the time he said to her, "What day is it?"

"The sixteenth," she answered.

"What day of the week is it?" he said impatiently.

"Monday."

He rushed into his office, slammed the door behind him, shouted, "Fuck!" as he threw his briefcase onto the desk. This was just unfair: Somehow he'd slept for nearly forty hours. It certainly explained why he'd awakened feeling so reinvigorated, he noted bitterly. So much for that. He sat down at his desk, looked at his inbox on his phone again—it made a lot more sense, knowing that these messages had been piling up for almost two days. He counted at least five from Sylvia.

Dolores knocked and came in. "Mr. Chen wants to see you this afternoon," she said.

His eyes fell on two towers of boxes of unread BBEC files that had been stacked by his door. His iPhone began to ring. It was Sylvia. "See if he has anything after four," he said to Dolores.

"Would you like to see him at four-thirty?"

"What did I say?" he answered hotly. "Anytime after four." She turned and left and he answered the call. "Hey," he said into the phone.

"Hi," Sylvia said evenly. "So I guess we're not talking right now, but I just wanted to know if you'd heard from Brett."

"Brett?"

"The loft."

He covered the phone, shouted out the door, "Dolores!" He removed his hand. "Look," he said to Sylvia as he opened his briefcase, "it isn't that we're not talking, but I had a . . ." Dolores appeared in his doorway—he shuffled hastily through the papers in his briefcase, looking for the rental application.

"You said you wanted to work on things, Jonah, and I believed you meant it. But I don't see how you think that's accomplished by ignoring my calls and emails."

"No, I agree, I agree," he said, finding the application.

"You agree?"

He handed the application to Dolores, put his hand over the phone. "Fax that to Corcoran. Brett somebody, on Bond Street." Dolores nodded indifferently and left. She became taciturn whenever he was short with her, which was not often—but it happened often enough that he recognized she might keep this up all day.

"If you agree, then why did you do it?" Sylvia was saying. "I just want to know if we're actually on the same page."

"We are on the same page," he said, "but I've been buried in work since—"

"You think I haven't?" she said exasperatedly.

Dolores reappeared in his doorway. "Mr. Chen has time at four-thirty," she told him.

"Fine," Jonah answered, and she left.

"What?" Sylvia said.

"No, Syl, I'm sorry, this day has just been, just been . . ." He was staring at the BBEC files. It was now eleven-thirty. What percentage of these thousands of documents could he read in the five hours before the meeting with Doug Chen? Ten? Fifteen?

"If you're too busy to talk, all you need to do is send me a two-line email."

"Right." He'd thought of something else. "Dolores!" he shouted again. "Sylvia, I'm sorry, I can't talk now." Dolores was back. "I love you, we're on the same page, I promise." Dolores smirked. Of course he didn't want her to hear him trying to placate his girlfriend, but one man could only multitask so effectively. He glanced down at his desk so he at least didn't have to see her watching him as he spoke.

"If you are having cold feet, Jonah . . ." Sylvia said.

"Of course not. I faxed over the paperwork to Brett, and I will let you know as soon as I hear. Can I call you tonight?" Sylvia sighed heavily—and he had to stifle rising impatience, not just because he needed to start reading immediately but also for all the phone calls he had uncomplainingly allowed her to cut short when her work demanded it.

Maybe she thought of this, too. "Okay," she said, in a tone suggesting she'd agreed to be mollified. "You'll call me tonight?"

"I swear on our rental application that I will." Fortunately she laughed a little, and he got off the phone.

He looked up at Dolores, who was still smirking. "Sorry," he said. She shrugged in a minimal way, as if none of this made any difference to her. "And I apologize for being short with you." She produced an identical shrug. Again his impatience rose up—but he knew circumstances demanded he ignore it. "Look, Dolores, I need you to buy me a suit."

"A suit?" she said dubiously.

"Yeah, shirt, tie, suit. Go to Macy's, put it all on my card."

She frowned skeptically. "I don't even know your size."

"I'll email it to you while you're on your way."

The frown deepened. "What color suit?"

"Salmon and taupe," he said sarcastically. "Navy blue, what color do you think?" He had allowed himself more impatience than he should have—she folded her arms, made a face of disappointment in him. "I'm sorry, I'm sorry. Work with me here, Dolores, I woke up thinking today was Sunday. Okay? Please?"

She unfolded her arms and held up her palms. "I just come in to work on time and do my job." And she left.

He did triage on his inbox for twenty minutes—felt lucky that he at least hadn't missed any client calls as he'd slept. Then he finally had the chance to approach the BBEC boxes. He opened the one on top, took out the first manila folder—Dolores appeared in his doorway, wearing her coat.

"I'm leaving now," she said. "I don't know the men's section of Macy's at all, and you still haven't emailed me your measurements—"

"I will, I will," he told her.

"So it may take a little while."

"I'm counting on you, Dolores, please get back as soon as you can." He returned his eyes to the BBEC folder, thinking that while he could appreciate the rationale for not having a secretary you were at all attracted to (because where else would that lead?), a twenty-two-year-old who wanted to sleep with him might have shown a little more urgency in attending to his needs in this moment.

"There's something else," Dolores said.

He neatly placed the BBEC folder back on top of the box. "Yes?"

"Daniel Coyne is here to see you."

"Who the fuck is Daniel Coyne?"

"Mr. Jacobstein, I am a Christian. Please don't use that language in front of me."

"Okay, okay, okay," he said. "I'm sorry." *I thought Christians were supposed to be charitable,* he just stopped himself from muttering under his breath.

"He says he knows your cousin."

Daniel—Danny—Jesus Christ, he thought. "He's here?"

"He's at the front. He told Angelica he's happy to wait. Angelica is the woman who sits at reception."

"Yes, Dolores, I know who Angelica is."

"I only mention it because you didn't put in for her birthday gift last year."

"Yes, because I am the worst human being in the world, I get it. Like I said, I am sorry for being impatient today." Dolores shrugged as if she didn't know anything about it. He sat back down at his desk. "You can tell Angelica, who will be receiving a very generous Christmas gift from me, by the way, that she can send back Daniel Coyne." Dolores shrugged one last time and left.

He'd forgotten that he'd seen his cousin's fiancé making out with another man in the stairwell—and was very unhappy to be reminded of it now. He told himself that he would have been equally unhappy to have remembered Danny cheating on Becky with a woman—but then wasn't sure what point he was trying to prove with this assertion, liberal egalitarianism pretty clearly irrelevant in this case. He cast a forlorn glance at the BBEC boxes. He knew he wasn't allowed to smoke in his office, but—whatever, extenuating circumstances, and he lit a cigarette.

Danny appeared, dressed with predictable accountancy in a pressed navy blue suit (exactly the suit Jonah hoped Dolores would return with, it occurred to Jonah). Danny looked a bit taken aback to find Jonah smoking—then smiled in a way Jonah could best describe as brave, shook Jonah's hand firmly, looking him directly and sturdily in the eye, and sat down in the chair across from his desk.

"It's great they let you smoke in here!" Danny said with a terribly forced chuckle.

"Look, Danny . . ." Jonah began. But he wasn't sure what to say next—and Danny jumped in immediately.

"I'm really glad you had a chance to see me today, Jonah," Danny said rapidly. "I've been thinking a lot about our conversation on Friday and I actually think my organization has a lot to offer you."

"You—what?"

"I'm sure you're a net saver and maybe you've been reluctant in the past to invest, especially given what's happened, in the economy." He cleared his throat; the tone he was attempting was sensible, businesslike, he maintained the strong eye contact, made stiff gesticulations on the nouns—but he couldn't seem to control a shaking in his left knee, a general jitteriness to his whole mien. "But what we at Windstaff can offer you is the chance to get into funds that have performed consistently even over the last five years. Now, normally there is a minimum investment to enter these funds, but our wealth management, ah, my colleagues would be prepared to waive that. We could get you into our strongest performers at really, any investment level you were comfortable with." Jonah shook his head, not following. "And because," Danny continued, clearing his throat again, "as we're family, we could work out something on the fees."

"The fees?"

"The fees would really be negligible, is what I'm saying. In fact, to get you in immediately, ah, I myself could put up the initial, ah, and the returns would go directly to you, and, y'know, we could revisit repayment, or not, being that it's all in the family."

"You want me to invest with Windstaff?" he said slowly—but by this point he realized he was only clinging desperately to his confusion. Danny's proposition was clear enough.

Danny forced another deeply uncomfortable laugh. "No, no, not with Windstaff directly, you don't invest in Windstaff, we manage your, but, ah, actually, if you'd prefer, what happens is, we audit of course the books of course of many of the biggest—I couldn't want to name names, uh, here, but, of course, informally, it would be simple enough if we had some indication of what performance might be, it isn't uncommon, I could, for example—"

"Jesus, Danny, stop it!" Jonah finally said.

Now it was Danny who feigned confusion. "I only thought because of what we talked about on Friday—"

"You understand that if you offer me a bribe and I don't report it, I could get disbarred?" He wasn't sure this was true, but it sounded good.

"Bribe? Bribe? What—bribe? Ha-ha-ha!"

"Look, I'm not retarded, Danny."

"Ha-ha-ha!" Then abruptly, Danny's cheeks and brows began to work together spasmodically, and he pressed his palms against his face—made choked sobbing sounds into them. Jonah considered what he must have been through for the last two days: not knowing whether Jonah would say anything, whether he had said anything already, not knowing what Becky knew and if his secrets had been exposed and if his life as he'd known it was over. And, despite himself, Jonah felt sorry for Danny—though this only served to redouble his annoyance at him for coming.

Danny began to take long, snuffling breaths behind his hands. When he'd finally composed himself enough to lift his face, his eyes were bloodshot and puffy, his cheeks moist. Jonah opened a drawer in his desk, thinking he might have some tissues—he didn't—looked around his desk for something else, and then finally just tossed Danny the pack of cigarettes.

"Oh, I don't smoke," Danny said weakly.

"Start." Jonah tossed him the lighter, too.

Danny pulled a cigarette from the box, put it in his mouth uncertainly, and lit it. He took a few coughing puffs. "I can't believe they let you smoke in here."

"Yeah, we're pretty progressive."

For several moments they smoked in silence. Danny did seem to get the hang of it. Slouching forward, face hangdog and pale where it was not splotchy with redness, he finally said, "This is a love story, Jonah. I know that sounds ridiculous, but it is. I've struggled my whole life with these—urges. Wanting to be one way, knowing I had to be something else. But then I met Becky, and I really, truly fell in love with her. She's so caring, and energetic, and positive, and kind, and . . ." He looked at Jonah pleadingly. "I got drunk and fucked up. Doesn't everybody do that?"

"Having one too many tequila shots doesn't make you gay."

"I mean, I honestly do not even believe I am gay. I was just . . . born with a really strong attraction to men."

Jonah could only rub his forehead at this, and resist a lawyerly instinct to ask Danny exactly what he believed the definition of "gay" was. "Look, why don't you come out?" he asked. "It's not exactly 1955 out there."

"It's too late for that!" He wiped his nose with vigor and repeated, "It's too late for that. I've been managing this ever since high school—with only a few slipups, Jonah! It's different in Boise. It's . . ." He spun his hands rapidly before him, as though trying to churn the words out of the air. "My family does weekly Bible study."

"And?"

"And they expect things of me! I know I'm a coward, but I can't let them down!"

He looked on the verge of tears again, so Jonah said, "Okay, okay, I'm not going to call your mother, just, calm down." Try as he might, Jonah could not sustain much scorn toward Danny. He had to admit: Gay in Boise did not sound like a lot of fun—nor did a life of denying your most basic sexual urges. Hell, he hadn't even been able to confine his own sexual urges to a single, very attractive partner. But, he reminded himself, there was more at issue here than Danny's repressed libido. "So don't come out to your family," he said. "But you have to come out to your girlfriend."

"Like I said, I'm a coward," Danny answered with a feeble smile. "I've never come out to anyone. You're the only one who knows."

"Yeah, me and the slipups," Jonah muttered. "Anyway, it doesn't matter if you're scared or not. You have to tell her the truth."

"But we're happy together!" he cried. "I make her happy! Family is very important to me, and I will take our marriage very, very seriously."

"Marriage?" Danny glanced away. "What was that bullshit before about us being family, we're not . . ." Danny still didn't meet his eye. Unwanted revelations were coming fast and furious today. "You fucking proposed to her," Jonah said.

"I already had the ring! I panicked! I thought you were going to say something, and if I—"

"And you figured if you were already engaged, I wouldn't say anything." Here it was: the scorn, the disgust—the righteous indignation. "You fucking asshole . . ."

"You can't say anything!" Danny exclaimed. "We're in love! And—

besides." His eyes darted up to Jonah's, then quickly away. "It's none of your business."

"She's my cousin, remember?"

"You never see her. You're not part of her life! You had no idea how screwed up she was when we got together. Did you know she was cutting herself then?" Jonah did not—and the news had the effect of pulling his indignation up short. The girl who'd bopped so happily through Cat Stevens songs on her acoustic guitar cut herself? "I'm thinking about her," Danny said, looking at Jonah a little more firmly now. "She's happy with me. And I'll take care of her, you know that. I'll always make plenty of money. We can live wherever she wants. I'll put her through law school if she decides to do that, or she can get an MFA. Or she can raise our kids. I will be a wonderful husband to her."

"Minus the occasional stairwell."

Danny nodded quickly, as if in agreement. "I deserved that. But I am telling you, that was the only time since we've been together. And I will work so, so, so hard to make sure there aren't any more."

"You're supposed to say there won't be any more at all."

"I want to be honest with you."

"Why do you want to be honest with *me*?" Jonah said in exasperation.

Danny looked at him with a small, tentative smile. "I don't really know. You just seem . . . like a good guy."

"No," Jonah shouted, suddenly furious—leapt to his feet. "No, no, no. I do not seem like a good guy. I am a corporate lawyer. Do you know what we do here? When companies put lead in baby aspirin, who do you think they call? That's who I am." He realized he was leaning forward, fists balled on his desk, and he must have actually been scaring Danny a bit, because Danny was pressing himself into the back of his chair, cringing as if he were worried Jonah was about to jump over the desk and start pummeling him. Jonah forced himself to sit back down. "I am not someone you need to be honest with," he concluded. He was a little unnerved by this reaction himself—lit a new cigarette.

"I'm sorry I said that," Danny said after a few moments. Then in a quiet, hopeful voice, he added, "Then I don't need to worry that you'll say anything?"

Jonah stared at Danny blankly—stared as he did at the chessboard when he found himself in utterly unexpected checkmate. He hadn't necessarily planned on saying anything to Becky—but he hadn't decided not to, either. Until Danny showed up, he hadn't thought about it at all, his weekend having been consumed by—other concerns. But now that he did think about it—he saw that Danny made a good point. As he had just been so adamant in explaining, he was not some sanctimonious moral crusader—and certainly had not become one over the weekend. Who was he to make judgments as to what was right and wrong, what should be revealed and what remain hidden? Besides, if he did tell Becky, what would he really accomplish besides ruining other people's happiness: breaking up an engagement, perhaps even inducing a relapse into neurotic self-harm? Such outcomes were precisely the reason why you should not take it upon yourself to intervene in other people's lives, he thought. And while he sensed there was a counterargument to be made here, he did not see that he necessarily had to be the one to make it. The bottom line, he told himself, was that he wanted Becky to be happy—and Danny made her happy.

"It never happened," Jonah said.

"It never happened," Danny answered promptly.

"And nothing ever will happen."

"I swear to the Lord in heaven, I will do my best."

"Remember what I said about being honest with me?"

"Nothing will ever happen again. Or nothing will happen. Nothing happened. Got it."

"Fine," Jonah said. Still dissatisfied, though, with his relative goodness or badness in this situation—unclear, actually, on which side of this scale he was trying to align himself at this moment—he added, "And if you ever say a word to me about any company, any fund, any earnings report you got hold of, I will—"

"Never. Never. As far as you're concerned, I work on an ice cream truck. Ha-ha-ha." The fake laughter was back. This was odd, thought Jonah—and he suddenly wondered if he'd been hustled. Regardless, he was ready for Danny to leave, and this seemed to be Danny's thinking, too. He'd already stood up, was moving backward toward the door.

"Thank you, Jonah," he said. "This really is what's best for everyone." He still had the burning cigarette in his fingers—he looked at it, he looked at Jonah, he looked around awkwardly, finally decided to take the cigarette with him, and left.

He had no right to ruin Becky's happiness. Danny was right: This was what was best for everyone. And this was exactly what he would have done before Friday night, he assured himself. But then Jonah put out his cigarette underneath his desk, and gave up pretending that he'd done either right or wrong, or what was best, rather than exactly what Danny had wanted him to do: what was most convenient for himself. He walked gratefully to the boxes of BBEC files.

It took Dolores two hours to return with the suit, but it was navy blue and the correct size and the tie matched and she even smiled as she handed him the Macy's bag, maybe signaling that all was forgiven. He shut his door after her, pulled the pins and tissue paper from the new clothing, started to undo his belt. But it felt inappropriate, some-how, to be undressing at work—the way he imagined texting during a funeral might. So he put on the new suit quickly, his back to the door, just in case. As he tightened the tie, though, shoved his jeans and polo into his briefcase, he had the sense that maybe, just maybe, he had finally regained some kind of control over his life—put the last of the weekend's pandemonium behind him.

Several uninterrupted hours of studying the BBEC files helped affirm this, too. As he made his way through the stacked boxes, the files made a steady exodus from the corner, spreading all across his desk, the chairs, the floor. When he took a moment to look up and sur-veyed this, he found something heartening in their migration—a visible symbol of what he'd accomplished.

He was still only at the beginning of the work of reading, skimming, assimilating the total, but he already had, he believed, the gist. Dyo-max, a biotech start-up founded by MIT researchers and California venture capitalists, was claiming that BBEC had stolen a molecule they had patented in 2001 and used it as the basis of the blockbuster eye drug Lumine. Hence, Dyomax argued, they were entitled to hundreds of millions of dollars in Lumine revenue and unrealized revenue and compensatory damages and so forth. BBEC, on the other hand, argued that Lumine was in fact based on a molecule they called 5F-LUM6,

which BBEC had created and patented in 2002. BBEC argued that
5F-LUM6 was "wholly and demonstrably different"—a phrase that
recurred frequently in the files—from the Dyomax molecule. It was
an apples-to-oranges defense, essentially: BBEC wasn't disputing that
Dyomax held the patent for an apple; they were just saying they'd
invented an orange. Theoretically, it would be up to the courts to decide
what sort of fruit 5F-LUM6 really was—but that, the files made clear,
was only theory. The research of Cunningham Wolf litigators showed
that Dyomax could never survive a trial that might play out over the
course of twelve or eighteen months, plus however many more months
before judgment. Minority stakeholders were already demanding a
settlement; the company had made it through the previous year only
because one of the partners had sold his stake on terrible terms; all the
old VCs wanted out, no new VCs wanted in. The show of the trial was
simply leverage toward a better settlement. Dyomax would walk in to
court and, after a couple of weeks of being outmaneuvered and out-
fought and outgunned by Doug Chen and Jonah Jacobstein and the
seven Cunningham Wolf attorneys sitting behind them, concede that
whatever 5F-LUM6 really was—they couldn't win.

Jonah guessed Dyomax had held out this long only because BBEC's
theft had been so transparent. The internal documents showed that
BBEC had made only token efforts to hide that the genesis of 5F-LUM6
was their attempt to create a version of the Dyomax molecule that
was just different enough to be called different. And when that didn't
work, they simply called one iteration 5F-LUM6 and patented it. The
BBEC correspondence he reviewed was full of what outside legal
counsel would call "imprudent language"—phrases like "the science is
pretty damning" and "we have about seventeen different ways we need
to cover our ass."

None of this was any some sort of John Grisham, proof-they-knew-
the-brake-pads-were-defective! revelation to Jonah, of course. He had
guessed BBEC had stolen the molecule almost from the moment he'd
heard about the case. And most of the truly imprudent language came in
emails with or between in-house counsel and hence could never be
admitted into evidence, regardless. More fundamentally, it was all water
that could easily be muddied by any lawyer with half Jonah's ability—to

say nothing of Doug Chen's. All it would take would be a few dependable expert witnesses, twenty or so insinuating questions. After all, when it came to the molecular level, who could really say what was what, and whose was whose? One thing Jonah had learned early in his career at Cunningham Wolf was that the legal system—with its insistence on precision, exactitude, comprehensiveness—rather than brush away ambiguity actually tended to create it where none had existed. Firms like Cunningham Wolf had for generations been monetizing the manufacture of ambiguity. If BBEC needed a little doubt cast in order to save maybe a quarter billion dollars, then they had come to the right party.

Closing another file, Jonah glanced out his window: the surrounding buildings had a tabular, fixed look against the bare and bright afternoon sky—appeared dense and intractable in their concrete hides. He watched as an airplane banked away toward the East River, the airports in the outer boroughs. The sight of airplanes over the skyline had made him nervous for a few years after 9/11—but he was used to them again. This one, in its silence, looked almost peaceful.

He felt secure enough seated there at his desk—in his suit, amidst the files—to light a cigarette, and let himself consider, for a moment, what the end of the ambiguity he would manufacture for BBEC would be. He didn't feel any particular moral repugnance toward BBEC for what (he was now sure) they had done—and certainly no more than he would have felt before the weekend. This was just how these companies operated. His Roxwood upbringing had taught him to expect nothing else. And it was not like the crime—if you chose to call it that—had hurt anyone; not physically, anyway. Quite the contrary, in fact: Lumine, the drug BBEC created from 5F-LUM6, had saved the eyesight of hundreds of thousands of patients suffering from macular degeneration—this according to the glossy Lumine marketing brochures. All a loss at trial would mean was less Lumine in the world, more macular degeneration, and fewer dollars for BBEC to invest in R&D so they could create and distribute new medicines. It wasn't the most sophisticated moral calculus, Jonah recognized, but neither was it wholly inaccurate.

He lifted a folder from the stack on his desk, this one filled with Dyomax annual reports—opened the most recent one and flipped through it until he came to a three-inch-by-three-inch picture of Dale Compstock, the Dyomax CEO. He was in that stage of middle age that has just surrendered the last intimations of youth: His carefully combed dark hair was thinning, a pervasive pudginess bordered his smile. He looked, overall, like a friendly, geeky man. Jonah knew there were tens of thousands of such men, with their pictures in tens of thousands of annual reports. But this was the man who would lose his business due, to some indefinable degree, to Jonah and his firm's actions. For exactly this reason, he felt compelled to look Dale Compstock in the eye—or in the digital facsimile of his eye, at least. He need not feel guilty, Jonah told himself. The two-paragraph biography beneath the picture mentioned that Dale Compstock had already launched and sold two prominent biotechs prior to cofounding Dyomax. He was rich, in other words, and he would remain rich, regardless of the company's fate. And more, a man now running his third biotech start-up would understand as well as anyone that he was a CEO, and Jonah was a lawyer, and they were both involved in a system, a way of doing business; and every day there were winners and losers, new partners, new counterparties, mergers, lawsuits, settlements—and in the end, they all got rich anyway. It was the promise of white-collar America—and the only morality any of them were interested in applying was the system's own internal logic.

But rather than the reassurance Jonah had expected to take from these reflections, he instead felt an uneasy correspondence between these thoughts and his conversation with Danny; between himself and the man in the picture. But it was a darting, nebulous feeling, he couldn't pin it down and finally didn't want to. He closed the report. He was seeing secrets everywhere today, he thought.

There was a brief knock on his door and Doug Chen walked in, as usual polished to immaculate tidiness. Evidently, Dolores was not at her desk; evidently, he had not been grated absolution after all. The good news was that Doug Chen had come upon him in a suit, clearly at work on BBEC. The bad news was he had a cigarette in his hand.

Doug Chen crinkled his nose in cartoonish repulsion. "Smoking is a workplace health liability," he stated, with the authority of one quoting gospel.

Jonah looked at the cigarette in his hand, considering all manner of excuses, justifications—decided if he was going to lie, he might as well go for a Hail Mary. "It's unusual circumstances," he said. "My girl-friend walked out on me. Apparently I work too much. There goes three years and ten thousand dollars of jewelry, but at least I can cel-ebrate my new freedom." And he held up the cigarette.

As lies go, it was not terribly sophisticated, but his instinct had been that someone who liked strip clubs so much might be a misogynist, and apparently he was right, because Doug Chen nodded in dispassionate acknowledgment—as close to sympathy as he probably got. "Those who don't work rarely understand what is required of those who do."

"I know what you mean," Jonah lied again. "Still, I apologize." He put out his cigarette.

"I am flying to Washington this afternoon to prepare a client for congressional testimony. This was unexpected, and unfortunately it is necessary to cancel our meeting scheduled later today." He made a small but precise gesture of his hand toward the BBEC files. "Do you under-stand the tack we are taking?"

"I wouldn't want to be a Dyomax attorney."

Doug Chen observed Jonah for a moment and then said, "On Tuesday, the twenty-fourth, there will be a meeting of BBEC in-house counsel in Los Angeles. I will be going to California ahead of that meeting with Kevin Phillips and Frank Chapman. I believe it would be helpful for you to join us on the flight, as we will be discussing general strategy."

Jonah had learned from the files that Kevin Phillips and Frank Chapman were the Chief Legal Officer and the CEO, respectively, of BBEC. "I'll ask Dolores to get the specifics from your assistant and have her book my ticket," said Jonah.

"That will not be necessary," Doug Chen told him. "We will leave from the office Monday and fly on the BBEC corporate jet." He said this as though flying on a private jet were as routine as taking the express train from 14th Street.

Jonah managed to nod with parallel equanimity. "Sounds good," he said.

"I will be back from Washington on Thursday. We will start

preparations then and through the weekend. Give some thought to any additional associate support you might need."

"Absolutely."

Then, with no visible alteration in mood or mind, Doug Chen added, "Gifts of jewelry rarely bring a satisfactory return on investment." He left and shut the door silently.

Jonah stared at the closed door for a moment—and then began to laugh: at the absurdity of this last statement, and more—at how well his career was suddenly going. Something in his work must have impressed someone in the upper echelons of the Cunningham Wolf hierarchy—Doug Chen or Aja Puvvada or someone even higher up than that. And the greatest irony of all was how poor his work performance had been for the last several days. It was a joke, really: He'd been scrambling all afternoon after sleeping through the morning and the whole previous day, and now he would be taking the BBEC private jet with the BBEC CEO, picking the associates who would report to him.

He realized: He was going to make partner. He'd known—he'd assumed—but it now attained some greater form of certainty in his mind. He really would ride on private jets, become a millionaire, accomplish what he'd spent so many years trying to accomplish—after all. "Those who don't work rarely understand what's asked of those who do, Doug?" he said, laughing. "You don't know the half of it." He felt so triumphant, so relieved and obliquely grateful, that he laughed almost to the edge of tears.

When this laughter finally abated, it was with a kind of generosity of spirit that he reopened the Dyomax annual report—looked again at the picture of Dale Compstock. Sure, he could acknowledge that he was sorry for him, in some abstract way. It was his turn to lose. But sooner or later everyone took that turn, and losing might only inspire him to start another biotech and maybe this time to do the stealing instead of being stolen from—and to hire better lawyers.

Jonah leaned back in his chair, and decided to celebrate his latest success by smoking another cigarette. It was too bad he'd gotten addicted all over again, but that only meant he'd have to do the work of quitting all over again. He'd done it once, he could do it again. This cigarette, he decided, would be his last.

Now that he had days instead of hours to finish reading over the BBEC files, he found it harder to sustain the motivation to continue plowing through the thousands of pages of documents. He looked at the clock on his phone: It was almost four. He decided to have another cup of coffee. He took the Vassar mug on his desk and walked out of his office. Dolores was still not at her desk—was either at a late lunch or simply not doing her job. He smiled at this, though—identified something amusingly ironic in the fact that even as he ascended the Cunningham Wolf ladder, Dolores's performance only declined. In any case, as a partner he would have an assistant who would never turn apostate on him.

To reach the kitchen and the coffeemaker, he had to walk down a corridor bordered on one side by ten-foot-high filing cabinets and on the other by a hive of cubicles. As he turned down this corridor, he saw a naked man pull open a drawer and lean scowlingly forward to examine its contents. The man stood in perfect silhouette to Jonah—such that Jonah could follow the line of bare skin from the man's neck down his shoulder and curved back and rib cage to his waist—ass and dick—thighs, calves, feet. Jonah's first thought was that the i-bankers had taken their bonus ritual to the Cunningham Wolf floors, but when he turned his head he saw that all the cubicles, the passages between them, the corridors beyond and the office doorways were all filled with naked people: naked lawyers, assistants, paralegals, associates, and yes, partners—all working with no attention to their nudity. A fifty-ish bald securities lawyer scrunched his paunch into folds as he slouched at his desk, holding a phone against his ear with his hairy hand; the long, narrow breasts of an M&A attorney dangled from her chest, flapped gently against one another as she took a phone from her tan-armed and pale-chested colleague. Two lawyers from Jonah's summer associate class, Steve Weisman and Rich Cameron, despite the exposure and nearness of naked genitals—circumcised and uncircumcised, respectively—sipped steaming hot coffee as they nodded seriously to each other. Everywhere Jonah looked: Folders were tucked into the hairy bend of armpits, belly buttons pressed into the edges of desks, arm flesh shook as fingers typed, legs were folded across pubic hair—asses spread doughlike against nylon seats and skin was squeezed waffle-like into the mesh of chair backs.

"Can you do a five o'clock TC with Scott and the LJP team?" asked Veronica Snyder, a petite redheaded lawyer with an arc of moles and freckles across her chest and small dark areolae capping her breasts like tiny yarmulkes.

Without answering Jonah headed to the elevator, which had pro-vided escape from the last vision. But as the doors opened he saw that the janitor inside was naked, too—short, Indian, with little tufts of white hair above his ears and a kind face and his chest had an almost perpen-dicular slope starting at the nipples and everything else was luckily hidden by the four-foot trash bin he had before him. Jonah got on and pushed L and stared at the floor. But the elevator floor was tile polished to reflection, and as the janitor walked off Jonah saw the mirrored image of the V-shaped sagging of the flesh of his back, a vitiligo-white splash across his right calf—he caught a glimpse—brief but long enough—of the underneath of the man's ball sack and his perineum.

Once, Zoey had mentioned to Jonah that when she walked down the street in New York, she always felt she was the only person heading in whatever direction she was going—that every other person on the sidewalk was coming toward her. This was in the early, halcyon days of their relationship; the comment had struck Jonah as both very reveal-ing (about Zoey's psychology) and very insightful (about New York's)—and it had the effect of pushing him even deeper into love with her—love for Zoey in those days being the only thing he seemed inter-ested in feeling. Those days were long since over, of course—but when-ever he observed this sidewalk phenomenon himself, he always thought of her, fondly. It was not, he didn't believe, that New York necessarily made you feel isolated—though it often did—but rather that New Yorkers always walked with decided purpose: with a great belief in the importance of getting wherever they were going. When you stood in the way of such people, you inevitably noticed them more than the people walking beside you, behind you. Very often, too—they were the people between you and the very important place that you had to go.

So as Jonah stepped onto the sidewalk and was confronted with a crowd of naked pedestrians moving toward him, he thought bleakly of Zoey—with a pang of nostalgia for better, simpler, more prosaic times. He was then swept up in a wave of masses and stretches and gatherings of flesh—juxtaposed against one another in size and shape and tint—a great farraginous jumble of white arms and darker arms, a leg here, naked arms there pushing a stroller and a naked toddler—a stomach across which black hair crept like a weed over unearthly soil. He started forward in what was his best guess as to the direction of home. Wasn't this a fantasy? he asked himself—being able to see any person he wanted naked? But that fantasy proved a very different proposition from having to see every person naked: the nude street vendor whose shoulders contorted as he fished with tongs for a hot dog in steaming water—the protruding bumps of spine of a nude delivery man, tracing an arc toward a dropped quarter. When he did see young women, attractive women, something in the profusion, in the lack of awareness of their nakedness altered it—made the tautness of stomachs, the fullness of breasts, the firmness of thighs and coils of pubic hair more a simple fact of their bodies than features to be admired by him. Whatever might be attractive, erotic in a particular body was lost in the general wash of bodies—the commonality of all the bodies around him: all things soft, all things pendulous. He saw in it something terribly sad—because this was how these people were. Only the thinnest stretches of fabric hid them, protected them from this. Beneath the clothes of every New Yorker, beneath their job and title and urgent reason for being on the sidewalk—was a naked human being: and him, too—

And Jonah found it heartbreaking.

6. TREMENDOUS PROMISE

One late August Sunday before Judith's senior year of high school, she and her parents went to see a movie at the independent theater that had recently opened in the center of town. It was already dark out

by the time the movie was over—the evening air "more fall than summer," Hannah, Judith's mother, commented. They walked across the
town common to a Chinese restaurant they often ate at, shared vege-
table lo mein, chicken with broccoli, steamed dumplings—their usual
order. Then they drove home—David, Judith's father, letting her drive
the new Saab he had just bought. Back at the house, Judith's parents
settled in the living room: Hannah sitting on the couch with the galleys
of an anthology of twentieth-century women's poetry she had edited;
David answering emails on his laptop, typing with two fingers, every
now and then asking his wife a question of phrasing or tact. Judith put
a James Taylor CD on the stereo, took her copy of the Sunday *New
York Times* crossword puzzle (all three of them liked to do the Sunday
crossword, so they got three copies of the paper delivered to the house
on weekends), and lay down on the living room floor, knees bent and
ankles crossed in the air, occasionally tapping her pen lightly against
her nose in absent contentment as she made her way through the
puzzle. At one point she looked up to see her father watching her.

"What is it?" she asked him.

"Just taking mental pictures," he told her, smiled a little wanly,
glanced at his wife, and went back to typing. College—the great trauma
of American family life—was fast approaching.

Judith had already taken her SATs and SAT subject tests, half a
dozen AP courses and exams. She had exhausted Gustav's course offer-
ings in French, and so had arranged an independent study with a professor at the college where her parents taught. That summer, she had
spent six weeks at a program for high school students at Yale.

This last experience had cinched her decision to apply there early.
She had been leaning in that direction, anyway—it was where Hannah
had gone as an undergraduate—but mounting the steps of templelike
Sterling Library, feeling, not unrealistically, that as she crossed its thresh-
old she was entering the presence of the most accomplished, the most
distinguished, the most promising minds in the country, stirred her zealotry pleasantly. And as she walked beneath the vaulted ceiling of the
reading room, light pouring through great traceried windows onto rows
of tables filled with students bent over notepads and laptops, flanked by
stacks of books—she concluded that this was where she belonged.

The application was a team effort. In a detail that would seem to her in later years touchingly anachronistic, they had to use a typewriter to fill it out: set up on the dining room table the old Olympia SM9 on which Hannah had written her dissertation, spread out around it all the forms and essays and recommendations and transcripts. Slowly, they assembled Judith's entire academic life—which represented more or less her entire life—in a single envelope. Then they "sealed it with a kiss," as David said—and sent it off to New Haven.

Those in her class at Gustav's who hoped their valedictorian would get her comeuppance when it came time for college acceptance letters were disappointed. She and her mother were cooking dinner together in the kitchen when her father came home from teaching—the propitiously fat envelope adorned with the blue Yale seal on top of the pile of mail. She remembered hearing the familiar, marchlike chords of "All Things Considered" on the kitchen radio as she tore it open. There wasn't much doubt as to its contents, of course; but then, had there ever been any doubt? She had gotten gold stars, glowing assessments—A's, 1600s, 5s, 800s—her whole life. She was the daughter of two PhDs, both of whom knew a thing or two about college admissions—knew a professor or two, for that matter, at Yale. It would not have been much of an exaggeration to say that they considered her getting into the college of her choice Judith's birthright. But even if none of them was surprised, when she read from the top page of the bundle of papers inside the envelope the word "Congratulations," they all wept and held one another.

It was strange, Judith observed, as they ate ice cream from the freezer, their eyes still red, how they had all worked so hard to get to the point that would mark the dissolution of their family as they knew it. "It's the way of things," Hannah replied. "All we can do is prepare you as best we can for the life you're going to have. We wouldn't want to lock you in your room for the rest of your life."

"Pushing you out of the nest!" David added—but he couldn't sustain the jocular tone with which he'd started, and as he finished he began to cry again.

Over the following months, Judith at times did feel mournful at the prospect of leaving her childhood home, her parents. More often,

though, she felt excited: for new challenges—for the next step. She
read and highlighted the Yale course catalog; she emailed with professors in the departments she was considering for her major (English,
French, Religion); she read about Puritanism, the New Haven Colony,
the founding of Yale in 1701. And when she did feel worst about being
separated from David and Hannah, she would remind herself, or they
would remind her, that they would all always be only a car ride apart.

In the spring, she got an email from her future roommate. This was
a girl named Milim Oh: Korean, from northern New Jersey, also
graduating that June from an all-girls private school. She seemed as
concerned as Judith that they establish their room as a sanctum of
mutually comfortable tranquillity: lights out at eleven, music they didn't
agree on in headphones. Suffice it to say, they hit it off from the start.

On an appropriately sunny and clear-skied summer afternoon,
Judith graduated from Gustav Girls' Academy. She and her classmates
dressed in white, wore garlands of white gardenias in their hair. White
was not a good color for Judith. In the pictures she looked a bit like
a giant candle with a stumpy, bulbous black wick. A former Gustav's
graduate, now a justice of the state supreme court, gave the commencement speech. "Wherever the years ahead take you," she told them, "the
lessons you have learned here at Gustav's will be a wind at your back."

That afternoon, David and Hannah threw a party for Judith in the
expansive backyard of their two-story brick Colonial home: hired cater-
ers, had a tent set up, invited friends of the family, Judith's friends and
classmates, her favorite teachers (most of them, anyway). Everyone
hugged Judith, told her how proud they were of her, how bright her
future was. She did not quite know how to conduct herself as the center
of all this attention; she was not arrogant enough to take it all as a matter of course, nor was she exactly humble enough to be genuinely embarrassed by it. She ended up making frequent trips to the bar for plastic
cups of seltzer and then repeatedly needing to go into the house to pee.

Judith's aunt Naomi and her daughter, Margaretha, attended the
party, as well. Judith's mother and her sister did not get along well—
were, as David put it, "incompatible at birth." David and Hannah
were reticent about the details, but from what Judith understood,
Naomi had always positioned herself as the free-spirited ying to

Hannah's tightly wound, conventional yang, which for decades had been infuriating Hannah as nothing else did. And because Hannah and Naomi rarely saw each other, Judith rarely saw Margaretha, her only cousin, despite the fact that they were the same age.

"Your house really kicks ass," Margaretha told her as she sat cross-legged on the the lawn, away from where the other guests were mingling. In contrast to Judith's white-and-lace, Margaretha was wearing a billowy tie-dye dashiki shirt and extravagantly ripped jeans.

"Thanks," said Judith.

"I can't believe you're going to Yale. I mean, who actually goes to Yale? Y'know?"

"Thanks," repeated Judith. "Do you know where you're going yet?" It was the middle of June, so if Margaretha was going anywhere she would know by now, but Judith was trying to be tactful.

Margaretha shrugged. "I might go live in Holland with my dad." She ran her palms over the tips of the grass. "I don't really believe in an ordered existence. No offense." Judith nodded with a certain unease—feeling she was enacting her mother's relationship with her sister in this conversation with her cousin. "Do you want to go up to your room and get high?" Margaretha asked. "I have really good weed with me." Judith had to admit she was intrigued—but the idea of smoking pot when all her neighbors and teachers and parents' friends had gathered at her house seemed dumb, inappropriate. (In later years, she would remember the offer kindly, though.)

"No thanks," Judith told her.

"That's cool," Margaretha answered. "Wait a minute, stand right there." She reached into the knit purse sitting beside her on the grass and took out a Polaroid camera. "I'm doing this art project. It's like, people's faces and the worlds they live in. And you and your house and the lawn and everything, it's totally perfect." Then, before Judith could respond, she said, "Smile!" and took the picture. "I'll send you the whole thing when it's finished," Margaretha told her as she waved the Polaroid in the air. Judith nodded—in spite of herself greatly skeptical that she would ever see this Polaroid again.

A few weeks later, the Bulbrooks took one last family vacation before Judith left home: went to Australia, snorkeled at the Great

Barrier Reef. When they returned in early August, they started in to
the practical work of getting Judith to college: loaded her belongings
into cardboard boxes, bought her a new computer and a new bathrobe and new sheets and new anything else they could think of. She
said her goodbyes to her friends, these girls scattering to elite colleges
of their own—Columbia, Harvard, Dartmouth, Wellesley, and the rest.
There was some sadness to these goodbyes, but it was a qualified sadness. They were all leaving for places they wanted to be.

The night before she and her parents were to drive to New Haven,
Judith found she couldn't sleep, her mind too crowded with thoughts
to be had—expectations, hopes, fears, remembrances—to find repose.
Finally she got up and, walking quietly through the sleeping house, took
the keys from the bowl in the foyer and got into the family's station
wagon, now packed with cardboard boxes they had filled with the
possessions she would bring with her to college. She drove for a while
with no destination in mind—simply retracing routes through her
hometown she'd taken for as long as she could remember, until eventually she came to the trailhead, to the trail that led to the creek: the
setting of the most potent, most piquant memories from what she had
already begun to think of as her childhood. Dressed in her Gustav's
cross-country shorts and the Yale sweatshirt her parents had given her
after her matriculation, she walked through the woods in the dark—
trying to take in the fear she felt as part of the night itself—came to
the edge of the water.

The moon shone through the gaps in the trees, its light silvery and
scattering over the creek's black surface. She identified an image of herself in this, in the interplay of blackness and light. The gurgling of the
creek was louder at night, she discovered—its sound as if echoing off
the larger silence in the woods. She took off her shoes—felt the pebbles
and soft ground giving against the soles of her feet—and then she
stepped into the water.

Every senior at Gustav's had to complete an honors project to
graduate. Judith had written about the Jewish conception of time. Since
her trip to Israel the summer after her sophomore year, Judaism had
become more central to her study, to her thinking. There were even

days when she toyed with the idea of becoming a rabbi. (And who knows, she sometimes thought later—maybe she would have.) In her honors project, she'd written about how the narrative of the Hebrew Bible was linear—how each event led to the next, and in all these events there was a progression, of genealogy and of history: God's promise to Abraham, the redemption of his descendants from Egypt, the gift of the Ten Commandments to Moses, and on and on and on. This notion of linear time contrasted with time as it existed within Jewish ritual, which was not linear but rather circular, cyclical, built around holidays that recurred every week, every year. These two kinds of time came together, she had written, in the life of every observant Jew, which was organized around the observance of key life-cycle events: circumcision or naming; bar or bat mitzvah; marriage under a *chuppah*; the circumcision or naming of one's own children. "Every week ends with Shabbat, the day of rest," Judith had written in her conclusion, the text of which had been heavily adorned with laudatory check marks by her teacher. "This gives every week the same shape, the same character, the same themes. In just this way, Jewish life-cycle events, from birth to death, give every life the same essential structure. Each life, whatever the differences in its specifics, is guided by the same essential story, across the generations, and all throughout time."

When she'd written these words, she had believed them—the concept of bullshit was anathema to Judith Klein Bulbrook. But she had believed them on the level of fact, of reason—she had not considered them as having a deeper truth—a truth the words themselves could only fail to articulate. She did not feel them as she did now: standing to her ankles in the cold water of the creek, a few feet from where she had lost her virginity—on her last night living in the only town where she had ever lived. She saw in her mind's eye an image of ascending spirals of every color—felt herself a part of this image—safely held within it. Time was not a chaotic tumble forward, nor was it a steady dwindling into death, she thought. Time was ordered, it was governed—it was Godly.

She knelt down, her hands and her knees now submerged. If the water had been deep enough, she thought she might have submerged herself fully, stripped naked—to feel herself, as much as possible, a part of it. "I offer myself to this," she prayed. "God, make me a part of your story."

She remained in this reverent crouch until she started to lose feeling in her toes and fingers, until her arched back began to ache. Then she straightened, and made her way carefully back to shore. She put on her shoes, tied the laces, returned to the car. She drove herself home, and went to sleep. The next morning, her parents took her to college.

Judith's parting from her parents was, in the end, fairly subdued. Her mother had made her bed in her dorm room; they had all met Milim Oh, who was as polite and agreeable and reserved as Judith was when she met Milim's parents. Then Judith walked David and Hannah back to the now-empty station wagon, hugged each of them goodbye—and that was that. They had all had so many crying jags over the last few months in anticipation of this moment, maybe they were relieved the moment itself had finally come—and to find that it was actually so manageable, could have the features of any other goodbye. They would be seeing one another again in only a couple of weeks, as well: Hannah, in support of her new book of poetry, would be giving a series of readings, one of which would be at an independent bookstore in New Haven. Her parents would have dinner with her before continuing on to Boston and then flying to California for a string of readings at schools on the West Coast. Academic life would offer them many such opportunities to get together, they all knew.

Judith had several days of orientation events before the upperclassmen arrived and classes started. She met with her adviser, heard speeches by various deans and administrators, ate lunches in the courtyard with her residential college. The school was unembarrassed in its attempts to inculcate its new students with the idea that, yes, this was the finest institution of higher education in the country, and, yes indeed, they were now among the academic elite—the elect. Predictably, Judith was unembarrassed in her embrace of these notions: They were more or less exactly what she'd been looking for in attending the school.

It was during orientation week that she got drunk for the first time.

Two boys on her floor managed to get cases of beer and a plastic bottle of vodka, and held an impromptu party in their room. Judith had done a little bit of drinking before: had snuck sips from the liquor cabinet at friends' houses during sleepovers, had drunk a couple of beers at parties during her senior year. But she'd never had sufficient will to get drunk to overcome her dislike for the taste of alcohol. Tonight, though—with the abandon of any freshman who'd just left home—she had the will. They played a card game that involved chugging and doing shots and ordering other people to drink, all the while listening to Wagner's *Die Walküre*. Later they played another game, called I Never, which afforded Judith the opportunity to impress her classmates with how sexually experienced she actually was. By midnight the party collapsed into what would colloquially be called a shitshow: nineteen-year-olds throwing up in the hallway, tearfully calling their long-distance high school boyfriends or girlfriends, Milim passed out on the couch in the lounge. Judith ended up in the bed of a soccer player who lived two floors above her—kept her underwear on and enjoyed herself just fine. The next morning she ran the perimeter of the campus until the skull-throbbing headache of her hangover (which she was even a bit proud of, recognizing it as the first of her life) had subsided, then spent the next three hours choosing her courses for the semester. As she walked among the stately cream-stone buildings to bring her adviser the appropriate form—the leaves of the trees on New Haven Green giving the first hints of their autumn colors—she realized she was in love with college.

By the time she had dinner with David and Hannah a few weeks later, this love had taken on the dimensions of near ecstasy. She told them about reading Proust in French, about her brilliant Philosophies of Religion professor. Hannah and David just smiled and nodded at this unusual bout of verbosity from their daughter. This dinner, David told Hannah that night in their hotel room, was the moment when he saw that their daughter really had graduated from high school—from their care.

At the end of the meal, as they were saying good night, Judith began to cry. "What is it, honey?" Hannah asked her. Misunderstanding the tears, she said, "You'll see us again for Parents' Weekend."

"No, it isn't that, it's just . . . I just want to thank you for giving me all this," she told them.

"We didn't give you anything," David said. "You earned it."

"No, I know, but . . ." Judith began, not quite sure how to articulate the nature of the gratitude she felt. She looked at her two parents—and felt she saw them, maybe for the first time, not only as her parents, but as people: a married couple getting toward the end of middle age, visiting their only daughter at college; her father's hair now closer to entirely gray than black, the deepening creases of his face giving him a sort of durable, late-in-life handsomeness; her mother, her hair having a touch of frizziness of its own, dressed with understated elegance in a light dress with a purple shawl wrapped around her shoulders, because it was chilly that evening. They had a long drive ahead of them that night to get to Boston for their flight to California the next morning. They had sacrificed a far easier trip to make time and have dinner with her. "I feel like everything you ever told me was true," Judith said.

The next day Judith woke up at 7:15 A.M.—went for a run, then sat at her desk in her dorm room, reviewing her Philosophies of Religion assignment for that day, sipping green tea. Milim's alarm went off at 8:30—the roommates said a brief good morning, and Milim went to the shower around 8:45. A few minutes later Judith went to take a shower herself. When she got back to her room she noticed that Milim wasn't there—but didn't think much of it. She might have heard some shouting in the courtyard outside her window as she got dressed at 9:15. Someone ran by her door as she was putting her books in her bag. She opened the door to go to breakfast just as Milim was coming in—towels wrapped around her chest and hair, her face wet beneath her glasses. "They crashed planes into New York," Milim said. It was several moments before Judith could decipher the meaning of this.

When she got to the lounge, half the students on her floor had gathered around the television. Many were crying; those from New York came in and out, trying over and over to call cell phones that didn't work. There remained, for Judith, something plausible—comprehensible—about the disaster as it unfolded on television. She had heard of buildings being on fire before. It seemed to her it was really a problem of engineering, of logistics: How do you put out a fire ninety stories up? She imagined that helicopters might be useful. Then, at 9:59 A.M., shrieking filling the lounge, filling the courtyard outside, the first tower collapsed.

It had been reported by then that one of the planes had departed from Boston, headed toward Los Angeles. But only when the tower collapsed did Judith walk to her room, and open her email, reread the itinerary her father had emailed her the night before. She saw that her parents had been booked on American Airlines Flight 11. She supposed they'd missed it. She looked at her watch, and saw that she still had a little time before she had to leave for her Philosophies of Religion class. She sat back down and finished going over the assigned reading.

As she walked across campus, the sky was incredibly clear, the campus incredibly bare, empty—the bright green grass and bordering stone buildings as if having been shaken free of people. But Judith was aware of a kind of frenetic movement at the edges of this blankness—as though just beyond her field of vision, people were running this way and that. When she got to the classroom, it was empty, the lights off. She checked her watch. She had arrived a few minutes early, she saw. She looked over the reading again. Finally a campus security guard came in and told her she had to leave: all classes had been canceled, all campus buildings were being closed.

This seemed wholly irrational to Judith—"hysteria unworthy of a school of Yale's caliber" was how she decided she'd phrase it in her letter to the *Yale Daily News*. She'd been thinking about becoming a columnist for the *YDN*. Maybe this letter could be part of her writing sample.

Milim was still in the lounge when Judith returned to her floor. When Milim saw her, she jumped up and ran after her as she went into her room—Judith could not quite close and lock the door in her face.

"Judith!" Milim said to her. "Your email—people are calling."

"They missed the plane."

"They missed the plane?" Milim stared at her worriedly—began to shake her head very slowly.

"Of course they missed the plane," Judith said furiously. She was finding breathing difficult. She had the sensation of falling. Where was

God? she asked herself. Where was God? "Of course they missed the plane. . . . They must have missed the plane. . . ." She was wheezing—she saw Milim and her bed careen up toward the ceiling—on television, she had seen people jumping—Where was God? She closed her eyes. She felt something constricting in her chest. An EMT was in her room. The phone was ringing. A dean was there. She was in and out, in and out—God—Hannah and David—Mom and Dad—. Where was the world she knew?

As she made her way blankly through the next days, it was remarkable to her that there were things to do. It turned out there was no one else to do them. She had never noticed before how small her family was. She had to return phone calls. She had to talk to lawyers. And all this activity seemed preposterous to her, given that David and Hannah Bulbrook had been murdered where they sat—burned alive in an instant, if they were lucky—or, if they were unlucky, their bodies crushed and compacted by steel, bones and skulls cracked by what was harder than bone or skull. Or else they had fallen. She could not help herself from dwelling on these possibilities—her mind unable to resist the habit of considering all possibilities. And still—there were phone calls to return. According to the email her father had sent, they had not had seats together: Hannah was in 27A, David in 16B. No one could tell her whether they'd changed seats—whether they had been apart, at the end, without even a hand to hold. Yet she was expected to sign her name. She was expected to talk. Some people were deluded enough to believe that talking remained necessary—that it remained worth doing. They sent her cards, they wrote her emails, they came to visit. They seemed to misunderstand, seemed unaware in some way that Hannah and David Bulbrook had been killed against the side of the World Trade Center. How foolish they were—how stupid—and how stupid she had been. How stupid, she thought at the funeral, looking at the pair of coffins before the *bimah*—how stupid, as she listened to the rabbi, and accepted what passed for condolences, and allowed herself to be hugged by all the same people who had hugged her at her graduation party. She watched it all as though from behind the pale mask of her face, and as she said the mourner's *kaddish* at the first *shivah* of her life, she realized now, at last—she had a secret to surpass all others. Her parents had been liars, and she had been a fool.

7. FOR YOU, LORD, HAVE DONE AS YOU PLEASED

As Jonah was overwhelmed by his vision, the tidal regularity of the city around him was no more disturbed than the ocean by the plight of a single fish. Shifts changed, happy hours began; on Wall Street, the markets closed. Buses made their weary way crosstown, uptown, and downtown, in their Sisyphean redistribution of commuters. Mailmen— with the dignity of the last American Indians—unlocked squat blue mailboxes and dumped the day's contents into white plastic tubs. Tourists finished up at Liberty Island, or Ellis Island, or Ground Zero, and boarded trains to Times Square, because there were shows to see that night. And because it was summer, the Great Lawn in Central Park was dotted with blankets and Frisbees in flight and women sunbathing and softball games being played with a goodwill that was almost indulgent. Among those in the park was Becky, who had taken the day off work to celebrate her engagement—the princess-cut diamond on her finger glittering in the sunlight with sparks of red and purple and blue. She was reading the *New Yorker* in a skirt and a bikini top— more skin than she usually risked, but she was feeling proud and exuberant to be getting married. Meanwhile her fiancé sat at his desk, staring blankly at his computer screen, not really seeing the Excel spreadsheet before him, realizing that the anxiety of the weekend had not been escaped but rather made permanent. Subway turnstiles spun in *click-clack, click-clack;* automatic doors of clothing stores sighed open, sighed shut, offering New York shoppers the full spectrum—in color and cost and fabric, in attention to fashion, in extravagance and utility—of dress. Dolores walked down the sidewalk with a bag from

Macy's, full of the three hundred dollars' worth of clothing she had bought on her boss's credit card—since he was too disorganized and generally foolish to check his own receipts. In the office of the mayor, a union official was making mildly veiled threats that sanitation workers might go on strike if their wages were not unfrozen. Philip Orengo, listening to this, was having trouble suppressing a smirk, because he knew that unions existed in name only now. Meanwhile Patrick Hooper was ordering online a five-thousand-dollar Hermès baseball glove, then decided to order two. And Aaron Seyler, in an office on Vesey Street, was on the treadmill, pushing to get his three-mile splits from six minutes down to more like five-fifty. His energy did sometimes flag in the late afternoon, so this was when he tried to get his workouts in. As he ran, his brows were knit, and even he recognized something savage in his focus. Traffic was beginning to accumulate on the FDR, and at the entrance to the Lincoln Tunnel, and on both levels of the George Washington Bridge, and beneath the stately neo-Gothic archways of the Brooklyn Bridge. Taxis converged on JFK and LaGuardia and Midtown. Where Hicks Street ran parallel to the concrete carapace of the BQE, drivers locked their doors as the woman to whom Jonah had given forty dollars—this money now long, long gone—passed by unsteadily on the narrow strip of curb. She stopped every now and then to assess the progress of withdrawal in her body, the attenuation of the chemical warmth—her head tilted and held still, as though she were listening for a distant storm, though the sky overhead was clear, its light a late summer blue-gold that would last for hours, everyone knew: They decided to walk home from work; they made plans to eat dinner outside. Sylvia was feeling pleased, because the meeting of the Chinese investors and the American lessees of the oil field they were buying and the Angolan ministers who governed the country in which it was located had gone well. They had just taken a fifteen-minute break; she could hear the voices of the men in the hallway as she washed her hands in the empty women's bathroom. And Zoey sat in her cubicle, pondering the naked body of the actress Katie Porter, displayed on the computer screen before her. Katie Porter, eighteen—crucially, from a legal perspective, not seventeen—had a cell phone camera in one hand, with the other she held her hair up behind her head, her mouth in a dewy, soft-core porn smile. The website for which Zoey worked had paid a thousand dollars for the image, with the promise of another four thousand if it proved genuine—and it was Zoey's job to study it, and scrutinize it, and determine whether it was real.

As all this occurred, Jonah was hiding in an underground storeroom beneath a restaurant on Lexington Avenue. The space was no more than a hundred feet square, crowded with cardboard boxes of paper products, jars and cans, cases of wine and liquor. The air was stuffy and close; a narrow crack between the metal doors at the top of a steep wooden stairway leading up to the street was the only source of light, but Jonah had his eyes closed anyway, just in case. He'd seen the doors standing open and fled down here: stumbled down the stairs and pulled the doors closed behind him. He had needed to get off the street, to get away from the sight of people. There had been only so much nakedness he'd been able to take.

Now he was hunched against a silver tower of beer kegs, his arms wrapped around his chest. A crescent of sweat was forming from his forehead down his cheeks, but he made no move to wipe it away. "I'm going crazy," he was saying to himself, over and over. "I'm going crazy." When he'd first spoken these words, he'd regarded them as an admission, an acceptance of something—a brave concession to the facts. But the longer he stood there repeating them, mantra-like, the more he understood that they actually provided a form of solace—a solace that diminished with every repetition. If he was going crazy, he could assign clinically defined labels to what he was going through, enact medically sanctioned solutions. He could assimilate what was happening to him in a way that would leave the world as he'd always known it intact. The problem was he didn't believe he was going crazy. He hadn't believed it after Becky's party, he didn't believe it now—and he believed it less the more he tried to convince himself he did.

An abrupt buzzing filled the storeroom. Jonah straightened, startled, flattened himself against the beer kegs. Several seconds of silence passed before he realized what he'd just heard was the buzz of a text message being received on his phone. He took the phone from his pocket, lifted it to his face. The text was from Sylvia: "APPROVED for Bond St. Brett says we need to sched signing ASAP. Tomorrow AM? Call me, love." He stared at the message, trying to gauge his reaction to it. Finally he couldn't, and returned the phone to his pocket.

As he did this, it occurred to him that he had a pocket, and so he was wearing clothing—maybe this meant the vision had ended. He hadn't really considered his own nudity, though, as he'd been witnessing everyone else's. One common feature of what he'd seen today and what he'd seen at Becky's party was how they both seemed to invert his consciousness—making him aware of himself least of all.

Maybe he should talk to a rabbi, he thought. But none of the rabbis he'd encountered in his experiences of institutional Judaism had been very inspiring. And as he imagined Googling "best rabbi NYC," eventually visiting an office bedecked with menorahs and *mezuzahs* and leather-bound editions of the Talmud and framed Chagall prints, imagined sitting down before the oaken desk of a bearded, yarmulked, amply nosed rabbi, and explaining that he'd been having "y'know, visions"—if he could even get this word out at all—he could not think of a single thing the rabbi might tell him that would give him any comfort, yield any insight. It wasn't like he needed advice on preparing for an adult bar mitzvah.

It was all completely unfair, he thought, as he now leaned his forehead against the cool surface of one of the kegs. He was not a bad person. Sure, he wasn't as good as he might have been, but then again, he was better than a lot of people: just like everyone else, in other words. Why, then, was he the only one who couldn't walk down the street without seeing the population of New York stripped of its clothing?

If there had been a discernible message, some purpose to these visions, he might have borne it all a little better. If he had to be afflicted in this way, was it too much to ask for the rationale? Or, barring that, why couldn't the visions be different? Why couldn't he see, say, harp-toting angels on puffy white clouds, lambs curled up with lions in some Edenic portrait of the Brooklyn Botanical Gardens? Hell, he might even have been grateful for that. Who wouldn't want confirmation of a greeting-card afterlife and a smiley-faced higher power? But there was something awful in the scenes that had been put before his eyes.

He could not say precisely what was so awful; but whatever it was, it was potent enough that even recollecting the details of what he'd seen in memory—New York reduced to a wasteland, everyone around him naked, equally and unalterably naked—an additional, cold sweat sprang onto his forehead, he had to tug away the knot of his tie and undo the button at his throat ahead of a gasping sensation.

He recalled the Hasid on the subway—his warnings, his story. Jonah was not afraid he was about to be swallowed up by a whale, of course (though he had to admit, his present circumstances resembled that predicament far more than he would have liked). But the whale, as the Hasid himself had explained, was not the point—was only a detail. Jonah sensed that there was something—Biblical—going on. And to find himself caught up in that mind-set, that order, was terrifying. That he didn't know how he recognized this, just that something in these experiences made it unmistakable, only added to the fear—such that the storeroom, as he looked anxiously around it, became eerie, forbidding, the way the inside of closets had looked when he was a child: its unidentifiable, shadowed contents suddenly imbued with sinister, uncanny possibilities.

Instinctively, he grabbed for the box of cigarettes in his pocket—but as he tried to take it out, the box turned sideways, and jerking it free the box slipped from his hand and dropped to the concrete floor. He reached forward to retrieve it, and as he did he knocked his head against the side of a set of shelves stacked with jars of mustard, ketchup, pickles. "Damn it," he said, and smacked the shelves—triggering another shiver of pain through his palm.

"Damn it!" he repeated, and started to shake the shelves—and as the jars shattered on the floor, he shook the shelves harder. "Damn it, damn it, damn it, fucking damn it!" he shouted, as he knocked over the tower of kegs, tossed boxes in the air, ripped open bags of whatever he found, threw soda can after soda can against the walls.

When he'd finished, he sank to the floor amidst viscous puddles and broken glass, his suit stained in a rainbow of colors—panting, his head hanging limp. "What am I going to do?" he said—quietly, sorrowfully now. "What am I going to do?"

The box of cigarettes was lying at an angle against a dented, fizzing can of Diet Pepsi. He wiped some mayonnaise from his fingers onto his pants, took out a cigarette, and lit it. He tried to concentrate on only the sensations of smoking: the filter between his lips, the warm smoke coming in and out of his mouth. He tried to envision the nicotine—soothing, steadying—being absorbed into his lungs, his bloodstream, coursing through his body. And by the time the cigarette was finished, he did feel buoyed a little. Maybe it would all just go away, he told himself. Maybe it would just stop.

At that moment, the metal doors to the storeroom rattled above him—Jonah raised his head as first one and then the other was lifted away and a tabular slab of light fell over him. He squinted and heard Spanish being spoken. He pulled himself to his feet as a Latino man in a Mets hat, apron, and cargo shorts appeared at the top of the stairs. This man's head made a bewildered semicircle as he took in the mess of the room, the food-splattered man at its center. "*¿Estás bien?*" he said to Jonah.

Jonah tried to construct a response from what he could remember of high school Spanish, realizing he had only a few moments before it was deduced that he was not the victim but rather the perpetrator in this post-food-fight spectacle. "*Necesario . . . médico . . . con permiso . . .*" he said, and then hurried up the steps and pushed past the still-befuddled man.

He had made a half-jogging walk across two avenues before he felt confident he wasn't being followed by the man in the Mets hat. And then he thought to himself, a Mets hat: a Mets hat, and an apron, and cargo shorts. He stopped, looked around: The people passing him on the sidewalk, going in and out of office and apartment buildings—they were all fully clothed. He felt like dropping to the ground and weeping with relief. He couldn't be sure, though, how long this return to normalcy would last, that he would not immediately be confronted with some new form of metaphysical exposure. He started to hurry again along the sidewalk, looking up and down the street for a taxi.

At a streetlight at the end of the block he had to stop. The other pedestrians gathered beside him on the curb gave quizzical looks to his Pollock-splatter clothing. He ignored them, kept his eyes on the street, still watching for an open cab. But as he stood there waiting—watching the cars, glancing at the traffic light—the solidity of these things began to assert itself. The mundaneness of it all—pedestrians clustering at the very edge of the sidewalk as they waited for the light to change; a mammoth red tourist bus now lumbering around a corner as every car around it honked; the green street signs with white letters meeting perpendicular near the top of the pole of the streetlight—the mundaneness was comforting, reassuring. What could interrupt this, alter this? Maybe he'd been crazy after all. Maybe, if he could hold on to the ordinariness, the inertial regularity of everything around him—he would be okay.

He spotted a bar across the street. Anyone would tell him he deserved a drink after what he'd been through, he thought. He crossed the street when the light changed with everyone else, went up the block to the bar. It was one of those faux-Irish places popular in Midtown: named O'Something's, with a neon Guinness sign in the window and a placard out front touting the Yankees–Red Sox game on eight HD flat-screens. It was not the sort of bar he typically went to; with Sylvia it was artisanal cocktail bars, with coworkers it was upscale places with good booze. Today, though, this characterless place, which could have existed anywhere in the city—maybe anywhere in any city—seemed to him exactly where he needed to be: a monument to the fundamental banality of life.

As he was pushing open the door, he noticed a man getting out of a taxi a few feet up the block. This man was heavyset, with a high, mottled forehead, wore a tie and slacks and had a suit jacket hanging over the crook of his arm, a bulging computer bag slung across his chest with a newspaper wedged into one of the outside pockets. There were two large rolling suitcases already beside him on the curb—and, as Jonah watched, he reached back into the open door of the taxi, began trying to yank out an oversize duffel bag. As the man pulled, his jacket fell to the sidewalk, his nostrils and mouth started to work silently. He gripped the handle of the duffel with both hands, yanked again. Beads of sweat sprang up on his forehead; his mouth bent into a pained grimace. "Uhh!" he cried, as the bag still would not come out after another pull.

Jonah stood with his palm holding open the door of the bar as he watched this. At last the bag came free. The man set it beside the others, shaking his head in an exaggeratedly dismissive way—as though to demonstrate his renewed self-mastery to anyone who happened to be watching. He picked his jacket up off the sidewalk and closed the cab door, and then he sniffed loudly—as if drawing a line between himself and all that had just occurred—took the strap of the computer bag off his chest and put his jacket on. As he straightened the jacket over his shoulders, he noticed that Jonah was indeed watching, staring at him from the doorway of the bar. They looked at each other for a few seconds—neither really knowing how to look at the other. The man raised his chin, opened his lips for a moment, like he thought he might recognize Jonah—and then a sort of instinctive hardening came over his features, and he turned back to his bags, slung the computer bag again across his chest, lifted the duffel onto one of the rolling suitcases, its edges drooping over the roller's sides, and began to pull the whole load down the street.

Jonah went into the bar. Inside were the mahogany booths and stools, the digital jukebox playing classic rock, the dartboard and row of taps lining the bar he'd expected. He didn't advance any more than a few steps past the doorway, though. He was thinking about the sound the man had made: the "uhh!" he'd let out. It was a universal cry among New Yorkers—guttural, visceral—you heard it on the subway when someone couldn't get through the crowd before the doors closed; you heard it in line at the grocery store when someone accidentally dropped his wallet on the ground. It was typically the most New Yorkers allowed themselves in terms of acknowledging discomfort, or disappointment, or embarrassment, in a city that so valued acting like you'd done it all, seen it all, conquered it all before. It was the sound of wits' end, of lost cool, of exhausted patience at the thousand tiny trials necessitated by life in New York, or anywhere else. It was, in so many ways, an awful sound.

Jonah turned around and walked out of the bar. He looked out at the city: his home. If this was his home, what did that make the man he had just seen, to him? What was the fellowship that existed between two people in the same home? It had to be fellowship of some kind. Hadn't he been that man—a thousand times?

He knew then what was so awful in his visions, what gave them their power to terrify, to torment—to make his life seem so peculiarly hollow all of a sudden: They were true. That fragility he had seen, the mortality, the vulnerability—they were everywhere. It was no great revelation that everyone was naked beneath their clothes, that the city and everyone in it would someday crumble into dust—except that it was.

He should have helped that man, he thought. If they were alike in—he should have done—

He clenched his teeth, squeezed his fists until his fingernails dug into the skin of his palms—willing this train of thought to come to an end. No, he thought. No, no, no. He was not the kind of person who spontaneously offered to help strangers with their bags. He was not the kind of person who reacted to an "uhh" with anything other than gratitude that he had not been the one who'd made it.

He saw that he was losing—was being robbed of—an essential capacity: the capacity to ignore. It turned out that you had to ignore certain things—a lot of certain things, in fact—just to be able to walk into a bar and get drunk, to say nothing of working 17,500 hours in a law firm. You had to ignore, for one, that you were surrounded at all times by fellow human beings whose lives had the same despairs, both minor and great, the same final brevity as yours, as anyone's. When you lost the anonymity of others—when you could no longer automatically filter out the peopleness of other people—then you couldn't function here. You had no place here. Jonah felt as if he had spent years, maybe his whole life, able to abide—to thrive!—on the finest surface of things, and having been plunged momentarily beneath this surface, he could no longer find it.

And that, he thought, was wrong.

Jonah got angry again—not in the manner of the temper tantrum he'd had in the storeroom; this was a deeper, a self-sustaining, indignant anger. Walking into a bar at any hour of the day to get drunk was the right of every New Yorker. Why was he denied it? Why couldn't he live his life however he wanted—with as much callous disregard for his fellow human beings as he wished?

He felt a wild impulse to demonstrate—to himself, and to whomever (or Whomever) might be watching—that he was the same person he had always been, would always be—for better, for worse. "*Non serviam*, motherfucker," he muttered under his breath.

Around this time, Zoey was leaving work. She knew she ought not have been, but staring at the digital picture of a naked Katie Porter—studying the individual pixels making up the flawless thighs, and flawless breasts, and flawless hair, and flawless stomach, and flawless on and on and on—had succeeded in depressing her. She'd recognized the image was real more or less from the moment it had appeared on her screen. Part of her job was to judge the authenticity of dozens of such pictures a week. And it was really too bad she had to see this, she'd thought as she examined it. Katie Porter was the celebrity Zoey had pegged herself against in recent months, since, in theory, they had very similar body types. So much for that theory, she'd thought dispiritedly. Everywhere Zoey was too round, or not round enough, or not toned enough, or somewhat disproportioned, Katie Porter presented the Platonic ideal. Zoey had considered whether it would make her feel better if the picture were shared with every pimply teenage boy and creepy middle-aged man on the planet—but it wouldn't, she'd decided. The instinct for revenge was not very strong in her, and more than that, she'd detected in herself an anticipatory sympathy for all the other girls in their cubicles who had a *Glossified* RSS feed and who would study this picture with the same masochistic scrutiny that she had, to the same dismaying effect. So she'd finally closed the picture and written an email to her boss, Anika: "Looks like a fake to me. Disney executives can exhale." Then she'd left for the day.

She now pushed through the revolving door of her building and walked out onto the stone plaza before it. Her plan had been to make a triumphant return to the gym she belonged to and which she had visited only once, the day she joined. She'd looked up the schedule online and picked out a yoga class to attend. This was in keeping with one of the clauses in the "contract with herself" that her therapist, Dr. Popper, had instructed her during her last session to write and sign: "Get more exercise & eat better." But as she stood on the plaza in the summer twilight, she felt drained from another day in B-girl purgatory—endured without even the consolation of cigarettes ("Quit smoking NOW" the relevant clause here). She reached into her purse for her phone—had pulled it out before she remembered that she couldn't call Evan to have dinner with her, because she'd broken up with him the day before. This had been in keeping with the third clause, "Take ownership of emotional well-being." Dr. Popper had suggested the language, but the impulse had been hers. She'd realized she didn't exactly know why she was with Evan. Sure, he was in good shape, and was unambiguous about his feelings for her (had even said "I love you" first), and was always happy to go to whichever restaurant/movie/bar she picked. But, as she'd said to Dr. Popper during the tearful Friday session, "Is that really all there is?" The fact that she'd forgotten about the four-hour conversation in which she'd ended it with him proved to her again that there had definitely been something lacking between them—on her end, at least. Even so, as she stared bleakly at her phone, recognizing she had no one to call, she wondered how much emotional well-being she had truly achieved here.

She realized, also, that, despite herself, she was disappointed That Person hadn't called her. He did, sometimes, in the immediate aftermath of dumping her, try to take it all back, try to coax her into forgiveness and reconciliation (emotional, physical). But she'd sensed that this time would be different, that there was something permanent in his intentions in this latest breakup—this feeling at least partly the cause of the tears and then the contract with Dr. Popper on Friday. She couldn't escape the sneaking suspicion that the next time she saw him would be on the "Vows" page of the Sunday *Times*, smiling next to *Schlampe*: blond, C-cup, Ellis–Michaels *Schlampe*.

Zoey had given her the full Google stalk, of course. She was, clearly, a Very Accomplished Young Woman. But from what Zoey could tell, that was all she was. And there was something so disappointing about that, like he wasn't even trying—like it turned out his favorite movie was *Titanic* or something.

She was chewing her thumbnail now, standing, she imagined, only a few feet from where she'd stood when he dumped her. She knew she couldn't be objective in this matter. And she would be the first to acknowledge she was not the easiest person to be with—that it took a particular kind of person to prefer an ulcer-ravaged, debt-ridden B-girl to a Very Accomplished Young Woman. The thing was—she had always thought Jonah was that sort of person. And if he wasn't, then who was?

She suddenly pictured her yoga class full of *Schlampe*s: fit, flexible *Schlampe*s in Harvard T-shirts. What was the point again of subjecting herself to that? Wouldn't her emotional well-being be better served by two slices of pizza and a pint of Häagen-Dazs and spending the next six hours watching Bravo on her couch?

But then, as she had been doing since she started high school at Dalton—still by far the most socially harrowing years of her life— Zoey gave herself a pep talk. Okay, she told herself, Katie Porter looks better than you naked. But she's a movie star, it's her job to look better than normal people naked. Plus, some of us have to ingest something other than salad and coke on occasion. As for Evan, it wasn't fair to either of you to keep dating him even though you thought he was a little boring most of the time and maybe not so smart. And all That Person did in choosing *Schlampe* was choose an unhappy marriage and an early heart attack. And maybe all the girls in your yoga class will look like the blond version of Olivia Wilde, but it's more likely they'll look like those mousy girls in Whole Foods who buy the quinoa salads. So cheer up, and yes, you can go to lululemon on your way to the gym so no one will see you in that NYU T-shirt and Evan's gym shorts, which is all you have to wear otherwise.

Fifteen minutes later, she was inside the store. She knew objectively that buying yoga clothes was a mistake, given that she had over $22,000 in credit-card debt. But some of the good health associated with yoga seemed to accrue to her just from being among the racks of fitness clothing, drinking the herbal tea she was offered when she came in. She did not correct the salesgirl's assumption that she did yoga regularly—successfully impersonated someone who understood the distinction between the words "ashtanga" and "bikram."

She was in admirably good spirits as she came out onto the street with her bag of new clothes. Then her phone rang. She tried to head off expectation by immediately checking to see who it was: Anika, her boss. *Oi,* thought Zoey. Anika was editor in chief of *Glossified,* basically a monster: six foot two, chiseled in features, statuesque in body, probably the only woman in the office or maybe the city who had nothing to fear from seeing Katie Porter naked, and who generally smiled only when an intern was crying.

"Hey, Anika," Zoey said, and forced a cough. "Sorry I had to duck out. I think I might have—"

"What the fuck made you think this fucking picture was fake?" Anika hollered. "Have you fucking seen TMZ?" *Oi, oi, oi,* thought Zoey. "We had this on a fucking exclusive two hours ago!"

"The neck looked a little weird . . . ?"

"The fucking neck looks fucking fine!"

"Well, y'know, I was also, like, is that the kind of material we want to post?"

"Material that drives traffic? Material that gets us on television? Yes! Yes, yes, yes! Where the fuck have you been working for the last two years? Are you a fucking deputy editor or not? You fucked this up, Zoey, you fucked this up."

This, Zoey supposed, was what was meant by the "mentoring" she had been promised when she was first hired at *Glossified.* She knew there was only one way to pacify Anika when she threw one of these tantrums: rip out her pride and stomp on it with her own foot. "I am so sorry," she said. "You're one hundred percent right. I completely messed this up."

"You absolutely fucking did!"

"I know, I can't believe it, I'm so sorry."

The conversation continued in this vein for several minutes: Anika swearing at Zoey, Zoey agreeing profusely with everything she said. Finally winding down, Anika said icily, "TMZ ate our lunch today. I hope that bothers you as much as it bothers me."

It didn't, but Zoey said, "I promise it won't happen again."

"It better fucking not, believe me." And she hung up.

Immediately Zoey started thinking of all the things she could have said, should have said, in her own defense: If Anika didn't trust her to make decisions, why had she made her a deputy editor in the first place? Did she really believe Gavin or Isaac or Aliza would do a better job? Had any of them worked until midnight for two straight weeks after three of the staff writers quit because Anika called them fags? And if Anika really thought Zoey was so irredeemably stupid, why didn't she just fire her? Most days, Zoey fantasized about getting fired. There even was a clause in the contract that read, "Take steps toward finding a more fulfilling career."

But really, Zoey thought, who was she kidding? She lived paycheck to paycheck. She had $22,000—make that $22,350—in credit-card debt, and another eighteen months on a two-year lease. What was she supposed to do if she got fired? Ask her parents for money? Again? She was over thirty, for Christ's sake (this not a comforting thought, either).

She glanced around, as if the others on the sidewalk might have been spectators to her ritualistic humiliation. She knew it wasn't good for her to be in public when these moods came over her: Even in jaunty commercial places like Union Square, the people around her seemed to enlarge, the shadows to darken worryingly. She hailed a cab and went home.

By the time she reached her apartment door, the gloom was full blown. She saw that the *mezuzah* she'd hung, the one that had belonged to her grandmother, had somehow come loose from one of its nails, and now dangled upside down on her doorjamb. She lifted it halfheartedly—watched it swing back down again. She had been pretty proud of herself for hammering it on. So much for that, too.

She unbolted her door and went inside. As always, her living room was a complete mess: clothes both clean and dirty strewn everywhere, an empty bottle of wine lying on the couch, the coffee table a small landfill of magazines and full ashtrays, her laptop open on the floor, its battery dead. She took out some of her new yoga clothes and changed into them, but it only made her feel ridiculous—as if she had just been trying to fool herself about something.

She was aware—had been made aware by Dr. Popper and by Dr. Popper's predecessors—of the character of the thoughts she was now giving in to: anxiety-driven, irrationally pessimistic, self-defeating.

They could all diagnose it, but none of them could cure it—unless she took psychoactives, which she didn't want to. She didn't blame them, however. She knew that Dr. Popper was right when she said that it was up to her: to manage the depressive thoughts, to cope with the inevitable setbacks, to stick to her contract and actualize the life she wanted. But she had been dumped by one guy and broken up with another, going from one-and-a-half boyfriends on Friday morning to being single on Sunday night. She had been bitched out by her boss and seen just how much hotter than her truly hot women were. Wasn't she entitled to feel like shit for a little while?

She went into the kitchen, pulled open the refrigerator—was greeted by boxes of leftover deliveries of indeterminate date, half-empty containers of condiments, an empty Brita. She didn't bother opening the freezer. In a more zealous moment, she had thrown away anything in there worth eating. She looked in the cupboard—found a jar of peanut butter. She opened it up and took out a spoon, scooped herself a dollop. Then she held it before her face, undecided. Couldn't her life be more than this?

Someone was knocking on her door. Given how her day was going, she figured it would be a home invasion. She went into the living room and looked through the peephole. It wasn't anyone in a ski mask, but somehow seeing Jonah's fishbowled image felt about like what she'd expected, too. She pulled open the door. "Before anything, will you fix Nana's *mezuzah*?" she said.

He looked puzzled. "Why are you dressed like that? And why are you holding that spoon?"

"I am going to yoga, *Arschloch*." She looked at the spoon and the glob of peanut butter. "And I was just making myself . . ." She trailed off. He looked very strange himself: his tie dangling untied around his neck, his hair mussed, his clothes covered with myriad stains she couldn't identify. "Did you get . . . mugged by painters?" she asked.

"No," he answered sharply. "I'm fine."

She studied him for another moment, and finally shrugged—walked into the kitchen and dropped the spoon into the sink. She heard him come in and close the door, sit down on the couch. She was feeling extremely horny all of a sudden—maybe this her body's panicked attempt to avoid going to the gym—and figured she could worry about her emotional well-being after he'd gone down on her. She went back into the living room, and apparently he was thinking the same thing, because he immediately stood up and grabbed her, a little roughly, around the waist. And here they were, she thought, kissing again. After ten years, he still kissed the same way: a bit clumsily, but eagerly, earnestly—like he thought it was important. And maybe there was in fact something special between them—notwithstanding Dr. Popper's skepticism—because after ten years she still liked kissing him: It still made her happy, in an uncomplicated way—it still turned her on.

She tasted tobacco in his mouth, and this seemed to both feed and transform her nicotine craving. The next thing she knew she had wrapped her legs around him, lifting herself off the floor. "Yoga!" she laughed, and then kissed him some more.

His clothes smelled like cigarettes too—cigarettes and maybe Tabasco sauce—but every sensation, every individual perception of her senses fed her arousal. Eighty percent of the time she didn't mind sex at all, 10 percent she found it sort of gross, and 10 percent it drove her to wild abandon and lachrymose orgasms. Happily, she could tell this was definitely going to be a top 10 percent moment. He threw her down on the couch, yanked off her top and sports bra, yanked down her stretch pants.

"Sylvia and I are moving in together," he said as he moved on top of her. "Do you know how wrong this is?" he said, pushing his fingers inside her. "This is so, so wrong."

It was a little strange as far as dirty talk went, but she was too busy having a tiny orgasm to care. "Tell me I'm hotter than Katie Porter," she said as he began biting her nipples. "Tell me I'm so much hotter than *Schlampe*."

"You're so much hotter than her," he said, taking off his jacket and shirt as she undid his pants. "I'm going to live with her, and I'm going to fuck you. I'm going to marry her, and I'm going to keep on fucking you."

This pushed the limits a little too far. "Maybe let's stop talking now." He pulled his pants and boxers off his ankles and lay back down on top of her—and, feeling the pressure of his naked body against her, she was ready to forgive any strangeness of conversation. "Fuck me, Yonsi," she whispered in his ear. She cursed in English only in these moments—only in these moments did it come naturally to her. She squeezed her eyes closed, waited.

"It's so wrong," he said, his lips beside her ear.

"Yup, right, got it."

She waited a few more moments—but the essential sensation was not being felt. She opened her eyes to see him looking down in a troubled way at her naked body. She reached down to his dick. "You have got to be fucking kidding me." She pushed him away with her leg. She considered masturbating, but could there be a more pathetic end to this day? She sat up and hunched forward. He had started to cry into his hands, but she felt an extreme lack of sympathy. They sat like that, naked, side by side, for several minutes. At one point his phone started to ring—he took it out of his pocket without looking at it and tossed it onto the coffee table. Someone named Brett was calling him; she watched the phone vibrate its way across the glass. "Okay, I know this is stupid," she finally said, "but it's not because I'm not shaved, right?" That only made him cry harder. She went back into the kitchen, retrieved her spoon, and ate some peanut butter. Then she went into the bathroom and put on her bathrobe, went back into the living room. He had his pants and shirt on, was smoking a cigarette.

"Don't do that in here, okay?" she said. He looked at her a little skeptically, but when she didn't smile he put it out in one of the four ashtrays on the coffee table. As if to further make her point, she picked his jacket up off the floor, folded it sharply, and slung it over the back of the couch. "This suit sucks, by the way," she told him. He didn't answer, just stared vacantly ahead, and there hadn't been any satisfaction in insulting him. There wasn't going to be any satisfaction of any kind today, she could tell by now.

"What are you doing here, Yonsi?" she asked him, feeling like crying herself. "I mean, seriously, what are you doing here?"

"We're all naked, Zoey," he answered. "The body is clothed, but . . ."

It suddenly struck her how strange it all was—the state of his clothing, his generally harried appearance, that he'd shown up unannounced outside her door.

"Nothing happened, did it?" she asked anxiously. She sat down next to him on the couch, put her hand on his knee. "You're okay, right? Nobody died or anything?"

"I wanted to prove what an asshole I am."

"Who said they still needed proof?" She'd said it as a joke—a fairly witty one, in her estimation—but the look on his face was so defeated that she immediately regretted it. "You're not an asshole, Yonsi."

"I just . . . I just wanted to prove that nothing had changed. Y'know?"

At this she pulled her robe a little more closed over her chest. "Don't worry, Yonsi," she said. "Nothing's changed."

His phone was ringing again—this time *Schlampe* was calling him. When it had stopped, he asked, "Do you still keep those tools under your sink?" She nodded, her eyes on the pile of crap on her coffee table. She heard him get up and shuffle around in the kitchen; she heard him go into the hall and nail the *mezuzah* back into place.

When he came inside, he said, "I'm really sorry. I won't bother you anymore."

"Yeah, I kind of figured that."

"You are hotter than *Schlampe*," he said to her. "And Katie Porter. It has nothing to do with being shaved, or whatever."

He seemed about to go, so she said, "Are those really going to be the last words?"

They looked at each other—as though across an ocean of memory and missed opportunity and regret and—Dr. Popper's skepticism notwithstanding, emotional well-being notwithstanding—love, she thought.

After a pause, he said, "Maybe in the beginning. Maybe that September," he went on, "I sometimes think if it hadn't been for—"

This brought on the tears—and she sobbed with all the force of the orgasms she hadn't had. He remained in the doorway until the tears had been exhausted. "I shouldn't have said that," he said. "I'm really sorry." And then he left.

She felt she could have successfully argued with any lung surgeon, public-health advocate, or cancer survivor in the world her case for having a cigarette right now. And for that reason she cleaned her apartment up a little bit and then put her yoga clothes back on. She figured she would never see him again. Then Zoey went to the gym.

8. JUDITH AGONISTES

Judith did not, as was universally recommended to her, take any time off from college. What exactly, she wondered, did people think she would do with time off? Her entire life, she had been prepared—absurdly, she saw now—to do only one thing: go to college. Just because she'd recognized the fallacy—the naïveté—of all this preparation didn't mean she knew how to do anything else.

But the attorney handling her parents' estate made it clear that she was the only one "empowered" to make the important decisions—and so Judith spent several weeks after the funeral in her hometown, if only so she would never have to return there again. She stayed at an anonymous Holiday Inn twenty minutes down the highway: She didn't want to be recognized where she stayed, she didn't want to sleep in her childhood bed—and the thought of sleeping in her parents' bed struck her as monstrous.

She could not avoid the house entirely, though. She had to be there for the assessment, she had to be there to tell the movers what to put into storage and what to leave for the estate sale, she had to search for papers in the filing cabinet in her father's office. The details to be attended to seemed only to accumulate, to multiply grotesquely. Her aunt Naomi might have helped with some of this, but immediately after the funeral she had absented herself to California. Margaretha, her only cousin, hadn't been able to attend at all. She sent her condolences, her aunt informed her, from Amsterdam.

One Sunday, Judith came to the house to see that three copies of the Sunday *New York Times* waited in their blue plastic bags on the stoop. It was the remnant of their little eccentricity: one copy of the Sunday crossword puzzle for each of them. Looking at the three untouched newspapers, Judith realized that the Bulbrooks had been more peculiar—rarer—than she had ever given them credit for. And now she was the last one. Walking through the house that day—great cardboard boxes everywhere with their tops gaping open, the china in the dining room encased in bubble wrap, the mattress on her parents' bed already thrown away, leaving only the wooden frame, the silence in all the rooms making the lack of occupants of the house somehow palpable—she felt as if she were making her way among the remains of some lost civilization.

Gabe reappeared around this time. He was not at the funeral, and later she wouldn't be able to remember if he'd arrived before the ceremony and hadn't been able to stay, or if he hadn't been able to make it out in time to attend. The days of her forced residence in her hometown blended together in her memory—were to her all equally funereal. And, in general after her parents' death, events would become progressively harder for her to sequence, to partition into discrete days, months, years.

She remembered, though, that she was at the house to pack up her mother's jewelry when they met. It was nighttime, and they spoke on the porch in the front of the house. The FOR SALE sign was already in the front yard; flies and moths circled the single porch light above their heads. Neither made a move to hug the other when they said hello.

"They really were wonderful people," Gabe told her.

"I know," she said. Out of respect for what they had once shared, she spared him the facile smile she'd mastered, which the people who said such things to her seemed so much to appreciate seeing. She figured if they were old friends, old lovers, she might as well do him the courtesy of showing him on her face all the comfort such words gave her. The calls she'd received from the president of Yale, from the president of the college where David and Hannah had taught, from the governor of the state and both its senators; the letter she got, signed in actual ink, from George W. Bush; the memorial service at which dozens of former students of the Professors Bulbrook came to pay their respects; the compliments everyone piled on her parents whenever they saw her, the carefully worded offers of sympathy: none of it was any more or less consoling. It was all, equally and unequivocally: Not Consoling. Her grief appeared incontrovertible to her in those days—she was even a little awed by its magnitude.

"I know they—well, I know they loved you." She nodded. "You know, you still . . ." he began, but trailed off. She had come to expect people to trail off when they spoke to her. It made her feel sorry for them—which she found another sad, dull irony.

"How's California?" she asked him. "Are you still writing?"

He nodded, but said, "No, not as much as I used to . . . I'm actually thinking about going to law school." She thought he was searching for her reaction to this idea—maybe even hoping for her approval—but the truth was she couldn't locate much of an opinion either way. Finally he said, "And you chose Yale, I heard."

"It seemed like a good fit," she answered—another rote response, which happened to be true.

A silence followed. He looked at her regretfully. "What have you been reading?" he asked with a sudden earnestness of caring, the same she sometimes heard when people asked her if she was eating. He looked older, she thought—a little heavier, a little balder. But, all things considered, if he'd walked into her English class that day and read a Whitman poem, and she'd still been a fifteen-year-old girl at Gustav's, she would have probably fallen in love with him all over again. But she was not a fifteen-year-old girl, and he was invoking a world—the world of the creek—that no longer existed for her, if she could believe it had ever existed at all.

"It was all pretty cliché, wasn't it?" she said to him. "You and me. A prep school girl and her English teacher. It felt so . . . important at the time. But we really weren't doing anything a thousand other people weren't doing, too."

"Judith . . ." he said.

"Anyway, thanks for coming by," she said to him.

He put his hand on her shoulder. "You're still going to have a wonderful life in the end," he told her.

Such sentiments, too, she believed served mostly as comfort for the comforters. It seemed as if people needed to think that she would be okay in the end. But what did okay mean? And, as she now asked him, "The end of what?"

They stood there for a moment, his hand on her shoulder—something that would have meant so much to her once, but was now so mutely, so sorrowfully unimportant. Then she thought of something else—went into her room for a minute, returned with the leather case from under her bed. "These are the letters you wrote me. I need to clean out the house, I wasn't sure what to do with them." He took the case, looked at it uncertainly. "Thanks for coming by," she repeated, and they said goodbye—again without hugging—and that was the last time she saw him.

As quickly as possible, she put whatever she deemed worth storing into storage, mostly photos and mementos she could neither look at nor bear to see thrown away. The rest she liquidated, sold. Then she returned to Yale.

Being a few weeks behind in her classes was actually a challenge she welcomed, though her professors fell all over themselves offering to make accommodations. She declined all these offers—just as she declined to be interviewed by *Yale Daily News*, or by *USA Today*, or to appear with other 9/11 orphans on *Good Morning America*, or on the *Today* show, or on *Oprah*; declined to sit in a luxury box at Yankee Stadium, declined to attend as an honored guest televised memorial services in New York or D.C. She had no intention of embodying for the public The Girl Whose Parents Died on 9/11: dressed in black, laying a wreath, brave in the face of tragedy. Even if she'd thought such gestures possible for her, her instinctive abhorrence of cliché—stronger than ever, as she'd found with Gabe—would not allow it.

She resumed her Philosophies of Religion class with the brilliant professor, went back to reading *À la recherche du temps perdu*. But there was none of the ecstasy she'd formerly felt in any of it; only a somewhat comforting familiarity in diligence, the minor satisfaction that she could get A's at Yale, too. Milim Oh, her roommate, seemed afraid of her at first, as did most of the others she'd met prior. Milim at least got over it enough to act like her friend, though in Judith's estimation their relationship would always have more of the outward gestures of friendship than genuine affection. Judith understood that Milim had judged it very important that they remain friends, and it was just this judgment that made authentic friendship impossible. The rabbi at the campus Hillel reached out to her—but her belief in God had blinkered out along with her parents. "Any God worth believing in wouldn't have let my parents be murdered," she told the rabbi. She knew this opinion was as much a cliché as anything—but she forgave herself for it, because it felt so manifestly true.

She'd expected when she'd started college to major in English. But reading literature, writing about literature, required something of her she was no longer capable of offering. All it took was one B on a paper on *The Canterbury Tales*—her professor explaining the grade by saying she had "failed to engage honestly with Chaucer's work"—to convince her she needed another subject in which to specialize.

It was a class she took called American Art and the Postmodern World that made her settle on art history. The other students struggled with the features of postmodernism: the piled layers of abstraction, the slipperiness of context. But Judith discovered she had an instinct for it, was not put off by the sterility, the abstruseness her classmates sensed. And she found that staring at art—staring at it until she could see it as merely an amalgamation of influences, intentions, trends and counter-ends—was somehow aligned with her present state of mind: something she could do honestly.

If anything, she worked harder than she had before. She did all the assignments for her courses, did all the suggested readings on the syllabus, even did a few readings she figured could have been suggested. Sometimes she would go directly to the library from an afternoon class, take a seat in some windowless corner of the stacks, and break off her study only when a librarian told her the building was closing, and would emerge into a chilly, thinly starred New Haven night. Again, she lacked the passion for academics she'd once had—but her resolve had taken on bleak new strength.

And, soon after she arrived back on campus, Judith started to have a lot of sex. In the crudest terms: Grief made her horny. She observed to herself that, from a Darwinian perspective, it was a fairly useful adaptation. If she allowed a slightly less reductive view of the matter, though, she could admit that she was profoundly lonely; she could admit she didn't know how to feel good. Sex solved both these problems, if only briefly. When the boys knew who she was—or, more precisely, knew how her parents had died—they generally seemed afraid of her, too. But a lot of them didn't know, and there were a lot of boys. She found all she had to do was remain at a bar or a frat party long enough, and eventually one of them would present himself. She became like one of those fabled people who actually doesn't care where the group goes to dinner: Judith was up for anything. She had no inhibitions regarding positions or parts of her body; she got into bed with guys and their girlfriends; she had sex with two members of the lacrosse team at once; she was content tying or being tied up. She found the variety in bodies and in preferences that she discovered surprising, even intriguing. You could never predict quite how people would look without their clothes on: where the hair would cluster, where their stomachs would fold as they turned or sat up, the way a penis would look relative to the rest of a male body—how people would conduct themselves when there was another naked human being beside them, willing to engage with them in whatever. There was, she sometimes thought, an essential truth to all this—as though bodies provided the full and final revelation of a person.

For a semester she took up with the graduate teaching assistant in her Art of the Etruscans course; he introduced her to BDSM. She would come home from his apartment and gaze at herself in the full-length mirror on her door—would look at her pale white skin here bruised, there welted with bite marks, belt lashes—and would see herself as if from very far away, as though studying her naked body from the end of a tunnel. What, she would ask herself, was the truth that her own body revealed to her? And as she would maybe trace the circumference of an egg-sized contusion on her thigh, she would conclude that her body told her only what any body could tell anyone: that this was what she wanted.

There were some boys who, when they learned what had happened to her parents (she was never quick to volunteer the information, but neither did she hide it), would try to console her, heal her—save her. They would substitute for caresses a sort of ostensibly reassuring petting, they would offer to "talk about it"—ask her questions about her parents, her feelings—would urge her to see a psychologist. While she knew this was well intentioned, she always felt embarrassed for them, at the thinness of their words of comfort—and more, annoyed that they would not simply give her what she wanted from them. "That sounds so awful," they would say. "I can't imagine it. Do you think you should talk to someone?"

And she would say what she always did when she was urged into the arms of psychotherapy: "What could they tell me about myself that I don't already know?" She knew she was drowning herself in self-degradation, in self-pity, in despair. But she believed she had finally found a state of mind equal to her voracious mental appetites.

She graduated Yale summa cum laude, with distinction in art history, and in three years, in fulfillment of the ancient plan. Milim, her parents, even Milim's teenage sister, attended Judith's commencement, insisted on taking her out to dinner that night—a kindness she finally decided not worth refusing. She would always remember the toast Milim's father—stooped, in his seventies—gave at this dinner. He spoke in Korean, Milim's mother whispering her translation in Judith's ear. "He is proud of you. . . ." she whispered. "He hopes you and Milim will always be great friends. . . . He knows your parents are proud of you, too. . . ."

After the meal, Milim's mother took a picture of the three young women, sitting side by side at the table. Judith was headed that fall to a PhD program at Princeton; Milim already had plans to attend medical school at Cornell after she graduated the next year. So the freshman roommates were ending up in something of the equivalent place— though it seemed to Judith you could tell just from looking at the photograph on the screen of Milim's mother's digital camera that their paths had been very different. Judith had wondered sometimes, in college, what others made of her—what they guessed about the girl going to and from the library at odd hours, or sitting mutely with her legs crossed on their roommate's bed the morning after; what they could tell of thoughts that tended to run far away from whomever she happened to be talking to, or fucking. This photograph, she believed, made it clear. While the smiles of Milim and her sister were bright, sincere, Judith's was distant, thin; she still wore the burgundy dress she'd had on under her graduation gown, its rich color accentuating the whiteness of her skin; her black hair was a dense mass above her forehead, her chin turned a bit away from Milim, making the mole by her left eye more prominent. It looked to Judith as if grief was written all over this strange, spectral face—as if it were the blackness itself of her hair and mole. Judith felt that anyone could see, just from the remoteness of her smile, that she had spent the ten minutes following the toast hiding in a bathroom stall and weeping, somehow gratefully. It had been two and a half years, and she could still feel the pain—could still see it in the picture—as though it were brand new: sharp, and undiminished.

Within three weeks of graduating Yale, she had moved to Princeton, started a summer research project for one of her professors. She'd chosen Princeton because of the reputation of its art history program, and because of the keenness with which the department had courted her. "Unlike many of your peers, you have an unusual capacity to critique art not in terms of what it aspires to be but rather in terms of what it is," the chair of the department had written in her acceptance letter. Judith regarded this as an insightful and greatly flattering compliment. Princeton also appealed to her because at no time during the admissions process had anyone suggested she would be an especially welcome addition to the school on account of her connection to 9/11. (Harvard and Columbia and UChicago had not been similarly restrained.)

Her life at Princeton quickly became so similar to her life at Yale—her weeks filled with thick, unmarked stretches of classes, professors, slides, reading, research, frantic but numbed sex—that she would sometimes forget to notice the difference. She would be walking beneath an archway of pale stone into a courtyard, she would be scanning a line of books on a library shelf, searching for a title, she would be making her way across a messy living room toward a narrow bedroom or a futon—and find herself surprised when she recalled that she no longer lived in New Haven. It occurred to her that all that had changed for her in these three years were the names on the doorplates, the numbers before the course titles on her schedule, the shapes and contortions of the bodies.

She knew she ought to give some attention to building a life for herself outside a university. But nothing that life might include held any particular attraction. She was at graduate school because she had to be somewhere. And at least graduate school allowed her to still be considered brilliant and hardworking, as she was by all her new professors, just as she had been at Yale, and at Gustav's—as she knew she would be for as long as she remained in school.

She began research for a thesis on Gothic architectural motifs in contemporary art, and won a fellowship to spend the summer after her first year studying at the Sorbonne in Paris. She had first visited the city with her mother when she was nine, and in order to confront any painful associations with this—pull the Band-Aid off in one rip, as it were—she spent her first day in Paris retracing the route she and her mother had taken among the tourist attractions of the city: the Arc de Triomphe and the Pantheon; Sacré-Cœur and Sainte-Chapelle; the Louvre, the Pompidou, the Musée d'Orsay; the Eiffel Tower and the Jardin des Tuileries. She wept as she went—moved to tears at every turn, at every memory, just as she'd anticipated. But she found something hollow in the force of this crying: It surprised her that the tears were not more violent, the sorrow not more intense. She realized that for her there would be no ghosts, no visions; the absence of Hannah and David Bulbrook was uniform across the world. This thought was the one that made her cry the hardest—with the force she seemed to have been seeking.

Classes at the Sorbonne were conducted in French, the faculty were of a more demanding frame of mind than those in the United States—but if any of this added another degree of difficulty to the work, it was not a challenge Judith had much trouble meeting. She was fluent by now: fluent in French, fluent in academia. As an ancient professor who had been a personal acquaintance of Braque praised her before the entire class for a paper she'd written, she suddenly had an image of herself as a sort of roaming academic game hunter: going from continent to continent, crossing names off a collectively understood list. Perhaps she would get a postdoc at Oxford.

During her first month in Paris, Judith got to know a girl in her program named Claudette Laurent. She had blond hair, cut very short, a classically French nose—widening down its bridge, elegantly curved along the nostrils—large blue eyes, large breasts. She was gorgeous, as a matter of fact—reminded Judith of the truly beautiful Ashleys and Beths she'd gone to high school with. She and Claudette would walk down the street, and Judith could watch as each man turned from whatever he was doing to stare. Claudette acted oblivious to this. She was engaged to an older man, a philosophy professor in Lyon, with a daughter of his own not so much younger than Claudette. She became schoolgirl giggly in her descriptions of his handsomeness, his intelligence, his *talents au lit*. Judith met him only once: tall, salt-and-pepper beard, casually brilliant and casually arrogant in a distinctly French way. She had to admit—she understood the appeal.

Claudette seemed surprised to find in Judith an American so intelligent, so insightful about art. And she admitted she was intrigued by the religion of her new friend's birth, notwithstanding Judith's abandonment of it; Claudette said Judith was the first Jewish person she had ever had the chance to get to know. Judith found this somewhat astonishing—realized that, having spent the vast majority of her life in the American Northeast, she'd been deluded into thinking there were simply Jews everywhere. But this was not the case, of course—in Europe in particular.

For her part, Judith found something intriguing about Claudette, too—as did most people. In addition to being genuinely beautiful, she was genuinely intelligent, and it was as though no one could quite believe the genetic miracle the young woman represented. Judith sometimes thought of Claudette as a sort of rare and lovely exotic bird, and the reactions of others to her—her own reactions to her—

were compelling in themselves. It was as if the combination of such physical beauty and such mental grace had the effect of altering the social gravity of everything around her: Husbands would break off mid-sentence the conversations they were having with their wives when she appeared at cocktail parties; the most austere and egotistical lecturers would not only deign to speak to her but would even attempt to charm her, to make her smile. And Judith herself—who had never been a very social person, in recent years even less so—felt undeniably drawn to her, to the point that she even noticed a certain warmth in her stomach when Claudette called her, or sat down beside her in class.

When they got to be better friends, Claudette invited Judith to the little country town where her parents lived, forty minutes outside Paris. Claudette led her up the dirt path from the road to the house, greeted her aged dog, Maxime, and Madame *et* Monsieur Laurent served them a five-hour-long lunch of duck cassoulet, ratatouille, fresh asparagus, local Merlot, cheese, and homemade bread. The Laurents were sweet, gray-haired people: Monsieur a schoolteacher, who complimented Judith continually on her accent, Madame a former stage actress—whose looks helped explain those of her *fille*.

During the train ride back to Paris from this lunch, Judith told Claudette for the first time about the death of her own parents. Claudette's eyes filled with sorrow—and, rubbing Judith's arm gently, she called her, *"Ma pauvre petite orpheline."* It was in this moment that Judith decided to seduce her. She had been with women before, and she had understood that her fascination with Claudette edged into the sexual. Whose didn't? But in that moment of hollow comfort— strangely naïve, strangely condescending—she apprehended a desire that was driven by more than mere attraction.

It was shameful, it was grotesque—Judith knew this—but she used her suffering to seduce her. Claudette's downfall, Judith thought, was that, despite her rare brilliance, despite her rare beauty, she was, finally, too much a cliché: just another overintellectualized French girl, fascinated by a pain that was, in her own life, merely an abstraction.

One night in Claudette's apartment, after an evening of drinking

wine with classmates in the 13th Arrondissement, another empty bottle of wine before them on the coffee table, Judith allowed herself to
start crying. It was not hard: She only had to think of her parents—
and of what she was about to do. But she couldn't help it. Her lust had
become entangled with jealousy, with resentment—creating an urge
that was too compelling to resist. As Claudette, crying herself now in
sympathy, took Judith's hand, Judith started to stroke her blond hair,
finding it had the ethereal softness she would have expected. Then she
pulled Claudette's head down, found the opening of her mouth with
her lips, pushed her hand between her thighs. Claudette pulled away a
little—but just a little. The sex felt to Judith both like a triumph and a
bottoming out of despair. She really couldn't tell the difference.

The affair lasted most of that summer. Despite the Parisian sophistication she displayed, Claudette turned out to be surprisingly imma-
ture emotionally. As Judith had learned well by now, though, you never
knew who someone would be when their clothes came off. Claudette
cried over her guilt at betraying her fiancé, cried over her confusion at
being attracted to a woman. She threw tantrums, she refused to get out
of bed, she drank wine by the bottle and then begged Judith to go
down on her. But it all combined in a strangely lovelike symmetry with
Judith's resentment and self-loathing over what she was doing to Claudette. They found a sexually charged harmony in their shared misery:
crying, fucking. And Judith could not deny an unmistakable feeling of
justice—even of revenge—in seeing Claudette's beautiful face either
choked with sobs or twisted in orgasm, and knowing she was responsible. She was learning there were ever darker and more captivating
shades at the bottom of herself.

She was shaken awake to her latest and most terrible theft of a *yad*
only when Claudette started talking about confessing everything to
her fiancé, about returning with Judith to America that fall. Judith
realized then—far too late, as usual—that she was ruining this unexpectedly fragile girl's life.

She told herself, with reassuring implausibility, that Claudette
would be relieved to have the emotional mess of the affair concluded—
and that a brief lesbian fling would fit seamlessly into the idyll that

was the narrative of Claudette Laurent. Years later, Judith would think how she had underestimated Claudette: how, even then, she had thought of her as merely a cliché.

On the afternoon Judith had chosen to end things, Claudette was sitting at the table in the narrow kitchen of Judith's rented flat, writing her parents a letter, longhand, as was her custom. This struck Judith as so insensitive, so needlessly cruel that, in retrospect, she was probably more abrupt than she ought to have been. Claudette had just signed her name in blue ink at the bottom of the lined piece of paper, when Judith said, in English, "I don't want to do this anymore."

Claudette glanced up, looked at her coldly, answered, "I don't know what you're talking about."

"I can't be with you anymore. I don't want to."

Claudette put the pen down on the piece of paper. *"Es-tu lassée, ma reine?"*

"Non, j'étais lassée bien avant." A tautness spread over Claudette's face, like she might cry. Judith asked herself why she could not stop hurting this girl. *"Je ne t'aime pas,"* she said, trying to be quick, merciful—pulling off the Band-Aid in one rip.

But for all Judith's brilliance, she found here, once again, that she had been born without anything like emotional intelligence. Claudette stood up, and Judith realized that the tautness she'd seen was not sadness but rather an emerging fury. *"Quoi de plus normal de la part d'une pute juive comme toi?"*

To Judith's amazement, she discovered that even now she remained an innocent—a child. This was the first anti-Semitic remark anyone had ever made to her—and as an avowed atheist, she was stunned by how immediately humiliating these words were to her. She pulled her hand back as far as she could behind her shoulder and she slapped Claudette across the face. The sound had a cracklike sharpness that filled the kitchen; her palm stung.

For several seconds Claudette remained bent forward, rubbing her cheek, almost ponderously. For a moment Judith felt victorious—a new, barbaric, singing form of victory she'd never known before—thinking of Hannah and David Bulbrook. And then she burst into tears, cried, "I'm so sorry, oh, God, Claudette, I'm so sorry." She moved toward her, but as she did, Claudette took hold of the black square-edged bottle of balsamic vinegar that sat on the kitchen table. She intended only to throw it in Judith's direction (or so she claimed later), but as she thrust her arm forward it crashed into Judith's advancing nose—shattering both glass and bone in a racket of splintering and blood. And as Judith now crumpled over, pain spreading across her entire body from her nose downward, all she could think was, So this is what I wanted.

The doctor at the hospital Claudette took her to had a red-splotched, fleshy face, a palsy tremor in his right hand, unkempt shocks of gray hair poking from the sides of his head and from his ears. As Claudette rested her hand on Judith's shin, he reset her nose, wrapping it in a great bandage and splint. She knew it was a clumsy job, and the shaking of his hand triggered constant little waves of agony. But she felt she deserved no better.

She and Claudette parted on the street outside the hospital, Judith's face now partially wrapped in a bandage. "Sleep at my flat tonight," Claudette said.

"No," Judith said. "This was all a mistake."

Claudette began to cry—hopeless, unrestrained tears. *"Pourquoi tu m'as fait ça?"*

It was, she thought, a fair question: Why had she done it? Reasons came tumbling to mind. She was lost, she was lonely; she was cruel, she was heartbroken. She had been brought up sheltered, coddled, had no capacity to deal with life when it was anything but kind and gentle—could not cope with death even years later. She had done it because she had wanted to ruin not Claudette's life but rather her own—the life she might have had if her parents had not arranged their trip to visit her and then fly from Boston on the morning of September 11, 2001. The line between a Judith and a Claudette was that fine, that narrow, that absurdly drawn. How could she not wish to drag Claudette over to her side? She was addicted to suffering, she was bored; she had never grieved properly, or else she had never grieved at all. It was the twists in her DNA: who she was. For all these reasons she had done it, and for a thousand others—or for none of them. She didn't know why, and she couldn't explain it in English, let alone in French—why anything happened, why anyone did anything. *"Le terrorisme,"* Judith said.

She spent the rest of the late afternoon walking around the city, with no destination in mind—simply walked, a dull throb in her nose with each step she took. Eventually she crossed a bridge onto the Île de la Cité and stopped before Notre Dame, the sun setting by now—and sometimes when she would look out the window on one of the upper floors of the Colonel's casino in Las Vegas, and watch the strip and its array of spectacles and the desert and mountains beyond slowly be coated in pinkish-red light, she would remember how the cathedral was as though painted in this same lovely pinkish color: the pair of towers and trio of portals, the rose window and profusion of carved figures—saints, sinners, kings, angels. The plaza before Notre Dame was surprisingly empty that day—the milling tourists with cameras slung across their chests, tour groups on the march, the odd devout Parisian, all gone to home or hotel for the evening.

A memory came to her mind—one that had eluded her during that first, emotionally indulgent day in the city. She remembered that, when she and her mother had visited Notre Dame thirteen years before, her mother had been so moved that she sat down on the gently sloped cobbles of this same plaza and wrote a poem. Later the poem was published in *Harper's,* then reprinted in one of her mother's books. But neither on that day, nor on any day that followed, even years later, could Judith remember the name of the poem, or whether she had ever read it. She did remember, though, how magical her mother had seemed in that moment: the master, the keeper of great secrets.

But now, standing before the cathedral, she knew there were no secrets—her mother was just another person who would die. There was no magic in the poem, or in the act of writing it, or in the cathedral itself—erected for worship of a God in whom she did not believe. Judith knew also that it was time to drop out of school. She had followed the faith of her parents as long as she could, long past the point of believing in it. She had kept to its rituals because they were the only ones she had. But it was a story she no longer recognized herself in: Judith Klein Bulbrook, and all her tremendous promise—all the great things she would accomplish in her life. In the end, Judith Klein Bulbrook had revealed herself to be something of a terrorist, too.

A nun appeared beside her—tiny, wizened—staring rapturously at the cathedral's façade, her black wimple worn almost to the line of her eyes. Judith wondered if she had ever seen a nun who wasn't old. Then a stiff wind picked up, and this pressed the bandage against Judith's face so painfully she groaned, tucked her head against her shoulder. When the wind died down and she looked up, the nun was watching her with a small, sympathetic smile. "English?" the nun said.

"American," Judith answered.

The nun nodded, as if this explained much. "We suffer so little for Him, who suffered so greatly for us," the nun told her consolingly. Then the old woman toddled off.

Looking back at the face of the cathedral, the pink of the evening now darkening into a bluish red, Judith puzzled over this sentence—began applying some of her greatly lauded intellect to parse the words. By "we," the woman likely meant humanity; but suffering, Judith had learned, was individual, and where it was collective, it was great, not little; and as for Him— She stopped herself. She turned from the cathedral and concluded the sentence was exactly what it sounded like: bullshit.

9. THEY TOOK UP JONAH AND CAST HIM FORTH INTO THE SEA

Jonah awoke on the floorboards of his apartment. He'd succeeded in getting drunk enough to fall asleep the night before—had methodically made his way through a bottle of Jack Daniel's he'd bought on the way back from Zoey's. His phone was ringing from somewhere among the cushions on the couch above him. He sensed, as he lifted his leaden and throbbing head, that it had been ringing for a long time. He reached up for it and studied it: Sylvia was calling him. The phone was unmerciful—to her, to him—in informing him precisely how many times she'd already called, and how many times Brett had called, and how many texts and emails they'd both sent. The gist of what he read was that he needed to be at the Corcoran offices at 9:00 A.M. The clock on the phone's screen told him it was now 8:30. He looked over toward the windows. Bright canary yellow sunlight spilled in across the floorboards.

He staggered to his feet, went into the bathroom, opened the medicine cabinet so he would not have to look at himself in the mirror, turned on the sink. He was surprised at the minor cacophony the rushing water made in the small room, and he stood there for a few moments, listening to it vacantly. Then he leaned forward, put his lips to the cold stream, drank for a while, then splashed some of the water onto his face. If he'd hoped this would give him a modicum of clarity as to what he was supposed to do now, he was disappointed. He turned off the water and went into his bedroom, closed the door—wasn't sure what he'd intended to do in there, and then just sat down on the floor.

The light in the room was a deep, murky blue coming in through the closed navy curtains. He couldn't remember when he'd closed those curtains, when he'd last been in this room. He felt as if the rhythms of time that his life had previously followed, that most everyone's followed—waking, working, sleeping—had been drowned out in some other, more domineering mode of time. He could no longer muster the anger, the self-pity, of the previous day, though. He understood that all he'd accomplished by swathing himself in these emotions was to humiliate himself, cheat on Sylvia again, and hurt the person he would have least wanted to hurt. But really, he asked himself—what else was there left for him to feel?

His closet door stood open, and before he could look away he saw in the full-length mirror inside the reflection he'd had an instinct to avoid. His face in the mirror looked weary—aged. He still had on the suit Dolores had bought for him—most of it, anyway: The stain-dappled shirt was open to his belly button, the tie was missing, he wore only one shoe, while the other foot was bare. And he thought he could see in the slump of his shoulders, in the thick black-red bags beneath his eyes, in the dull, open-lipped inexpression of his mouth—see, as though it were as literal and permanent an aspect of his appearance as his nose—just how weighted down he felt: with exhaustion, with the physical toll of the endless drinking, the endless smoking, with the arguing and lying and bargaining that suddenly seemed like all he'd been doing for days. He closed his eyes, waited for sleep—but his phone was ringing again.

Of course it was Sylvia. But what could he tell her? That he couldn't live with her on Bond Street because—Why? Because he'd been rendered metaphysically incapable? Because he just didn't want to? He didn't know that he didn't want to. He only knew that his desires had become difficult to parse, had become fraught with all manner of risk and ambiguity. Perhaps this was the intent—the source—of the visions: his mind's way of telling him that he didn't know what he wanted. It wasn't a very convincing rationalization, though—indeed, one of the less convincing ones he'd come up with. Didn't his mind have more direct routes for delivering such basic information, ones that didn't involve so much collateral damage to his life?

He'd been looking at the face of his iPhone as he had these thoughts, staring absently at the announcement of Sylvia's Incoming Call—and when this announcement vanished, he found himself studying the screen more closely, peering into the device's little pixilated world. It was so quaint, so tidy, so hopeful in its way: the time across the top in sturdy, soothing Helvetica, the pictogram icons for maps, for messages, for games—whatever you might need to get you through your day. This was, it occurred to him, another version of the puffy-clouded heaven with the rosy-cheeked angels that it gave people such comfort to see depicted—to believe in. This was the version that had given him comfort.

For the third time in as many minutes, Sylvia called. It was reasonable to think she might be worried about him. It was reasonable for him not to do any more harm than he'd already done. And when all else failed—and all else did seem to have failed at this point—he could at least try not to make things worse.

"Hey," he said into the phone.

"Jonah, Jesus," she said, distressed. "Where have you been?"

"Working. Out. I don't know."

"But you'll be at Corcoran in twenty minutes, right? I'm in a cab from LaGuardia now."

"Look, Syl . . ." But he didn't know how to finish this sentence.

"Do not tell me you won't be there, Jonah, do not say that to me." There was an unfamiliar commingling of worry and anger in her voice—strained in a desperate way. "I canceled a meeting with the president of the Bank of China and the finance minister of Angola for this." The fact that she had divulged the players in the deal she was working on was more striking to him than their titles: It meant that much to her. And why shouldn't he live for other people? It seemed he was no longer permitted to live for himself.

"I'm heading downstairs to get in a cab," he told her.

He allowed himself time to change his clothes—knew as he walked out his apartment door he ought to have said something about being late so he could have showered and shaved, too. But what difference did it make anymore? At least he could get there on time, for her.

He actually ended up arriving before she did. He was led by a receptionist into a conference room decorated with framed maps of New York at various stages of its history, with a long table where Brett sat waiting. He was stapling the lease with an electric stapler as Jonah walked in. "Jonah!" he said, predictably upbeat. "Great to see you." Something in Brett's sunniness exhausted Jonah all the more. He let himself drop into a swivel chair on the other side of the table. "Jonah, how are you?" Brett now asked, his voice taking on tones of tremendously sincere concern. He probably should have showered, Jonah concluded. "Did you get any sleep last night? Did you call Guru Phil? I promise you, he will put you in touch with the universal."

Jonah rubbed his forehead with the heels of his hands, effecting minor, momentary relief of his headache. "I don't need a guru for that, Brett," he said. "When the universal has something to say to me, it comes down and kicks me in the balls."

"Exactly," Brett said. "Exactly! It sounds like you've had an epiphany."

"That's the least of what I had . . ."

"You know how I felt when Lehman closed?"

"Like you'd been kicked in the balls?"

"Like I'd been kicked in the balls."

Jonah lifted his face and looked at Brett—smiling encouragingly and as if he knew exactly what Jonah was going through and that it was all no big deal. It was the sanctimony, he decided, that he couldn't stand. "Y'know, Brett, you did help trigger a global economic collapse, so maybe you deserved to get kicked in the balls."

Brett nodded assentingly. "Maybe so, Jonah, maybe so. But what matters is what we do with that kick. Where does that kick take you? I know where it took me."

Clearly, Brett's sunniness was not to be defeated, no more than Jonah's blackness. "Can we talk about something else?" he muttered, rubbing his forehead again.

"Sure," Brett agreed. "Take a look at that map," he said, indicating one on the wall near where Jonah sat. It was hand drawn, black and white, titled "New Amsterdam, 1660," and portrayed the tip of Manhattan as a modest collection of docks and farmland, with little penciled ships sailing off the coast. "Most New Yorkers don't appreciate the maritime history of the city, but you have to remember that this was a port city, first and foremost, for almost all of its existence. Now, what is really interesting to me is that you're starting to see that nautical flavor in the architecture in a lot of the newest developments in—"

"Sorry, sorry," Sylvia said, hurrying into the room. "I had one of those cab drivers who can't drive." She had her impressively sufficient day bag with her, looked well put together, as always—in a tan jacket and skirt and a pale-blue shirt, ironed and collar straight, heels on her feet, her hair organized in its bob with military precision. Then Jonah did have an epiphany: He was going to live with this woman. She must have caught something in his look, because she returned it with a puzzled frown, which deepened as she took in his appearance. She sat down next to him.

"So let's get started," Brett said. He slid the lease across the table. Sylvia seemed to wait for Jonah to take it—which surprised him until he remembered that, oh, right, he was a lawyer. After another moment when he didn't pick it up, Sylvia started to read it herself. "There's nothing exotic in there," Brett said as she read. "It's a boilerplate Manhattan lease. Termination fees, pet restrictions, liability limits. Once you sign, the owner will countersign, and I'll FedEx you both a copy, hopefully by tomorrow afternoon. Your move-in date is September first, but your payment today of first month, last month, and security deposit will cover you until October first. You remembered to bring your checkbooks?"

Sylvia nodded—glanced at Jonah. Under the circumstances, he could hardly be blamed for forgetting this detail. Sylvia said to Brett, "I'll write our check for the full amount."

"That works for us," said Brett.

"Jonah, do you want to take a look at this?" Sylvia asked him. She held out the lease. He glanced at it and looked into her face. He'd been avoiding this—her perplexed, frustrated, anxious eyes. He looked away.

Brett patted at the pockets of his pants and said, "You know what, guys? I forgot a pen. I'll go get one." He stood up and left. Jonah had to give him credit: Sanctimonious or not, Brett was incredibly tactful.

Jonah was expecting an immediate, no-holds-barred tongue lashing, but instead Sylvia turned toward him in her chair and said in a concerned way, "Talk to me, Jonah."

"I've had—I don't know, Syl."

"I know it's been hard with me gone. You think I don't miss you, too?"

He looked at her again: Her face was more worried now—supportive. Yes, he thought, he could live with this woman. "I think I've been working too much," he said quickly. "I've been stressed and I've been, drinking and shit."

"I can smell it on you, Jonah."

"But you know that is not who I am."

"Yes, I know," she answered.

"And I can—I can be what you want me to be, I think, if we work together."

She took his hand, squeezed it in hers. "Look, don't get mad," she said. "I was talking to Emily about, well, our problems. She and her husband had some marital problems, too, and they saw a counselor, in Chappaqua, and from what she said . . . I think he could really help us, Jonah."

Sylvia's father was an alcoholic—a mean-spirited, misogynistic piece of shit Jonah had met once and had no interest in ever meeting again. He'd made Sylvia and her mother and her two younger sisters as miserable as he could, short of doing anything strictly illegal. Sylvia had fled to boarding schools, to Harvard, to New York and Wells Fargo and then Ellis–Michaels. How hard it must have been for her to come into this room on this day and find him in this state. Was that the message of all he had been put through? That he was a piece of shit, too, just like Sylvia's father? Fine, he thought, he got it. He would change. "We'll see that counselor in Chappaqua," he said—and as he pronounced the words, he felt an incredible upsurge of hope and optimism. Yes, he thought, the counselor in Chappaqua! "We'll go five times a week if we have to."

"We will get through this, and we will start making our life together," she told him. She kissed him, put her hand on his heart. At that moment Brett returned. Jonah concluded that either there were cameras in the room or Brett's sense of timing was impeccable. Either way, this man really had to be the greatest broker in the city. He seated himself again, straight-backed and formal, giving the occasion the ceremony he must have believed it deserved—handed Sylvia a black uni-ball Vision pen (Micro).

Sylvia opened the lease and, still holding Jonah's hand, signed her name. Then she slid the papers and the pen to Jonah. "Sylvia J. Quinn," she had written. Jonah lifted the pen. There was a thin black line where he was meant to sign—and above it a blank space.

He glanced to the neat loops of Sylvia's name. He found himself staring at her middle initial. Her first and last names she'd written in cursive, but the *J.* was done in simple print. And he'd never seen her include it in her signature before: not on any check, or letter, or anything else he'd seen her sign. There was something so touching in its presence now—something so honest and forthright—as if in this tiny upward-reaching hatted letter were encapsulated all her hopes for them, her allegiance to him—her wish for a home together on Bond Street. Only when he saw that letter did he understand how badly she wanted a home.

"I cheated," he said. He wasn't looking at her, at anyone, was still looking at her signature in black ink, the vast empty space beside it, above the line where his was meant to be. There was silence in the room. Apparently, not even Brett was tactful enough for this.

"Who?" she finally asked.

"Zoey."

"How long?"

"Months."

"You are so stupid," she said simply. "You are so, so stupid." She sighed audibly. Then she picked up the electric stapler on the table and slammed it against Jonah's face. "You are so fucking stupid!" she screamed as he nearly tumbled over in his chair. She threw the stapler on the table and it exploded apart in a cloud of staples, Brett shielding his eyes. She took her bag and left the room.

There was something exquisite, something tremendously sheer or total in the pain in Jonah's face. She had hit him squarely in the nose—he reached up tentatively to it, and as his fingers brushed its tip, his entire field of vision was swallowed in searing white pain. When he looked at his fingers, there were droplets of blood on them.

"Okay," Brett said. "Let's all stay calm." He was on his feet, very pale, arms raising and lowering at the elbow, like a drama student gesticulating through a high school play.

Jonah knew his nose was broken.

Brett wasn't much use after that. He kept insisting on the need for calm, then finally had to sit down with his head between his knees. From this position, he revealed that he always got light-headed at the sight of blood. The most helpful person was the receptionist who had led Jonah into the room. She had a couple of semesters of nursing school, she told him, and she examined his nose in a professional manner and confirmed that yes, it was broken, and yes, he would need to go to the hospital. Soon after that, a manager appeared with some sort of waiver for Jonah to sign. But Jonah remained sufficiently conscious of being a lawyer to refuse to sign anything while bleeding from the face—though in a different mood he might have assured the manager that it would be difficult to build a tort case around the presence of a stapler. The manager took his refusal to sign angrily and then said something rude to Brett—whom Jonah had acquired a strange fondness for—and when Jonah told the manager that he should stop being a dick to his employees, he was asked to leave the Corcoran premises. Before Jonah went out, the receptionist handed him a frozen veggie burger from the kitchen freezer, and Jonah held this gently against his nose for a while, sitting on the curb.

It was now mid-morning, on a fine summer day: hot but not humid, the sky a deep and cloudless blue. Jonah was reminded of sitting on the porch of the house he'd grown up in, in Roxwood—and perhaps because of the iciness of the veggie burger, he was reminded of eating Popsicles. He could not deny a sense of peace, sitting there on the narrow street. He regretted the hurt he'd caused Sylvia. But by now it seemed clear that hurt was all he had to offer her—and vice versa. At least that hurt had reached its end point—or perhaps its inevitable climax. Either way, it was over.

He recognized that if he'd felt compelled to make a confession, he ought to have waited to make it: found a more appropriate time, a gentler manner in which to tell her the truth. When the moment had come, though—he really hadn't felt he'd had a choice. It was as if the visions and all that had followed had been steadily gathering into a tide, and in that conference room he found he could no longer resist it. Maybe he had never been able to resist it.

And this, he sensed, now switching the veggie burger from one hand to the other, was the true source of his unexpected contentment. The relief was more than satisfaction at the end of a punishing relationship. It was the relief of giving in, of surrender—of being buoyed by a current he had been struggling against, vainly, for so long.

He looked around: The street was too small to be anything but a tributary of the city's din and traffic; cars passed him so infrequently that he could hear each one as it drove up, and then rolled away. The late-summer sun seemed to touch every surface with the subtlest tinge of gold. And taking all this in, he asked himself: Why resist at all?

Why not, he thought with gathering fervor, admit to the enlarged sense of humanity he'd acquired? Why not accommodate his chronically distressed conscience? Why not yield to these spastic urges to be better than he wanted to be? Wasn't this the meaning—the message—to which all his recent experiences amounted? Why not just give up, and do good?

The simplicity, the clarity, with which this idea struck him was such that for several moments he forgot about his nose, sat staring across the street with the veggie burger resting on his knee. Then his phone—foghorn or siren of the world not circumscribed by a quiet street on a sunny day—chimed from his pocket. He took it out: He had an invitation to a meeting with Doug Chen that afternoon. He recalled the circumstances of the BBEC case: 5F-LUM6, and Dyomax, and Dale Compstock. He recalled the theft that BBEC had committed—and the role he was to play in helping them get away with that theft. He understood this was an overly simplistic accounting of things. The moral complexities he'd gratefully observed in his previous analysis of the case were still there, even if he now wished they weren't. But that didn't matter. He would hold himself to a higher standard—obviously, he had to. He had to think of the scientist whose labor had been wasted, of the dozen or more people who would lose their jobs, of the angel investors and the . . . These were the only examples, however, he could come up with of individuals who might really suffer if BBEC prevailed. But they were enough, and besides, the point was that he would no longer reason as he had before—would no longer content himself that the ambiguities inherent in a dispute between a multinational drug maker and a biotech venture absolved him of any personal, ethical, moral responsibility. He would embrace that responsibility. He would run to it.

He discovered that setting up a new Gmail account on an iPhone was logistically a little complicated, but eventually he managed it. Next he did a Google News search for "BBEC"—found an article in the *Wall Street Journal* titled BBEC CLOSES IN ON COURT DATE WITH CAMBRIDGE START-UP. The use of the phrase "closes in" suggested the reporter had some idea what was going on. He wrote her an email from the new dummy Gmail account, BBECsource123@gmail.com:

> i have access to documents related to bbec/dyomax . . . including internal bbec correspondence btwn upper leadership . . . should be of interest to wsj . . . 100% anonymity a necessity . . . pls advise with next steps . . .

He figured he was probably being a little overcautious with the cryptic language, with the lowercase letters and the ellipses. But why take chances? He wanted to do the right thing, but he did not see that he should sacrifice his career in the process.

As he stood up from the curb, he found that his tranquillity had blossomed almost into happiness. At last he was free of the guilt, he was free of the lying, he was free of the moral degradation that he had too easily allowed to become a part of his career, his relationships— his life. He would leave all that behind him now—just as he left behind the veggie burger, which had gotten rather unappealingly bloody, tossing it to the curb.

He got into a cab and told the driver to take him to Beth Israel. It was not the closest hospital, but it seemed appropriate. As he rode uptown, he scrolled through his emails—saw that he'd received one from Becky:

> Hi Jonah!
>
> I've been calling, but no answer! I guess you are buried at work. I wanted you to hear the great news from me, tho . . . Danny proposed over the weekend!!! Of course I said yes. :-p Anyways, let's get together soon and I'll tell you the whole story. (You would not believe how nervous he was.) I'm so glad we got to hang out on Friday & you got to know Danny a little better. Let's all get together soon!
>
> Love, your newly engaged cousin,
> Becky

Jonah thought for a moment, and then replied:

Hey Becky,

Good to hear from you. There's something I should have told you a couple days ago. I saw Danny kissing a guy in the stairwell at your party. I wasn't going to say anything, but I realize now that wouldn't have been right. Give me a call so we can talk further.

Love,
Jonah

Only later, when it was far too late, would he realize that one obvious indication he was maybe not thinking too clearly when he wrote this email was the fact that he'd begun it, "Good to hear from you." But as he hit send, all he felt was a further unburdening, a greater affirmation of his thinking, and—worst of all, it would seem in retrospect—a stirring of pride at this latest evidence of his new-found integrity.

When Jonah arrived at the ER, his injury was deemed noncritical—or anyway, not so critical that he wasn't made to fill out insurance forms and then sit for an hour beneath a TV blaring *The Price Is Right* with an ice pack pressed to his nose. When a nurse finally called his name, he was led into a little curtained treatment room, then waited there for twenty minutes. Eventually an extremely harried doctor appeared—an Indian woman, about his age, in a white jacket and glasses. She asked him a few cursory questions, didn't really seem to listen to the answers, studied his nose from various angles. After about a minute of this, she injected anesthetic into his face, then left the room for another twenty minutes. When she returned, she immediately took his now-numbed nose between her fingers and began shifting and pulling at it, sensations Jonah could feel only as a phantom tugging at his neck.

"You won't need surgery, so that's something," she said as she worked on him. "Though there may be some crookedness. But that's what plastic surgeons are for." She placed a splint over his nose and began to wrap it into place. "Leave the splint on for at least twenty-four hours," she said. "Try not to get it wet." She spoke with a lovely accent, British with Southeast Asian inflections—reminded Jonah of a reporter on the BBC. "I'll write you a scrip for the pain. Have you ever taken any prescription pain medication?"

"No," he answered.

"I'll make it mild, then. The nurse said someone hit you? With a stapler?"

"Mmm-hmm."

"You should file a police report," she said perfunctorily, and began to write the prescription.

She was a little plain, maybe—but with her precise elocution, the small silver-framed glasses she wore, she had an undeniable librarian cuteness. "Where are you from originally?" he asked her.

She glanced up from writing and scrunched her brows behind her glasses, as if she didn't quite follow. "India," she answered.

A doctor was just the sort of person he should have in his life now, he thought. And considering the fact that he was single as of this morning, he said, "I know with the nose I'm probably not looking my best, but when this comes off, maybe we could have dinner sometime?" He was feeling liberated indeed.

She gave him a witheringly disinterested look. Maybe this happened to her often. "I'm married," she said. "Take the Adonine once every four hours, no more." She handed him the prescription and left.

He didn't take the rejection too much to heart. For all he knew, she really was married—and besides, his nose was broken. In any event, he'd just been exercising new freedoms, rather than making an earnest attempt to pick her up. And if he did decide he felt any lack of companionship in the wake of breaking up with Sylvia, he could always try to resurrect things with Zoey. Maybe this time it would even work out.

He picked up his prescription and went home. He showered with his bandaged face stuck out on the other side of the curtain, put on a clean suit, took an Adonine, went into work. He'd left early the day before, he was coming in late today, but those facts dovetailed nicely into a single lie he'd devised in the shower: that he'd slipped and fallen on the subway stairs and broken his nose. As he rode the elevator up to the twenty-ninth floor, he thought about the changes he would make in his career. Going forward, he would work exclusively on cases in which clients were trying, say, to protect themselves from ongoing patent infringement, or to redress brazen acts of intellectual property theft—cases, in other words, in which Cunningham Wolf was helping an indisputably wronged client obtain justice. There weren't many of those cases, of course. But he was willing to accept a more humble career in order to adhere to his new values.

As the elevator doors opened, he felt a sudden twinge of anxiety, and realized that at least some of this thinking had been preemptive bargaining. But as he stepped out of the elevator, the first person he saw was a summer associate he'd worked with over the last several months—and he was dressed in charcoal suit and polished brown shoes. The associate said hello to Jonah, and Jonah responded with a *de rigueur* nod—and he was satisfied that he had finally found his way back to the right side of things, that his sacrifices had been acceptable.

Then, as he walked down the hall, his phone chirped with a voice-mail message, caller unknown. He experienced a new foreboding over this—but dismissed it as maybe an effect of the pain med he'd taken. He listened to the message. "You are a terrible person, Jonah," the caller said—a male voice he didn't recognize. "You are a terrible, terrible person. Just remember, one day you will stand before Jesus and answer for all you have done." That was it. Only on the third listen did he realize that it was Danny.

He supposed this meant the wheels were in motion. This reaction, however, surprised him—though obviously it shouldn't have. But somehow he'd assumed his email would just—dissolve the whole issue. Regardless, Jonah reminded himself, Danny was the one responsible, and if Danny was angry, he should be angry with himself. Jonah was only the messenger. And as for Jesus, well, Jonah felt he was a greater authority on such subjects than Danny was.

Well-being thus preserved, Jonah continued to his office. Dolores was at her desk—made a show of busily typing as soon as he approached. "Good morning, Dolores," he said. She didn't answer. "I want to apologize again for yesterday." She seemed only to type harder. It made him uneasy, though, to think that she remained unhappy with him, so he said, "Again, I really am sorry, and it won't happen again. I promise." Still she didn't acknowledge him—and finally he went into his office and closed the door.

He looked to the corner where the BBEC files had been stacked—they were gone. He turned and saw that his desk was empty, too: the computer, papers, books that had covered it all missing. For a terrified instant he thought he was having another vision, this one more thorough in the bareness of things it exposed—but he recognized almost immediately that the suffocating intensity of the other visions was lacking. More, his phone was still on his desk, his law school diploma was still on the wall. But the immediate terror only gave way to sinking dread—which was not much of a relief. He didn't need the instincts he'd developed over 17,500 hours to know what was happening here. As omens went, a cleaned-out office was as bad as it got. He opened his office door—now Dolores was gone, too. He saw her hurrying down the hallway toward the bathroom.

"Oh—" and before he could say "fuck," the phone on his desk was ringing. He considered not answering it—but not answering wouldn't change anyone's mind, wouldn't undo anything that had been done. "Hello?" he said into the phone.

"Hi, Jonah, it's Scott Baker," the man on the phone said affably. "Why don't you come over to Doug Chen's office so we can talk." Scott Baker was a partner, but he never took cases, he never met with clients, he never appeared in court. He was, as the hallway knew well, Cunningham Wolf's internal fixer. A phone call from Scott Baker: That was as bad as omens got.

"Will there be an . . . HR representative there?" Jonah asked, his nose suddenly aching.

Scott Baker laughed. "Seriously, Jonah?"

"What I'm asking is, do I need an attorney?"

"Well, there are lots of them in the building. See if anybody wants to come with you."

You will stand before Jesus and answer for all you have done, he thought as he hung up the phone.

What the fuck had he been thinking?

It had been only a few days since he last visited Doug Chen's office, and the scene inside was nearly identical: the Mondrian, the stone sculpture, Doug Chen silently typing at his spotless desk—everything pristine and spare and smooth. The only difference—not an inconsequential one, unfortunately—was that Scott Baker was perched on Doug Chen's windowsill, swinging his legs insouciantly. He was dressed in khakis, a shirt with no tie, sneakers. You had to be a very, very good lawyer to get away with charging tens of thousands of dollars in lap dances on your firm's credit card; you had to be an even better one to be a Cunningham Wolf partner and get away with wearing that. I am so fucked, Jonah thought.

But Scott Baker smiled pleasantly as Jonah came in. He had a puffy face and a doughy build, his cheeks and nose very red—like a hapless middle-aged man who always comes back from vacation sunburned. "Have a seat," he said, gesturing to the chair across from Doug Chen's desk. Jonah did; Doug Chen went on typing.

"Well, first things first, you're fired," Scott Baker began, swinging his legs. Jonah nodded grimly. He had his hands folded in his lap— had to make an effort to keep from slumping forward in the chair. "So what happened to your nose?" Scott Baker asked.

"My ex-girlfriend hit me with a stapler."

Scott Baker chuckled with amused sympathy, as if he were hearing this story over drinks at a bar. "Jonah, this is not your day. So was it before or after you got your nose broken that you emailed Ashley Salomon at the *Journal*?"

Jonah sighed heavily. "That was fast," he said.

"Next time you're sending an anonymous email, do it from an iPhone that your employer doesn't own. Jonah, if you had been Deep Throat, Richard Nixon would still be president." And he chuckled again good-naturedly.

The phone, Jonah thought. Of course. "You really track all of that?"

"I don't know what you mean by 'all of that,' but put 'BBEC' into an email and send it to the *Wall Street Journal*, and yeah, we'll take a look. So anyway. You wrote the email, and then your ex broke your nose?"

"She broke my nose, then I wrote the email."

For the first time, Scott Baker glanced at Doug Chen, who continued typing as if the room were empty, silent. Scott Baker looked back at Jonah. "And you didn't actually send anything, right? I mean, that would make this all a lot simpler." Jonah shook his head. "We figured that," Scott Baker answered. "By which I mean, we didn't find anything missing. You can't Xerox those files, by the way. Special paper. They won't scan, either. Did they put you on any pain meds or anything like that?"

"Adonine," he answered.

"You took one of those and wrote the email?"

"No, I actually wrote it before I . . ." Jesus, he thought, as Scott Baker glanced again at Doug Chen—why didn't he just plead guilty to breach of contract right now? "I don't think I should say anything else."

Scott Baker made a waving gesture with his hand. "We'll assume you didn't send anything. That's really the most important point." He hopped up, took a manila folder he'd been sitting on from the windowsill, handed it to Jonah. There were two stapled documents inside. "So here's how this works," Scott Baker said. "In the first document you attest that you didn't send any material documents, BBEC or otherwise, to anybody in the media, or anybody not in the media, for that matter—you know, anybody sentient or otherwise—and we'll agree to refrain from jumping on you with both feet for violating your NDAs, which, incidentally, have bite, and I know because I drafted them. Of course, if it turns out you did send anything . . ."

"I didn't," Jonah insisted, actually offended by this—and for no good reason, he recognized, because this had been exactly what he'd planned to do.

"Like I said, we more or less believe you," Scott Baker replied. "But sign that and we'll feel a lot better. And then the other document is a fairly standard severance: three months paid, never darken our doorway again, and so forth. From our end we'd be much happier to give you nothing, but you know how this works: It's all a little neater if it looks mutual. Juries do the damnedest things."

"I'm not going to sue," he muttered.

"We don't think you will, either, but it's signatures that help us sleep at night," he replied. "Also, Jonah, this is one of those offers where we expect you to accept right now. Otherwise, well, let's just say this has gone to some of the very highest people in the firm, and those are always the last people you want jumping on you with both feet."

Jonah noticed Doug Chen had stopped typing—was staring at him, his face passionless, inscrutable as ever. Jonah knew he ought to at least read the two documents. But he also knew that his best chance of getting out of the room without being the subject of a lawsuit he could neither win nor afford would be to sign these papers as fast as fucking possible. He took out a pen he found in his pocket—realized it was the uni-ball Vision (Micro) from Corcoran—allowed no further consideration, and signed the BBEC document. He flipped to the last page of the severance— couldn't stop himself from stopping. His eyes had again fallen on the blankness above the line on which he was supposed to write.

"If I sign this, I'll never work in a New York firm again, will I?"

"Nope!" said Scott Baker cheerily, and somehow without malice. "And I wouldn't get your hopes up for L.A. or Chicago, either."

He lifted his hand, but it was trembling. This was it: his career, every one of 17,500 hours—of his life!—all his plans. "I can't do it," he said.

"You really should," Scott Baker responded.

He looked at the stark black line, the tip of the pen shaking weakly over it. He imagined this was the same difficulty he would have had if he'd been asked to sever one of his limbs with these pen strokes. "Can we . . ."

"Afraid not," Scott Baker answered. "You sent the email."

Again he made a motion to sign, but his hand was trembling embarrassingly. He tried to steady it with his other hand. This didn't help. He finally put the pen down and rested it on top of the paper. He saw that Doug Chen was still watching him.

"Bear in mind, the firm made a significant investment in you,"

Doug Chen said, with all his usual emptiness of intonation. "Perhaps, while recognizing your promise, we paid insufficient attention to other of your qualities." Jonah could only stare back uncomprehendingly.

"I think the idea is, we're sorry this happened, too," Scott Baker said. "After all," he continued, making a circle in the air with his finger, suggesting the outline of Jonah's face, "we had you sized up for partner."

"Regardless, at this point it is in your best interest to sign," Doug Chen told him. "It is in all of our best interests."

Jonah knew he was right, and—in what he realized would likely be the last demonstration of his "promise" as an attorney who might one day ascend to partnership in an elite New York law firm—he understood the argument that was being made: He owed it to them. He took a deep breath—he chopped off his leg at the knee. He handed Scott Baker the documents and started to cry. The tears were so pure in their sadness, in their remorse: For the second time that day he felt like a child—now one crouching in the living room beside a broken lamp. To the humiliation of this was added the pain he felt in his nose with every sob. When he'd pulled himself together enough to look up, Doug Chen was typing again; Scott Baker had hopped back up on the sill, was swinging his legs. "Don't worry," Scott Baker said. "We won't tell anyone. But out of curiosity. Were you going to try to sell the documents to the *Journal*? They don't really pay for that sort of thing, not enough to make it worth it, anyway. Or was it you imagined yourself testifying before Congress and going on *60 Minutes*? Some guys do get that when they're your age. They have to prove how much smarter they are than the rest of us."

"I just . . . I was trying to do the right thing."

"Conscience!?" Scott Baker cried, in parodic shock. "Didn't you have that removed in law school?" He glanced at Doug Chen, but he continued typing. Scott Baker looked almost disappointed that Doug Chen hadn't laughed. "In any event, Jonah," he went on, "there's only one more thing. You know the scene in the movie where the cop has to turn in his badge and gun?"

"Yeah," Jonah said, not getting it. Then he got it. Scott Baker nodded in confirmation. Jonah reached into his pocket and opened his wallet, took out his firm credit card and his building ID, put them on the spotless surface of Doug Chen's desk.

"There's nothing hinky on the card, right?" Scott Baker asked.

"No. I mean, no, my assistant does my receipts . . ."

"No one's accusing you, just curious. We'll check anyway." There was a pause. "And the phone," Scott Baker said. Jonah reached into his pocket and placed the iPhone on the desk—hesitated a moment, then removed his hand.

"So that's it!" Scott Baker said. "Now if you'll permit me a personal suggestion. What with the broken nose and the attempted illegal dissemination of documents and the getting fired, you seem like a man who could use a vacation. So take the three months, get out of Dodge, drink a few mai tais, and try to adjust yourself to the way things are, rather than how you'd like them to be. And when you have your head screwed on straight again, maybe take another run at a less ambitious law career. The feds are always hiring."

Jonah was still looking at his phone. It was as if the amputation he'd imagined earlier had been made literal, and he was left to stare forlornly at the abandoned limb. "I'm really sorry," Jonah said. "I'm really sorry." And he had to fight off another bout of tears.

"Well," Scott Baker said, "remember that the next time someone tells you to do the right thing." Then he laughed, and maybe even Doug Chen's mouth moved a half inch.

When Jonah returned to his office, Dolores was still not there. He supposed this was for the best; he figured she was the one who'd called Scott Baker or whomever when he came in, and he couldn't help but see this as a kind of betrayal. But of course, she had only been doing her job—and what had they been to one another, really, besides two people doing their job in the same place, who had never liked each other very much?

Someone had placed on his desk a single Post-it note. On it, in handwriting he didn't recognize, was written, "People are waiting for you at reception." This, he supposed, would be security. They might have spared themselves the trouble. After all, they'd already cleaned out his office; they already had his signature on the documents of castration, assigning to them anything of his career at Cunningham Wolf they could make assignable. Did they really think, after he'd signed that, he had it in him to make some sort of scene?

He went through his desk, didn't find anything worth salvaging, didn't see what good ostensibly lucky Knicks ticket stubs, an extra mouse pad, would be to him now. He glanced for a moment at his framed diploma (Columbia, '05)—decided it would be too pathetic to walk out with it under his arm. As he was about to leave, he noticed he had a new message on the phone on his desk, from Sylvia's work number. With an eagerness and hope he would find embarrassing later, he grabbed the phone and checked the message: "Hello, this is Linda in Ms. Quinn's office. Ms. Quinn asked me to make arrangements to pick up her personal effects from you. If you could call me back with a time that would be convenient, I'll send over—" He hung up. She'd had her assistant call. It was, undeniably, very Sylvia. From her, there would be no tearful voice messages, no late-night confessions of remorse or regret. Whatever tears or regrets there were, she would be, for better and worse, too prideful, too strong—too smart—to share them with him. And he suddenly had a powerful urge to call her, to tell her—that she was the strongest person he had ever met.

He got as far as lifting up the phone again before realizing this would be pointless. He would never get past her voice mail, would never get further than Linda. What would she care now, anyway, how strong he thought she was?

He tried not to meet anyone's eyes as he walked down the hallway to the elevators. He supposed everyone knew at this point, and he couldn't face whatever reactions to him they had, or had settled on: He didn't want to see embarrassment for his sake, he didn't want to see insincere sympathy, he didn't want to see barely disguised satisfaction that there was one less comer, one less rival to deal with. He didn't want to see them all naked again.

He came down the hall and pulled open the glass door to the reception area, wondering how the security guards might handle him (rudely? deferentially? He'd never been escorted out of anywhere by anyone before), and then saw that it was not security guards waiting for him but rather his cousin Becky, in an oversize sweatshirt with the hood up, her eyes covered with large black sunglasses; her fiancé, Danny, dressed in a neat black suit, his hands on his hips, as though to project Jonah doubted even Danny knew what; and Becky's roommate, Aimee, who had an arm around Becky and glared disdainfully at Jonah as he appeared. It was such a strange tableau that at first he had no clue what to say. The woman sitting at reception was taking curious, surreptitious glances at the group, at Jonah, apparently trying to figure out how all these people fit together.

But after his initial bewilderment, Jonah understood very well what they had come for—and rather than begin this conversation just yet, he turned to the receptionist and said, "Angelica, right?" She was a round-eyed, Hispanic young woman with black straight hair, dressed in a pink blouse. She nodded at his question with confusion, clearly surprised that, of all those gathered here, she was the one he had chosen to speak to. "Sorry about not putting in for your birthday."

"That's okay," she said quickly. She was now giving him a look that suggested she thought he might be deranged. He wondered what Dolores had told her—then he remembered about the bandage on his face.

He turned to the others. "So I understand congratulations are in order!" It was, he realized immediately, a heartless joke, and if he hadn't realized it, the looks on their faces (despondent, disgusted, wrathful, respectively) would have told him so. But it seemed to him that at best the situation was farcical, though evidently no one else was prepared to see it that way—and he couldn't blame them.

"Is that what this is to you? This is all a big joke to you?" Aimee started. "Don't you realize there are people's feelings—and I mean, like, this is your family? I mean, seriously? There are people like that in the world? Seriously? Wow. Y'know? Wow."

"Jonah," Danny began, in a voice that was stern but suggested he was prepared to be reasonable—Jonah would have found this impossible to take seriously even if Danny's hands had not remained steadfastly on his hips. "Maybe you had a good reason for telling the *lie you told,*" he said. "And maybe you didn't have a good reason for *lying.* But you need to realize how damaging your *lie* was." If he was trying to communicate the line he expected Jonah to take, he was not being very subtle about being subtle.

"I mean, your cousin has been sobbing for hours," Aimee said. "Does that even mean anything to you?" She still had her arm around Becky, who had her face, her covered eyes, toward the floor. Jonah had managed not to look closely at her until now. He noticed that she had on pajama pants. Seeing this, he suddenly understood how humiliating coming here like this must have been for her—how humiliating all of it must have been for her: getting the email, telling Aimee, talking to Danny. Obviously, as little as his attempts at goodness had done for him, they had done even less for his cousin. "Becky, can I talk to you alone for a minute?"

"I don't think that's a good idea," said Danny.

"Really?" said Jonah, with open disgust. The tremendous remorse he felt had triggered commensurate contempt for Danny for his role in all of this.

"It looks like you've been injured," Danny offered. "Maybe you have a *concussion* . . . ?" he added helpfully.

"No, I don't have a concussion, my nose is broken." He turned to Aimee. "Just give me five minutes."

But evidently Aimee and Danny were coconspirators at this point—conspiring for the well-being of a girl who, Jonah could now readily believe from her ashen face and crumpled form, had indeed cut herself for a time—because Aimee immediately said, "No one wants to hear any more of your bullshit. I don't know if you're a sociopath or whatever, or you just have a really, really sick sense of humor, like, but all you get to do right now is admit that everything in that email was a lie."

Jonah studied her face: cheeks flushed, eyes wrathful, determined. If it was an act, it was a good one. But no, he concluded, Danny had probably convinced her, too. Or rather, she hadn't needed convincing. It was simply that no one believed him.

"Look," Danny said. "Maybe you were messed up on Friday night, or maybe there is something else going on with you, but you have to understand that doing things like what you did, out of the blue, whether you are joking or not, Jonah, that behavior is just really, really wrong." He was actually meeting Jonah's eyes as he said this, and with a reasonable approximation of conviction, too. Jonah might have been impressed if he was not so appalled. "All we want—the only reason we're here," he continued, "is for you to admit what you wrote in that email is not true, so Becky can hear it for herself, and we can put all of this behind us."

Jonah looked over to Becky again. She still had her face toward the ground, but her mouth and cheeks were working, as though struggling against the sobbing they'd mentioned. "C'mon," Aimee said to him. "Don't be an asshole. Okay?" With this last question, her look shifted, some other form of appeal entered into it—more earnest, less hostile. Perhaps she was in on it, too, even if Danny didn't realize she was. It occurred to Jonah that this scene had the overlapping layers of deceit of a show trial. "She won't stop crying. Okay?"

"You all can't do this in here, though," Angelica now said from the reception desk. She might have said this sooner, but Jonah guessed she had gotten caught up in what was happening, too. "You're all going to have to leave."

"Let's just agree to put this behind us," Danny said.

Jonah gave a final look at Becky. It was too bad, he thought, that he hadn't gotten to know her better. "It's only a sick joke," he told her. "Why don't you forget all about it."

Aimee pulled her a little closer. "Okay, honey? We can go home now?" Becky moved her head in a way that might have signaled agreement, and Aimee immediately started pushing the elevator button, again and again. Jonah thought he could see in Danny's face a flicker of relief, or gratitude—some acknowledgment of what they both knew to be true—but he turned away before it might develop into anything more than a flicker. Likely there were things Danny did not acknowledge even to himself.

Danny now took a position behind the two women, facing the elevator, waiting. Apparently there was nothing further to say. But then, Jonah understood: When you got the deal you wanted, you didn't wait around for the other party to change his mind. Finally the elevator doors opened—but as Aimee moved forward, Becky stayed where she was, and then she turned her face toward Jonah. "Stay out of my life, Jonah," she said. Then the three of them stepped into the elevator, and the doors closed.

Jonah waited for a few minutes, giving them time to get across the lobby, to get into a cab. After a while, Angelica asked, "Was it true?"

He looked over at her. "Yup," he told her. "It was."

Angelica nodded, taking this in. "What did—" The phone at the reception desk rang. "Cunningham Wolf," she answered. "Mmm-hmm, this is she . . . No, actually, he's um . . ." She turned away from Jonah in her chair. More quietly, she continued, "He is standing right here, as a matter of fact, would you . . . Mmm, is he . . . ? Okay, I will . . . Mr. Jacobstein?" she said, addressing him. "We need you to vacate right now, Mr. Jacobstein, otherwise we—"

He pushed the elevator button—got on when the doors opened, rode down to the lobby.

It was now approaching the middle of the afternoon. Whatever mildness Jonah had sensed of the day that morning had been succeeded by a pure ninety-five-degree heat—undiminished by wind, unadorned by humidity. The heat seemed to collect in bright shards and slivers of sunlight on all the metal surfaces—the hydrants, the roof racks of parked cars, the horizontal flagpoles at the entrances to Midtown buildings—to gather in a uniform layer over sidewalk and street. Jonah had been standing a few feet from the entrance of 813 Lexington for several minutes before he noticed he had sweated through the bandage, that it was sagging down his cheeks. But he made no move to adjust it, remained where he was. When he'd walked out of the building, he looked up and down the sidewalk—stretching off in both directions to a heat-hazy vanishing point—and had been struck by an unfamiliar dilemma, one he did not remember ever having faced in his entire life to that point: He had nowhere to go.

"We," Angelica had said to him. "We." He kept thinking of this, over and over. Almost instantaneously, Cunningham Wolf had become "we," and he had become Mr. Jacobstein—an outsider, as much as a stranger to them. It was the same with Becky and Danny and Aimee: He had been as though pushed through some permeable membrane, and they had re-formed as something new without him—or maybe something the same without him: a family. Danny and Aimee—they were Becky's family. And he was the asshole that they had bound together to confront.

Was he supposed to go back to Roxwood now? Move in with his mother? Besides how unmitigatedly depressing that idea seemed, he knew it wouldn't do her any good to have her adult son suddenly move back in with her. She was an anxious person, had grown more so with age. She'd spend a lot of time asking him if he was okay and not-so-subtly implicating his father's influence in whatever story he came up with to explain how the fuck he'd ended up there. The idea of moving in with his father wasn't any more appealing. He wouldn't want to be on the couch of his father's apartment when his father brought women home, and his father wouldn't want him there, either. The fact was, he and his parents were three adults who had been living separate lives for a long time now.

Two laughing men brushed past him and went into the lobby. They were bankers from the upper floors—Jonah knew because he had seen them, more than once, running naked around the lobby tree on bonus day. He watched them as they carried their briefcases, their cups of coffee, their phones, past the tree, into the elevators.

When they were gone, his eyes lingered on the tree. As always, its foliage was resplendent in green, its thick and twisted trunk evocative of immovable permanence. He had always seen the tree as a symbol of something, he realized—though he could not say exactly of what. It was not something to be admired, necessarily, though neither something to be disdained. But it was something he'd imagined he would always be a part of. He supposed, finally, that he had had a kind of faith in the tree—a faith that had been misplaced. He had never guessed at the fragility of his place in things.

He remained outside 813 Lexington for a long time—finally started to walk, more from a desire to avoid being seen by his former colleagues in this state of defeated immobility than from an urge to be anywhere else. He walked without any idea of direction or destination—merely let himself drift up one avenue, down the next. Eventually, the blue of the summer sky thinned; the sun sank lower, the shadows lengthened, the heat relented and everyone who had to be outdoors suffered a little less. In cubicles, people logged out of accounts and turned off their monitors for the night; Penn Station and Grand Central and every subway station swelled with those heading home; the more cautious decided it was time to leave Central Park. As Jonah began to make his way among the vending carts being hitched to the back of cars, the growing knots of people beneath bus stop signs, a destination started fixing itself in his mind, soon more firmly with each step. By the time he arrived, the stone of the plaza outside Zoey's building had taken on the faintly orange hues of a New York dusk: the amalgamation of all the headlights, the fluorescent lights in office windows, the burning tips of cigarettes, the neon signs, great and small, and—somewhere beyond the horizon of buildings, some-where out over Hoboken, Jonah imagined—the sunset.

As he waited for Zoey to appear, he sat down on one of the con-crete planters that dotted the plaza's border. The planter's stone was hot, and its edge pressed uncomfortably across his buttocks, but he was too worn out to stand any longer—his legs aching, his nose keen-ing with every breath. He would have called her, of course, but her number, all her numbers, were ensconced in his iPhone, which was ensconced in the offices of Cunningham Wolf—in a drawer in Doug Chen's desk, he pictured, like where teachers kept the magazines and candy they'd confiscated. There was nothing he could do but wait for her.

But by the time dusk had given way almost completely to evening, he still hadn't seen her. At first, the foot traffic across the plaza had been steady as people left for the day, alone or in tiny groups, but now it was virtually empty. His fear was growing that he might have missed her, or that she hadn't even come to work that day. Soon he would have to look for her at her apartment. But what if she was there with Evan? What if she refused to open her door to him at all?

Then he saw her: a slender figure, more recognizable for her frame and distinctive gait than for what he could see of her face in what was left of the twilight. She crossed to about the middle of the plaza, stopped—and then did not, as he expected, immediately reach into her purse for a cigarette. Instead, she stood still for a few moments, and then she put her hand against her mouth, just below her nose, rested it there, her face set in a look of delicate concentration—as if she were trying to remember something, or were on a beach, searching for the lights of a distant ship. He saw something tender—touching—in this pose, and he had an impulse simply to leave her alone, as he'd promised. But, he thought, if they only gave it one more try—if only it wasn't too late—

She lowered her hand, took a few steps across the plaza. Her first look as she saw him approaching was terror, and she even took a step backward; he supposed this was a reaction to his bandaged face. Then she recognized him, and her mouth bent with concern—but she seemed consciously to push this expression and whatever thoughts inspired it aside, and her face settled into marked irritation. She started to walk quickly away.

"Wait—Zoey," he said, following after her. "I have to talk to you." She didn't stop. "Please, Zoey," he said, trying to keep pace beside her, but walking quickly was difficult, because each step sent a jolt through his nose.

"I have such a good guess what happened to your face," she muttered, still walking.

"Please, just give me a second," he said. "Zoey, I—I—" But how could he convince her it would be different this time, that he wouldn't fuck it up, like he always had—like he had even the day before in her apartment? How could he explain what he'd realized as he'd made his way there, as he'd surveyed what was left of his life: that he was in love with her, had always been in love with her—that everything that had happened had happened because he had broken up with her—but it could still be undone, could still be made right? "I want to marry you!" was what he came up with.

"*Jesu Christo,*" Zoey answered in response, not breaking her stride.

"I mean it!" he said. They had crossed the edge of the plaza, he was following her down the sidewalk. "I was living the wrong way, I see that now, but I can change, I want to change! I want to be whatever you want, I swear, I want to have a family—I want to have babies with you. Jewish babies! I want them to have bar mitzvahs, I want to keep kosher, I want to take vacations to Israel, I . . ." He knew he was babbling—and could see how crazy he looked by way of the uncomfortable glances the shouting mummy chasing the young woman down the sidewalk was getting from everyone they passed—but he went on: Every motion of his mouth redoubled the pain in his nose, but he went on. He didn't see that he had any other choice. "We'll live in a house. In a neighborhood. We'll leave New York."

"I like New York," she said, not looking at him.

"Yonkers," he said. "I could practice law there. Or where you're from, we'll go back to Larchmont."

"Oh, now this is getting really romantic."

"Please, Zoey, please!" he cried, and something in his tone—its desperation, or how stark and uninhibited this desperation was—made her stop, at last, though she didn't look at him, kept her face turned away, had her arms crossed over her chest, her purse dangling from her hand. She was standing beneath an illuminated streetlight; he saw all along the block, the streetlights were coming on for the night. "I know I made mistakes," he said. He did not know which mistakes he was referring to, but undoubtedly there had been many. "And I want you to know how sorry I am, for all of it, for everything. Zoey, I never . . . I never understood . . ." For his own sake, he wanted very badly to be able to finish this sentence. But the truth was he felt he understood less than ever. "Maybe, maybe if in the beginning . . ."

"Please don't," she said, shaking her head. Fine shadows cast by the streetlight above crossed her face as it moved back and forth, so that he could make out only the shapes of it, intermittent and indistinct: lips, eyes—beloved nose.

"We can start over," he told her. "It can be like it was before." She was still shaking her head. "Please, Zoey," he said. "Marry me. You're my last hope."

She probably didn't mean to hit him exactly in the face, but then again, it was a large purse, it was a large bandage—she really might not have hit him at all. In any event, in the next moment his entire head was bursting with pain, he was crouched on the ground, knees to chest, forearms over his face—as if he were doing a cannonball into a pool.

"Y'know . . . sorry," she said, without much conviction.

He managed to say, "So you'll think about it?" And she laughed. It seemed so long since he'd heard her laugh—and he realized he'd done everything wrong again.

"So here's my guess," she said. "*Schlampe* found out you were a philanderer and beat you with her Louboutin. Since I'm sure my name is going to come up between you two again and again from now on, and, I'd wager, get slandered mercilessly, please mention to her that I always imagined her as the kind of woman who wears beautiful shoes.

"As for me, I quit smoking, I ate kale for lunch, and I'm no longer going to be the girl you run to when your real relationship gets too complicated and you're in the mood for someone with exactly zero demands and expectations. And yes, you've been that person for me when I've wanted that, but the whole point is that I don't want to want that anymore, because I know it isn't good for me. And someday someone I love is going to propose to me and actually mean it, and when that happens you know what they're not going to say? They're not going to say, 'You're my last hope.' I hope you remember, Yonsi, that's not altogether flattering to us girls." He lifted his face to try to answer, but she continued. "The simple truth is that I've given up hoping you'll ever stop trying to become a bigger asshole than you are. I mean, if all you want to be is a corporate lawyer who cheats on his girlfriends, why should I think you'll end up any different? And that's certainly not the kind of father I want for my Jewish babies. But really, if that's all you're looking for, believe me, there are plenty of Jewish *Schlampe*s out there. And while I obviously don't want to get into anything now, I mean I absolutely refuse, let's just admit that when it comes to Jewish babies, our ship sailed ten years ago." He could see the familiar trembling in her forehead that signaled she might start to cry—but she didn't, she kept talking instead. "I mean, does it matter that it was pretty great, in the beginning? Does it matter that I've been more or less in love with you for a decade? I dunno.

Maybe in theory. But in practice it just seems like . . . It just seems like . . ." Whatever force had propelled her speech gave out. More quietly, and with a certain puzzlement—as though what she said perplexed her—she resumed, "You said you wanted to marry me, Yonsi. You talked to me about having babies. . . . And you know me better than any single person in the world." She had started to cry, though with a lightness he had never seen before: tears in fine, slender lines sliding down her cheeks. He got to his feet; he reached out to touch her arm, but she jerked it away from his hand. She avoided looking at him, too—stared at some invisible point on the sidewalk before the point of her shoe.

"I've been trying to change," he told her. "You have no idea how much I want to change."

She shook her head toward the sidewalk forlornly. "Don't you see? I don't want you to change. I never wanted you to change, Yonsi." The shaking of her head stopped; she sighed in and out through her nose. "It's just, why do you have to be so selfish? You're just so goddamn selfish."

"I've been trying to—I want to do the right thing!"

She finally looked at him—with irony, with regret, with weary affection, with scorn. "This was your idea of the right thing, Jonah?"

He didn't know what to say—sensed that he shouldn't say anything else. And as if in acknowledgment of this, she brushed the tears off her face quickly with her fingertips and lifted her purse up onto her shoulder. But even though he knew she was right—about all of it—to have these be the last words was more than he could bear. "I saw you, standing, on the plaza," he said. "I thought you looked so beautiful. What were you doing?"

She smiled faintly at herself. "I was praying," she said. "I don't want to be so scared all the time." For a moment she seemed to turn this smile in such a way as to make him its object—and then she walked away. He watched until the top of her head, the last thing he saw of her, disappeared among the crowds on the sidewalk—like she had drifted away over the horizon.

————

It was fully night now: the street as Jonah looked down it an unwinding scroll of doorways and lights, taxicabs and illuminated storefronts. It's going to be okay, he said to himself. It's going to be okay. He did not know why he thought so, nor could he imagine by what course of events "okay" would be achieved. He did not even really know what "okay" would look like anymore. He understood, with a stark clarity of perception, unshaded either by hope or self-pity—a clarity he was aware he had rarely allowed himself—that he would never be asked to return to Cunningham Wolf; that his career as a white-shoe attorney was over; that Sylvia would never speak to him again; that he had managed to betray Becky not once but twice; that Zoey was right to think she was better off without him. And somehow, all this had happened in the space of time between a Friday and a Tuesday. And confronting all these facts, all his mind could come up with was the dull, convinctionless assurance—that it would be okay.

This thought, he realized, was a sort of reflexive solace, a last defense: the comfort you offered—offered someone else, offered yourself—when there was no other comfort to give. It was going to be okay: This too, he saw, was a kind of faith—a blind faith—that by some immutable quality of events, something tolerable would emerge. It was the faith of the lucky—those for whom things had always been okay before. It was the faith of Aaron Seyler, and Philip Orengo, of everyone who walked daily past the tree in the lobby of 813 Lexington, the faith of those who did not feel they had or needed any faith at all, exactly because, whatever happened, it was going to be okay—or, more precisely: It would be for them. It was a faith, Jonah now discovered, you didn't even notice you had until you'd lost it.

No, he said to himself, it was not going to be okay—at least, it would not be for him. And the city, as he looked around it, suddenly appeared as it was often described to him by those who didn't live there: vast, and bewildering.

He turned and started walking in the opposite direction from Zoey—and as he walked, he could hear—faint at first, but as he listened—growing, gathering—a roar—a storm—rolling beneath the sidewalk—rolling across the sky—red and electric blue and aqueous green—shaking up and down the faces of buildings—shaking up and

down his spine, rumbling under the soles of his feet—through the
shattered fragments of his nose—and then he saw the rain of it: roar-
ing, hot, ceaseless—water falling from the sky—bubbling up from
the storm drains and subway mouths and bursting from hydrants
and gushing from the windows of the buildings—and every person
caught in it—drenched, soaking—whether inside or out, whatever they
wore—water against their skin, and water in their eyes—in everyone's
eyes—and his, too—the roar of it only increasing—until Jonah had to
cover his ears—but pressing his hands to his ears only made it louder—
until in the midst of the roar—a voice, still and small—in words he
couldn't understand—and then in words he could—

יונה הנני

Jonah: Here I Am. Go There and Offer the Words
Inscribed in Your Heart.

He was blinking away tears—his pulse hammering in his ears and
in the veins in his neck. He felt himself toppling over and grabbed
onto a streetlight. He looked around. It was a warm August night in
New York City. Its bustle was predictable, it was unremarkable: people in restaurants, people in taxis; chatter on the sidewalks, chatter in
the bars; this one cheerful, this one distraught, this one listening to
headphones, this one heading to a first date, and to a child's piano
recital, and to a baseball game, and to a subway. But if he listened, he
could still hear the roar of it: that need; if he looked closely, he could
still see—everyone soaking wet—just like him—

Jonah began to laugh.

Offer words inscribed in his heart? He laughed harder, and it hurt
his nose more, but he didn't try to restrain it. Indeed, he reveled in the
laughter. He was supposed to talk about a relentless storm? About a
universal nakedness? To what end? The little good he had tried to
do—even if it was done out of pure terror and self-interest, as Zoey
had deduced—had destroyed everything he'd known of his life, maybe
destroyed the lives of a few other people, too. He was meant to do
more? Of that? No, he thought, looking around the sidewalk, fuck
these people. Fuck their trees and their show trials and the nakedness

that they were obviously much, much happier ignoring—just as he had been. Fuck all of it, and fuck the notion that he might have anything to offer to anyone—whatever that meant. And, he thought further, laughing hysterically now, fuck whatever power actually conceived of any of this as a good idea—as anything like wisdom, or justice.

No, he would not be offering any words inscribed in his heart. What he would be doing was drinking mai tais or their equivalent, and adjusting to the world not as it was, but rather as everyone wanted it to be.

And Jonah decided to take a vacation.

II. "IN CASE OF LOSS,
PLEASE RETURN TO _____"

9/2

Went for a run today. Defunct towpath along a canal through the woods south of Princeton. No one else on the trail. Sound of my breath through my mouth (nose still painful), footfalls on the dirt. Exhausted after only five or six miles, stopped to catch my breath. Leaning against a tree, palm pressed to the bark. The late-afternoon sunlight turning red between the branches overhead, leaves in their late summer colors: fulvous, ocher, vermilion. Delicate cooling in the air, so familiar it seemed to echo some seasonal cooling in my own body. Thought appeared in my head: school starting soon. It was several more breaths before I noted my error. This morning, sent formal letter requested by dean, renouncing all rights and privileges. Received a letter from housing office, informing me I must vacate student housing, as I will no longer be a student. The anticipation of another year of school was just a trick of association: contemporaneity of a certain quality of air, a lifetime of first days of school. Need to disentangle myself, my sense of time, from the rhythms of the academic year. Surely everyone has to do this, at some point, to some degree? The emptiness of the woods became ominous next, though, the disappearing light forbidding. Turned around and ran back to the street, walked the rest of the way along Alexander Road, finding reassurance in traffic. Hadn't been frightened of the conventional things, nothing so particular as the fiend behind the tree with the knife. More fundamental fear, more nebulous feeling of pursuit.

9/3

Began to pack my apartment. Incapacity for practical tasks again rears its ugly head. In the course of assembling a box, managed to tape all the openings closed. (Apt example of Pyrrhic victory?) The rooms filled with cardboard bring back unpleasant memories of packing up the house in B. Mom's papers bursting out the bottom of an overstuffed box. This afternoon, went through my own papers. Tests, essays, going back to elementary years at Gustav's. Odd to see that it all ended up here, in the present. I suppose I assumed it would be of interest to someone else (scholars? mate?) at some point. Sufficiently humbled to recognize this as narcissism. Opened a plastic-sheathed report, 6th-grade Judith's take on the Battle of Gettysburg. Tumbling out comes Dad tromping around the battlefield that spring. Muddy, wearing green rubber boots. That and a long car ride. Interesting what floats on the sea of memory, when so much else sinks. In any event, plan to leave most of the essays, etc., behind.

Resisting strong impulses to make edits on entries thus far. No instructor to please, in the first place, and, in the second, do not want to make this a journal about me journaling. Tedious, again narcissistic.

9/4

Dream about Claudette: cutting each other's hair. Not savage, not sexy. Weirdly intimate, though. Relief we were back together, sad to admit. Also sense of unnaturalness to the event. Grotesque piles of hair at our feet. Signal that I am not, finally, bi, despite evidence to the contrary? More likely, simple recognition of how *wrong* we were for each other. Cutting each other to pieces. She'll marry Gilbert, I suppose. And I'll spend the rest of my life tearing up every time I sneeze. This is justice, *oui*? Surprised I've turned out so angry. Surprised by all of it. And she was the last friend I made. Looks a little melodramatic on the page, I admit, but, reader, how does one make friends? Outside of a school, I mean. Out here in *le monde réel*. I look at people and don't know how to see them. Schools provide context. They affirm similarities (affiliation, interests), they categorize difference (grade level, major). I look at people and see on their faces the pressure of my looking at them. They don't know how to look back. And then I find myself too dumb to know what to say. Starting a conversation seems lately an epic task. Entering into communication with another person, crossing that . . . gulf? breach? distance? I glance away, I scurry away. I open this Moleskine and find I am the last person I know how to talk to, and with more self-pity than eloquence, as these pages show.

9/5

This morning tried for an hour to rent a van. Called six different numbers, reached six different answering machines. Finally thought to look at a calendar. Labor Day. Becoming increasingly clear that even as I cultivated a specific kind of intelligence, I also fostered a specific stupidity. Perhaps the same is true, inversely, for those who don't bother with education at all. They never learn what the aorist tense in Greek is, but they know how to rent a van. Later, on my way to Small World for coffee, passed a family coming out of Labyrinth. Impossibly young-looking daughter, though must have been a freshman. Loaded with books. Displaying in all ways the heady feeling of first arrival. Admittance, belonging. Her parents proudly draped in orange and black. Had strong and sudden urge to berate them. To *explain* something to them. But what? That everyone dies? That you end up stupid, one way or another? At bottom, probably just wanted them to know how unhappy I am. Watching them from across the street, became dizzy, short of breath, throat constricting like from thirst. Panic attack? Similar to the sensation in the woods, but more immediately physical. Returned without coffee. I would like to procure a bottle of wine for the night but can never get the cork out, end up having to push a broken chunk through with a fork. Reader, I don't even know how to get drunk properly.

9/6

Ran again this morning. Didn't feel like it, but no better ideas what to do. Down Stockton, up Russell. Passed the Hun School, über-elite prep school, even by Bulbrook standards. Saw some children (eight-year-olds?) scratching around in the dirt, planting a garden amidst posters diagramming photosynthesis. I think I would have been at home there. Occurs to me now I never envision motherhood. Always identify with the children I see. Some type of psychological malformation I could identify if I were a Freudian, I suppose. Mom said she lacked the propensity, too, until my arrival, but not convinced this is parallel. Imagine pregnancy as a feeling of unwelcome crowding, another person swimming inside me. Closest thing to a maternal instinct I can detect in myself is that I would not want myself as a mother. And now a thought that makes me bark with laughter. Better off if I *had* been pregnant in high school? Carting my brat through the aisles of a grocery store, while *Grand-mère* looks on with vivid disappointment. This a very odd form of wishful thinking.

9/7

Rented the van. A minor victory, yielding a greater challenge. Namely, where will I *go* in this van? Yes, until now I had succeeded in not thinking about it. So, reader. Where does one live? How does one locate oneself? Again, problems I imagine are easy for other people to solve. But is it merely self-pity, worldly incompetence, that make me think these questions are especially difficult in my circumstance? No close friends. No contact with family, aside from the odd email from Margaretha. Went so far as to take out a map to aid me. Failure of this predictable in retrospect. Scores of tiny dots beside places I have never been, have no conception of: Santa Fe, Milwaukee, Boise, Kansas City. In between rivers, lakes, mountains, deserts. Or else bare stretches of color the cartographer did not even bother with. All of it looked more vast than it ever had before. Like France could fit snugly in the jutting corner of Texas. Felt another choking, dizzy spell incipient. Turned the map over. Looked around to see myself surrounded by cardboard. Retreated to the closet, eventually turned on the light to do this. However one might characterize *this*.

9/8

Going through last of the books this afternoon, came across Dad's copy of Rilke, *Selected Poems*. German verso, English recto. *Duino Elegies* (German & English) adorned with checks, circles, brief notes, all of it in his hand. Cursive left-to-right tilted, loops narrow, stars beside passages made in one motion of unlifted pen. I had forgotten what his handwriting looked like. And, seeing it again, I could *remember* seeing it. Notes he used to leave for Mom on the refrigerator door. Lists of what he had to pack for vacation. Comments in the margins of the papers he'd edit for me, and the peculiarly optimistic nervousness I would feel, reading over those comments. There was such warmth to these memories. To be plain, they made me *happy*. When I looked up from the book, it was already 4 o'clock. Not that 4 o'clock is one thing or the other to me. But it was like the time had been swallowed into the past, sweetly.

I find there is a hangover to this, however. How lonely I feel, ashamed, even, reading this over. My reverie over a dead man's book. All I can do not to rip the page out.

9/9

Finished packing. Obvious I was drawing the task out, to fill the time. Now it is done and tomorrow I leave. Still lack a destination. In sudden burst of anxiety over this, sent emails to former professors, former classmates, inquiring about work opportunities. Attempted neutral phrasing. Tried not to announce myself as one with no place to be tomorrow. From a financial perspective, I do not need a job. No more tuition payments to make and, as a percentage, have spent almost none of the money Mom and Dad left me. But I understand that a job is what you hang your life on, outside of a school. It is the something that tells you where to go each day, what to do. Three hours since and no replies. Hitting refresh like one of those rats to whom they give cocaine.

Three hours further, still nothing. What did I expect? People I haven't deigned to speak to in years. Why should I assume they even remember who I am?

9/10

Picked up the van promptly at 8. Then spent hours going up and down stairs, carrying one box at a time. Didn't think to hire movers, *bien sûr*. Eventually two neighbors I had never met volunteered to help. Grad students, poli sci and comp lit (Spanish), respectively. Introduced themselves as lovers. Former chatty enough my intractable reticence mattered less, latter described himself as "obsessed" with contrast of my hair, skin tone. They asserted genuine disappointment to be only meeting me on the day of my departure. I refrained from revealing I was almost tearful over it. Over the dumb, antagonistic irony of it. Hid also the impulse to discard all my plans and stay because I had met them. But I am, finally, not *that* stupid. My near breakdown on Nassau Street was proof enough that my presence here is not only pointless and unwelcome but also unhealthy. Their descriptions of their thesis work sounded juvenile, silly. Had to bite my inner cheek at times to stop myself from smiling (though in retrospect it would have been a smile I'd have been curious to see). The ash-colored stone buildings on campus put me in mind of mausoleums. When I see professors, or anyone in my former department, I experience an indecipherable shame. Turn my back and walk the opposite direction rather than have to make an accounting of myself. Have nowhere to go but at minimum understand I can't be *here* any longer. Will be forced to navigate by dislocation. It is time for Judith to stand up from the closet floor and depart.

8:02 PM by the digital clock on the bedside table. Glowing red numbers composed of elongated trapezoids meeting at right angles. In a

Hyatt, I believe in southern New Jersey. Though possibly Delaware? Maryland? Curtains and bedspread an eggplant shade, at once both overdark and washed out. Ceiling fan over queen-sized bed. Window overlooking a parking lot. Little desk and a chair. A bathroom that illuminates brightly. Not much else. Chose this hotel because its name evokes safety, cleanliness to me. Credit to those whose job it is to establish such connotations in my head. Realize I ought to have brought in at least some of the things from the van, but find I lack the energy. Not sleepy, though. Drove south from Princeton for hours with a feeling of . . . Sorry, not able to describe it. My mother was the poet of the family. My father was an essayist, critic, but had a gift for prose (vivid, nimble, funny) that has not proven hereditary. My own writing often praised for clarity, precision, but I have long understood it lacks artfulness. Never quite felt this deficiency as I do now, though. Trying to describe how it felt to drive out of Princeton with all my earthly possessions, or all the possessions I had elected to keep, with no idea where I ought to go. Must I say it felt frightening? Lonely? Must I specify it lacked anything like a sense of liberation? Of a new beginning? And whatever I say, how can it be taken seriously, given how farcical it all is? The incompetent postgrad driving off into a foreign, forbidding "real world." Reader, it felt like failure. Feels like failure.

And only now do I receive the final knife twist: reading this over, take note of what tomorrow is. But isn't this a sign of persistent narcissism, too, to take this as assault? The universe's cruelty. It is not a knife twist at all, simply another fluctuation of randomness. What the date happens to be tomorrow.

11:14 PM. No sleep. Ceiling fan spinning above my head, silence from the other rooms. Patch of parking lot behind the window not producing any sound, either. Oblique sense it would be easier to sleep if it were louder.

12:07 AM. Glad I stayed awake. Would have been worse to wake up and have to realize it again. As though entering the day twice. Four years. Won't waste paper & ink trying to offer insight into what the

day "means." For me, it will always be a personal tragedy. I don't pretend to know the contours of anyone else's grief, much less a city's, a
nation's. Have my doubts such things can be felt collectively. Do find
myself wondering, Is this what they intended? They, the terrorists.
Four years later, an emotional cripple trapped in a hotel room.

7:58 AM. Shallow, intermittent sleep. Gave up hope for better at five.
Checked email. Inbox unchanged as a stone. Showered, went for a run.
Woods behind the parking lot. No trail, sore when I began, ran for
hours anyway. Scenery never appeared to vary. Black pine trees, fallen
needles, broken branches. Knees, feet, nose aching by the time I got
back. Hobbled across the lobby. Checked email again. Showered again.
Lying in a towel on the bed.

12:18 PM. Fell asleep for a little while. Woke up, and none of it had
budged an inch. The fan overhead. The shit purple curtains. The digital clock with the square red numbers on its face. Can you believe it? I
used to believe in miraculous things. I miss that, too.

4:27 PM. Called down to the front desk, inquired about a local bar, a
taxi to take me there. Lonesome enough to be glad for merest bodily
companionship. Bodily accompaniment. Hopeful I can achieve at least
that. Would have left immediately, but, in jolt of shame, told the desk
clerk I wanted the taxi for 7. Still light outside in the parking lot.
Evidently the desk clerk is the only person I have left to impress. Will
spend the intervening time in meticulous preparation. Slowly drawing
the pencil across my eyebrows, counting the strokes as I yank the comb
through my hair.

8:32 PM. Bar was called the Skybox. Squat, brick, freestanding building, sharing its parking lot with a laundromat. Inside, broadcast of a
sporting event played over the speakers. Not sure what sport. Sat down
at the bar. Even I knew better than to ask for a glass of red wine from
the bartender (female, middle-aged, frowning with hostility). Ordered
a gin and tonic, waited. Made an honest effort to follow the sporting
event, but difficult when one can't identify sport, rules, teams, players.

Finally (and that is just the word, though it could not have been more than ten or twenty minutes), a man took the stool nearest me. My age or just older. Red baseball hat turned backward, earrings in both ears. Stocky. Waggish grin as he sat down. Inquired about my rooting interest in the sporting event. Confessed my total ignorance of professional sports. He laughed as though I'd told a joke, offered to buy me a drink. Recognizing this as the first step in these mating rituals, I agreed. Thought, Isn't this what I came for? Bartender placed two shot glasses before us on the bar, filled with a yellow liquid. Flavor lemon, syrupy. He suggested I imbibe more quickly, I obliged. More glasses of lemon syrup were brought. Next asked if I had "walked into a wall" and laughed again. Then expressed smiling contrition, assured me that he was "just fucking with" me. Pointed to my nose. Reader, I never knew. It is so crooked other people notice. He asked, with superficial sympathy, "Did you get into an accident or something when you were a kid?" Considered abandoning the whole endeavor then, but thought of the clock. The fan. Even this, describing my failure to make even the most ephemeral connection with another human being. Again in my head, like a rote response, Isn't this what I came for? Continuing mating rituals as they were practiced in early 21st-century New Haven, Connecticut, I stated I was bored. I stated I wanted to get out of there. He smiled as though this confirmed some assumption he had made about me. (But what had he guessed? And how?) Followed him out of the bar, through the parking lot. Kept expecting him to stop at one of the cars, take out keys. Instead, he stopped behind the building. Simultaneous visual, olfactory, tactile sensations: dumpsters, urine, tongue in my mouth. Again, though, Isn't this what I came for? Back up against the dumpster. Wordless, pleasureless. Violent but in an unaccustomed way. Indifferently violent. Realized I had been stupid enough to think every bar was an Ivy bar, the boys so respectful you have to ask them not to be. Earful of seething breath when he finished. Turned away as he pulled his pants up. While I put my underwear back on, he said something about needing to watch the ninth inning. "Who did you think I was?" I asked him. He shrugged, disinterested, impatient. As if he were always hearing this question from women by the dumpsters. Reiterated necessity of watching the ninth inning. Walked several steps ahead of me back into the bar. I called a taxi. I waited. And here I am. 8:48 PM, sayeth the clock. And the hardest part, reader: I have to do it all again tomorrow.

Showered and stood before the mirror. Attempted to give myself an honest look. Thinner than perhaps I have ever been. Elbows jutting out from the middle of my arms. My finger disappearing almost to the second knuckle in the depression between neck and clavicle. Breasts a modest disruption of white skin across chest and stomach. Hair on my head and hair on my pubis differing only in scale. Color the same, texture the same. And nose unmistakably, unmissably crooked. Only somehow I had missed it. Recalled a joke Dad used to tease Mom with. "When they chose Klein, they weren't talking about the nose!" Smiled for a moment, thinking of it. Then watched the points of the smile slacken, my lips bend, my chin push itself up a little. I watched the whole affair contort and contract into weeping. All my features crowding together spastically, like for warmth. Sheen of water down my cheeks. I cried and I cried because . . . Because I don't have a nose like my mom's anymore, because I had humiliating sex, because I'm living in a hotel with no reason to stay or to leave, because it all got so fucked up four years ago. Because, because, because. My eyes fell on the razor I'd used to shave my legs, on the raised lip of the shower where I'd left it. Plastic, red and green and blue. I could envision it, so easily. A flick down each wrist. Crouching to the bathroom floor, watching the cascade of blood. And, soon enough, nothing more. It was as though the moment lengthened, broke apart into its constituent elements. The mirror. The sink. The tile. The glow of the fluorescent light from above the mirror. The weight of my body distributed between the soles of my feet. My two eyes blinking. My two lungs swelling. Heart beating. Neurons firing. All these facts, these arrangements of the physical world. It is only the neurons that name them, organize them into a moment. I thought how easily I could become merely another aspect of the room: a corpse crumpled on the floor for the maid to find. I thought how smoothly the world would continue to spin in the seconds, in the eons after my death. Then I came out here to sit beneath the fan and record the chattering noise the firing neurons make. Maybe the cliché was simply too abhorrent: some Plathian surrender to despair, and on the anniversary, no less. Reader, I do not know. I can't say if it is bravery or cowardice that makes me cling to something I have no earthly idea how to do. If it is bravery, it is no more than the same bravery that keeps the eyes blinking, or the fan spinning. Call it a preference. Some small but irreducible preference for life over death. Perhaps there, my true heritage as a Jew. That enduring preference, the six thousand years of clinging dumbly to existence, despite all reason.

And now an email. A girl who had been in my residence college at Yale. She works at a gallery in Los Angeles, she informs me, is now going on to graduate school herself. Was just beginning to search for her own replacement when my email arrived. "What a lucky coincidence!" she writes. I knew her only tangentially, I have no graduate degree, I have no experience with or interest in commercial art. So I doubt very much her enthusiasm has much to do with my merits as a job candidate. Or anything like luck. It has to do with what she thinks the date means. But I find I am in no position to refuse. Maybe there is a person the world expects you to be, and all your struggles not to be that person are in vain. In any case, I find there is something I can't escape. I have turned the lights off in the room. Writing by the glow of lights in the parking lot outside. Next I'll close the curtains. Make of the room something dark and narrow. Then I will go to sleep. And in the morning, I will leave as much of this behind as I can. All the people I would have been, should have been. I will leave them here, like a gathering of ghosts. And you, too, reader. I will stop staring at my life and weeping over it. I will accept it as what it will be, I will make a virtue of what it lacks. And nothing more.

III. AMSTERDAM, OR
THE BELLY OF THE WHALE

While he lived in Amsterdam, Jonah was plagued by a recurring dream. The dream took place in a banquet hall of fantastic luxury: chandeliers spreading octopus arms dripping with sparkling diadems above a room lined in molded walnut paneling; tables arrayed with gold flatware, china plates, crystal vases capped with roses of pink and red— all of it of a class he would have thought had sunk with the *Titanic*, as it were; waiters in black tie circling with green-glass bottles of champagne or with trays of caviar and lobster tail poised on the pads of five white-gloved fingers. The guests at this banquet were dressed immaculately in tuxedos and evening gowns, and Jonah found himself seated at a table with Doug Chen, and Aja Puvvada, and other Cunningham Wolf partners. Sylvia was sitting beside him, resplendent in a shimmering dress of pale green, smiling with warmth and satisfaction.

At the front of the hall was a stage and dais, and after a time Lloyd Davis Cooper himself appeared: managing partner of Cunningham Wolf for the last two decades, dressed in a white tuxedo and carrying a large and propitiously ribboned envelope. "The time has come to announce our newest partner," he declared, speaking in the absurdly dignified Boston-gentleman's-club accent familiar to Jonah from the speeches he gave at the firm's annual holiday parties. At his words, the lights dimmed, and spotlights began to wheel across the hall, as though searching for the anointed associate.

At this point, it would occur to Jonah that this was a very unusual way to announce partnership at a law firm. But this thought only sent ripples across the surface of the dream—didn't shatter it—nor did it stop him from feeling a breathless, heart-gripping elation when Lloyd Davis Cooper tore open the envelope and read, "Jonah Jacobstein!" As the spotlights surrounded him and applause filled the hall, tears of happiness would spring to Jonah's eyes—in the dream, and where he slept on the couch in the back of the houseboat.

The partners rose in a standing ovation, Doug Chen nodded in approval. Sylvia beamed, and Jonah kissed her on the lips. Then he stood and walked onto the stage. Lloyd Davis Cooper produced a green jacket and slipped this over Jonah's shoulders. (This latter detail, apparently drawn from watching golf highlights on SportsCenter, was especially baffling to Jonah in his waking life.) He took his place at the dais—triumphant, grateful, ready to thank everyone: his parents, his colleagues, his law school professors, his elementary school teachers, friends, Sylvia, everyone—thank them all so earnestly.

And then he noticed, at the back of the room, a Hasidic Jew, smiling devilishly at him. This man resembled not so much one particular Hasid as he did the idea of any Hasid: He had a Hasid's distinguishing characteristics but in exaggerated, almost caricatured form—like the costume Jonah had worn in eighth grade to play Avram the Bookseller in his junior high school's production of *Fiddler on the Roof.* He was dressed all in black—black overcoat, black hat, oversize black boots—his beard had a sort of gaudy charcoal blueness to it, his *payos* dangled in wild curls. As Jonah met his eyes, the Hasid wagged a finger at him, tapped his nose, wagged his finger again, sharpened his devilish grin. Jonah cleared his throat, returned his attention to the other guests. The spotlights seemed to have brightened; he felt himself getting hot.

"I just want to say . . ." he began. His eyes darted nervously to the back of the hall—but the Hasid had vanished. Relieved, Jonah continued. "I just want to say, that I've learned if you work hard, if you dedicate yourself to a goal and—"

Plunk! Something had struck him on the cheek—soft, round,

somewhat slimy. He looked around, but saw only the expectant faces of partners. "If you dedicate yourself to a goal and commit yourself to—"

Plunk! He was struck again! And this time the off-white, grease-dripping sphere bounced from his forehead and onto the dais—and Jonah saw: He had been hit with a matzo ball.

He quickly wiped the grease from his face, glanced anxiously in the direction of his table. Sylvia was frowning; Doug Chen lifted and lowered his hand in disappointment. "What I mean is, becoming a partner was an ambition of mine for a long time, and if you believe you can accomplish—"

Plunk!

This one struck him right on the nose.

He spotted the Hasid ducking behind a table to the right, tittering fiendishly. "Security!" Jonah yelled. "That man is attacking me!"

The crowd started muttering—and Jonah could tell these were the uncomfortable mutters of an audience losing faith in the speaker. Had no one else noticed the Hasid? Had no one else seen the matzo balls? He plunged ahead. "I worked very hard for this!" he declared.

Plunk!

Jonah looked frantically around the room—the Hasid was nowhere to be seen. "Because I . . ." he resumed, hurriedly wiping his face. He spotted the Hasid doing a leg-kicking Russian folk dance, a bottle balanced on his head. "That man!" Jonah shouted, pointing.

Lloyd Davis Cooper put his hand on Jonah's shoulder. "It would be best if you returned our jacket, young man," he said.

"No, that isn't necessary," Jonah said. He risked a look at his table: Sylvia was gathering her things to leave; Doug Chen went so far as to shake his head perceptibly. Jonah took a wary step back from Lloyd Davis Cooper. "If you just let me—"

With surprising agility for a man in his late sixties (it was known in the office that he remained an excellent tennis player), Lloyd Davis Cooper lunged forward and grabbed the lapel of the jacket. "Our jacket, young man!" he said, pulling.

"It isn't necessary!" Jonah said, pulling back.

As the tug-of-war continued, from the corner of his eye Jonah saw the Hasid poking his head above the lip of the stage, and then, with one flick of his finger, he rolled a matzo ball underneath Jonah's foot. Jonah slipped—he tumbled off the stage and crashed to the floor.

By the time he sat up, the crowd had turned on him fully. Partners started toward him menacingly, made to remove the jacket—and now Scott Baker appeared, smiling amiably as he waved a contract over his head like a pitchfork. Jonah struggled to his feet and ran, the crowd following in hot pursuit.

As Jonah came out of the hall, he found himself running down a stairway—and this ended in an elevator—which brought him to another stairway—which led to still another elevator—and on and on—and never did Jonah feel himself getting any farther from his pursuers. Finally he entered some sort of lobby—vast and deserted and fronted with glass windows many stories high. He raced to the revolving door at the front of the building and pushed through it.

Outside, it was nighttime, and Jonah recognized a busy New York street, across from it the edge of Central Park, at this hour dark past the first clusters of trees. The crowd had started to pour into the lobby behind him. Jonah ran for the park—dodging taxis as he crossed the street—leapt over a low stone wall around the park's edge, and began running blindly over the grass. At last he took refuge behind a tree, panting. For a moment all was quiet. He no longer heard the demands, the complaints, the shouted disappointments of those chasing him. He looked up and saw stars twinkling overhead (the sky in the dream differing in this way from the real, light-polluted sky of New York). Briefly, he felt a sense of escape—an unburdening—a sort of deliverance from—

Plunk!

The Hasid had followed him!—found him!—somehow. He took off through the park, running as fast as he could, but the Hasid was just as fast. Jonah ran and ran—desperately, frantically—enduring continual matzo-ball plunks, moaning in his sleep now—the faint buoyancy of the floorboards in the narrow and low-ceilinged houseboat room perceptible as he awoke, gasping for air.

———

With a wheeze, Jonah jerked up to a seated position, looked around. He took in the foot of the couch where he'd been sleeping, the sheet he'd been sleeping under kicked into a clump at his feet; he took in the thin red curtains, illuminated to a pale pink, over a trio of portholes on the opposite wall. It was several more agitated moments before he could recall where he was, how he had gotten there. He had been in Amsterdam for weeks, and his mind still grasped this fact only imperfectly. Even when he wasn't jarred awake by the dream of the Hasid, he might open his eyes in the dark and flap his arm out, his hand searching for a nightstand and an iPhone that weren't there.

Recollecting now that he was on a houseboat on a canal in Amsterdam—and how this had come to be—he leaned his shoulder back against the couch cushions, caught his breath. Whenever he had the dream, the emotions of it would cling to him upon waking, like cobwebs: the embarrassing joy at being named partner; the anxiety at seeing the Hasid from the stage; the panic and desperation of flight. These dissipated quickly enough, though they gave way to a more durable feeling: bitter vexation that he had had the dream, again. He should have remembered to get high before going to sleep.

He lifted one leg and then the other over the side of the couch—pushed himself up to his feet. He had slept in his clothes, which was not unusual. He picked up his coat from the floor, climbed the narrow spiral stairway in the corner of the room—the only way in or out—and stepped onto the deck of the houseboat. Newsprint-gray clouds hung low and thick overhead. He could tell it had rained earlier, as the wood of the deck was slick and darkened with moisture. He guessed it was mid-afternoon, though it was hard to be certain from the sunless sky; jet lag he had never overcome and smoking weed five times a day had made his sleep patterns irregular.

The houseboat was docked (it hadn't moved in the time Jonah had lived there) on a canal called Brouwersgracht, in a sedate, mostly residential neighborhood northwest of Amsterdam's center. On both sides of the canal stood three- and four-story houses in distinctive Dutch style: narrow and peak-roofed, with painted, thrown-open shutters, tightly crowded together, like dollhouses lining a shelf. Though it was not yet fall, there was an aqueous chill in the air. Jonah put on his

coat, pulled it closed across his chest. He had found this coat at the
Albert Cuyp Market one Saturday, among stalls of cheeses, pirated
European soccer jerseys, faded enamel cookware. It was a Russian
Navy coat, the man selling it had told him in fractured English—was
thick, midnight blue, with ten gold-colored buttons across the front,
each decorated with a tiny anchor. Jonah hadn't brought any warm
clothes with him from New York—nothing so practical as packing
for the weather had been on his mind as he'd dumped armfuls of
clothing from his drawers into a suitcase—and though he understood
its effect was somewhat to make him look like an extra in a low-
budget submarine movie, he'd bought the coat anyway. It evoked for
him a hardiness, a military sufficiency, that he liked to think trans-
posed to him whenever he put it on.

He was bearded now—had stopped shaving when he'd left New
York—this beard dark and full and flecked here and there with individual hairs of gray. He was aware that the beard added to the B-movie
sub-captain impression, but the mass of facial hair gave him a feeling
of sufficiency, too. And anyone who had known him in New York
would have immediately noticed that his nose had acquired a curve
toward its bottom—as though it were fashioned in the shape of an
upside-down question mark. But the only person who knew him prior
to his arrival in Amsterdam was Max, and if Max had noticed, he
hadn't mentioned it.

In one of the pockets of the coat, Jonah found a pack of cigarettes
he didn't remember buying. He hesitated, and then took one out and lit
it. He'd been trying to quit, but smoking as much pot as he did usually
dulled his self-discipline. Anyway, it was a morning after the dream, a
cigarette was forgivable. It would help brush away the cobwebs.

He smoked the cigarette to the filter, made to flick the butt into the
canal. But then he stopped, the butt poised between his thumb and
index finger. The old Roxwood guilt around littering he'd acquired as
a child had kicked in. He looked into the canal: Its water had a kalei-
doscopic quality—might appear brown or green or blue depending on
the time of day, the light in the sky; toward noon it acquired a stripe
of bright reflected sun down its center, at night presented itself as inky
black, edged in plumes of amber street light. He finally put the ciga-

rette out on the bottom of his shoe—looked around with annoyance
for somewhere appropriate to dispose of it, then just shoved the butt
in his pocket.

He walked around to the houseboat's bow—felt fresh annoyance
when he saw Max come up the gangway from the street, lean against
the railing beside it. Jonah had met Max, the renter of the houseboat,
in college. He had a portly build, sandy-blond, unkempt hair, a large
and notably expressive mouth, a round-tipped boyish nose; today was
dressed in jeans and an unbuttoned yellow cardigan. He spread a rolling paper in the palm of his left hand, with the right began breaking up
marijuana buds above it.

"All the great questions have been answered, Rabbi," Max said.
"And it turns out there were no questions at all. Morality is just selfishness by another name, a trick we play on ourselves to give our
genes the best chance of reproduction. Art is sublimated sexual energy,
lust misplaced in clay and sheet music and whatnot. Love is more
sexual energy and reproductive advantage-seeking, it's not even worth
discussing. Humanity itself is just an accident, the result of disinterested physical forces operating the only way they could possibly work.
And as for God? Well, now that IBM has perfected the art of creating
computers whose only function is to demonstrate how dumb we are,
we are fast approaching the moment when a robot opens its eyes,
hears about God, and bursts out laughing because we've held on to a
concept that only ever came about because our prehistoric ancestors
couldn't explain thunder.

"Fortunately, now we can explain everything. How we act is Dar-
winism, how we think is psychology, reality is all in the mind, which is
all chemicals, which is all DNA. And why are we here? Well, there are
an infinite number of universes, so we had to be somewhere."

As he spoke, Max had started rolling the broken-up weed into a
massive joint. "These are wondrous times, Rabbi," he continued. "By
which I mean, they aren't wondrous at all. All the myths have been
dispelled, all the superstitions have been dragged to light, every mystery
can be explained right down to the specific gene sequence from whence
it came. It's like at the end of a *Scooby-Doo* episode when the monster's mask has been pulled off: It was never really a monster, because

there are no monsters, or anything like them. The fear Descartes articulates in his 'First Meditation,' that there is some demon god deceiving his reason, has been entirely put to rest because, needless to say, there are no gods of any kind, demonic or otherwise. Scooby and the gang, in the form of rational, materialist thinking, pulled off God's mask to reveal a mechanism of social control that dovetailed conveniently with a collective fear of death.

"Naturally, there is some melancholy to our era. Of course we miss Santa Claus. Of course we miss the romance of the uncharted, the unknown, the Loch Ness Monster, transubstantiation, the joy of the laughing Buddha, wishing on a star, and so forth. Remember prime time, Rabbi? Remember when the good shows were on? Now we can TiVo it. And yes, our generation had VCRs, but who could work them? Time is irrelevant now, it's just another aspect of the physical world that we've conquered and put entirely to our own uses, like fire."

He licked the joint horizontally, continued. "But even granting the nostalgia for belief, which, I'll add, we'll be the last generation to feel, even granting that, Rabbi, we're better off. We're better off knowing there's nothing else out there. Who wants to be forever searching the sky for locusts and frogs? Who wants to check under the bed every night for monsters?

"And don't misunderstand me," he said, waving the finished joint for emphasis. "I freely concede we have no shortage of monsters. I am the first to admit to all of humanity's barbarism, its innate cruelty, its unquenchable bloodlust. But at least we've given the problem the clarity of cliché: The enemy is us, man's greatest predator is man, the fault not in our stars but in ourselves, and so on. When we consider the cycles of genocide, the torture memos, the suicide bombers, isn't it better to know that it's just us? That we're doing it all ourselves? Not to mention the calamities of the physical world, the tsunamis and famines and African pandemics. Isn't it preferable to know that it isn't malevolence we're facing, but simply indifference? That the volcano wiping out your village has no more malice than gravity?

"No, what is scary, what is truly terrifying, is to think there could be some higher power that allows it. A higher power that wills it!" He lit the joint, took a long hit—his face was entirely still for several seconds, then he exhaled through his nose. "It's the ultimate fear, Rabbi. It's the old Cartesian fear. At the bottom of all of it: God's winking emoticon."

He shook his head hastily, as if shooing the thought away. "Rabbi, your beliefs are like the creepy old uncle at the family reunion everyone wishes would hurry up and die. This notion that there is a God. That under the monster mask is a real monster. That there are vast tracts of existence we have no idea about. It's frightening, it's undemocratic, and it's anti-humanist. Really, it's offensive. You're a traitor to your species is the bottom line. To say that there are things we don't know, when everyone knows we now know everything . . ." He shook his head again, this time with shame. "Honestly, Rabbi, who do you think you are?"

"Don't call me 'Rabbi,'" Jonah muttered—knowing this injunction would be ignored, just as it always was.

Jonah often thought that if he'd made one mistake since coming to Amsterdam, it had been telling Max, shortly after his arrival, about the circumstances of his departure from New York. But he had been a wreck during those first days: by turns manic, weepy, enraged, despondent. Finally he had needed someone to talk to, and Max was the only person in the city he knew.

They hadn't been friends in college, exactly. There was a consistent slipperiness to Max's character that Jonah had always found a little off-putting. At Vassar, Max had a reputation for getting into shouting debates with professors in the most banal of courses (Spanish I, Introduction to Structural Engineering); for chanting lustily at campus protests, abruptly joining the counterprotests, then chanting just as lustily for the other side. Since college, Max reported he'd hiked the Annapurna Circuit in Nepal, worked at a start-up in Silicon Valley, most recently won a Fulbright to study Spinoza in Amsterdam, with which he funded his life on the houseboat—none of this suggesting to Jonah that Max had embraced a newfound earnestness in his postgrad existence. Still, they'd had a few long and memorable dorm room conversations in their time, and when Jonah had contacted Max, he'd welcomed him to live in the houseboat's back room.

Jonah hadn't told him all the details of what happened in New

York. Even if he'd wanted to describe the specifics of what he'd seen, and all it had led to, he'd been too drunk and high at the time of telling to relate it coherently. But Max had gotten the essentials: visions, voices, Hebrew. He had at least respected Jonah's request not to tell anyone else, though he had decidedly not respected his request not to bring it up at every turn: calling him "Rabbi," delivering discursive monologues on religion and Scooby-Doo and whatever else came to his mind, and generally prodding Jonah and pushing his buttons in order to elicit—Jonah was not sure what, exactly. It was possible that Max didn't know himself.

In any case, nothing Jonah said in response to the provocations ever satisfied Max, so Jonah had given up trying. "Can I have a hit off that?" he asked, nodding his chin toward the joint.

Max let out a predictably disappointed sigh and took a hit himself. "Why don't you just curse God and die, already?"

"What, and miss these little chats?" Jonah responded.

Max smiled at this. Then, brightening further, he said, "I had good luck at the Van Gogh Museum this morning, Rabbi. An exercise-science major from California." Max often trolled Amsterdam's more popular tourist attractions for American women abroad, frequently with great success. "Really, with these college girls, it's so easy even you could do it. Just mention you know where the locals smoke and they're ready to take off their North Face jackets and money belts and go at it right there underneath *The Raising of Lazarus*."

"You should write that up for TripAdvisor."

"Why don't you come with me today, Rabbi?" Max offered. "I'm sure she could produce a friend-for-my-friend from the hostel. We're eating at De Bolhoed, and then we're coming back here to get high." He grinned and said, "Well, Rabbi?"

Jonah had long observed that Max's face had an unusual capacity to form two expressions at once: an expression and a comment on that expression—as though the look in his green eyes could effect a footnote to the look on his face. The smile he now gave Jonah was most immediately lascivious, suggestive, but it also managed to be a caricature of such a smile—as if to mock the smiles that men gave each other to indicate their intentions toward women.

However the smile was meant to be taken, though, the invitation didn't appeal to Jonah. He had no interest lately in meeting women, flirting with women—nor even in sex: He found he'd developed a strong aversion to seeing anyone new naked. On the few instances when he had given in and accompanied Max on his rendezvous with tourists, been matched with a friend-for-my-friend, he'd felt uncomfortable the entire time, increasingly dispirited—not least because one of the women inevitably reminded him of Sylvia, or Zoey, or both. "I think I'll pass," he said.

"Better things to do?"

Jonah shrugged. "I was going to smoke, then maybe check out the botanical gardens." He hadn't specifically been thinking of visiting the botanical gardens, but they were on the vague list of potential activities that represented the closest thing in his life to a schedule.

Max tapped ash from the joint thoughtfully. "Who knew you had an interest in horticulture?"

"Right, I'd be better off spending my time cruising for girls outside the Heineken Brewery," Jonah answered, irritated.

"That would be a good place to do it," Max mused. He took another hit, then asked abruptly, "Rabbi, do you remember History of Western Philosophy, with Professor Marquez? The week we covered Nietzsche, you were practically delirious with indignation. All that will-to-power stuff, it was like you took it personally. You wouldn't stand for it. Even Marquez was impressed with your *contra* Nietzsche diatribes." In fact, Jonah didn't remember: didn't remember any diatribes, barely remembered anything about Nietzsche. "Or do you remember how you used to stand on the bar in the Mug and do Jäger bombs? You used to do Jäger bombs in the Mug with such conviction, Rabbi."

Max had assumed an almost wistful look. All Jonah could think to say was, "What the fuck does that have to do with me going to the botanical gardens?"

Max opened his mouth to answer—then made a show of changing his mind about whatever he was going to say. "Nothing. Of course nothing. Have it your way, Rabbi," he said. "Smoke your weed, stroll among your exotic trees. Who did it ever hurt, right? As for myself,

I'm going to get ready to introduce a young lady from California to dear, dirty Amsterdam." He casually dropped what remained of the joint into the canal, then pulled open the door at the bow to the stairs beneath, walked down into the houseboat.

Jonah remained on the deck, pulled uneasily at one of the buttons of his coat. He took out and lit another cigarette—for warmth this time, he told himself. The problem was that you could never precisely trace the trajectory of Max's innuendo, his irony. This was intentional, of course—tactical: He didn't want you to know what the fuck he was getting at. And this inevitably left you feeling exposed— even if you had no cause to.

Besides, Jonah thought further, there was a quite obvious reason he might be feeling anxious, beyond anything Max had said, beyond even having woken up from the dream: He hadn't gotten high yet today. Smoking as regularly as he did now, sobriety inevitably became a little uncomfortable—its perceptions a bit too aggressive, too sharp-edged. He wasn't proud of this, but at least there was a simple solution. Within a ten-minute walk of where he stood there were a dozen coffeeshops, each with its own menu of among the best strains of marijuana on the planet. He didn't intend to spend the majority of his waking hours stoned for the rest of his life—but for as long as he was doing that, he was in the right place.

So, he thought, weed, but breakfast first—a good way to start any day, and indeed, the way he started nearly every day.

He buttoned his coat, then walked down the houseboat's gangway and onto the cobbled street running beside the canal. The streets of this neighborhood were always quiet, but were especially so at this hour of the afternoon, in this weather. Only occasionally did people ride by him on bicycles; other than an elderly woman carrying bags of groceries over a half-moon bridge up the canal, he didn't see anyone out walking. He could hear birds chirping—still a pleasantly unusual sound to him after so many years of living in Midtown Manhattan— the distant low of a canal boat's air horn.

At Lindengracht, he turned and came to the little red-awninged bakery he preferred, went inside and ordered from the apple-cheeked, middle-aged woman behind the counter. He'd come in enough times that she recognized him—always smiled with nebulous sympathy when he tried to order his coffee and croissant in Dutch. He was aware his accent was terrible, and this handful of words represented pretty much all of the language he knew, but even so—it still felt like an accomplishment when she handed him the steaming paper cup, the bag with the warm pastry inside. He took these back onto the street, and ate, as he always did, leaning against a lamppost overlooking the water.

This experience of Amsterdam was far different from his previous visit, backpacking through Europe after his junior year of college. Then he and his friends had spent their time getting drunk and high in the noisy coffeeshops around the train station, wandering the Rijksmuseum while tripping on mushrooms, gawking and laughing at the prostitutes in the red-lighted windows in the Red Light District. He'd imagined finding that sort of drug-fueled oblivion when he decided to come here. Instead, he'd found a much more pacific existence: living on the couch in the back of the houseboat, getting high alone as often as with anyone else, and spending his days in pursuit of whatever he identified as his whim—which typically meant spending his days not doing much of anything at all: sitting in Vondelpark and listening to Toots and the Maytals, working on the KenKen in the *International Herald Tribune*, or, as today, visiting the botanical gardens. It was still drug-fueled oblivion, only in a much more tranquil key. And—dreams and Max's soliloquies notwithstanding—he believed this version of Amsterdam had turned out to be just the refuge he'd needed after the disasters of New York.

It wasn't only refuge from the visions he felt he'd found here, either. It was refuge from the whole of his New York life. Indeed, from the perspective of munching a croissant at some indeterminate hour of the afternoon—watching, as he did now, a pair of ducks paddling up the canal—that life seemed ludicrous to him: getting up in the dark to work an eighteen-hour day at Cunningham Wolf; going to sleep on the floor in front of his desk, waking up three hours later to do it all again; meeting Zoey for an hour in her apartment, showering, taking a cab to be on time for dinner with Sylvia that night. It had even occurred to him that the visions had simply been his overburdened brain's way of crying uncle. The fact was, since he'd come to Amsterdam, there hadn't been any visions. He didn't think there would be any, either. The weed, he sensed, had a suppressive effect here, but even more than that, the atmosphere of Amsterdam didn't seem conducive to them—to the sort of pitiless exposure that characterized them. Everything here felt less urgent, less consequential: the canals, the cobblestones, the long northern twilights, the uniform flower boxes beneath every window. He perceived a kind of gentleness, a safety to the city, even on the rare occasion when he wasn't stoned. Amsterdam's very location reinforced this idea for him—tucked, as it were, in an upper corner of Europe.

He didn't plan on remaining here forever, of course. He figured that at some point he would return to America, start up again with his career, with dating, with all of it. But really, these plans were no more specific than those he'd had for what he'd do today when he'd gone to bed the night before. He sometimes imagined building a new life for himself in San Francisco—that city had a reputation for gentleness, too. There was no rush to decide anything, however. Every two weeks his checking account was fattened with another direct deposit from Cunningham Wolf. He could live in Amsterdam for a year off what he made in a month—easily—and that didn't even take into account his savings. He was single, he was unemployed—he owed nothing to anyone. He was allowed to get high in Amsterdam for as long as he wanted. As Max himself had said: Who did it hurt?

He threw out the croissant bag and empty cup in a wastebasket on the corner (every day the same wastebasket) and from Lindengracht headed east, into the Canal Ring—the quartet of canals radiating from the teardrop-shaped center of the city. It had gotten colder; a mistiness filled the air. He pulled the collar of his coat closed tighter around his throat.

Walking south down Herengracht, he arrived at a coffeeshop called Amnesia. It occupied the ground floor of a narrow building on the corner of the block—its door and the frames of its windows painted black, the windows themselves and a sign above the entrance etched with the coffeeshop's name in stately gold lettering. It had the look of a place that in New York would have been in the West Village, sold bespoke shoes, and Jonah had always appreciated the sophisticated restraint of this exterior—in marked contrast to the façades of so many other coffeeshops, seeking to lure in tourists with neon and cartoon animal logos.

He was reaching for the door when a group of people came out. He recognized them as being among a loose collection of expats Max had introduced him to; they often came by the houseboat for afternoons of bong hits, chess, and alt hip-hop. It was a sociable, easygoing crew—about what Jonah would have expected of people who had made getting high every day the practice not of weeks, but of years. And as they greeted him with an assortment of nonchalant heys and pats on the shoulder, Jonah found he was enormously glad to run into this group of his fellow travelers.

"Why are you out in this shit weather?" asked one, named Rafik, scowling up at the misty sky. He was Turkish, about Jonah's age, his head shaved and a Rastafied lion tattooed on the back of his neck.

"I was just going in to buy a gram of something, then go to smoke in the botanical gardens," Jonah answered.

Rafik let out a dubious chortle. "In the rain, man?" Somehow it hadn't occurred to Jonah that this would, in fact, be a terrible day to visit the botanical gardens.

"I think there'll be greenhouses and shit," he mumbled.

They were joined by another member of the group, named Geoff— British, an aspiring filmmaker, with a mop of curly brown hair that in appearance shaved even another year or two off his twenty-odd age. "Max was here before," Geoff told Jonah. "Had a girl with him, too. Wasn't half bad."

"Only an American girl would go to Amsterdam and hook up with the first other American she meets," Rafik snorted. He had varied— and, to Jonah's mind, not altogether consistent—complaints about America. He'd described his background to Jonah once: had left Turkey for Sweden with his brother when he was a teenager, bounced around Oslo, Copenhagen, London, briefly held some regional position in the German Green Party—at some point had made his way to Amsterdam. "American girls only ever look at white guys, anyway," he added.

"Yeah, but I'm fuckin' white, too," Geoff responded, and he and Rafik laughed.

Cigarettes were being passed around. Jonah was glad for the excuse (sociability) to have another. "Forget about the fucking gardens, though," Rafik said. He gestured with his cigarette to where a few others were standing nearer the canal. "Paul got some coke. A lot of coke. Good coke." Paul, an American who had only recently started coming by the houseboat, presently stood—hovered—near the edge of the cluster of people Rafik had indicated, wearing a grease-stained sweatshirt and torn cargo pants. He was spindly, fidgety, and had an unswerving puppylike friendliness—but was maybe a bit too friendly, a bit too puppylike in demeanor; he lacked the patina of cool the others had. And, it occurred to Jonah, he was almost always broke.

"I'm glad we ran into you, matter of fact, Jonah," Geoff now said, in a not quite offhand way. "What did you think of the new draft of *The Quest* I dropped off?"

The Quest was the movie Geoff had (ostensibly) come to Amsterdam to make; Jonah had already acquiesced to reading two different versions of the hundred-seventy-five-page script, knew there was a third waiting for him somewhere on the houseboat. The movie told (in great detail) the story of a young British man's road trip across Europe, and his search for love, or nirvana, or something; there was a lot of sex, and a lot of descriptions of sunsets. The others in the group showed a lot of enthusiasm for the project—had all been promised roles on set when the time came to make it—but Jonah couldn't help feeling skeptical about *The Quest*'s prospects. From what he could tell, the script was never finished, and only the actresses had been cast.

"I actually didn't get to it yet, I've been . . ." Jonah began—but could hardly claim to have been busy.

"Right, right, when you get the time," Geoff said, nodding sharply with each monosyllabic word. Jonah had observed that Geoff had the fragile ego of a much more accomplished artist.

"So how'd Paul get good coke?" Jonah asked, trying to change the subject.

"Sold his bicycle," Rafik snickered.

Paul, as if sensing that they were talking about him, left those by the canal and walked up to the three of them. As he raised his hand in greeting, he dropped the cigarette he'd been holding. Rafik snickered again. Paul smiled sheepishly, glancing into each of their faces in turn, reached down to retrieve it.

"We were just talking about how we're going to party tonight, brother," Geoff said.

Paul broke into a wide smile. "They told you, Jonah?" Paul asked. Jonah nodded. "We're going to go over to Marcus's and just do the coke I got for, like, three hours. You're gonna come, right?"

Jonah had done coke a couple of times during his summer associateships, when it had appeared at parties. He'd liked it well enough—though its brain-buzzy, hyperenergized high held absolutely no attraction for him now. But more than that, as he looked at Paul's eager smile—something troubled him about the whole situation. "You should just make sure you save some for yourself, since you paid for it," was what he came out with.

They were not a group prone to awkward silences—but Jonah had evidently managed to create one with this comment. Rafik folded his arms, scowling; Geoff eyed him with undisguised hostility. For his part, Paul looked almost hurt. "Why would I want to do that?" he said to Jonah. "These are my friends."

"Yeah, of course, no, I only meant . . ."

He was rescued from having to finish this sentence when one of the group by the canal called, "Hey, shut up you guys, listen." A woman had spoken; she had pasty skin, long, unwashed blond hair, wore an oversize Melvins T-shirt. "Listen, listen," she urged. Watching her gaze down the canal with a stoner's airy fixation, stalks of greasy hair falling across her face, Jonah couldn't help thinking that there could not be a woman more different from Sylvia—that she was almost a parody of Sylvia. But why the hell was he thinking about Sylvia? he asked himself. From somewhere, Jonah heard faintly a synthesized beat, melodic piano, a rhythmic male voice.

"American corporate rap," Rafik announced.

"Tupac got shot, how could he be corporate?" another in the group answered, and they all laughed.

"No, shut up, shut up, I love this song," the Sylvia doppelgänger said. She closed her eyes, smiling placidly, tilted her cheek toward the canal—where on the opposite side, Jonah now recognized, the music was being played from a radio strapped to the back of a bicycle. The rider had stopped for something, but now he got back on, and began to pedal leisurely again. The blond woman kept pace with the rider, with the music—started to dance in a slow circle, her eyes still closed. The others laughed some more at this, and a few started dancing, too—Paul jumping around the street rather in the manner of a bee's waggle dance—while others began to sing the chorus.

And watching them all singing and dancing their way down the canal, Jonah suddenly wondered: Who are these people? A Turkish leftist Rastafarian bully; a would-be filmmaker endlessly tweaking the dialogue of his mammoth movie script; and Paul, a very kind person who in his kindness had just sold his only possession of value for a night's worth of coke. It was as though they had all washed up on the shore of the city, on the banks of the canal—refugees—castaways. And no, no movie or anything else tangible would likely come from their time here. But what did they care? This smidge of Amsterdam—circumscribed by this street, this afternoon, this fun—was enough. And Jonah felt jealous, watching them dance.

Soon the bicyclist headed down a side street, and the group rounded a corner in the opposite direction and was out of sight. Jonah stood looking down Herengracht for another moment. Then he turned toward the door of the coffeeshop.

And then he saw him!—the Hasid!—standing on the deck of a passing canal boat—tapping his nose, wagging his finger. Jonah took a lurching step forward. But no, it wasn't—no, of course it wasn't. It was just a man dressed in a dark overcoat, smoking a cigarette as the canal boat disappeared beneath a bridge.

As always in these moments, Jonah first looked around in embarrassment to see if anyone had noticed his distress. But even as he did, he understood that the only person there to comprehend the embarrassment of it, and the perturbation, and the fear, and the pall of futility it seemed to leave hanging in the air like the present mist—was him.

No, there hadn't been any visions in Amsterdam. But the day after he'd had the dream—sometimes, if he was honest, even several days after—he might catch sight of the Hasid: spot the devilish grin among the crowd waiting for a tram, or see him in the window of a distant Dutch row house, holding up a matzo ball—teasingly, tauntingly. He always vanished in an instant, almost in the moment of apprehension turned out to be someone else. Yet this never stopped Jonah from reflexively believing in the next sighting—or from feeling inexplicable instants of surprise when the Hasid turned out not to have been there once again.

He grabbed in his pocket for a cigarette, realized he already had one between his fingers. He took a drag until he began to cough—shallow, rasping. He didn't know when he'd developed a smoker's cough.

There were moments in Amsterdam—when he would unthinkingly lift two euro coins from his pocket, identifying them by weight, not finding in them anything unfamiliar, exotic; when he would be on his second joint of the night in the back of a coffeeshop, and a Bob Marley song would come on, and meet his high at just the right point—and in such moments Jonah could believe he occupied his life as fully, as naturally, as any of those he'd just watched dancing along the canal. He could believe he had gotten far away from everything he'd sought to escape.

But then he'd see the Hasid again; he'd notice a clock and subtract six hours and imagine what was happening right then, in New York. And in these moments—which had the force of unlooked-for clarity— he would apprehend himself as having established nothing, escaped nothing, having merely hidden in the midst of it—and in a hiding place so fragile, so tenuous, so alien to himself, that it was only a matter of time before it collapsed around him. He didn't know what this collapse would look like: further visions, deeper visions; or a giving over to the churn of emotions that had accompanied losing Sylvia, losing Zoey, losing his career, the whole catastrophe. Whatever it might be, though, it felt suddenly, ominously imminent as he stood there on the damp street.

How would this end? he asked himself.

There was really only one thing to do, though, when these moods came over him—only one way he'd found to steady his nerves, regain

what passed for his peace of mind: get high. He had been on his way
to do this anyway, of course—but you could grow weary of your own
pleasures, he'd learned. He still liked smoking pot, in a straightforward way. But getting high defensively, needing to do it in order to
feel better—at some point, it became pretty depressing. But then, for
better or worse, getting high would help mute these feelings, too. After
a couple of hits, he'd be able to convince himself that the Hasid was
just a typical, tolerable symptom of ordinary bad dreams—something
that could happen to anyone. He'd reaffirm that he liked being here,
that it made sense. And in the end, he would still go to the botanical
gardens.

He had his hand on the door of the coffeeshop when he realized
for the second time he'd forgotten about the cigarette he was smoking. Coffeeshops didn't allow cigarettes—a rule the logic of which he
could appreciate, but which in practice struck him as utterly absurd.
He took a last few impatient puffs, and fat, cold raindrops began to
fall on the cobbles at his feet, into the canal, down his nose. He lifted
his arm to toss the cigarette away—was seized by the same ingrained
reluctance as earlier. He let out an audible, frustrated growl—at, he
supposed, the inescapability of being himself. The rain started to fall
faster. He saw that a few doors down was the recessed entrance to a
hotel, and he ran over to take cover.

As he huddled into the alcove of the hotel's doorway, the rain
began to come down so heavily the water looked as if it formed a
great unbroken stream from sky to street. Its spray still dampened
his coat and face; he pressed himself more closely against the wall.
Someone hurried into the alcove and stood by the glass of the hotel's
windows a few feet away from him: a woman, tall, with short blond
hair, wearing a belted trench coat and carrying a blue purse that he
recognized (from being dragged into Saks on umpteen Sundays) as
being very expensive. She brushed some of the water from the top of
this purse with the back of her hand, then opened it, took out a slender guidebook—its title, *Amsterdam's Museums and Galleries*, written in English. She opened the guidebook to an illustrated map of the
city's larger streets, scrutinized it for several moments, then lifted her

eyes, her brows knit ruminatively—as though trying to decipher something in the wall of rain before her.

If not for the English guidebook, he would have assumed she was Swedish or Danish, as there was a precise, modeled quality to her features, which he associated with Nordic faces. When she looked back down to the map, he saw a black mole set on her cheek like a tiny flake of ash.

It occurred to him that he was staring—and as it did, she noticed it, too—glanced briefly, unwelcomingly, in his direction. But then her gaze lingered—she looked over his face as though she suspected she knew him from somewhere. He realized it was this suspicion that had made him take an interest in her, too, though with her face's various peculiarities—the scalp-short hair, the mole, the black eyes—he figured he'd have remembered her.

She turned back to the map. Then, without looking at him, she said, *"Ihre Nase war gebrochen."*

"Sorry, I don't speak . . ," he answered.

She looked at him again for a moment. "Your nose was broken," she said, with neat elocution and vaguely academic disinterest.

It was undoubtedly an odd way to strike up a conversation—and maybe because it was so unusual, he replied with unusual frankness, "Yeah, about a month ago."

"Mine was, too," she told him, studying the map again. He took this as permission to study her nose more closely, and as he did, she said, "I had rhinoplasty."

It was this nose, he deduced, that gave her face the prevailing synthetic look he'd observed: ruler straight, mathematically symmetrical. "How did it happen?"

After hesitating a moment, she said, "Someone hit me with something."

"Yeah, me too," he answered—finding this coincidence odd, as well. She had returned her attention to the street before them. "Where are you trying to get to?" he asked her. "I actually live in Amsterdam . . ."

Again she hesitated—then reached into her expensive purse and handed him a torn piece of paper with an address written on it. "You're on the wrong end of the city," he told her.

"I thought if I followed Herengracht . . ."

"You must've followed it the wrong direction." She nodded, looked back at the map with a certain antagonism. The rain had started to taper off a little, the cigarette had by now burned almost to the filter: He'd soon be able to head into the coffeeshop. But on the other hand— he had nothing urgent to do that day; had nothing urgent to do for the foreseeable future. And whether because she was American, or because of their noses, or because of the prevailing peculiarity of the whole encounter, he found he'd developed some affinity for her— though only, he thought, to the degree that he'd prefer not to smoke his first joint of the day while imagining her wandering around in the rain. "It's not very far, if you want I can show you," he offered.

She glanced back and forth from street to map repeatedly, then pulled back the sleeve of her coat, as well, to check her watch: elegant, with an orange strap, also clearly expensive. He was about to tell her it was all the same to him whether she accepted his help or not, when she finally said, "Yes, that would be very helpful, thank you."

The rain was still coming down heavily enough that they had to wait at least another minute or two before setting out. They stood side by side, watching the rainy street—as if waiting for elevator doors to open. "So is this an art gallery you're going to?" he asked her.

"My cousin has an art show here," she told him. "I worked in art for many years, and there were other pieces I wanted to see while I was visiting."

"You don't work in art anymore?"

"I work in real estate in Las Vegas," she answered, in a mechanical way—as though it was an answer she'd rehearsed.

The reply was another surprise, though he wasn't sure at this point what answer he'd expected. Somehow the details of her appearance, her behavior, weren't cohering into a personality he could make sense of. But at the same time, there remained something ticklingly familiar about her.

The rain had soon dwindled to a light drizzle. "Well, if you're in a hurry, you want to get going?"

"Yes," she answered, "let's."

"I'm Jonah, by the way."

"Judy," she said in reply.

He led them from the doorway, south down Herengracht. The air remained misty, the cobbles of the street slick beneath their feet. His companion kept her eyes down, walked in her high heels with a certain conscientiousness, neither clumsy nor graceful, her trench coat falling abruptly down the slope of her thin shoulders. Jonah still had the cigarette butt between his fingers—eventually stamped out the last of its embers on one of the metal posts demarcating the sidewalk, put the butt in his pocket. She watched him do this but didn't comment. "Sorry, but I keep thinking I know you from somewhere," he said to her. "Did you go to Vassar?"

"Yale," she replied, and seemed to observe how he would react to this. It was a tic he had noticed in many Ivy League graduates—Yale and Harvard alums in particular.

"Well, I'm pretty sure you didn't go to Jewish summer camp," he continued.

But here she smiled a little and answered, "Camp Ramah, as a matter of fact."

"No shit? I did three summers at Tel Yehudah."

"I was a BBG girl."

"I was in BBYO."

They had reached Raadhuisstraat, the major thoroughfare on the western side of the city. It was only two lanes of car traffic and a pair of tram tracks, but it was still the street in this part of Amsterdam that reminded Jonah most of New York. They waited for a tram to pass; then, as they continued along Herengracht, she said, "Did your rabbi ever tell those Yiddish folk stories? And no matter what else happened, they always ended in complete ambiguity?"

"Yeah, my rabbi used to love those. 'And then Rabbi Ben Shmuel looked at his donkey, and it was already sunrise. The end.'"

She smiled more fully. "That stuff was fun, wasn't it?" Jonah recalled climbing into a sleeping bag with Shira Friedburg at a BBYO initiation sleepover. Yes, he thought: fun. But from the pensive look that had entered her face, it was clear she had a different kind of fun in mind. "They make it simple, don't they, when you're young?"

"Make what simple?"

"Belonging, I suppose," she said after a moment. "Belief. They don't have to account yet for the fact that the most potent experiences in life end up making what they tell you less believable, not more." She appeared to reconsider with embarrasment what she'd just said. "Sorry. I don't usually get the chance to talk to . . ."

He guessed she meant "other Jews"—but the conversation was now approaching topics he had absolutely no interest in pursuing. They crossed a bridge where Herengracht was intersected by an east–west street, Huidenstraat—and Jonah saw they were only a canal east of an alley, halfway down, which was his favorite coffeeshop in the city: a three-tabled space with wooden floors, a vaulted wooden ceiling, dim lighting—the overall impression cozily reminiscent of a nineteenth-century inn. A few steps from this, at one end of the alley, was a bakery that made fresh *Stroopwafels,* thin, crunchy waffles enclosing a layer of caramel—a sort of gastronomically elevated Twix bar; the alley's opposite end opened onto a small stone plaza, lined by shops and cafés, never crowded, with benches and pigeons and a bookstore that sold English-language magazines and newspapers. You could spend hours, entire days, even—and Jonah had—smoking in the coffeeshop, eating warm *Stroopwafels,* reading a magazine in the square, watching the pigeons, going back to the coffeeshop and doing it all again. The urge to do this now manifested itself as a physical tug, as though the alley had taken on the physics of a black hole. They were not far from the street she was trying to reach, it would be difficult not to find it from here; the rain had stopped, the light behind the cloud-domed sky had even brightened a little. This would, in other words, be a reasonable place at which to say goodbye.

But instead, Jonah decided to keep walking with her—and before he could ask himself why, he reminded himself he didn't need a reason.

The canal they followed began to loop gently to the east, turning like a second hand sweeping the wrong way down the bottom of a clock. "What do you do in Amsterdam?" she asked him.

"Well, right now I'm sort of—taking a sabbatical," he told her, settling on the term he'd used to explain what he was doing here to his parents.

"You're a professor?" she asked.

"Uh, no, I'm a lawyer. I mean, I was a lawyer. Well, it's not like I got disbarred or anything, I mean I used to be a corporate lawyer, in New York. But now I'm . . . on a sabbatical." He recognized how uncomfortable he sounded—but if the answer struck her as strange, she didn't show it. And so, almost as a test—to see if he could—he told her, "My life got pretty fucked up a little while ago. My job, too. It was the same day my nose got broken, if you can believe it."

"I can believe it," she replied matter-of-factly—as though the question hadn't been rhetorical, as though he'd really been asking.

And he didn't break out in a cold sweat, he didn't feel compelled to make a beeline for the coffeeshop in the alley. It was a good sign that he'd been able to share this, he told himself, even if only with a stranger. It showed he was—settling into things. But he'd risked as much as he was prepared to risk, and as they turned down Nieuwe Spiegelstraat—the street written on the paper she'd shown him—he felt prepared to return to his accustomed comforts.

The designated door was metal, unmarked, stood among a line of shops and galleries in the colonnade of a brick building, stretching almost the length of the short block. They stopped before the door, not speaking. By rights it was an awkward moment, though it did not feel exactly awkward to Jonah—more that they couldn't quite find a way to resolve it.

"Thank you for walking me," she said at length.

"Yeah, it was nice talking to you," he told her sincerely. He didn't really talk to anyone in Amsterdam, he recognized, not in any meaningful way: certainly not to the expat crew, and his interactions with Max were in many ways the opposite of real conversation. But this lack was hardly accidental, he reminded himself. "Good luck with everything in Las Vegas."

"Thank you."

And that, he figured, would be that. Whatever was to be gained or lost by never seeing her again, he would gain or lose it now. He would head to the coffeeshop in the alley—and, he thought without much enthusiasm, he would go to the botanical gardens. The only consequence of their meeting would be that he'd want to be sure to get high before going to sleep tonight.

"I don't suppose you like art," she blurted out. And to his greatest surprise yet, she blushed—blushed through her determinedly neutral expression, through the makeup he now noticed covered her cheeks.

He was struck by the bravery this blush suggested had been required of her to make this half offer—and, in a rush of sympathy, he leapt out to meet her the rest of the way. "Of course, who doesn't? I'd love to see your cousin's stuff."

And they went inside.

Immediately behind the door was an alcove of heavy curtains, and beyond this the room was dark—the lights lowered to an indistinct glow, the walls painted black. All around the dim space were hung Polaroid photographs, each one illuminated by a single spotlight. A female voice spoke over a sound system in hushed tones, and after a few moments Jonah recognized that this voice was reciting biblical verses. Looking closer, Jonah saw that on the Polaroids were drawn graffiti-style renderings of religious iconography: halos, crosses, a caricature Jesus, and so forth. The first picture he studied closely showed a group of young women smiling as they danced on a table at a club, each adorned with a pair of angel's wings.

He would have found all this more uncomfortable if he had not regarded it as so thoroughly bad. He had no pretensions about understanding modern art—he figured it was possible that this show was actually brilliant by some aesthetic principle he had no idea about. But as far as he was concerned, it just wasn't any good—and this opinion provided him a kind of safety as he moved around the space. He passed an apple orchard with snakes drawn around the trees, a haloed Taylor Swift playing guitar onstage.

Judy moved more slowly through the room, giving each Polaroid more attention. If it had been his cousin's artwork, he figured he might have done so, too. But now he was stung by another group of thoughts he tried to avoid: He'd sent Becky a dozen emails since he'd left New York, called her as many times. She hadn't responded to any of it. His father told him that, from what he knew, she was doing fine—whatever that meant.

A young woman in a navy dress now approached him—dyed cherry-red hair piled on top of her head, a mélange of brightly colored tattoos running up and down both arms. "Do you want some wine or anything?" she asked him in accentless English, evidently guessing he was not a Dutch native.

"No, I'm all right," he answered.

"Okay. Thanks a lot for coming," she said, with a light, sincere smile.

"Oh, you're like a . . ."

"I'm the artist. Margaretha Klein van Dijk."

"Oh, cool. Yeah, this is all . . . really impressive."

She shrugged good-naturedly. "It's no big deal. The sublime and the mundane or whatever. My dad paid for it. He feels guilty about everything."

Jonah didn't know how he was meant to respond to this, so he told her, "I came here with your cousin, Judy."

She looked puzzled for a moment—then parted her lips in comprehension. "She told me people call her that. It didn't really register as something that could actually happen."

"Right," Jonah said.

"I can't wrap my mind around her hair, either. Like, what that whole process must have been like."

"I only just met her."

She looked at him kindly. "I'm glad. You have a really nice aura."

"No, no," he clarified quickly, "we really only just met, we're not—anything."

But she had turned to look over to where Judy—or whatever she ought to be called—was studying one of the Polaroids. "She never got over what happened to her parents. That's why her hair is all fucked up." She looked back at Jonah. "Don't tell her I said that, okay?" He nodded. He wanted her to think he knew what she was talking about so that she wouldn't tell him what she was talking about. "The one thing I learned in rehab is that it's the people who have their shit together who take that stuff the hardest. Have you noticed that?"

"Yup," he said, again hoping agreement would preempt any elaboration.

"I know you guys can't stay long. I'm going to go say goodbye. But I'm going to tell her what a good aura you have." Then she smiled again, and walked over to her cousin.

He watched them exchange a few words; Margaretha gave Judy an eager, full-bodied hug, which was returned stiffly. If there was a family resemblance, it was difficult to see, even assuming the noses had been a closer match pre-rhinoplasty: They seemed so starkly different in disposition, in mannerism. Margaretha, for instance, would have fit in well with the expat crew—while Judy—who the fuck knew where she would fit in? He began coughing his smoker's cough. How had he ended up in this art gallery? He headed to the door to save everyone this disruption of the show's atmosphere.

"Is it nothing to you, all who pass by?" the disembodied voice said over the speakers as he went out.

There remained a general dampness to things outside. Water dripped from the front of the colonnade, tiny rivulets flowed into puddles at the edge of the street. Jonah's coughing petered out. Then he lit a cigarette, because—because he fucking wanted to. He leaned against one of the colonnade's pillars as he smoked. He felt tired in a nonspecific way—tired of all of everything.

A few minutes later he heard the door open behind him, and Judy appeared. One of her hands was balled in a fist at her hip, and, makeup or not, her face had taken on a perceptible pallor. "Are you okay?" he asked.

She turned and looked at him as though she'd forgotten he might be there and, reminded, wished he wasn't. "You didn't have to wait," she said coldly.

And Jonah found he was ready to return this coldness. "Yeah, well," he said, and held up the cigarette.

The silence that followed was awkward—and it was too bad their encounter would have to end this way, he thought. Something sterile and amicable would have been preferable—what they would have had if they'd parted at the alley, after all.

She stared down one end of the street, turned her head to look to the opposite end. Then she said to him, "You asked before what I did?" He nodded. "I work for a shell company that's secretly buying property in downtown Las Vegas for one of the biggest casino developers in the country."

"So you buy out, like, bankrupt condo developments?" he asked after a moment.

"Right now I'm buying out a church," she said simply.

Jonah frowned at this. "Why'd you tell me that?"

"Because I wanted you to know what I was really like."

He studied her carefully composed face—and then he did understand something new about her, though he doubted it was what she'd assumed, or intended. Characteristics that had seemed so strangely incongruous in her—the aggressively styled hair, the luxury accessories, the remarkably unremarkable nose—suddenly fell into place. She was wearing a costume: She was dressed up as a Las Vegas real estate investor.

It was getting later in the afternoon—the air was becoming colder, the mist thickening. He saw that she'd started to shiver a little in her trench coat. "You're sure we've never met before?" he asked.

"No, Jonah," she said. "We don't know each other." She continued, "I have to go back to my hotel for my things. I'm leaving for the airport soon."

He supposed she'd be able to find her own way to her hotel. But then, why should he feel so reluctant to ask? Either way, she would be out of his life forever in twenty minutes. As she'd just said: She had a plane to catch. "You know which way to go?"

She worked the fingers of the fist at her side. "My hotel is near the train station."

"If you want, I can show you."

And, after a pause, she said, "Okay." (In later months, back in Las Vegas, she would wonder why she had agreed to this offer—which he had obviously been so reluctant to make, and she had been so disinclined to accept. She supposed, in the end, there had been some refusal with regard to each other that they had not yet been prepared to make—though that refusal would come soon enough.)

Jonah led her to Prinsengracht, the outermost canal of the Canal Ring, and then they started back northward. It was not the most direct path to the train station—but he figured if he was walking her, he might as well take a route he liked. Trees, their foliage still green, lined both sides of the canal; brightly colored rowboats and tarp-covered speedboats were tied in long rows at the edge. They didn't speak as they retraced their path back up the clock face of the city, though the silence was more comfortable now. He sensed they were both able to enjoy this stroll up a charming Dutch street on the most straightforward terms, and were capable of enjoying it this way because they both knew it would soon be over.

They crossed Westermarkt, the western continuation of Radhuisstraat, and as they resumed their course northeast, Jonah's nose started to hurt. It didn't often anymore, except when the weather was like this: cold, and wet. He might have asked her if hers did, even after having had the surgery, but he didn't think it was worth breaking their mutually sustained silence to find out. She walked, as before, with her face down, arms now folded across her chest—the one fist clenched tightly in the crook of the other arm.

They went up a bridge arching over Bloemgracht, a canal that branched off to the west. Then, at the top of this bridge, Judy stopped; looking across to the opposite side of the water, she asked him, "What's that?"

He looked over. "The Anne Frank House."

It was a nondescript building—handsome, but in the same way as every other building on the street: three stories of dark brick, large black-and-white casement windows. It would have been difficult to pick out if not for the long line of tourists waiting outside—carrying guidebooks, umbrellas, a cluster near the front in matching rain slickers. Jonah had never been inside the house: hadn't gone during his college trip, had seen absolutely no advantage to going now. It wasn't far from the houseboat, though, and he passed it fairly frequently, usually without giving it much attention. He regarded it mostly as another place Max went to meet women. But Judy seemed to have taken an interest in it—moved up to the bridge's metal railing to study it. He watched as her head followed the line of tourists stretching down the block, around the corner. "What do you think it is they're looking for?" she said.

He was inclined at first not to answer—but, finally, he knew what she meant. "You know how it is, half of tourism is just saying you've been there," he said. "You go, you take a couple pictures, you cross the name off the list. I remember after 9/11, seeing tourists posing for photos in front of the rubble at Ground Zero before it had even stopped smoking. Smiling, even."

"You were in New York then?" she asked, still looking across the water.

"Yeah, but, y'know, fifty blocks away," he said. "Still, it was shitty. Where were you?"

"College," she answered.

She was young, then—or not even young, only younger than him. He'd been just out of college himself, dating Zoey for the first time—by September, breaking up with Zoey for the first time. She'd lived on Christopher Street then, and that far south you could smell it in the air: electrical burning and God knew what else. Outside her subway stop, one of the vendors who had appeared in the city as if by spontaneous generation to sell bullshit gewgaws and commemorative bumper stickers would set out his wares every night. "Remember! Remember! One dollar! Remember!" the vendor would repeat, sing-song, as Jonah came up the subway steps. And then he and Zoey would spend the next five hours fighting and crying, while on television they showed as if on a loop the towers burning, the towers falling—or else people jumping, some holding on to sheets, like they hoped they could just sail away. Here was another set of thoughts he didn't like to revisit—not now, and even less when he'd been sitting at his desk on the twenty-ninth floor of 813 Lexington. Yes, he thought: shitty.

He began to study the line of tourists himself: the rowdy college students, possibly or probably high; the Chinese tour group ranged behind a woman holding up a purple umbrella. Maybe the point of visiting these places was so that you didn't have to remember—or rather, it made the memory manageable—finite. You paid your visit, you spent your thirty minutes, and then you were allowed to head to the next site—you lived your life as though these things didn't happen anymore: belonged to some other time, some other place.

He spotted him!—in the back of the line!—grinning—tapping his nose—

But it was just a man in Hasidic garb—a normal Hasid, as it were—shuffling forward to fill a gap in the line ahead of him. Jonah saw that he had grabbed onto the railing—as if he might leap over the side, or he feared a wave was coming to sweep him off. He'd dropped the cigarette he was smoking, too—fumbled in his pockets for another, dropped the box, and the cigarettes spilled out into the canal, floated away.

He could sense Judy's eyes on him. But he felt so distressed and ashamed by what had just occurred he couldn't look back. He waited for what she would say. All she said, though, was, "Why don't we keep going?" Then she headed off the bridge. After a moment he followed her—the line of tourists still shuffling one by one into the Anne Frank House.

Regular gusts of wind had started up—blowing water from the trees, shaking the boats in the canal against the side. She was shivering again. "It isn't too much farther," he told her. "We cross over at Herenstraat, and then the train station's right up the street." She nodded. "Look, about what happened on the bridge," he began, suddenly identifying something—unwanted, in their silences. "It's just, I have bad dreams sometimes."

"What about?" she asked.

He heard her teeth chattering behind her lips. "There's someone chasing me."

"Freud said we're everyone in our dreams."

Jonah thought about this. "I think Freud and I had very different experiences of puberty." And she laughed, fully, for the first time since he'd met her: clear, surprisingly light, mezzo-soprano, like her voice.

They passed a bench at the edge of the canal, before which no boats were tied. "Can we sit for a bit?" she asked.

"You don't need to get to the airport?"

"I have a few minutes."

They sat down, the wind driving ripples up the canal before them. He could still hear the faint clicking of her teeth. He unbuttoned his

coat and put it around her shoulders. She hesitated, then pulled the
lapels closed around her, pinching one with the thumb and forefinger
of her closed fist. "Thank you," she said. But then she seemed to feel
the need to compose herself—sat up a little on the bench, pulled the
coat straighter over her chest. "You're probably disappointed we won't
have time to fuck," she said tersely.

He stared at her, startled—offended, even. "You think that's what I
wanted? Is that what you wanted?"

"What more could this have been?" she replied.

He thought of what her cousin had said about her, about never getting over it; he thought of it like a warning. But he asked her anyway,
"How did you end up in Las Vegas?"

"Everyone ends up somewhere, don't they?" she answered after a
moment. "How did you end up in Amsterdam?"

And Jonah wanted to tell her the whole story—not the despairing,
truncated version he'd told Max: He wanted her to know all of it, fully.
But then it seemed too much to begin, he wasn't sure there'd be enough
time—he worried she wouldn't believe him. His nose was aching by
now, his hands nearly numb. He shoved them into the pockets of his
jeans. He could see Judy, even in his coat, still shivering—as if even
between the two of them there wasn't warmth enough for either one.
He leaned forward, and she slid from out of the corner of his eye.
What was he waiting for? he asked himself. What was he hiding from?

He turned around to look at her and was struck by how small she
appeared: her blond head poking above the coat, bulging in empty
folds around her torso. A faint blueness had entered her lips. Behind
the bench up the street, he saw a bakery, not unlike the one on Lindengracht he visited. "How about I go get us some coffee?" he offered.
"Help warm us up a little bit for the rest of the walk?" She nodded,
and Jonah hurried across the street.

When he had gone, Judith tucked her elbows closer against her sides,
crossed her legs at the ankles, pulled them underneath her on the
bench. It seemed to her like some strange indictment that she'd traveled
so far from where she now lived and only here met someone so easily

recognizable. He was intelligent, he had gone to a good liberal arts college, he was a Jew who had been raised in the Northeast. He was familiar. More than that: She liked him. But then, who was she kidding? she
thought. He had been nice to her—and these days, that was all it took.

She took her fist out of the coat—she unfolded the balled-up Polaroid that she'd pulled from the wall of Margaretha's exhibit, smoothed
its creases as best she could over her thigh. Margaretha probably
assumed she'd taken the picture and stormed out because she was
offended that the photograph had been included as part of the show.
But it hadn't been that. The shock of it had been that when she first
saw this image of a young girl in a white dress, standing on a grassy
lawn—to which Margaretha had seen fit to add a crucifix in the
background, a crown of thorns around the girl's head—she hadn't
recognized that the girl in the picture was her.

Now looking at it a second time, there was a second, passing disbelief, like a momentarily obscuring cloud. But she knew—this was her:
standing on the lawn of the house she'd grown up in, at the party on
the day of her graduation from high school. There was the unflattering
white dress she'd worn, the garland of gardenias in her black, wiry
former hair, her overlarge, unbroken former nose—all of it as it had
been when Margaretha had pulled the camera out of her knit purse
that afternoon in June 2001.

She thought of the hotel room in New Jersey, where she'd gone
after leaving Princeton—the compromises she had made, had been so
deliberate in making, in order to leave that room: The Septembers
passed now without her noticing; she didn't suffer so much from the
lack of companionship in her life; she had even made a fine career for
herself, first sitting behind desks in Los Angeles art galleries, lately
engaged in far-different activities. It was to that girl's credit all she had
managed to leave behind in that room. She only wished she had held
on to the journal she'd kept then. She would have liked to encounter
that girl, at least one last time. She knew there were not many of these
revenant Judiths left for her to run into.

She licked her thumb, and tried to wipe away Margaretha's dumb
embellishments. She succeeded only in smudging the colors of the forehead beneath the crude crown of thorns. But even so: In the face of

this girl—formal, somewhat self-conscious, looking back at her from across an ocean of years—she could see, could feel in the texture of the memory it elicited, not just the immediate pride of the moment, or the luxurious gratitude the girl felt for everything in her life, but most potently of all, the promise she sensed in everything to come: the unquestioned faith that ahead of her, beyond this afternoon, beyond the passing discomfort of posing for this picture—was so much more—

Jonah came out of the bakery, carrying two cups of coffee; he had packets of sugar in his pocket, in case that was how she took it. As he approached the bench, he saw she was shaking violently—at first he thought with chills, but then he recognized with sobs.

Here it was, then: everything she had never gotten over. And wasn't it like this for everyone? Scratch beneath the barest surface, and you found it—could see it: that gaping need.

And then Jonah saw the street before him—Amsterdam—engulfed in scorching sunlight—felt the furnace heat of it on his face—the sun burning the moisture from the air—heat rising in waves from the cobbles, the shingles on the rooftops smoldering—the canal dry, its stone bed cracked—the boats tipped sideways into it, ropes tying them impotently to their moorings. And she sat there in the midst of it— eyes sunken, tongue swollen, lips parted and cracked—her hair abuzz with flies—so thin the coat seemed to fold shapelessly against itself— shaking with tearless sobs. He sensed there were others—hidden in attics, huddled beneath the bridges—but he saw only her—the undulating waves of heat rising from the cobbles thicker, faster—distorting what he saw—she was there, she was gone—she was white as a pillar of salt—and before he could take another breath she had vanished— became indiscernible among the rising heat, the searing sunlight. Then the light became duller, weakened into the gray of the clouds—the canal grew placid and darkly green, and he saw people walking into the bakery behind him, carrying umbrellas across the half-moon bridges over the water. And there was Judith, crying.

He remembered her—he knew her. He had seen her before, in the photograph on the bookcase in Becky's apartment, the night of Becky's party. She was the woman he had thought of when it all began. This was Judith.

He knew it could have been anyone: an apocalypse could occur in any life, any two lives could meet in a doorway. But she was the one he had seen, she was the one sitting on a bench, crying—waiting for him. Go there, he thought. Go there and offer—something. Was she not, in her way, soaking wet, just like him?

He recognized he had come to this point again—was faced again, with this leap. He dropped the coffees and ran away up the street.

And in the only instance of moral judgment in the entire period of what might be called his prophecy, Jonah would conclude that if such a thing as sin existed, then this had been it.

It had started to rain again by the time Jonah arrived back at the houseboat. He heard music from below as he descended the steps at the bow, sounds of laughter. He came down into the main living area—a rectangular room with a low ceiling, filled almost to the walls by a great central table of rough-hewn wood. Max was seated at this table with two young women Jonah didn't recognize—and even if one of them hadn't been absently leafing through a copy of *Lonely Planet Europe*, even if they hadn't both been wearing North Face jackets (red and blue, respectively), he believed they would have been easily identifiable as American tourists. He detected a distinctly American freshness, an eagerness, in the frank prettiness of their faces, in the practicality of their pulled-back hair, even in the cheerfully colored Post-its sticking out of the guidebook.

"Rabbi!" Max cried amiably. He and the young woman nearest him at the table—round-faced, her hair brown with blond highlights, wearing the red North Face jacket—were playing a card game, an ashtray with two burning joints between them. An iPod dock on the table filled the room with something light and poppy. "Joints and Uno, Rabbi," Max said. "What could be better? Deal you in?"

The woman in the red North Face jacket regarded Jonah with amusement. "He's not actually a rabbi, though, is he?" she asked.

Max frowned at Jonah with concern. "You didn't do any ritual bathing in a canal, did you? And what happened to the *Battleship Potemkin* coat?"

Jonah looked down at himself. His sweater and jeans were soaked; he touched his beard and felt water dripping from it. It must have been raining harder than he'd noticed. "I . . ." he began, but didn't know what he was trying to say. He saw that his hands were shaking. He sat heavily in a chair at the table, shoved them under his thighs.

"He's not actually a rabbi, though?" he heard the red North Face repeat as he stared down at the grain of the wood table, the undulations and swirls of the darker lines across the surface.

"Not technically," Max answered. "But he suffers from a rare affliction. He believes in God."

"I believe in God," the red North Face said.

"No, no," Max corrected her. "He doesn't believe in the warm feeling you get after you do yoga. He believes in God in the old, obsolete way: old white man, long white beard."

"Okay, so he's just, like, really traditional," the red North Face said, satisfied. Then she added, singsongy, "Draw two, skip you."

Jonah wanted to reach for one of the joints, but he could feel his hands even under his legs shaking violently. How long would she sit on the bench? Was she still sitting there now? He thought of the alley—the coffeeshop. But spending a day getting high, eating *Stroopwafels*, contentedly watching pigeons in the square—these now seemed like someone else's idea of time well spent, amusements borrowed from some other life. He might as well call up Sylvia and tell her he wanted to live with her on Bond Street after all.

"Is he okay, though?" asked the woman in the blue North Face jacket, looking up from her guidebook.

Jonah had been hoping they wouldn't notice his agitation, or at least would ignore it. This, of course, was wishful thinking. And next he felt like crying—clenched his teeth to stop it—because whether he drank Scotch until he passed out on the floor of his apartment, whether he bargained with Becky's marriage and the details of his career, whether he spent weeks (weeks! It seemed incredible now) hiding in a cloud of marijuana smoke in Amsterdam—it was all the same: rationalization piled upon rationalization, fear tied in knots of fear until he could believe it was something else. All of it was wishful thinking. In the end, these visions—the Hasid—Judith—they would always find him.

"Should we get him, like, a tea or something?" the blue North Face continued.

"I'm sure he'll be alright," Max answered her—maybe for once showing some sympathy for Jonah. "He's well acquainted with the costs of religious life. What are you learning about Europe from your guidebook?"

"Just looking for places in Germany that aren't too touristy," she responded.

"The last thing a tourist wants is to be around other tourists," Max said. "Too bad they all use the same guidebooks to decide where not to go."

"Ha-ha," the blue North Face replied, unamused.

Never one to be deterred by the unamusement of others, Max asked, "So what non-touristy places will you be visiting next?"

"We already did England, Spain, and France," the red North Face answered, putting down her cards and pointing in the air, as though indicating an invisible map. "In two days we take the train to Germany, and then it's Switzerland, Italy, and all around Eastern Europe. Then we'll do Turkey, Israel, and maybe Egypt, y'know, depending."

"Obviously," Max said.

"For the winter it's India and Southeast Asia, like Thailand and Vietnam, then Australia, New Zealand, some islands in the South Pacific, Hawaii, and finally home to California." Reciting this list seemed to build up some momentum of joy in her, and as she finished she burst out laughing.

And Jonah could picture the two young women, in all these places: in a gondola in Venice; strolling the Old Town Square in Prague; posing before the Taj Mahal; in a tuk-tuk in Bangkok; hiking up to Angkor Watt; river rafting in New Zealand; wearing matching bikinis—red and blue, naturally—on the beach in Fiji. Travel was such a rite of passage for Americans of his generation—and in the end, where did it take you? How far had Judith traveled, to break down into sobs once again? How far had he gone, to end up back in this place?

"It's all about having experiences," the red North Face said. "And that's what I feel like right now, y'know? This is one of those crazy experiences that we'll always look back on."

The blue North Face closed the guidebook. "You want to go to the bathroom, Bonnie?" she asked her friend.

"Hmm? Oh, yeah, right," she answered, standing up.

"It's through the door on the left, though you'll find it's a bit cramped for girl talk," Max told them. The two women left. Max smiled placidly at Jonah. "This is the 'If you're going to do it, then do it already, because I'm getting bored' conversation. The fact that you're such a terrible wingman might actually work in my favor, Rabbi."

"Will you stop fucking calling me that . . ." Jonah said, his shaking hands still shoved under his legs.

"What did happen to you today?" Max asked. "Did they try to drown you for a witch? Or did you accidentally take a bite of a ham-and-cheese sandwich and from out of the whirlwind—"

With sudden ferocity, Jonah shouted, "What the fuck do you want from me?" He lurched forward, swinging his hands up to bang them on the table—succeeded only in smacking them against the bottom. The stinging pain of this only intensified his wrath as he repeated, this time almost screaming, "Tell me what the fuck you want from me!"

Max had a look on his face as if an unpleasant odor had entered the room. The jolt of fury drained away; Jonah leaned back slowly—sat on his hands.

Max took a moment to rearrange the disrupted piles of cards. It appeared that, for once, he didn't know what to say. Predictably, though, this was not a condition that persisted for long. "You know, Rabbi, as King Kong said to Fay Wray, we actually have a lot in common," he began. "The same college, mostly the same friends. And I'd say we both see a little more of things than most people do. The difference is I could never believe all the nonsense you do. And the truth is, Rabbi, I envy you. You really think that out of the thousands of millions on this planet, God chose to whisper in your ear and say, 'Here I am.' Do you know how many people wish they could think something as preposterous as that? So of course it disgusts me the way you skulk around this city in sackcloth and ashes, draped in the cowardice of your convictions."

Whether any of this was meant to be taken seriously or not, it struck Jonah that he had always envied Max, too—for how comfortable he seemed, in his chameleon's skin. "Yeah, you'd see it differently if the situation were reversed," he mumbled in reply.

"We'll never know, will we?" Max answered. "I'd like to have been a believer for a minute or two. But I just don't have it in me. We all suffer what our faith demands, Rabbi. Or else we suffer from the lack. Or did you really think you were the only person on the planet with no fucking clue how to live?" They heard the North Faces coming back down the hall toward the room. "Anyway, try not to screw this up for me. I've been playing Uno for the last two hours."

The two women reentered the room. The North Face in the blue jacket sat down at her guidebook, but the red North Face remained in the doorway. "This ship is really cool," she said.

Max grinned. "Would you like a tour?"

"Okay, yeah, sure, yes, that sounds great."

Max got slowly to his feet—making a show of savoring the moment—winked at Jonah, and they went out. Well, Jonah thought: She was having an experience.

Jonah and the blue North Face didn't speak for a few moments. Eventually she said, "He shouldn't be too proud of himself. She does this all the time."

She was brunette, with an olive complexion, her face narrow, freckled, her eyelids resting low on close-set eyes, giving her a somewhat sleepy appearance. Something in this face surprised him, though he couldn't say exactly what; maybe simply that it had the specificity of any face—a specificity he'd ignored until now. "What's your name?" he asked her.

"Lindsey," she said. "Look, I'm not going to hook up with you or anything, if that was the plan," she went on. "It's nothing personal I'm just, like, trying to do me on this trip."

"Why?" he asked her.

"Oh, y'know," she answered, smoothing her ponytail through her hand. "Bad breakup."

"What happened?"

"The asshole cheated," she said. "Bonnie basically came to my rescue with this trip, though, I probably wouldn't have come if it hadn't happened. So I guess it's all for the best."

He could imagine Sylvia saying something like this; he could imagine Zoey saying it, too. Had it all been for the best? He doubted it. Not when there were so many ways it could have been better. "I'm sorry," he said.

"It's not your fault. All guys do it, right?" she said with a shrug. "So what's your deal? Are you like a . . . sorry, this is a stupid question, what's Matisyahu again?"

"No, I'm not a Hasidic Jew," he answered with exhaustion.

"Then why does he always call you 'Rabbi'?"

But Jonah didn't have the energy—couldn't locate the will or the reason—to deny it anymore. "I have visions," he said. There was no relief in the confession, though; it only seemed to reaffirm it in some new way.

"Visions . . ." she said, as if she'd suspected he was crazy, and now she was sure. But then she asked, "What are they like? What do you see?"

"I'm supposed to offer . . . something . . . to help . . . someone."

"Why don't you do it?"

"Why don't I do it?" he asked with a scoff. "Why don't I do it?" he repeated, with desperation. "Why don't I give in to some totally insane, these ridiculous—I mean, do I look like a Hasidic Jew? Do I look like the sort of person who would go around and—and—and, not for nothing, but I am angry! I am very, very fucking angry! I mean, this happened to me! And now I'm supposed to just give up and—and what? Seriously, I'm asking, what the fuck am I supposed to do? What do I have to offer—to anyone? I mean, look at me! Look at how I've ended up! And my nose is fucking killing me!" She was observing him worriedly—had her hands on the table, like she was thinking she might need to make a run for it. But the words were coming out in a flood now. "None of this was supposed to be this way," he said, tears forcing themselves from his eyes. "I was supposed to be a success! I was supposed to accomplish things! Do things! Things that matter! But instead I'm—instead I'm . . . None of it makes any sense," he said, sobbing. "None of it makes any fucking sense . . ."

She stood up from the table. He figured she was leaving—and why shouldn't she? She had her own problems, her own disappointments, failures, losses—as anyone did. She had been dumped, she had been deceived—she would suffer worse than that. So much of it was just a matter of time.

She came around the table, leaned over and hugged him. She pressed her face into his shoulder, and after a moment he realized she was crying, too. "It's going to be okay," he heard her say.

He'd been certain in New York that these words meant so little—contained so little of use, of value. What difference did they make beside even the smallest tragedies, touching a single life—to say nothing of all the greater ones? But as they hugged each other—strangers in a strange city, crying for their own reasons, or for the same reason—he understood that she didn't say it because she believed it would be okay, or because she had any reason to think so: only so that he would know—that she wanted it to be okay, too. There was something irreducible in that. There was something you could call holy.

They hugged for a few more moments, then she straightened and drew away, and wiped her eyes, and he wiped the tears from his. And that was all.

In the Amsterdam twilight, silent and still, the bench was empty, as Jonah had known it would be. He had run the whole way, as though spat from the houseboat—but she was at the airport, she was on her way back to Las Vegas. The emptiness of the bench was so complete it was possible to believe she had never been there at all—but Jonah knew she had. The setting sun cast swaths of red across the white and charcoal blue of the clouds—and he imagined he could see in these folds of light the fullness not only of the sky but of the city beneath it, and all its people—all the people he knew, and would never know: his parents, and Zoey and Sylvia—Philip Orengo and Aaron Seyler—Becky and Danny—Brett and his guru—Doug Chen and Scott Baker, Rafik and Geoff—Lindsey and Bonnie—and Max—Judith—and him, too—

And with longing and with fear, Jonah said, "Yes, I'll go, I'll see what good I can do there."

IV. NINEVEH, LAS VEGAS

1. JUDITH AND THE KING

Prior to moving to Los Angeles from Princeton to begin work at the art gallery, Judith's experience of living in large cities was limited to her brief stint in Paris—and there, of course, she had been a student. She wouldn't have guessed that a city of so many millions would furnish her such privacy—and privacy was what she was seeking (that was one word for it, anyway). She discovered that in Los Angeles, people didn't bother you. Every day she drove her car to work, and every day she got caught in traffic—and everyone in the cars around her kept their eyes straight ahead. Only she looked briefly at the faces suspended beside her, until she learned not to.

The galleries she worked at were all clustered downtown, among white stone buildings that glowed uniformly in the uniform sunshine. Walking in in the mornings, she might glance up and see in the distance the ice-blue glass of the Gas Company Tower, sheer and mirror-gleaming. She did her job competently, which seemed to distinguish her among her peers, and soon won praise for her "eye"—having learned that the trick to creating a successful gallery show was not identifying what was actually good but rather identifying what would be considered good by the kinds of people who bought art in down-

town Los Angeles. She was promoted; she was hired away by competing galleries. Her success gratified her, to an extent, but she understood
that it was the familiarity that really pleased her—the echo of other
praise, other accomplishments that had once meant much more.

In the Los Angeles art world, a silent, solitary figure was not so
unusual, and it turned out she had a lot in common with the younger
ranks of the L.A. art crowd, many of whom had fled to the city from
some childhood distress, whether tragic or banal (or, as in her case,
she thought, both). But this similarity somehow made her feel even
less inclined to spend time with her peers. She endured the opening-
night receptions she was obliged to attend, the after-work drinks she
consented to, with discomfort, impatience.

Men and women made passes at her, asked her out on dates from
time to time. In high school, she'd imagined her chiaroscuro looks
might one day be appreciated, and in the Los Angeles art scene, they
were. The dates she agreed to would typically end in sex—she wanted
them to end that way—but she never agreed to a second date, or even
a second hookup. Those she'd spent the night with didn't object much
when they were rebuffed. Her attitude in this regard seemed familiar
to people—acceptable.

During the years she lived in L.A., she rented a one-bedroom apartment in a complex in an undefined neighborhood east of Fairfax, fur-
nished it during one long afternoon at IKEA. She forgot to buy a
hamper—but after six months of piling her dirty clothes and underwear at the foot of her bed, it struck her she hadn't needed one, after
all. She didn't know any of her neighbors, they didn't seem to know
one another: One of them played thumping techno on weekends;
another smoked marijuana she could smell whenever she walked by
his door.

And—the time went by. A rhythm developed in her life, of daily
obligation, of task following task—and then she'd see a wreath on the
face of a door and realize it was December; she'd get to the gallery and
find it closed and an hour later be told Daylight Savings Time had
ended. On her days off (another reason she did well at her jobs was
that she never asked for any), she would run parts of the California

Coastal Trail, from Venice Beach north past Santa Monica. The farther she ran, the fewer people she saw, and sometimes she would stop
on an empty stretch of sand, succumb to the trite inducements to
contemplation she observed there—the distant horizon, the waves
crashing and receding—and take stock of her life. She didn't think
much about the past anymore—considered this a relief, a type of
freedom—nor did she think much about the future. And as for the
present: Judith regarded herself as content.

Once she had moved to Las Vegas, she would reconsider this sense
of contentment. She did not believe it was facile, did not think, in retrospect, that it was a lie she had been telling herself. What she asked of
her life in Los Angeles, it gave her. But there must have been something missing, some need must have gone unfulfilled, because the Colonel seemed to find it so easy to lift her out of this life and place her in
a new one—like he was picking up a coin off the sidewalk and putting
it in his pocket. (She would observe that he did this with a lot of people.) Her best guess was that it had been her zeal: that old, insatiable
longing for something, anything, still lurking inside her without her
knowing it—indifferent to the limits that she'd prescribed for her
modest existence—waiting to fix on whatever object it could find to
inspire it.

On the afternoon Judith met the Colonel, she was sitting at her desk
in the back of the gallery where she was working then, writing a
press release, a typical task for her. The weather was bright and
sunny and clear; the events of the morning had been routine. It was,
in other words, an unremarkable day—and she would think later
that if some omen presaged the Colonel's entrance into her life, she
had missed it or forgotten it. (Though, of course, she knew better
than to believe in omens.)

The press release announced the gallery's upcoming exhibition of
ink and pencil portraits of American movie stars. And it was just as
she was trying to formulate a way of saying these works had artistic
legitimacy because Andy Warhol had used celebrities as subjects, too,
and everyone knew who Andy Warhol was—though without actually

saying this—when the appearance of someone in the gallery caught her attention. He was dressed in a dark tailored suit, shirt open at the collar, a small American flag pin sparkling on his lapel—his head shaved and a neat auburn goatee surrounding his mouth. He was accompanied by a young woman Judith assumed must be sickly in some way, as, despite the afternoon heat, she was wore a jacket zipped up to her collar, a baseball hat, dark sunglasses.

Judith was by then the assistant manager of this gallery; Sonya, her junior colleague, was responsible for speaking with those who came in, sounding out as subtly as possible whether they had any intention to buy. Judith might be called upon to close the sale, to talk with anyone who showed more than a passing knowledge of art. She didn't have any of the social skills associated with a good salesperson, but she had what one of her employers had once called "artistic gravitas": Buyers took her seriously, which Judith attributed to the fact that she didn't smile.

Sonya was speaking with the bundled woman—and, watching them, it occurred to Judith that this woman was not sickly but instead famous. This was how famous people dressed in downtown L.A.: conspicuous about being inconspicuous. It made sense, then, for Sonya to focus her attention here. Typically with these pairings, the model or actress or whichever settled on something she wanted—based on color if for any reason at all—and then the well-dressed man accompanying her took out a credit card. Often, no one bothered to remove their sunglasses. But Judith found that her own attention was drawn to the man, and the longer she watched him, the more intrigued she became—which was itself intriguing, as she took a certain pride in being able to assess, fully, with a single look, those who walked into the gallery.

He was large, in a brawny way—the roundness of his torso powerful, trunklike. The skin of his face was featureless from the crown of his shaved head down across his broad forehead to the sharp, dark slashes of his eyebrows; his nose was large, flat, fleshy, rather like a bull's. What was most compelling to Judith, though, was the way he moved through the gallery: pacing the room in long, unhurried strides, his small, round eyes turning slowly left and then right, giving more attention to the physical aspects of the space than to the works on the walls—his gaze rising with a support beam to the ceiling, following the path of the exposed ventilation ducts—a slight, sardonic grin fixed on his lips, as if something in all he saw amused him. And though he did little but stroll the room, survey it with this expression of subtle mockery, he managed to convey in these gestures a certain authority—as though, just by occupying the space, he owned it.

Evidently, the swaddled star found him to be the most interesting thing in the gallery, too; she regularly turned her head from the canvas Sonya was explaining to watch him. And Judith had the peculiar thought that, whatever else this man was, he was powerfully—unmistakably—American: in the breadth of his gait, in the manifest self-assurance of his face, in his casual disregard for everyone else in the room, all these combining to make the American flag pin he wore superfluous—and this superfluity struck her as somehow American, too. These were not the only characteristics she associated with her native country, of course, but she had observed them to be strong in the national character, especially after her time in France. The French walked into a gallery so differently—with a certain reverence, even if they ended up sneering at what they saw. Whatever this man evinced was the opposite of reverence.

Now his eyes fell on Judith—he approached the desk, giving her the same look of mocking assessment with which he'd studied the ventilation ducts. There was something unsettling about his eyes, she thought: deep-set, almost perfectly circular, their color a dark blue that lightened through shades of indigo to paleness at the pupils. His unashamed stare was causing her an almost physical agitation—but maybe for just this reason, she didn't look away. He smirked, as though impressed by this—the corner of his goatee-ringed mouth jutting sharply into his cheek. "You have a price list?" he asked.

She handed him the two stapled pages. He glanced at the first page, flipped to the second, dropped them back on her desk. "So how much did they cost to make?" he asked.

"Excuse me?"

"These paintings. How much did it cost to make them?"

She hesitated—no one had ever asked her this before. "For the artist?"

"Sure, let's start there."

The paintings were nonfigurative, oil on canvas: swirls and waves and jutting arcs of color executed in globs, in splatter-thin lines, in quarter-inch-high ripples of paint. In the exhibition brochure, she had written that these works "rendered the chaos and confusion of human emotion with subtle, perceptive beauty." Whether or not this was true (Judith had her doubts), she was aware they had been made quickly, with an intentional sloppiness—the West Hollywood–based artist who'd painted them had told her so himself—and in terms of materials, their most expensive elements were almost certainly their frames. "Two or three thousand dollars, I suppose," she said—knew this was being generous.

"For one of them?"

"For all of them," she conceded.

He snorted through the broad nostrils of his nose. "That's quite a markup, considering you're selling the cheapest one for twenty grand. It makes you wonder why they call them 'starving artists.'" He watched her, apparently waiting for her response. "But aren't you going to tell me you can't put a price tag on art?"

"You just saw the price list," she answered.

His smirk deepened, and he narrowed his eyes, as if studying her in a new way. "A girl could get herself fired talking that way." Judith shrugged—because she sensed that this, too, was a form of a challenge, and did not want to be seen as backing down from it. "Okay, then," he continued. "You tell me why someone should pay a ten thousand percent markup for one of these . . . works of art." And he tied this last phrase in a neat bow of derision.

Half-formed thoughts tumbled to her mind: explanations of the aesthetics of abstract art; a history of American painting as it evolved after World War II; a more general defense of nonrepresentational art as a means of portraying the nonmaterial dimensions of existence. But as she looked up at his burrowing eyes, at his persistent smirk, which seemed a preemptive contradiction of anything she might say, even at the American flag pin—composed, she now noticed, of tiny sapphires, rubies, diamonds—she could not muster these thoughts into a cogent reply. Glancing at the paintings themselves didn't help, either: They had always struck her as being a bit needlessly muddy. The pin he wore had more evident craftsmanship, if not necessarily artistry, to it. The truth was, she didn't like most of the works she sold. It occurred to her he made a good point.

When she didn't answer for another moment, he let out a loud, staccato laugh that seemed to strike and echo against the gallery walls. Sonya and the presumed celebrity had begun to stare at them, apparently having lost interest in their own conversation. It discomfited Judith, though, how easily he'd been able to wrong-foot her in an environment with which she was so familiar—felt she had to make at least some defense. "This isn't a hardware store," she said. "It's not a question of pricing the materials."

"No? What is it a question of?"

"It's a question of . . ." But again, under the force of the eyes, the smirk, the lambent pin—she trailed off.

He took obvious pleasure in seeing her lapse once again into silence—let her sit in it for a few moments before he said, "That's all right, I know exactly what it's a question of." The smirk vanished, his voice became harsher. "It's a question of giving your customers what they're looking to buy. If it's not expensive, they can't brag about it at art parties, they can't put it on the wall to remind themselves that they're the sort of people who pay twenty grand for something that cost maybe two hundred bucks to make. That's why they're happy to pay whatever markup you decide to charge. You sell them something that tells them who they are."

She sensed she had some objection to this—felt she must have had some objection. The best she could do, though, was, "The price also includes the gallery's costs."

"Oh, I know," he replied dismissively—implying he could both make her argument for her and undermine it in the same breath. "There's overhead: You have to pay the rent for the downtown gallery with the eighteen-foot ceilings. You have to pay the girl to sit behind the desk and hand people a piece of paper. Tell me something," he said. "Where did you go to college to learn to do that?"

Now she felt the unaccustomed sensation of heat entering her cheeks. "Yale," she said.

He smacked his hands together, laughed again triumphantly. "Yale! Beautiful. Your parents paid $150,000 so you could sit there and do a job a—"

"I'm sorry we don't have any more garish pins to sell you, but if you don't see anything you like, why don't you and your friend please leave."

To that point, she had taken a certain pleasure in how uneasy he was managing to make her feel. The anger had risen so suddenly, so forcefully—as if it had taken its place undetected with the redness in her cheeks—that she spoke in almost the same moment she was aware of it. And as quickly as it had arisen, the anger vanished—leaving her stunned at her outburst, embarrassed enough that she finally needed to look away from his gaze.

When she looked back, he was smirking more sharply than ever— like this was an outcome that pleased him. "Clearly at Yale you weren't a marketing major," he said. Then he added, "And who said I don't see anything I like?"

"Colonel," the star said from across the gallery. "Are you going to buy any of these, or . . ."

"They're terrible," he replied without turning to her. "They're all terrible. Even the girl thinks so." But how had he known? Judith wondered.

The woman sighed behind her sunglasses. And now the man smiled fully at Judith: spreading his lips to reveal rows of small white teeth. This smile had an ominous quality—all his smiles were ominous, she would learn—and the ominousness fascinated her all the more. "You have a card?" She took one from the silver tray on her desk, handed it to him. He studied it. "Judith Klein Bulbrook," he said. "That's a lot of name for such a spindly little thing." He put the card into his jacket pocket. "I'm guessing you don't know who I am." She shook her head. "Go out to Las Vegas sometime and ask who that hundred-story tower belongs to. That's who I am." The casual pride he displayed in making this pronouncement, undiluted by any trace of irony, was more impressive to her than the fact itself. He turned to leave, then added over his shoulder—in a way that was still more ominous, and so to Judith still more fascinating—"I like that I can make you blush." He walked out the door of the gallery, the woman in the sunglasses following behind.

When they had gone, Sonya immediately approached Judith's desk and said, "So can we talk about that? She was that actress, y'know, the one who's always topless on that HBO show. And he's a casino mogul or something?" When Judith didn't answer, she asked, "What did you two talk about?"

"Nothing," Judith told her. "Nothing interesting." It surprised her that she'd said this, because she knew it was a lie. This was the most interesting conversation she'd had in years.

The next morning, Judith got a phone call in her apartment from Edgar, the owner of the gallery. "So, Judith," Edgar began uneasily. "I'm afraid . . . Well, you don't need to come in today."

"Why not?" she asked.

"Judith, so, here's the thing . . . We won't be needing you anymore."

She had already dressed for the day—had her phone in her hand as she stood in the middle of her box-shaped living room, her purse on her shoulder. "I don't understand," she said, confused.

"So there is good news," Edgar said, brightening. "We sold out the entire Knauer exhibit! One buyer!"

Judith sat down on her couch, placed her purse on her lap, no longer confused. "I see," she said.

"You know how the art world is," Edgar went on. "Buyers are always . . . eccentric. It's the business we're in! I'm sure you didn't mean to say anything insulting. I mean of course you wouldn't. But the buyer was very insistent. You understand, don't you?"

"I do."

"You're a cat with nine lives!" Edgar reassured her. "You'll land on your feet! This is just . . . it's just art, honey!"

"Will I get my commission for the sale?" She didn't really care about the money, was more curious about what he would say.

"Oh, Judith, you understand," he answered. "The buyer really made it very clear. . . . Obviously you didn't exactly . . . *help* make the sale. . . ."

"Of course."

"You understand."

She hung up the phone. To buy out the entire exhibit would have cost close to $100,000. And she found that in addition to being stunned and shaken and angered—and, yes, fascinated—she was flattered.

Several days later, a courier arrived at her door. She signed for a small box wrapped in ivory-colored paper, tied with a black ribbon. She sat down on her couch and opened it. Inside, resting on a velvet pillow, was a golden butterfly pendant on a slender gold chain: art nouveau in style, very elegant, very lovely, the wings dotted with deep-crimson rubies. Beneath this was a card with a name embossed in the center, all in capitals: COLONEL HAROLD FERGUSON. She turned the card over; on the back, in spiky script, was written, "Something less garrish for you. —C." He had spelled "garish" wrong—but she got the point.

As she held the butterfly in her palm, feeling its unexpected heaviness, it occurred to her that she must have understood something of the way he thought, because it seemed so clear what he was doing: seducing her. And, she thought as she now rested the butterfly gently on its little velvet cushion on her IKEA coffee table, he must have understood something of her, as well—because she found how willing she was to be seduced.

The next day she received a phone call—one that, when she answered it, she realized she had been expecting—from a woman who identified herself as "Mr. Ferguson's executive assistant." She was informed, rather curtly, of a meeting she had with the Colonel that afternoon "at Mr. Ferguson's club." She wore the black dress she used for openings, her only pair of high heels, and the butterfly necklace. A car had been sent to pick her up. She was driven to a glass-faced, rectangular building on Sunset Boulevard, its architecture of a refreshed mod style regarded as very hip at the time. She rode the elevator up to the thirty-second floor, came out into a reception area that interwove more refreshed mod with old Hollywood flourishes: dark-wood paneling, chairs upholstered in zebra print, mirrors in gilt-gold frames—all this also very hip, decidedly *au courant*.

She told the predictably lovely young receptionist whom she was meeting. The receptionist made a brief phone call and then asked Judith to wait. For the next hour and a half she sat in a great, high-backed leather chair, the dimensions of which made her feel a bit like a shrunken Alice. There was a salon wall behind the reception desk, covered in photographs and paintings—she spotted at least one piece that had been sold at her gallery. Members of the club came and went—Judith saw many high cheekbones, many luxury logos. A very famous movie star was permitted by the receptionist to smoke a cigarette while he waited for the elevator.

Finally, a woman walked out into the reception area: six foot in her high heels, wearing a heather-gray skirt suit, probably in her mid-forties but with the toned physique of a much younger person, her eyebrows plucked over her eyes in an arched shape that gave her face a look of permanent disdain. She greeted Judith with a perfunctory nod, followed by an almost imperceptibly brief up-and-down look of evaluation. "I'm Mr. Ferguson's executive assistant," she said. "We spoke on the phone. You can follow me." (This interaction would prove the high point of their relationship: This woman's enmity toward Judith would be unremitting, and progressively more severe. She would learn this was merely typical, though, of the way the Colonel's employees treated one another.)

As she led Judith up a white marble staircase—this another strand of old Hollywood DNA—she instructed her, "Remember, 'Colonel' is Mr. Ferguson's given name. He has no formal military affiliation. While it's appropriate for his employees to refer to him as 'the Colonel' in talking about him or as 'Colonel' when talking to him, you should address him as Mr. Ferguson, or sir. If he invites you to call him Colonel, then call him Colonel." This final injunction was the first indication—and there would be many—that this woman regarded Judith as incredibly stupid.

They came out onto a rooftop garden, with glass walls overlooking the green, mansion-pocked Hollywood Hills. There were tables and print couches spread beneath the leafy branches of olive trees; in the center of the space was a circular bar, behind which a bartender was grating ginger over a trio of martini glasses. A house reconfiguration of a Rolling Stones song thumped gently. Everywhere Judith looked, she saw blond hair crowning lustrous skin. She felt by now she was being escorted deeper and deeper through the nine circles of hipness.

The Colonel sat at a table by the wall on the western side of the roof. He was dressed as he'd been in the gallery, in a tailored suit without a tie, the American flag pin on his lapel. Spreadsheets and maps and blueprints covered the table before him; he held a phone to his ear with one hand, with the other clutched a red pencil, with which he occasionally marked one of the papers with a number, a line. He actually looked a little overlarge for the armless chair in which he sat, and the sides of several of the papers hung limp over the table's edges—but the effect was of a man whose surroundings were insufficient to his needs, rather than of a man out of place. He had that way, she would find, of redefining the spaces he occupied around himself.

Taking her guide's cue, Judith waited silently as he spoke into the phone, not acknowledging either one of them. "And do we know how many of those units are occupied? . . . As of when? . . . Good. Let him know I know he's tied up with the NGCB, and you can tell him I know why. Tell him everything between that lot and the 215 on-ramp is mine already, and now it's just a matter of time. . . . If he stalls we'll go down to eighteen. I want this all finished by the end of the year. . . . That's right. I know." He hung up. "You can take all this out of here," he said to his assistant. She began to gather up the papers before him. "You, sit," he said to Judith, giving her only a cursory glance. She sat. "Stephanie, see if you can get me some coffee." His assistant nodded and headed toward the bar. The Colonel now turned his eyes on Judith fully, scrutinized her across the bare table. "You wore the necklace," he said at length. "Not too garish for you, then?"

She responded, "Yes, I wanted to apologize for—"

"Don't flatter yourself," he said, cutting her off brusquely. "I didn't bring you here for an apology, and I didn't get you fired because my feelings were hurt." He gave her one of his sinister-compelling smiles. "What about this place?" he asked, gesturing in a way that encompassed the whole of the garden, everyone in it, perhaps the views of the hills besides. "You think this is garish, too?"

Judith took the time to look around again—sensed there was a right answer to this question, didn't want to get it wrong. The olive trees were hung with round wicker lanterns; in a corner behind the Colonel was a four-foot-high statue of a Buddha—smiling serenely, hands folded—done in artfully weathered gold paint.

"I wouldn't say garish," she answered. "Though it certainly isn't my sort of place."

She had intended to continue, but he released a howitzer blast of laughter. "Of course it's not your 'sort of place.' Your 'sort of place' is a small dark room in a library somewhere. That's not the point."

"What is the point, then?" she answered sharply. She realized he'd already succeeded in wounding her pride—and she had been so determined not to let this interaction go as their first one had. But she would find he had this way, too: of defining interactions—people, even—around his purposes.

"The point," he answered, leaning back in his chair, assuming an overtly professorial pose, "is that this place and your gallery are two different versions of the same thing. Twenty-thousand-dollar paintings, or two grand a year for the privilege of sitting up here and drinking an eighteen-dollar cocktail. Different packaging for different customers, but the same product, for the same reason."

His assistant returned with his coffee. "Should I have them get the car, Colonel?" she asked as she placed the cup and saucer on the table, giving Judith a thinly disguised look of disdain.

"Go down and have them wait," he answered. "I need to have a chat with her." Judith watched his assistant absorb this like a physical blow—though of course she didn't protest—and she walked away.

The Colonel studied Judith's face in a more leisurely way now, as though he was examining singly her lips, cheeks, forehead, nose. Staring firmly back at his eyes didn't lessen the discomfort of this: It was as if their lightening color—the dark blue of their outer rings sliding progressively through lighter shades to something almost white around his pupils—gave them a disorienting concave depth.

Finally he released her from this tyranny of his two eyes—took a sip of his coffee, lifted a briefcase from beside his chair, and took out a plain manila folder. He opened it and made a show of examining its contents. "Judith Klein Bulbrook," he began. "Born June 8th, 1983. Ages five to eighteen, attended Gustav Girls' Academy. Graduated class valedictorian, plus a whole list of other things besides. Went to college at Yale, graduated from there summa cum laude"—he mangled the pronunciation— "and wrote a thesis titled 'Sacred Architectural Motifs and the Modern Artistic Mind,' which I'll bet is just as much of a page-turner as it sounds. Parents, David Bulbrook and Hannah Klein Bulbrook, both PhDs of English literature at Evans College, both killed on 9/11. Sincere condolences, by the way," he muttered, his eyes on the folder. (These were the only times he ever appeared uncomfortable: when he had to show, or dissemble, anything like pity.) "Dropped out of a PhD program at Princeton," he resumed, "moved to Los Angeles six weeks later. Registered Democrat since April 2001, but at least you've never voted. No medical history of interest besides some work on your nose at a French hospital"—he glanced up at her— "non-cosmetic, from the looks of it." He flipped a page. "Most of your credit-card charges are for groceries and delivery food, and you're fairly well set for money, although I'd advise you not to keep $876,342.39 in a single Citibank checking account that only accrues .05 percent annually. But then, it's obvious the nuances of personal finance are lost on you, considering you've spent close to eighty thousand dollars to rent a one-bedroom off Highland Avenue. What else . . ." He flipped another page. "You have an aunt who works at a Bikram yoga studio in Denver, but there's no reason to think you knew that, since you two haven't spoken in years. You have a cousin in Europe you email with sometimes, but that's the only family there is to speak of. No close friends, no one you call regularly. Recently unemployed"—here he smirked— "but that's hardly your fault. Prior to that a consistent employment history,

though no one you worked with had much to say about you personally, good or bad. Sex here and there, but only sex, and only here and
there." He closed the folder, dropped it on the table. "So it would
seem to me your life consists of dinners alone in a shitty apartment, a
job you just lost that was the only reason you had for getting up in
the morning, sex let's say six times a year, and if you got hit by a bus
tomorrow, there'd be one or zero people at your funeral, depending
on whether your aunt could get time off from the yoga studio. That
about the size of it?"

She had found it riveting to hear herself explained to herself in this
way. Her eyes had fallen to the folder where he'd dropped it on the
table. Her entire life had fit in that folder. It was another moment
before she looked up at him and answered, "Yes, that's the size of it."

"Shows what a degree from Yale is worth," he snickered.

She didn't know whether she'd been able to resist his gaze before,
but she felt herself yielding to it in some new way now. "I didn't know
what else I was supposed to do," she told him.

He nodded his shaved head, as though acknowledging something
to himself in this. Then he folded his hands over his sizable stomach,
and told her, "Here are some things about me. My father worked at the
Denton poultry slaughterhouse in West Texas. He was drunk, and then
he was dead before I was eight. My mother was born again and tried
to make a living as a Christian music singer. I spent my childhood in
the back of a Chrysler Sedan, driving to revivals and church picnics,
anywhere we could eat for free. When I was twelve I went to live with
my uncle in California, who owned a two-hundred-person bingo par-
lor. And despite the heartbreaking tragedy and crippling poverty of
my upbringing, I somehow managed to get into the gaming business
myself. When the state of Mississippi in its wisdom legalized gambling
in Tunica County in 1990, I had ground broken before the Vegas casinos could even find it on a map. Gambling revenue in Tunica went
from ten million dollars a year when I started to a billion a year today.
That's profit even someone with your limited understanding of finance
can appreciate. Today I own the tallest building on the Las Vegas strip
by about twenty floors, plus nineteen other casinos from New Orleans
to Michigan. I have five private residences, my own jet, a horse that's

going to run in the Kentucky Derby, and a hundred-foot yacht. I'm a proud George W. Bush Pioneer twice over, I've slept in the Lincoln Bedroom, and I sit on so many boards and panels and industry associations that even Shelly Adelson has to kiss my ass at parties. And again, I miraculously accomplished all this without the benefit of even a single semester at Yale.

"So pop quiz, Miss Summa-Whatever-It-Was, Miss Daughter-of-Two-PhDs who grew up to hand people a piece of paper in an art gallery. Which of us knows more about life. You or me?" When she didn't answer right away, he grinned with satisfaction. "Exactly. And now if you listen closely, I'll explain something to you." This injunction was unnecessary: Judith was listening closely.

"Every person lives by an idea," he declared. "And I'll prove it to you." He reached into the inside pocket of his jacket, produced a checkbook and a pen. With a few strokes, he wrote out a check—held it up. "This is a check for two million dollars, made out to Judith Klein Bulbrook. Do you see this?" She did: In handwriting she recognized from the back of the card he had sent was her name, and beneath it the words "Two million dollars and 00/100," signed by Colonel Harold Ferguson. She had to admit, it was a compelling sight—a check with her name on it, for that amount of money. "I'm just going to assume you understand by now that I'm honest. I'm going to assume you understand that if I gave you this check, you could go down to your local Citibank and deposit two million dollars in that dusty checking account of yours. You understand that, don't you?" She nodded. "Good. I'll give you this check if you crawl under the table and suck my dick. Don't worry, no one will stop you. The owner wants to build one of these in my casino on the strip. I'll pay you two million dollars to see that overeducated head of yours bobbing up and down in my lap while I sit here. What do you say?"

Judith's face darkened. "No," she said.

He let out his burst of laughter—slapped the table in a sort of angry delight and ripped the check neatly in two. "Exactly. Exactly! Because you live by an idea. And your idea is that you're sad. You're so, so sad that you believe money doesn't matter to you. $876,000 or $2,876,000, it's all the same because your parents died." He leaned forward in his chair. "Well, guess what? Fuck your parents. Fuck David, and fuck his wife Hannah." She actually felt herself begin to tremble as he said these things; the immediacy, the physicality of her response was shocking to her. "Like I told you, I'm honest," he said— not as apology, of course, but as explanation. "And I am going to tell you what every other person in this room and in that city down there is thinking. They don't give a fuck about David and Hannah, either. Two strangers who died almost a decade ago? They don't care. You know what they care about? Eighteen-dollar cocktails. Twenty-thousand-dollar paintings. Getting a blowjob, or a promotion, or another gram or second or inch of whatever it is they've decided they can't live without. Because that is how the world works." She noticed that redness had appeared at the crown of his head. "All your Ivy League friends and your art-gallery pals would like you to think there's so much more to it than that, but in fact it's all very simple. This world spins based on one principle and one principle only: Accrual. Getting More, having More. That is what makes the world go round." The redness had now spread down to his forehead. "Forget your paintings of nothing, forget the sadness you think you owe to your dead parents. It's all bullshit. Let me tell you something: Your boss fired you like that." He snapped his fingers—loud, cracking. "He didn't ask a question, I didn't even have to insist. How many people in your life do you think wouldn't fuck you over for a couple hundred thousand dollars? You think that aunt wouldn't? Or that cousin in Europe? How much do they really care that your parents died? Do you actually believe they matter to anyone anymore but you?" The redness had spread to his face—darkened his nose across the gaping nostrils. "Not many people have the courage to live by my idea. They'd rather tell themselves fairy tales: God's grace, universal brotherhood, human kindness. I bet your parents were big believers in human kindness, right up until the moment the five most devout people they ever had the bad luck to come across crashed their plane into a building. I think that tells you everything you need to know about God's grace right there. In the end, my idea is the only one that matters. The only one that counts. And you want to know how I know?" He placed a single finger on the table—the coffee cup rattled in its saucer. "Me, sitting here. I am here because I'm not afraid of how the world works. I made myself how the world works."

He leaned back in his chair, folded his hands across his stomach again. The redness of his face slowly receded. Then his eyes went back to work on her face. "I admire you for having the courage to live by your own idea," he continued. "It's the wrong one, of course, but either way it takes courage. And you don't come across many truly courageous people." And now she felt herself blush again—deeply, uninhibitedly—because to be called courageous by him struck her as the answer to a problem she had had with herself her entire life. "And I know what a person with the strength to devote themselves fully to an idea can accomplish, provided it's the right idea. Provided it's my idea. Provided," he said, "you're interested."

A glint near the pale rings of his pupils suggested to her that he knew she was interested—was more than interested: enthralled. But it seemed necessary—to him, to her—that she say it. Her eyes fell on the Buddha statue behind him: the calm, pupilless eyes, the drapery, the serene indifferent smile. She looked back at the Colonel. "Yes, I'm interested."

He opened his briefcase again and took out a single laminated page, placed it on the table between them—did this almost gently. Evidently, there were some things that commanded his reverence. On the page was a digital rendering of a tower: widest at its base, rising in stacks of tapering circular floors, each floor lined with arched black windows, the cream-colored façade toward the bottom deepening into blood red at the top, suggesting a gathering momentum in its ascent. Around this tower were clustered several smaller buildings—a concert hall, a shopping center, a sports arena, she would learn. Directly in front of the tower was a lake, dotted with tiny sailboats. "This is the Babylon Center," he told her. "Twenty million square feet of gaming, entertainment, retail, and residence. It's going to be the largest development in Las Vegas history, a city within the city: my city. Right now downtown Las Vegas is nothing but pawnshops, meth dens, vacant lots, and city land they don't even know how to get rid of. I'm going to turn all that into this." He tapped the page. "Everyone else in my industry is running for the hills—or to Macau. I'm not. I'm staying.

I'm building. People don't seem to realize we're running out of America. There isn't much of it left. And the time to get the remainder is when you can buy it for thirty cents on the dollar."

"Jesus Christ," she breathed quietly—not at any one aspect of what she'd seen or heard, but rather at all of it: at the scale of this *ex nihilo* creation.

"What I am offering you is an opportunity," he told her. "You can go on nursing your secret sadness until you end up as an old woman buying a week's worth of cat food at the grocery store because you don't like leaving the house. Or you can help build a city."

She was hardly unwilling—but a practical problem presented itself to her. "But I don't know anything about . . . the gambling industry. What would I do for you?"

"First of all, it's the gaming industry," he corrected her roughly. "Gambling is something the Mafia runs and you can get your thumbs broken doing it. Gaming is fun for the whole family. And in the future, you never have to tell me any of the long list of things you know nothing about. I'm well aware. For starters," he continued, "you'll buy art for my casinos. I may actually be able to get some return on your $150,000 degree, believe it or not. If nothing else, there are dealers who'll be impressed by the sound of the word 'Yale.' After that," he said with a loose shrug, "we'll see. Not everyone has the stomach for Las Vegas real estate. But I have a feeling you just might." Already he was artful in pulling the threads of her emotions—yanking her with an insult, drawing her back with a compliment—playing herself against herself. And already, too, she was aware he was doing it—but found she didn't have it in her to resist. "To begin with, I'm going to move you out of your one-bedroom off Highland and into one of my properties in Las Vegas. I'll have one of my personal shoppers work with you to create a look that won't remind people of an Oreo cookie. If you're going to represent me, you need to look expensive. I'll also set you up with a financial planner to do something real with your parents' money. I'll even pay you a salary. But what I'm really giving you is an education. Not the one you got from your history of modern whateverthefuck professor, or from your parents. A real education. Think of it as enlightenment."

He picked up the paper, returned it to his briefcase; he stood up—she did, too. He surveyed her again, with a certain finality now: standing in the rooftop garden, wearing the butterfly necklace he'd given her, having agreed to go to Las Vegas and enter his employ. "Not many people would have turned down the deal I offered you," he told her—and his smile spread across his face. "Even a lot of men would have at least tried to negotiate a little. Maybe you think that proves something. But someday you're going to suck my dick for free. Because that's just the way the world works. And when that happens, I'm going to remind you of this conversation." He extended his hand, she shook it; he seemed to make a point of surrounding hers completely with his own. "I'm glad to have you," he told her. She was blushing again when he let go. He picked up his briefcase and left.

She stayed in the garden for a long time—felt the need to pay for an eighteen-dollar cocktail. She sat at the table until the sun began to dip behind the rarefied real estate of the Hollywood Hills, and watched the light of the sunset on the Buddha's face—sparkling orange and red withdrawing down the profile before shadow. Then she stood up and left. She had not been able to resolve a question she had posed to herself—couldn't resolve it then, or any of the other times it came to her mind over the following months: not as she watched her belongings packed once again into cardboard boxes, this time by movers he'd hired, for her relocation to Las Vegas; not as she flew on his private jet to Berlin, or to Hong Kong, or to Art Basel in Switzerland, to purchase art for him; not as she sat in the waiting room before the surgery on her nose—which she was made to understand was a condition of her employment—or as she was wheeled around in the salon chair to see her new hair in the mirror. She didn't know the answer on the night they slept together for the first time, and when she awoke to see him standing naked before the full-length mirror, staring at himself with an almost savage rigor. And she didn't know when she flew back from Amsterdam, and landed in McCarran Airport, felt the blast of dry, desert air as she came outside, and got into the car that was waiting for her—the Polaroid left crumpled in the pocket of the seat in front of her on the airplane.

In none of these moments, or in all the time she worked for the Colonel, was Judith ever certain whether what she had consented to was more like captivity, or liberation.

2. JONAH UPON THE DRY LAND

Ash-colored mountains, stark and jagged and still, stood in the far distance before a cloudless sky of dilute blue. From these mountains, unfurling like a carpet or seeking the foreground like ocean to shore, were miles and miles of uncultivated valley, murky yellow-green in color—interrupted at some unremarkable point by the farthest sloped, cracked curb, the final chain-link fence that represented the outer edge of the exploded sprawl of Las Vegas across the desert. And several miles of asphalt and strip mall and tract of identical ranch-style house and body shop and windowless strip club and billboard (gun show, restaurant, divorce attorney) inward from this was the corner on which Jonah found himself—standing beside a telephone pole to which was taped a handwritten sign on yellow paper, with a phone number and the words, WE BUY HOUSES! CASH!

Heading down the street from the bus stop where he'd disembarked, he passed several homeless men—hunched on the curbs, or standing near the middle of the sidewalk amidst overstuffed plastic shopping bags. The homeless tended to congregate in this part of the city, as this was where most of the city's homeless services were located: the soup kitchens, the shelters, the food pantries. The neighborhood was for this reason called the "Corridor of Hope"—though whom this epithet was meant to impress or encourage, Jonah couldn't guess.

He arrived at the church that was his destination this morning. Before he'd come to Las Vegas, he'd thought of churches as ornate European cathedrals, or quaint New England steepled structures, or the gaudy-luxe megachurches in California. The Greater Love Hath No Man Church was one story of painted red concrete, L-shaped around an empty parking lot, surrounded by a wrought-iron fence, a cinder block holding open the front door. Jonah pressed a button at

the gate; after a moment he heard it unlock with a clack. He pushed it open, crossed the parking lot, and went inside.

He'd learned also not to expect long rows of wooden pews, an altar beneath a cross flanked by stained-glass windows. The interior here was entirely white—painted white walls, white ceiling, white vinyl floors—fluorescently lit, with a few rows of folding chairs set up toward the front, more folding chairs stacked in a corner. There was a cross, but it had a rather perfunctory appearance: two slats of polished metal bolted to the front wall. The overall effect put him in mind of a waiting room in a dentist's office—but he'd seen worse. If it was antiseptic, it was also clean.

As he came in, a Hispanic woman—short, plump, in a turquoise sweater and slacks—appeared through a door in the front of the room. "Oh, sorry," he said—not sure what he was apologizing for, but he always felt uncomfortable when he first walked into these churches. "I'm looking for Pastor Keith, I called yesterday. . . ."

"Mr. Jacobs?" the woman said in a thick Spanish accent.

"Jacobstein."

"You called, talk to Pastor Keith," she affirmed.

"Yes, that's me."

She gave him a look he'd gotten used to: bemused, curious—the "how did he end up here?" look. Not that he wasn't generally welcomed in the churches he visited; indeed, he was often greeted by a sincere squeeze of his two hands, an assurance that "everyone" was glad he'd come. He understood, however, that he didn't fit the profile of the person who typically wandered into a downtown Las Vegas church, seeking time with the pastor. And, to be fair, if she had questions about what a young, white, conservatively dressed, now clean-shaven former corporate lawyer was doing in her church—he did, too.

She led him down into the church's basement—a much more inviting space, in Jonah's opinion: the vinyl floors a woody brown color, the walls papered in orange. One half of the room was occupied by furniture covered in dust cloths, bookcases stacked with worn prayer books, a refrigerator that buzzed tinnily. Across from all this was a door, a piece of masking tape stuck to it with the words "Pastor Keith's Office" written in red Sharpie. The woman knocked and said something in rapid Spanish; a male voice answered back in Spanish, and the woman opened the door, smiled, and gestured for Jonah to go inside.

The room Jonah entered was so small he suspected it had been built as a closet. The floor was piled with leaflets, sheaves of paper bound in rubber bands, more broken-spined prayer books. The small metal desk toward the back was similarly cluttered, the computer monitor sitting on it no less than ten years old. Above the desk on the back wall was a purple cloth banner stitched with the words JESUS SAVES!

Pastor Keith stood up as Jonah came in. He was a heavyset African American man, stooped, with bottle-bottom-thick glasses, wore a tie and a sweater vest, had a cell phone clipped to his belt. He came around the desk to shake Jonah's hand.

"You're welcome here," he said.

"Thanks, I . . . appreciate your taking the time," Jonah answered. He noticed a conspicuous floral odor in the room—a heavy dose of air freshener.

The woman at the door exchanged a few more words of Spanish with the pastor, and then went out and closed the door behind her. "You'll have to excuse Fernanda," the pastor said. "We begin our daily meal service soon." His voice was a raspy bass, and he formed his words slowly, as though he had gotten used to talking to people who might not understand what he was saying. He motioned to two folding chairs leaning against the front of his desk. "We'll sit here," he said. The room was cramped enough that when they sat down their knees were almost touching. "How can I help you, son?" the pastor began.

"There's someone I'm hoping you can help me find," Jonah answered.

After the many weeks in Las Vegas, the many visits to churches— large and small, rich and (mostly) poor—after all the conversations that had begun just like this one, he'd found this was the most effective way to start. The request seemed not unfamiliar to the heads of Las Vegas churches.

"And who is this person?" the pastor asked.

"She's a friend, and I know she's working in real estate in Las Vegas."

"You think she might be a parishioner here?"

"No, but I know she's working on a real estate deal that involves a church." The pastor nodded. "She's tall, maybe five-eight or five-nine, short blond hair. She's sort of . . . reserved. Her name is Judy, or Judith. . . ." The pastor waited for him to continue. And he felt ridiculous whenever he came to the end of this meager description of her—but after all the weeks of searching, this was still more or less all he knew about her. He hadn't been able to find out anything, in fact, besides what he'd learned about her in Amsterdam. It was as if when she'd left the bench that day, she'd slammed some sort of door behind her.

"You can't tell me your friend's last name?" the pastor asked.

"I can't," Jonah admitted.

The pastor pushed his glasses up his nose. "I'm afraid I can't help you with that."

"You're not working with any real estate companies or anything?"

"I'm sorry, son," the pastor replied, gently consoling.

By now, though, Jonah had gotten past feeling disappointed when the pastors, the priests, the doctors, the reverends (there were far more forms of address than he would have guessed; far more churches in the greater Las Vegas area, too) told him they didn't know anything about her. All he felt, really, was that he'd heard what he'd expected to hear. "I knew it was a long shot," he muttered.

"You only came in to see us today because you knew this woman was doing a deal on a church?" Jonah nodded, fully aware how unlikely it sounded. "Why this one and not some other church?"

"I've been trying the other churches," he said.

The pastor peered at him. "This woman must be important to you."

"Well . . . it's important to me that I find her."

"What are you really looking for, son?" the pastor asked him benignly. "What do you want with this woman you're hoping to find?"

The synthetic floral smell was tickling Jonah's nostrils; he rubbed his still-tender nose carefully with his hand. This was the part of these conversations he always hoped to avoid: the questions of Why. But he had learned they were as inevitable as being told that no Judys or Judiths of that description had ever set foot in the church. "I just want to apologize to her for something."

"You hurt her?"

"Yeah, maybe, I think so. But really I only—"

"And you want her to forgive you?"

"Look, it's very complicated," he told the pastor.

"No, son, it isn't." He pointed a fleshy finger toward the cloth JESUS SAVES! banner. "Seek your forgiveness there, and you'll be forgiven for all things. You messed around on her? Got caught up in dope, or booze, or gambling? You beat her? Weren't a father to your child with her?"

"I actually only met her one—"

"Jesus will forgive you for all of it." The pastor put his hands on his thighs, leaned forward in his chair. "The love you're seeking is the love of Christ."

He'd thought about wearing a Star of David to these meetings— finding some way to announce from the outset that he was Jewish and therefore not interested in the Christ the Redeemer package. But if he found the evangelizing tiring, awkward, he also sensed—in this case, anyway—there was something sincere in it. This man wanted to help him, and this was the best way he knew how. Unfortunately, it was the wrong help, for the wrong problem. "Look, I'm really only seeking this one woman. Judy, with blond hair?" he tried one last time. "She speaks German . . . ?"

The pastor took off his glasses, wiped them with a handkerchief from his pocket. "I'm afraid I can't help you with that," he repeated. Without the glasses, his face looked weary: There were thick bags beneath his eyes, darker than the tone of his skin. A lot of church leaders looked this way, he'd found. Jonah almost wanted to apologize for not being more receptive to the evangelizing.

"Like I said, I appreciate your taking the time," was the most he could offer, though. "Can I at least leave my name and contact info, in case . . ." But "in case" what? In case Judith turned up here wanting to buy a second church, on behalf of whomever she was buying them for? He tried not think of the search as futile, though. Yes, there were a lot of churches in Las Vegas—but she had to have some connection to one of them. "Well, just in case," he finished.

The pastor returned the glasses to his face. "Certainly," he said. He took a piece of paper off his desk, glanced at it briefly, then handed it to Jonah. It appeared to be the middle page of a sermon, presumably (hopefully) long since delivered. Jonah wrote his name, his email, where he was staying, on the back. Then he returned the page to the pastor.

"They'll be needing me over at the kitchen," the pastor said, folding the piece of paper neatly and putting it into the breast pocket of his sweater vest. "I'd be glad to show you out."

They walked from the closet-cum-office back upstairs, through the white hall of the church. As they passed the stacked chairs in the corner, the pastor said, sounding a bit embarrassed, "We don't have so many folks on Sundays as we did five years ago. Ten years ago we had more than that."

Stepping over the cinder block in the doorway, they came outside. Jonah blinked against the sunlight. The sun seemed brighter to him in Las Vegas, the desert air more translucent. When his eyes had adjusted, he saw that a line of people had formed along the fence around the church—stretched around the corner to the side of the building, where the entrance to the soup kitchen must have been. They were almost all men, though there were a few women, a variety of races, ages, though most of them were middle-aged or older. There was one man with bulbous red lips and cheeks, his hair sticking up from his head in greasy curves, eyeing Jonah and the pastor suspiciously; another man appeared almost cheerful, wearing a blue-and-orange basketball jersey, a backpack on his shoulders, bouncing sprily from one foot to the other; another wore a corn yellow sweatshirt and jeans, his hands shoved in his pockets, muttering with his eyes closed. Jonah didn't see Judith standing among them—though he hadn't really expected to. He realized, however, that as he'd been searching the line, he'd been looking for something all these people might have in common. But aside from a pervasive dirtiness to their clothing, there wasn't anything— except that they were lined up outside a soup kitchen. "We serve over a hundred a day," the pastor said, observing Jonah looking down the line. "Though we're only set up for fifty. But nobody gets turned away here."

"How do you manage that?" Jonah asked.

"Fernanda," the pastor answered. "Good Christians like her. You know, she lost a boy of her own to the streets. But she makes miracles happen here every day. God works through people, son."

Jonah was not sure the line before him was really evidence of that. He and the pastor watched as a family joined the end of the line: a man, sharp-eyed and rail-thin; a woman leading one child by the hand, carrying another, dressed only in a shirt and diapers, in the crook of her arm. "You see a lot of the same faces, of course," the pastor said, in the same self-conscious way he'd explained the stacked chairs inside. "We've had a lot more out here than in the church these last few years. I do my best to give them the spirit. It's hard to preach to a hungry man, though. A hungry man wants food, even if that won't save him in the end."

"Yeah, but, this is clearly, like, very important work you're doing," Jonah responded—not entirely sure what the point of this reassurance was.

"A lot of people out here are doing their best for their brothers and sisters," the pastor answered. "The Salvation Army down the block, the Catholic Charities on Owens . . ." He pushed his glasses up his nose again. "Twice as many out here, half the number inside on Sundays," he muttered. The fatigue looked like it had thickened on his face—or maybe it was just more noticeable in the sunlight. He lifted his chin toward the chain of mountains above the flat-roofed, single-story buildings of the neighborhood. "The desert's coming in," he declared. Then he added, apropos of Jonah didn't know what, "I've been in the church since I was eight years old." Jonah could only think to nod. "You can at least set my mind at ease by promising me you don't wish any ill will on this woman you're trying to find," the pastor said, turning to Jonah.

"I'd say ill will is the opposite of what I wish her," Jonah answered.

"Then I'll pray that you find her. And if it's in God's plans, I'm certain you will."

Jonah was skeptical, having his own ideas about the predictability of God's intentions. "Well—thanks," he said.

"God bless you, son," the pastor told him.

"Right, um, same to you," Jonah mumbled—still not sure how to reply to these words, though he heard them at every church. He cast a last look at the line of people—which now extended past the front of the church to the boarded-up gas station beside it—finally started down the street, back toward the bus stop where he'd begun.

Jonah rode the bus south, in the direction of Las Vegas Boulevard—the strip. He could measure the bus's progress by the increasing frequency of motels and quickie wedding chapels visible out the window. On the strip he would change buses and, he'd decided, return to the apartment he'd rented. Sometimes he did two churches in one day, but the effect of this was always pretty discouraging—doubly discouraging, as it were.

He got off the bus across from the Wynn, one of the higher-end casinos on the strip—a smooth, fifty-story curve of brown-and-gold glass. This was of a piece with the Las Vegas he had experienced on his previous visit, made with some friends during college: carefully managed glitz, expensive restaurants and nightclubs, the loss of several hundred dollars of his parents' money—lots of alcohol. One early indication of how vastly he'd underestimated how long he'd be in Las Vegas was his decision when he'd first arrived from Amsterdam to stay on the strip, as he had on that earlier vacation. He'd gotten a room at the Mirage, a resort with a muddled desert oasis and Polynesian(ish) theme, only a notch below the Wynn on the luxury scale. It took less than a week of returning there from failed church visits for the casino's affectations of ceaseless revelry to become powerfully depressing. Jonah discovered there were only so many times a day you could walk past an empty bar playing "Don't Stop the Music" before you wanted to bang your head against the nearest wall. The apartment complex where he lived now was pretty depressing at times, too—but at least it offered a reprieve from the willed fairy tale of the strip casinos.

He began walking south, to his next bus stop. He passed the usual assortment of people on the strip: the hatted Latino men slapping together their glossy cards with pictures of glossy hookers; a bachelor party in matching T-shirts, armed with drinks in novelty plastic cups; a clutch of gray-haired tourists, happily gawking left and right; and stony-faced locals just trying to get from point A to point B—the way he used to try to cross Times Square when he lived in New York.

During his first days here, he would attempt to study all the faces
he passed, thinking that finding Judith could be as simple as bumping
into her again. (He'd had a lot of confidence then—a lot of momentum of faith.) But all this fruitless scrutiny proved dispiriting, exhausting. It was stunning to him, the variety, the combinations he discovered
possible, among noses, eyes, hair, teeth, cheeks—each face inscribed
with its own ideas, its own story, its own conceptions of itself—and
each one wholly, stubbornly: not Judith. And a place like the strip
was so densely packed with cars, bars, restaurants, casinos, elevators,
escalators, malls, shops, stands, arcades—all of it crawling, teeming
with people—that for every face he did see, he sensed he was missing
a dozen others: groups disappearing into a food court, the backs of
blond heads rising up an escalator, pedestrians on a footbridge too
distant to be made out clearly. Worst of all were the false alarms:
moments when he would suddenly be convinced he'd found her, feel
himself shot through with an adrenal mix of joy and terror—but even
by the time he was saying "Judith," realize it wasn't her. The cascad-
ing disappointment of these errors was worse than a dozen unavail-
ing church visits. Finally he'd decided to spare himself this
all-too-literal search for a single face in the crowd—though even now,
when someone slender and blond approached, he couldn't resist staring with blunt, ephemeral hope.

It was getting toward the end of November—the strip had begun to
put up the holiday decorations. He passed a man in a Santa suit taking
pictures with tourists for a dollar each; the trunks of the palm trees on
the medians had been wrapped in plastic strings of lights; on the other
side of the strip, the fifty-foot video billboard outside Treasure Island
announced a $100,000 Christmas Eve free roll in the poker room. But
there was (as with most things on the strip, in Jonah's opinion) a certain unreality to all these seasonal touches. Not least, it was hard to
muster much holiday spirit when it was sixty-eight degrees out, the
air so dry he woke up most mornings with a bloody nose.

He thought of the New York holiday rituals that would be starting
up then: the string of boozy office parties, the elaborately decorated
department-store windows, the lists of gifts clutched in gloved hands.
Maybe there was something contrived in these traditions, too, but he

felt the holidays always succeeded in infusing the city and its residents with a red-cheeked, seasonal *joie de vivre*—or as close to *joie de vivre* as New Yorkers ever got.

He understood he was homesick. But as he stopped at a traffic light—waited beside a woman pushing a stroller with a baby in it dressed in a 7-7-7 Onesie—it occurred to him he didn't know which home it was he missed. He didn't really want to resume his life in New York, as it had been—and knew he couldn't, even if he had wanted to. He certainly didn't want to move back to Roxwood, or return to the houseboat to live with Max (who had gone so far as to choke back tears when Jonah left). He still thought fondly of Zoey—but he believed leaving her alone these last few months was maybe the one inarguably correct decision he'd made. As the light changed and he crossed the street—watched the woman push the stroller and the lucky baby clumsily up the curb—he thought what he actually longed for was a life that felt familiar: one that felt natural—normal. Half the time being in Las Vegas seemed absurd to him; crazy, as a matter of fact.

But it wasn't as if he hadn't tried simpler ways of finding Judith. The day after he met her in Amsterdam, he had returned to Margaretha's art space, but it was closed, and on the following day a different art show had opened there. He eventually got in touch with the owner of the space, who had an email address for Margaretha, but she hadn't replied to any of his pleading requests for more information about her cousin. He doubted Margaretha was the sort of person who kept close track of her inbox, and he recognized it was possible that even if she had seen his emails, Judith had asked her not to reply, had told her she wanted nothing more to do with him. As for his other tenuous connection to Judith, Becky still wasn't talking to him, and Aimee hadn't responded to the notes he'd sent her via her food blog. He understood that if they took him for a creepy asshole, requesting the contact details of a woman they barely knew probably didn't help.

He hadn't been able to find her on Facebook, or on LinkedIn, or on any of the other sites seemingly every other person on the planet used. A lot of Judiths turned out to have been at Yale in September 2001; even more had gone to Camp Ramah in the previous decade. And the fact was that he might have found her name in his hours of Google searching—might have been staring right at it—but without a picture, how could he know?

Eventually he'd gone through every reasonable approach he could think of—and at that point, he didn't see what other choice he had. The one thing he knew about her present life was that she lived in Las Vegas, and she was working for a real estate company that was buying a church. So he'd come here and started making his way through the list of churches in the yellow pages. How long could it take? he remembered thinking. Again, he'd enjoyed a lot of certainty then.

He walked by an outdoor bar where a man with slicked-back hair and an earring was shouting into a microphone, "We got three-dollar kamikaze shots all day long!" Then Jonah came to another intersection, had to turn the corner to an escalator up to a pedestrian bridge above the street in order to cross. One of the (many) things he'd grown to dislike about the strip was the fact that you couldn't walk in a straight line from one end to the other: navigating it required passing through a maze of skywalks, escalators, moving sidewalks, so that you might think you were walking along the strip, only to find yourself halfway down a covered bridge to the entrance to Harrah's—which, of course, was the whole point.

On the pedestrian bridge, a man in a black bandanna and a tattered motorcycle jacket, his forehead dotted with scabs, eyes squeezed to slits, squatted in the sunlight on a dirty American flag towel beside a cardboard sign that read, PLEASE HELP! VIETNAM US VETTERAN. GOD BLESS USA. Visiting the churches, Jonah encountered people in the extremes of poverty fairly regularly—but seeing it again and again didn't help him get used to it. In many ways, it had the opposite effect. He doubted very much this man was a Vietnam veteran. Even by the most generous estimate, he would probably have been about twelve when the war ended. But Jonah knew it didn't really matter. He took a dollar out of his wallet, put it in the crumpled paper cup at his feet. As the man muttered a croaking "Thank you, brother," Jonah thought abruptly of the woman on the subway he'd given forty dollars to that afternoon with Sylvia. It was hard to believe the forty dollars had done her much good—or that this dollar would do this man much good, either. And there were people like this sitting on every pedestrian bridge on the strip, and many other places besides. He remembered something the pastor had said, which hadn't made much sense to him at the time: The desert was coming in.

Jonah had felt moved to volunteer at some of the churches, at other charitable organizations; he gave money whenever someone even hinted that his or her institution was in need of funds. It all seemed, viscerally—the right thing to do. He'd even arranged with one church to provide *pro bono* legal advice to the local community. Theoretically, this was the most valuable service he had to offer, but it had yielded the least in terms of results. There was simply not much he could do for someone with no picture ID, no birth certificate, no Social Security card, who'd had the car in which he was living unlawfully impounded. Jonah wasn't trained to help someone in that circumstance. He was trained to help BBEC.

The frustration of it was that he knew he had, objectively, so much more than so many of the people he encountered here: more money, more education, more familiarity with the law and government and employment and all these other systems. Yet he managed to do so little for any of them—little more than whatever had been achieved by giving this faux veteran a dollar. And, too, how many people had he missed walking by as he'd bent down to put the dollar in the cup? How many of them might have been women, how many with blond hair?

He rode the escalator down off the footbridge, arrived at the entrance to the Venetian, a Brobdingnagian complex of cream-colored arches and columns in high Renaissance(ish) style, fronted with an outdoor canal of swimming-pool blue, in which costumed boatmen in gondolas sang (real!) opera. To continue around all this would require him to immediately go up another escalator, onto another footbridge. Instead, he decided to go inside the casino. He was feeling hungry—and if nothing else, the strip offered a lot of good places to eat. There was a deli he'd been to once somewhere in the Venetian that could approximate a sandwich he might have gotten in New York.

He walked under an archway to the double set of doors at the casino's entrance, their inlaid glass tinted to protect those inside from the light, or the dark, or from whatever was happening outside. For a moment he caught sight of his reflection in this darkened glass—looking maybe a little haggard, a little thin, even, his nose a sort of abstract-art installation in the center of his face. Now it was November—in July he had spent the weekend of the Fourth with Sylvia and Philip Orengo and a few other couples at a house they'd rented in the Hamptons. They'd thrown a catered lobster bake on the beach, and he'd been introduced by Philip to Georgina Bloomberg. He'd gotten drunker than he should have, he and Sylvia had gotten into a searing fight about it the next day, and he recognized he was hardly in a position to complain about his quality of life—but even so—Jonah couldn't help feeling a little—diminished—as he looked at his reflection. He pulled open the doors and went inside.

He was greeted by a forty-foot Christmas tree arrayed with chubby-cheeked ceramic angels in the style of Raphael, ornamental bulbs of gold and silver; an instrumental "God Rest Ye Merry Gentlemen" was playing. As he rode the escalator behind the tree down to the casino floor, the orchestral music was replaced by the inchoate jingle-jangle of hundreds of slot machines, punctuated by regular, recorded cries of "You win again!" and "Wheel! Of! Fortune!" He instinctively glanced around the alleys formed by the slot machines. He doubted very much Judith was a gambler, though he figured that if she was, she was a slots player. But some mental rejoinder immediately noted she might also be a slots player who was playing that day at one of the twenty other casinos within a mile of where he stood. It isn't futile, he reminded himself.

He began walking down the aisles of slot machines: based on television shows, movies, sports; island-themed, fantasy-themed, cartoon-themed; or not themed at all—just machines that let you push a button and maybe win some money. He was already turned around trying to find the deli. The principle of design was the same one that governed the strip: If they could get you lost, they could get you gambling.

All around him as he walked, all manner of people were sliding money into the slots—the machines banging away happily in reply. There was an obese man with a walker here; a bride in her wedding dress and a groom in his tux there; he saw an Asian woman who was maybe eighteen, nineteen, in a very short cocktail dress, smiling across the casino floor as she sat at a slot machine, not playing. Sometimes someone won; at most they would throw their arms up and cheer for a moment. More often, a person who won just pushed the Bet Max button—the same button they pushed when they lost.

Eventually, Jonah sat down before a machine topped with a digital screen showing Rudolph the Red-Nosed Reindeer, for no reason in evidence armed with a machine gun, chewing a cigar. He felt exhausted, as though he'd absorbed all the fatigue he'd seen on the pastor's face. What was he doing here? he asked himself.

He hadn't had any visions since he'd left Amsterdam. He hadn't had any dreams. He hadn't noticed the Hasid lurking behind an Elvis impersonator or ducking into a buffet. He didn't feel like he was avoiding any of this, either, as he'd been in Amsterdam. Rather, it seemed that these things just weren't there for him to see any longer. At first, he'd taken this as confirmation that he was finally on the right track, at last doing what he was supposed to do. But increasingly he suspected the opposite: that if he'd stopped having visions, it meant he'd managed to get it wrong once again. Maybe his visions hadn't been pointing him toward Judith; maybe they hadn't been pointing him toward anything at all. He'd even tried praying—but his prayers, which he felt the clumsiness of even as he was saying them, had gone wholly unanswered: as unanswered, as unacknowledged, as the prayers he said before had always been, as he'd once assumed all people's prayers were.

Standing beside the empty bench in Amsterdam, he'd been sure. But that moment of knowing had turned out to be so brief—had started to vanish almost as he became aware of it. Soon it was all he could do not to doubt it out of existence. The only thing he still felt truly certain of—as certain as he'd been then—was that Judith had needed him, and he'd let her down.

But didn't people let each other down every day?

As he surveyed the vast sea of slot machines, all the players swimming in it, it seemed obvious: He would never find this woman. She'd said she worked for a shell company—the entire premise of her job was secrecy, deception. Even if he found the right church, its pastor or priest or whatever might not know she was involved in its sale—might

not know there was a sale in the works at all. Or even if he had somehow known she was in the Venetian at that precise moment—if the
Hasid had appeared, tapped his nose, and given him that assurance—
his chances of finding her would have still been almost nil. This hotel
had dozens of floors, tens of thousands of square feet of casino, an
entire shopping mall attached to it—and the city was full of such
places, and full of people like her opening new ones all the time. Why
did he assume he would even recognize someone he had known so
briefly? Wasn't it possible he'd passed her a dozen times, and not
known it?

He looked again around the casino floor. He wondered how many
of these people he saw playing slots were gambling addicts—how
many of them were giving away dollars they desperately needed to
eat, to pay a mortgage, to make a child-support payment. And how
many of them were gambling the way he had in college—knowing he
could only win, not lose in any real way? He didn't feel any sort of
moral superiority over those he saw gambling: He didn't condemn
them, he didn't pity them for their errors. What he felt was the broad,
willy-nilly sympathy he had somehow acquired: for the homeless
people lined up for food, for the poker dealers carrying around their
seat cushions, for the children he saw being led into bars on the strip—
even for the parents who led them there. When he looked around the
casino at the Venetian, he saw himself in New York, pushing buttons
at Cunningham Wolf—with such ambition!; he saw, too, himself
wandering all of Las Vegas, searching for someone he'd met once, for
less than an hour. What was the longer shot—being the couple who
won the two-million-dollar progressive jackpot on their wedding day,
or him finding Judith?

He put his hand to his face, rubbed his eyes—drew his palm carefully over his nose. "Give up," he said to himself. "Forget it." And
yet—and yet—

There was always an "And yet." He had seen things so real, so
vivid—he could not simply walk away from it. He could not simply
abandon the hope of it.

"Can I get you a drink, sir?" A cocktail waitress had approached
him. She wore a short gold-and-silver skirt, had a tray of a dozen

empty glasses balanced on her palm above her shoulder. And she was pregnant—her stomach roughly the size of an elementary-school-classroom globe.

"Uh . . . I'll just have a coffee or something," Jonah told her.

"Coffee, no problem!" she said, decidedly chipper. "Cream and sugar?"

She was strawberry blond, probably in her later twenties, had a thin, drawn face; her smile seemed to be trying to push all of her other features out of sight. "What are you doing here?" he couldn't stop himself from asking. She crinkled her nose uncertainly—the smile weakened a little. But he could guess: a stripper, or a hooker, or just someone's girlfriend, who'd gotten pregnant, and because she couldn't be a stripper or a hooker or someone's girlfriend anymore, she'd been set up as a cocktail waitress. It was not an uncommon story.

"Oh, wait," she said, now frowning apologetically. "Sir, if you aren't playing, I can't . . ."

"Forget it, it's okay . . ." And then he reached into his wallet and put a five-dollar tip in the cup on her tray. She thanked him profusely and walked off—her stomach protruding at least six inches before her.

Jonah stood, resumed wandering around the casino—past the slot machines, the craps and roulette tables, the bars, the poker room. He studied as many faces as he could, but after a while he wasn't looking for Judith anymore—or at least, not only for her—but for something else, and something of himself, of all of them, he was terrified to lose.

3. JUDITH OF THE MOJAVE

Judith turned on the video camera in the computer monitor on her desk so she could see the digital image of herself—used this as a mirror as she ran a tube of red lipstick across her lips. She'd considered this a pretty clever trick until she saw someone doing it in a five-year-old movie on television. It was another reminder: she had come late to the working world. She squeezed her lips together, sandwiching them between her teeth; she puckered them out, as if offering herself a kiss. She looked over her face more generally. She'd never thought she looked exactly pretty with the new nose and the rest of it, but she could tell by the reactions of people who had typically ignored her in the past (older men, the drunker young ones in bars) that she had achieved some other quality of appearance. "Well put together" was perhaps the most apt description for her now.

There was a knock on her office door. She closed the video display as a man stuck his head in. "Ready to do or die, Judy?" he asked, with a characteristically cloying grin. His name was Jerry Steadman; he was one of the Colonel's attorneys.

He came in and swung the door closed behind him. He had a bright red sneer of a mouth, thick cheeks, a half crown of reddish-brown hair. "I tell ya, I cannot get used to the sight of you behind a desk," he said with a chuckle. His head made a full hundred-eighty-degree turn from the bare wall to the left of her desk over the beige-gray carpet to the bare wall to the right, and he commented, "For a former decorator, you sure haven't done a lot of decorating." She might have corrected him that she had not been a decorator, she had been an art buyer—but of course he knew that. "Nobody ever got further hanging paintings for a living, though, that's for sure," he added. He approached her desk, handed her a plastic folder, thick with contracts. "Now don't lose these, honey. More importantly, bring them back signed. Matter of fact, if you can't, maybe don't come back at all."

Like all the Colonel's personal attorneys, this man was consistently obnoxious, two-faced, vindictive, sycophantic, petty, mean. She'd mentioned this to the Colonel once, after one of their nights together, asked him how he could trust such people. The Colonel had agreed fully—even enthusiastically—with her assessment, and explained, "It's never a question of trust with someone who charges by the tenth of the hour. Just keep paying them, they'll keep fucking whoever you tell them." Judith also understood that for the Colonel to operate the way he did—for any real estate developer to operate in Las Vegas at scale—he needed lawyers like Jerry Steadman: ones who were not inhibited by legal gray zones—rather, relished them.

He now lingered in front of her desk, tapping its edge with his fingers. "You're all set, then?" he asked her. "Shaved your legs, put on clean panty hose, told your roommate not to wait up?" He winked. "Metaphorically speaking."

Unfortunately, she had to tolerate his condescension, his smiling misogyny, his barely disguised insinuations. The Colonel had charged him with keeping an eye on the "day-to-day" (this a rather artful phrase by the standards of corporate argot, in her opinion) at the Downtown Las Vegas Development Group, the real estate company where she was now technically employed.

"I don't anticipate any problems," she said.

"Look, Judy, I'm not gonna lie," he said, clasping his hands ceremoniously behind his back. "We all know the Colonel likes to keep himself amused, but you aren't picking out paintings for the high-roller suite at the Golden Goose in Jackson, Mississippi, anymore. It's a big mystery to a lot of us how you ended up here." To be fair, it was an abiding question for her, too, why the Colonel had selected her for this particular project. She wanted very badly to believe it was not merely because he thought the manner of her parents' death gave her some sort of moral credibility that would be useful in dealing with the head of a church. "You understand this is a multi-billion-with-a-b-dollar business, don't you? And that nobody wants to see that get hung up on a fucking church?"

"He's already agreed to sign," she replied.

"Oh, well, that and a piece of toilet paper and you can take a shit," he laughed. "The signature maketh the deal, sweetheart. I guess you didn't learn that taking art classes at Yale." All the people in the Colonel's circle knew the details of her background; it was even possible that Jerry Steadman had been the one who'd compiled the dossier covering her entire life.

She now stood up from her desk. "Thank you for the contracts. The car's waiting for me downstairs."

He sighed dramatically—resigned to her fate. "Have it your way," he said. "But from one kike to another, you don't want to blow this. I'd hate to see Judy Brooks, vice president of the Downtown Las Vegas Development Group, turn back into plain old Judith Klein Bulbrook." He smiled at her with stark insincerity—because that, of course, was exactly what he wanted to see. Some of her disdain must have worked its way into her face, because he said, "That's a girl. Now you're starting to look like someone who works in Las Vegas real estate."

When he'd left, she put on her coat, took her purse and the contracts to the elevator, walked outside the anonymous office park in Henderson where the group had its offices. The first touch of afternoon cool had entered the air. She buttoned her trench coat and fastened the belt around it—though not entirely because she felt cold.

The driver of the waiting town car opened the door for her—she got in, put her purse on the seat beside her, the contracts on her lap. The business aspects of the real estate industry, the gaming (never gambling) industry, had turned out to be relatively easy for her to pick up; indeed, to her surprise, she found the subjects fascinating. There was an almost Talmudic attention to detail in the way the Colonel built his casinos, she'd learned. He researched the precise number of feet from guest elevators to table games that maximized revenue, the average time to the minute a player would sit at a slot machine based on demographics and the specific tactics (a visit from a casino host, a five-dollar coupon for a buffet) that were most effective in lengthening that average. What she was finding harder to master, though, were the social dimensions of the working world in which she'd been placed: the politics, the maneuvering, the daily score-settling. She didn't know how to turn Jerry Steadman's saccharine menace, or the Colonel's assistant's unrelenting disdain, to her advantage—and this seemed in many ways more important than whether or not she had any idea how a casino was built.

She rested her hands on the plastic folder as the town car merged onto I-515, heading north toward downtown. Yes, she had come late to the working world—but she had always been a quick study. That there were so many people rooting for her failure today was motivating. Her success would prove something.

The car exited on North Las Vegas Boulevard, and from there it was only a few blocks to the church. For every lot the car passed occupied by a forbiddingly armored liquor store, a stark industrial storage facility, there were two others with only a boarded-up building or else vacant altogether. Most of the people she saw on the side-

walks were homeless—stood on the corners in an attitude of waiting—
though Judith did not pretend to have any idea for what. Much of the
area had now officially been classified as blighted, and the Colonel
would soon gain the rights to develop it via eminent domain. Achieving this designation of blight had been a massive legal undertaking—
one in which she'd had no part—but it seemed clear enough, just
looking through the window at it, that something in this neighborhood had failed. She'd asked the Colonel once whether the community
here would try to stop the construction of the Babylon Center. He'd
answered contentedly, "What community?"

The car came to the gates of the church. The driver got out, rang
the buzzer, then drove them inside. "I'm not sure how long I'll be," she
told the driver as she got out.

"Is no problem, Ms. Brooks," the driver answered, in a thick Russian accent.

She walked across the few feet of parking lot to the church's entrance,
carrying the contracts against her chest. The church's head, Pastor
Keith D. Tolson, had legal authority to sign over ownership of this
church and its land—Jerry Steadman and his cohort had made sure of
it. The church's leadership committee hadn't met in a decade, and in
such circumstance, the pastor had full rights of disposal, according
to the church's governance documents. Just to be sure, though, they'd
quietly gotten signatures from the surviving members of the leadership
committee, now living as far away as Delray Beach, Florida, and Hack-
ensack, New Jersey. The Downtown Las Vegas Development Group
had the resources to be thorough. She pushed open the door, stepped
over the cinder block in the doorway, and went inside the Greater Love
Hath No Man Church.

She'd been here half a dozen times by now, and as always, her first
impression of it was of a staggering emptiness—emptiness that seemed
to reverberate against every bare white surface. She sat down in the first
row of folding chairs, and waited. The pastor had an office in the basement of the building, but he didn't deem it appropriate for them to be
alone together there. "Perhaps when you're married," he'd told her
once—his a far milder form of sexism than Jerry Steadman's, but sexism all the same, she thought.

She felt nervous as she waited—but she liked that, she told herself. Jerry Steadman was reprehensible, but he wasn't wrong: There was a lot at stake—for her, and for the Babylon Center. While this was only one small piece in the vast project of acquisition—involving the eminent domain takeover of some properties, the outright purchase of others, the surreptitious purchase of still more by the Downtown Las Vegas Development Group and puppet organizations like it—the church had its significance. It had taken time for the pastor to come around to the idea of selling—and time was becoming short. Already a few journalists, a few local politicians, had begun to notice that real estate in the area was being snatched up, though they'd yet to put together how much and by whom. Any further delays, though, and the Colonel's intentions might become widely known—and if that happened before he'd secured all the land he'd targeted, the whole process would become more difficult, and vastly more expensive. The Colonel wanted the church and every other holdout crossed off the list by the end of the year. So she had her part to play—in building a city.

She ran her eyes over the slats making up the metal cross on the wall. As a girl, she'd always liked churches—to the point that she worried there might be something sacrilegious in it, given how strongly she identified then as a Jew. Her mother had reassured her: She could admire the peacefulness of a place, even share in the hushed reverence it impressed on those who entered it, without betraying her religion. Her mother had been a very accepting woman—tolerant of any thought, any emotion Judith expressed. But then, she was a poet, Judith reflected.

She had found lately she could think about her parents this way: cleanly, at a distance—even with irony. Ever since she'd returned from Amsterdam, she'd been doing this. It did not make her feel proud, exactly—strong, though, perhaps. She was involved in a multi-billion-with-a-b-dollar business, her colleagues were vicious and aligned against her. But she was a match for all of it. She could reduce this cross on the wall, this church—which didn't inspire much of any feeling in her anymore, one way or the other—to nothing. Here was another change she'd noticed in herself since her return from Amsterdam. She felt at times a passion for revenge. This revenge didn't have any specific object she could identify. But it seemed to take hold of her, or she could harness it, in working toward her goals.

"I see you're admiring that cross, Miss Brooks," the pastor, standing in the doorway in the front, said in his raspy voice. He always wore one of three sweater vests—wore them with surprising dignity, she felt. (The Colonel had found this idea uproarious when she'd tried to explain it.) "You're welcome here," the pastor greeted her as he shook her hand.

"I'm very happy to be here," she answered—not wholly untrue, she reflected.

He sat down beside her in the first row of chairs. "'To all who are thirsty I will give freely of the springs of the water of life.' So says the Lord, Miss Brooks."

"I've explained to you that I'm an atheist."

"I didn't forget what you said," he replied, sighing through his nose. She had to give him credit: She never budged, but he always tried. He patted absently the half ring of stubbly black hair that remained around the back of his head. It would have surprised him to know how similar their hair had once been.

"I have the contracts," she told him, lifting the plastic folder from her lap. "It will take some time to go through them, so perhaps we ought to get started?" He didn't answer, adjusted his glasses. He was prone to thoughtful silences; she'd learned it was best just to wait for him to reach the end of them for himself.

Though he did know a few facts about her by now, in this case, she was the one with the dossier on him. He was born in North Carolina, the son of a Baptist minister, had given his first sermons as a child, and by the time he was twenty was the head of his own church, in Fayetteville. He'd gotten married, had two children, but there was a falling out of some sort—the private detectives hadn't been able to uncover the details; alcohol or adultery, they speculated—and he and his wife had gotten divorced, and he no longer spoke to her or to his children. He'd come to Las Vegas after his marriage ended to lead the Greater Love Hath No Man Church, and had been here for over thirty years. He lived in a house around the corner, didn't have a second wife or a girlfriend, was sober now if he ever hadn't been, spent his time in his church and among his dwindling flock of parishioners: visiting the housebound, comforting the grieving, helping mothers write letters to their sons' parole boards. He'd even learned Spanish so he could teach a weekly ESL class, held for the few attendees in the church's basement. "He's a true believer," the Colonel had said as he'd handed her the dossier. "The last of the Mohicans," he added with a sneer.

But Judith had grown to like him. He was thoughtful, gracious, even when she rebuffed his proselytizing: He was decent, in the best sense of the word. And she had moments of feeling pity for him, that he would no longer have this church, which constituted so much of his life. But this pity did not extend to guilt for what she was doing. The facts simply did not warrant it. The truth was the Greater Love Hath No Man Church was dying. Attendance had declined steadily for more than a decade, the building itself was overleveraged even by Las Vegas standards, and what assets there were were steadily being drained away by the soup kitchen, which operated at a heavy loss. Barring some preternatural change of fortune on the order of a parishioner winning the lottery, the church simply couldn't last more than a year—likely wouldn't make it that long. Profiting from its sale was the best outcome the pastor could reasonably hope for at this point—as she'd explained to him, as delicately as she could, many times. He'd said he intended to donate the money from the sale to various other churches and charities in the area, but the contract would also provide him a pension (the Colonel had insisted on this, for some reason). The income would not be much—but it would be sufficient. The pastor had once mentioned the possibility of moving to Virginia, where he had some cousins. You could even say it would be a happy ending for him, if you wanted to look at it that way; or if not happy, then again—sufficient.

"We used to have a wonderful music program here," the pastor now said. She'd also gotten used to him breaking his silences with comments that lacked any apparent context.

"Is that right?" she answered.

"Time was we were very well known for it. It's quite a thing, Miss Brooks, when a whole congregation is praising together."

"I can imagine," she responded—though the musical aspects of Judaism had never been her favorite.

He pushed his glasses up his nose, smiled a little. "You're a well-mannered young lady," he said. "I understand you've got other things to do today besides listen to me hold forth on the good old days. Times change and they keep on changing, isn't that right, Miss Brooks?"

"Yes, it is." She shifted the folder on her lap again, felt her stomach tighten—with eagerness, she told herself.

"I want you to know I've prayed over what happened to your parents," the pastor said. "I've prayed over it many times." The thrill, or whatever it had been in her stomach, promptly vanished; she replaced the contracts on her knees. So she would have to endure this again. "Your face tells me you don't want to talk about it," she heard him say. "Your face says that about a lot of things. But I've been in the church a long time. I know you told me what you did for a reason." Yes, she thought—because she had been instructed to, in order to win his trust. And it had worked. The Colonel had been at this a long time, too. Still, she couldn't escape the feeling that there was something terrible in trading this information in this way. And if her face had shown unhappiness when the pastor brought it up, that was the reason: Here, she did feel guilty. "The Lord has a plan," the pastor told her. She nodded neutrally. "It isn't for us to know the whys or the wherefores."

"Yes, I've heard people say things like that."

"But every now and then the Lord reveals a small piece of his plan to us. And after a great deal of prayer, I've come to believe He shared something of his plans for you with me this morning." He reached into the breast pocket of his sweater vest, produced a folded piece of paper and handed it to her. She took it with sudden anxiousness: Was this a letter from a reporter? From another real estate company? Someone outing her—ruining everything? She was relieved as she began reading to find it was only a page from a sermon: "of Daniel's strength in the lion's den. How many of us walk daily with lions? They don't look like lions, brothers and sisters. They wear the clothing of—"

"The other side, Miss Brooks," he told her patiently.

She turned over the page—shook her head with confusion. "I don't know who . . ." The comprehension of it seemed to work its way backward from her pupils: she could feel it prick at the corners of her eyes, clench her jaw, send what felt like a wave of blood toward the back of her skull. How was this possible? How was this possible?

"Then you do know this young man," the pastor said.

"Very little," she said curtly. And yet, as little as she had known him, he had managed to hurt her so deeply that she could feel the rage of it crawling over her skin even now. He had abandoned her, and in the moment she had allowed herself to be most vulnerable to abandonment.

"I can see that you're angry," the pastor was saying. "I'm not going to ask why. But I can tell you he's sincerely sorry for whatever he's done to you."

How long had she sat on that bench?—hopeful, then still hopeful—that someone was coming to put his arm around her—like a dumb, expectant child. "Oh," she answered.

"He's trying very hard to—" She had lifted the paper and was on the point of ripping it to pieces when she heard him say sharply, "You want me to sign your papers?" She looked at him: Something hard—steely—had entered his face. "Then don't you tear that page in my church." She folded the paper and put it in her purse. "I'd hate to see you give in to despair, Miss Brooks," he said, more gently now. She'd underestimated him—or she'd underestimated something.

"Sorry," she said.

"You have nothing to apologize for," he assured her. "And I want you to know I kept your secret about what we're doing. I had to bend my word to do it, but I know some women are better off not getting found." He adjusted his glasses on his nose. "I'm no fool, Miss Brooks. I didn't ask that your people keep going with the meal service, or preserve any of our other works in this community. Business is business, and I know that's why you're here. The desert's coming in, and there's nothing I or anybody else can do about it. But I also know there's nobody comes through that door that's not in need. And the fact is, I've come to care about you, Miss Brooks. I'm going to ask you to try to forgive this young man. I'm going to ask you to hear him out. I'm asking you to try to put more love in your heart than you think you're capable of and forgive him, even if he doesn't deserve it. If you promise me you'll do that, then I can sign your papers in peace."

"Then I promise," she said. And that promise and a piece of toilet paper and you can take a shit, Judith thought.

By the time she came outside, the sun had set, and the sky above the mountains was a brilliant red. The driver got out of the town car and opened the door for her as she approached. "We're not done yet," she lied. "I was hoping you would get us some dinner."

"Of course is no problem," he answered. She picked a restaurant on the other side of the city—watched him drive from the church and down the street. She wasn't happy to trick him in this way—but she doubted he would have consented to leave her alone here. And she wanted to be left alone. Besides, wasn't it the case that she could send him driving across town if she wanted? He was paid by the hour—so weren't those the rules?

She pushed through the church's gate, stepped out onto the sidewalk. A few cars drove by, but the streets were otherwise empty—more in a deserted than in a tranquil way. There simply wasn't a lot here: an out-of-business gas station to her right, a single-story house with a low-slung roof and graffiti-covered boards in its windows to her left, directly before her a pawnshop surrounded by an imposing stone wall. And behind her was the foundering Greater Love Hath No Man Church. She had a vision of all of this gone—bulldozed, torn down, paved over—replaced by the Babylon Center. If the Colonel had his way, the stretch of street where she now stood would become the lobby of the concert hall. Yes, she worked with reprehensible people, but weren't they going to accomplish something—grand?

The last time she had seen the Colonel was weeks earlier, in his office in the Olympus, his casino on the south end of the strip. Its tapering emerald green spire towered knifelike high above any of the surrounding buildings—this a great source of pride for him. Never a man for subtlety, the Colonel had his office on the top floor—the entire western wall composed of floor-to-ceiling windows. From that height, the city of Las Vegas below looked like a mere discoloration of the desert valley: an ink stain, disordered at its edges.

She had come that day directly from meeting the pastor for the first time—was nervous as she sat down across from the Colonel at his desk. The Colonel still showed an interest, when they met, in talking with her—or, more precisely, talking at her—but their face-to-face meetings had become increasingly sporadic. Most frequently now she heard from him only through his assistant, or through a Jerry Steadman.

Some of this was attributable to a need for secrecy now that she had been positioned with the Downtown Las Vegas Development Group—but not all of it, she recognized. He was mercurial, unpredictable in his dealings with all those who worked for him. The fact that they were having sex merely added another dimension to this capriciousness. Sometimes he elected to sleep with her; sometimes he behaved as if he never had. The sex never led to anything like intimacy, either (though it had its other satisfactions). And she'd come to realize that he slept with many of the women he hired, and always in this same inconstant manner.

Whether all this was pure calculated manipulation, or a reflection of some real inability in him to form relationships (he had no friends she knew of, spoke of his deceased parents only with disdain), Judith wasn't sure. But she knew it didn't matter, either, because the effect of the behavior was the same: It created a constant itching for new proofs of his favor, in her, and in all his acolytes—particularly, she observed sadly, in the women. But perhaps her job's greatest appeal was that it fostered such urgency of devotion in her. And whether this devotion was to the work itself—to this grand project of creating a city—or to the person of Colonel Harold Ferguson: this was a distinction Judith didn't bother to make.

The Colonel leaned back in his chair as he listened to her recount her meeting with the pastor—fixing her with his round, striated eyes, the inevitable American flag pin on his lapel. When she had finished, he wanted further specifics: how the conversation had begun (with a sincere welcome and an urging toward Christ); who had spoken first after she'd explained what she wanted (she had, which she was told had been an error); whether they'd gotten around to money (they hadn't, which she was told was a good sign); what they'd both been wearing (this was when the Colonel had laughed about the dignity of the sweater vests); whether she'd followed his instructions and told the pastor about her parents (she hadn't, though she repeated her promise that she would, when she found the opportunity).

When he was finally satisfied that he'd heard it all, he asked her, "So will he sign or not?"

She hesitated. Of course she wanted to say he would—but she judged it more important that she be accurate in her assessment. "I think he will," she finally answered. "I think he realizes that he's . . . fallen out of step with things."

The Colonel nodded. "That's good," he said. "That's very smart." She had managed to stop blushing at the praise, the criticism, though she still felt them as powerfully as ever. "It makes sense you two would understand each other," he added. "After all, you're both Indians."

He took visible pleasure in her confusion at this comment. And she knew he was baiting her—but why bother pretending she had it in her to resist? Wasn't the fact that she was sitting there proof enough of her subjugation? "What do you mean?" she asked.

He acknowledged this latest concession by smirking at her for several moments before answering. "There are two kinds of people in the world," he began. "Cowboys and Indians. The cowboys want all the land they can get. The Indians don't want them to have it. It's not that the Indians want the land for themselves. That's not how Indians think. They just don't believe the cowboys should get it, because the world is all ghost shirts and ancestors and the Great Spirit and shit. Cowboys— they don't give a fuck about the Great Spirit. They just want the land for their cows. Cows and oil wells and casinos.

"Now, my family history isn't distinguished in most ways," he went on, running his palm from the crown of his head down the back of his shaved scalp. "But we've been killing Indians for generations. I had a great-granduncle who was a private at the Battle of Wounded Knee. One of my grandfathers was a Pinkerton who broke the railroad strikes. Even my father shot at a few commies in Korea.

And I like to think I've done my part, too, helping out in the fight against the Islamists in the Middle East and the dirt-worshippers in the EPA.

"Fact is, though, there aren't many Indians left. Nowadays, most people want to be cowboys. Fortunately for me, they usually don't have the stones for it, in the end. But it's hard to find a true Indian anymore. Especially in this city. A community organizer here. A pastor clinging to his church there. Sometimes the culinary workers' union sneaks someone into my casino. The last throes of a dying breed. In another generation, there'll be nothing but cowboys.

"Which brings us back to you," he went on, his eyes making a brief tour of her face—a face he had refashioned in so many ways. "You were raised by Indians. Reading poems, praying to invisible spirits. But you've always had the heart of a cowboy. That's why you're sitting here right now. That's why you took that white-man name I gave you. You may think like an Indian, but that'll never be enough for you. You'll always want more.

"And so, Judy," he concluded, pronouncing the name with relish, "that's why it's no surprise that you and Pastor Keith enjoyed your little powwow. You're a nice Jewish girl from the Northeast, he's a black man from the South, but you were born of the same race. Judith of the Mojave," he said—and he curled his mouth in an O and patted it with his hand. "Wah-wah-wah-wah."

The power of these homilies he produced was not in their logic, and certainly not in their consistency, one to the next. Today everyone was cowboys and Indians; tomorrow it could be hunters and gatherers, wolves and sheep. No, what made his words compelling—and she still found them compelling, even after all these months, after everything she'd learned about him—was the force of the ideas themselves, their violence: how they shoved together, tore apart—reimagined and restructured the world around him without regard for nuance or detail. All this was inseparable in its power, too, from the persona of the man saying it, a persona he so carefully cultivated: the tycoon, in his high tower. As he often pointed out, he was his own best argument for the truth of what he said.

He now turned his attention to a pile of blueprints on his desk. "We'll speak again once you've taken care of the church," he said to her. "I've always thought you had a lot to offer. Now we'll find out if I was right."

She waited for him to continue, but of course there would be nothing more. Finally she stood, and walked toward the door. But as she was about to go out, he said, "You just need to make old Pastor Keith understand he's on the wrong side of history. And if he doesn't believe you, ask him who this whole country belonged to before cowboys like me showed up."

Now, standing outside the Greater Love Hath No Man Church, Judith considered again these things he'd said: the sweep of history he'd alluded to, the "white man" name he'd given her—Judy Brooks. He hadn't offered much rationale when he'd told her to change it— said something about it being easier for "ethnic types" to pronounce. But she realized it had more to do with his compulsion to remake things: sever them from their pasts, re-create them in his own image. He'd done it with her, he would do it with the street on which she now stood. That was the way of cowboys. And that was the heart he'd said she had.

She took a few steps down the sidewalk—stopped. It had obviously been unwise to send the driver away. The light in the sky was already fading, and her whole job was based on the premise that this neighborhood was blighted, dangerous—undesirable. She reached into her purse for her phone—instead took out the piece of paper. She read, "of Daniel's strength in the lion's den. How many of us walk daily with lions? They don't look like lions, brothers and sisters. They wear the clothing of men and women and they have the faces of men and women. But brothers and sisters, they are lions. Pushers and pimps. Gangbangers and thugs. Those who call themselfs our friends, who say they are our brothers, who claim to be our sisters, tho they lead us into sin. These are the lions who smile at us even as they tempt us from the path of Jesus. And praise God, there are those among us who see a lion when they look in the mirror each day. Yes we walk daily in the lion's den. But what does Daniel say in his righteous strength? He says, They have not harmed me! They have not harmed me, because I"

That was all. She turned the page over: the name, the email, the address. Lions, she thought. It was childlike in its naïveté—had no more intellectual sophistication than something the Colonel would have said. Though he would have said that there were only lions—that all of them were lions.

"Jonah Jacobstein," she read, in sloppy print. She had no intention. She had no intention. What did he think he was doing here? He didn't know her—and had gotten to know her only well enough to hurt her. It was like he had tricked her into a certain form of trust, just so he could betray it. She was lucky she hadn't missed her plane!—though she could hardly pretend this represented even the smallest part of the betrayal she'd felt. The truth was, she hadn't offered the hope of that particular trust—in a very long time. And when she'd broken down over that fucking Polaroid—he'd disappeared. And now he was back. It wasn't fair. It didn't make sense.

She pulled one corner of the paper toward her with one hand, the other corner away with the opposite, poised to rip it apart. She didn't care about her promise. She'd made it with every intention of breaking it—even with an enthusiasm for breaking it. If nothing else, it would feed her omnidirectional revenge. But she was aware she was struggling against a sort of wonder—a curiosity: How had he found her? He couldn't have known her last name; she barely knew her last name. And how had he known this was the church? No one knew this was the church. "Jonah Jacobstein," she read again. It was all very—strange.

She was standing in the middle of the empty sidewalk, a few feet along the fence around the church, staring over at the fortresslike pawnshop. She knew she could tear up this paper, and all the scraps of letters and numbers would be scattered in a hundred different directions—and in a year every place they scattered to would no longer exist as it did now. In a year she would be doing—what? Whatever the Colonel told her to, presumably. She could leave whenever she wanted, of course: It wasn't as if he'd stoop to stop her, if he'd care at all. And she still had the $876,000 she'd inherited from her parents, in the same Citibank checking account, had never allowed him to touch it. But what good had money ever done her? No, she would probably stay. There would be other churches—other ways to win. He knew her well enough to give her that, if only that. And after everything, she still liked the feeling of winning, of achievement. Everyone ended up somewhere, as she'd said to Jonah that afternoon in Amsterdam. She would end up here.

But if she tore up this paper, she would never know anything more about him, and what had brought him here, and how he had found her, and why. And she wanted to know more.

So, she thought, what was it, finally: Judy or Judith?

4. WHO CAN TELL IF GOD WILL TURN AND REPENT?

The Aces High Apartment Complex had the virtue of being only a ten-minute bus ride from the strip. A resident of the Aces High could, if so inclined, stand in the empty lot behind the building among the weeds poking through the spider's web of cracks, the dappled accumulation of broken glass, and see the sprawl of outbuildings backing the casinos on the western side of the street—the offices, the kitchens, the laundry rooms, the garages—and, past these, the casinos themselves: the silhouette of the roofed coliseum of Caesars Palace, the obsidian-colored pyramid of the Luxor, the jagged green spike of the Olympus, the squat approximation of the New York skyline.

Conveniently, the Aces High was also located along several other bus routes: to north Las Vegas, to Henderson to the southeast, to Summerlin, to McCarran International, where a few Aces High residents worked in food service and baggage handling. There were churches all across the city, Jonah had learned quickly—so he had sought out a place that made it relatively easy to get wherever he needed to go on a given day.

In addition to the advantageous location, the Aces High featured

(ostensibly) FREE CABLE & INTERNET!, CLEAN & SAFE ROOMS!, WEEKLY
OR MONTHLY RATES!—these attributes listed on the sign at the entrance
to the complex's parking lot. In fact, Jonah had found that only the
super's cable worked, the Internet was spotty at best, the rooms were
not reliably safe, and they were clean only in the most superficial sense
of the word. Still, it was one of the nicer short-term apartment com-
plexes he'd found in central Las Vegas. It was not overrun with meth
addicts, as was a motel a few blocks down the street; the super, Francisco, did make an effort to keep the facilities at least minimally func-
tional. Sometimes when Jonah returned to the parking lot, the two
stories of apartments—in horseshoe configuration, mint-colored doors
facing into an outdoor corridor with aquamarine railings—looked
even somewhat inviting: the paint still relatively bright, the palm trees
at the elbows of the complex more green than yellow. As he arrived
today, however, he thought the Aces High looked exactly as inviting as
would any other low-cost, short-term residence on the juncture of
several Las Vegas bus routes.

It was by then approaching dusk. He had ended up going to a second church, more or less for the sake of doing so. But he hadn't called
ahead, and the priest wasn't there, and the custodian he spoke to
seemed increasingly suspicious as they talked that he was some sort of
undercover cop. It was actually a more plausible explanation for what
he was doing there than the real one, Jonah had to concede, as he
trudged inside the Aces High.

He climbed the stairs to the second floor, walked down the outdoor corridor to his room. Simon, his neighbor, was sweeping the
concrete in front or his door—clearing it of dried palm leaves and
cigarette butts. He did this every morning, every evening. "My friend!"
Simon greeted Jonah.

"Hey," Jonah replied.

Simon was a slender young black man, originally from Mozambique. He lived in his apartment with four other young southern African men, which was the only way they could afford the monthly rent.
One of the (many) ironies Jonah had noted about the Aces High was
that, for most of its residents, it was actually rather expensive. Simon,

dressed in a plain blue painter's cap, an oversize pink polo shirt that sagged at the collar, and the dusty blue jeans he wore every day, took Jonah's hand in a handshake, and as usual, it continued into a more amorphous hand grip. Simon did not seem to recognize that Western handshakes typically terminated after a second or two. "Did you find your woman today?" Simon asked him as he held Jonah's hand.

"No, I didn't find the woman . . ." Jonah answered.

"You will find her," Simon told him. "Tomorrow." Simon gave him this assurance daily, his faith in Jonah's half-explained project never wavering; Jonah could only wish he had the same confidence. "I sweep for you, my friend," Simon offered, finally releasing his hand. To say that Jonah was entirely indifferent to the cleanliness of the patch of concrete outside his door at the Aces High would have been an understatement—but he'd given up denying Simon this chance to help him.

During the first days of their acquaintance, Simon had advised Jonah that he shouldn't get his checks cashed at the check-cashing store on the corner, because they charged a higher percentage than the one a bus stop south. Jonah had asked Simon why he didn't simply deposit his checks into a bank account, as there they wouldn't charge him any percentage at all—and Simon had stared at him, flabbergasted. This led to a long and somewhat tedious discussion (Simon required facts to be repeated several times before he would believe them) about the American banking system, and interest rates, and the rights conferred by green cards, and the relative risks of bank robbery, and so on. It all culminated in Jonah going with Simon to a bank branch a few blocks away, walking him through the steps of opening a checking account, and standing there as Simon deposited for the first time his paycheck from his job in the laundry room at Caesars Palace. For this, Jonah had earned Simon's undying gratitude and, evidently, a lifetime of doorway cleanings.

"In the last night, my friend, I tell you who go," Simon said as he swept. At the Aces High, someone was always either coming or going—and Simon, despite having limited English and working six-teen hours a day, seven days a week, somehow kept up with all the building gossip. "In the last night," he continued, "Martha, children . . ." And he paused his sweeping long enough to make a gesture of his palm parallel to the ground, slowly rising—which suggested Martha and her kids had floated off into space—but Jonah got the point. Martha had crammed herself and her four children into a one-bedroom unit; Jonah had once given her some predictably useless legal advice regarding unpaid child support. "Left things, all things, in dumper," Simon went on. "Clothes, papers, fan." Simon spun his index finger, as though to show Jonah how a fan operated. "Still work!" he said brightly.

"I guess there's always a silver lining," Jonah muttered. Simon seemed immune to the assorted miseries of the Aces High. But then, from what Jonah had heard about Simon's childhood, they had very different standards for what constituted misery. Still, thinking of Martha and her four overweight, sullen children, all piled onto a bus headed somewhere with whatever of their things they could carry, did nothing to dispel the hopeless feeling he'd been wrestling with since his visit to the Greater Love Hath No Man Church. "That's probably clean enough," he said to Simon, opening his door as the sweeping went on.

"Tomorrow you find your woman, my friend," Simon said. "Or sooner!" he added.

"Right, count on it," Jonah said, and went inside and closed the door.

His room consisted of a double bed with a dark-brown comforter, a dresser with a television chained to it, a closet-sized kitchenette equipped with a sink, a three-foot refrigerator and an electric burner, a marigold-tiled bathroom with a curtainless shower, a card table and chair by the window—and that was about it. He tossed his wallet and keys onto the dresser beside the Bible he'd been trying to read; it had proved slow going—he'd gotten bogged down in Leviticus.

He could hear a man shouting in the adjacent room. The walls were thin enough that if he'd listened he could have made out every word this man said—but he had heard it all before by now. The man had been kicked out of his house by his pregnant wife, who suspected he was cheating. He spent at least a few hours a day on the phone with her, trying to shout his way back home. Despite his at times vicious, at times sobbing denials, he really was cheating: Jonah had met his redheaded, spray-tanned mistress smoking cigarettes in the outdoor corridor a few times. She was a baccarat dealer at the Golden Nugget, was actually pretty friendly—though from what he heard through the walls, he knew she was capable of viciousness, too.

"Is it my fault I'm fucking in love with you, bitch?" the man shouted.

Jonah opened one of the heavy dresser drawers, took his laptop out from under a pile of his T-shirts. It was a meaningless precaution; if someone broke into the room, they'd obviously search the drawers. But it was better than just leaving it out. Sometimes when people happened to see inside the room, their eyes lingered on it.

He sat down with the laptop at the card table, checked his email. He'd put ads in the newspaper, had posted them on Craigslist, seeking information about a Judy or Judith in Las Vegas. All this had gotten him was forty emails a day from prostitutes and phishers, claiming to be her or know her.

He had new emails from both his parents, continuing with their advice war as to what he should do with his life now that he'd told them he wasn't on a sabbatical but rather had "quit" corporate law. His mother thought he should take up a craft of some sort, something that would let him work with his hands—printmaking was her latest suggestion; his father thought he should go back to corporate law. Philip Orengo had written, as well, updating him on the New York gossip: Patrick Hooper had a twenty-three-year-old girlfriend who was "not even wholly unattractive"; Philip himself was considering a run for city council the following fall. And naturally, all this seemed at least a world or two away from the Aces High in central Las Vegas.

He clicked over to the list of churches he kept. He actually had only about a dozen left—couldn't tell whether he found this alarming, or a relief. Either way, he didn't know what he would do when he got to the end of this list. He'd thought about going through every real estate company in the city—calling each of them up, asking to speak to Judy. And when that failed? he asked himself. He knew he couldn't stay in Las Vegas forever—whether he found Judith or not. He just had no idea what he should do next. It wouldn't be printmaking or corporate law, though. In the heady days just before he'd left Amsterdam, he'd toyed with the idea of becoming a human-rights attorney—but that seemed an especially bleak prospect, as he sat there. But didn't whatever he did after this have to depend on what happened here, in the end? How could he know what came next until he found Judith—or didn't?

He clicked back to his email. Nothing worth reading had appeared in his inbox in the last ninety seconds. He was about to close the computer, when he did get a new message—from Becky, he saw. He hesitated a moment—then opened it.

> Dear Jonah
>
> First of all I got all your emails. And Aimee talked to her sister about that girl, but she said she hasn't heard from her in years. If you do track her down she wants her email. So that's that. The real reason I'm writing is to let you know that Danny & I broke up. I still think you're an asshole for everything you did, but I guess I see the whole thing a little differently now. Maybe someday we can talk about it. But not now. Anyway. I thought you should know.
>
> Becky

Jonah reread this email several times—but each time he read it, he only grew more perplexed. Did this mean he'd been right to tell her about Danny? Or did their breakup have nothing to do with him? And what was the "whole thing" she saw differently? And why did she think he should know? He was turning all this over in his head when he heard a knock on the door. He figured it was Simon; as he stood up and opened it, his eyes were still on the computer. Only when he didn't hear Simon greet him did he turn and look—and see in his doorway a tall, skinny woman with short blond hair in a belted trench coat.

And Jonah told Judith the whole story.

———

Jonah paced back and forth across the room as he spoke, Judith sat at the card table by the window, only listening, not asking questions—and by the time he'd finished, the last of the dusk through the window had faded from the room, and all the surfaces—bed, dresser, table, carpet—looked as though they had been splashed with shadow. He sat down heavily on the bed when he was finished—nose aching from talking so much, wishing he hadn't mustered the will to quit smoking after all.

For a few moments, Judith studied him: slouched forward, his elbows on his knees, hands dangling before him, the bed bent almost to a V with his weight. The beard was gone, which contributed to a generally more conventional appearance, though it also made the crookedness of his nose more noticeable. She looked over at the dresser with the television shackled to it, a Bible lying beside this, the ribbon tucked among the first quarter of its pages. Someone in the next room started shouting. She stood up, moved closer to the wall to listen. "You think this is a fucking game?" she heard a man hollering. "You think this is a game? This is my fucking life!"

"Why do you live here?" she asked Jonah.

"It's close to a lot of buses," he muttered. But he knew there was some evasion in this—and there was no point in holding anything back now. "There's less bullshit here than in a lot of places in Las Vegas."

"Do you consider yourself an ascetic?" she asked.

"What?"

"Do you consider yourself someone who renounces—"

"Yeah, I know what the word 'ascetic' means," he said with annoyance, carefully rubbing his face at the sides of his nose. "And no, I don't consider myself one."

Judith smiled a bit in response. She had been so nervous coming here—nervous enough that, standing outside his door, she'd considered not even knocking. But she felt almost giddy now—triumphant: because it had all turned out to be so ridiculous. Who would have guessed he was the sort of person who could hold such notions—prophetic visions, divinely inspired missions? From the looks of it, not even him.

And observing her persistent smirk, Jonah said, "You don't believe it, do you?"

"I understand you believe it. But as for myself, no," she said simply. "I don't." She now picked up her purse from the floor. "Well, thank you for satisfying my curiosity."

"Wait a minute," he said, getting to his feet. "You're leaving?"

"Why would I stay?"

"Because I . . ." But it was as though in telling his story he'd lost track of precisely what it was he wanted from her. "But—at least tell me how you found me."

"I didn't follow a pillar of fire through the desert, if that's what you were thinking." His face was increasingly anxious—she knew this had been needlessly cruel, even if there had been some satisfaction in it. She reached into her purse, took out the page of the sermon with his name and address written on it, handed it to him.

"I was there this morning, though," he said as he studied it. "This was that church off Foremaster."

"The Greater Love Hath No Man Church, yes, that's right."

"But he told me he didn't know anything about you."

"It would seem he lied." And for some reason, she found satisfaction in saying this, too. She moved again toward the door.

"Wait—wait!" he said, growing desperate. He'd known it was possible she'd be skeptical when she heard his story—but of all the scenarios he'd gone over in his mind, he'd never imagined this: that she would appear so wholly indifferent, so dismissive of what he'd told her. "Look, you can't just walk out of here," he insisted.

"No?" she asked, standing at the door, her purse hanging from her hands. "Why can't I?"

"Because you have to let me—I mean, you were obviously really upset that day. You have to let me—make things right."

She paused. She had been prepared to leave him to his little corner of oddness, but now she felt an impulse to explain certain things to him. He wasn't crazy, only wildly self-deluding. And she ought to cure him of those delusions—as recompense, she thought. "Despite what you may think, I wasn't put on this earth to vindicate what you perceive as your spiritual journey," she told him.

He watched her composed, neatly made up face uneasily. "That's not what I'm saying. . . ."

"But the fact remains, you need me far more than I need you. After all, if I don't play along, then what was the point of all the time you've spent looking for me? What was the point of anything you've been through? The truth is you might have fixed on anyone, identified some urgent reason for finding that person, placed her in the role of Lois Lane to your Superman. It only happened to be me, and for no better reason than because you say you remembered seeing my photograph once."

"When I left you were sobbing," he said defensively.

"Well, that—may be so," she answered, tripping only briefly—unnoticeably, really, she told herself—at the memory of being alone on that bench. "But even you have to acknowledge that what you're implying lacks anything like logic, or fairness, or justice. Why would God send you after me, and not after one of the millions of people on the planet who might actually want or need your help? Does crying make me more deserving of divine intervention than someone sick, or someone starving? You must see that the whole idea is simply absurd."

"Okay, I get that it seems crazy, I know that better than anyone. But . . ." But he realized that even now he didn't know how to describe his faith—knew this wasn't solely a problem of articulation, either. And he could not deny—she made a strong case.

"I don't doubt you've felt guilty for what you did," she continued. "But don't mistake your guilt for more than it is. Despite your purported visions, there's nothing I want or need from you, Jonah. And if you ever thought differently—you were mistaken," she concluded with a shrug.

He opened his mouth to respond—then didn't. She watched his eyes darting back and forth to look at hers. She felt sorry for him now. Even the pastor had made a better showing, and he had wanted to surrender. The Colonel had been right about her, she thought. He had been right about all of it. "They're all just stories, Jonah," she told him. "They're just stories we tell ourselves from the things that happen to us. We're the ones who give the events meaning or moral, who conclude that they unfold the only way they could unfold, as opposed to how they happen to unfold. And we're the ones who imagine that at the center of them is us, on our little journey, and that it's God's hand on the quill pen. But the fact is, if you'd done what any reasonable person would have, and started taking pills when you had your visions, so-called, you'd probably be living with one of those girls right now, and be at work at your law firm, and feel perfectly content that everything was going exactly according to plan."

The only light in the room now came from the dull glow through the window of the streetlamp in the Aces High parking lot. Jonah sat back down on the shadowed bed. He knew he ought to argue with her—but much of what she'd said had occurred to him at times, too. And to have finally found her—the central figure in so much of what he had come to believe—only to have her pick those beliefs apart, bit by bit, made her assertions very difficult to dismiss. It was true: There was no logic, no discernible fairness to what he'd described. It wasn't based on anything like logic or fairness. Maybe then, she was right—it wasn't based on anything at all.

And yet—and yet—

But why was his faith never more than an "And yet"—no more powerful than a caveat, a footnote, a suspicion? Why, when he tried to take hold of it, did it feel no more certain than grasping an icicle?

"I'm afraid I left your coat in the Amsterdam airport," she said. Watching him sitting silently on the bed, his face toward the floor, looking so thoroughly confounded, she'd felt she should offer some consolation—hadn't come up with anything better. "Perhaps you can claim it from their lost-and-found. There were only some . . . cigarette butts in the pockets."

"Why were you crying that day?" he asked after another moment.

She hesitated—but why shouldn't she tell him? Hadn't she promised herself she would never cry in that way—for those reasons—again? "I was thinking about my parents," she answered, very evenly, very cleanly—the way she'd practiced in the mirror before telling the pastor. "They were killed on 9/11." And she continued, in just the way she'd practiced, "But that was a long time ago. In any case, I was upset that day. That's to be expected from time to time. And I do—appreciate all you did to make amends for—departing so abruptly. But of course, you weren't responsible for—me. Regardless, I am glad we got the opportunity to resolve things. I wish you all the best. So, goodbye." She didn't move—as though in this unexpected stream of words, she'd forgotten what it was she was actually saying. "Goodbye," she repeated, reminding herself. She saw him studying her quizzically. "Oh, I suppose that fits your purposes very nicely, does it?" she said sharply. "The poor little orphan, and your divinely ordained mission to console me."

"It's just you didn't mention it."

"Didn't mention what?"

"We talked about 9/11, and you didn't mention it."

"Did we?" she said quickly. "I don't remember that." It was a stupid lie, a pointless lie—and, she recognized immediately, one that announced itself as false even as it left her mouth.

For a while neither spoke—they eyed one another with differing forms of suspicion. Jonah remembered what he'd concluded about her in Amsterdam: that she was wearing a costume. And here she was, with the same polished face and hair, the same purse, the same trench coat—which, he now noticed, she hadn't removed.

"Why are you working in real estate out here?" he asked her. "Why are you buying churches so a casino can secretly—"

"And why shouldn't I be doing that?" she interrupted. "Because I went to Jewish summer camp?"

"Because it's a fucked-up thing to do!"

She scoffed. "Would I be better off getting myself fired and going to look for a stranger because God said so?"

He stood up from the bed. "What point are you trying to make with all this?" he asked, waving his hand at her. "You know as well as I do all of this is bullshit."

She forced out a bitter chuckle. "Is that right? Then why don't you enlighten me as to how I might live a more authentic life."

"For starters, don't defraud some dilapidated Las Vegas church!" he shouted.

She reached into her purse and pulled out the plastic folder—threw it onto the bed. The contracts spilled out across the comforter. "You see? It's done. He signed. The Greater Love Hath No Man Church now belongs to Colonel Harold Ferguson. Thanks to me." Jonah looked at the stapled sheaves of paper—the pages askew, bunched into waves against the pillows, every inch covered in typed words. "Are you satisfied?" she asked. "Will you leave me alone now?"

In the vague light, he could see the fixity of her face as she stared at the contracts—her one fist clenched around the handle of her purse. "You came to see me," he said quietly.

She couldn't deny it—but she didn't know why she had anymore: some indulgence, of old, vestigial instincts. She knew she ought to leave at last, but there was something dismaying in seeing the contracts scattered across the bed this way; she found she didn't have the energy to gather them back into their plastic folder. "It's something to be a part of," she told him. "A way to be exceptional. And I always imagined I'd accomplish something—exceptional. Can you understand that?"

He thought of the 17,500 hours of his life he'd given to Cunningham Wolf. "Yeah, I can."

"What does it matter anyway?" she said. "One less church in the world."

Again they were silent. Jonah could hear the tinny, somehow hopeless whirring of the air-conditioning units in all the neighboring rooms, cars rolling by on the surrounding streets, someone watching television in an adjacent room—the sounds of the Aces High at night. "Judith . . ." he began.

"Please don't," she said. "There's no great tragedy here. This is just the career I'm choosing."

"But what if—"

"What if what? What if, instead of leaving that day, you'd stayed? And then? You'd have spent ten minutes consoling me and wouldn't have felt so guilty? Or I'd have changed my flight so we could have gone to my hotel room and spent a night together? I know it's tempting to think it could all have been different so easily. If I'd gone to a different college, then maybe my parents would have flown out of a different airport. Or I might have gone to college where you went. Then we might have met each other a lot sooner.

Two Jews at a good college, who knows? Fine, it might have been different. But it wasn't."

Her voice had remained even, controlled. But in her trench coat she looked to him the way he remembered her looking when he'd last seen her in Amsterdam: thin—insubstantial. He had never known exactly what he would do, was supposed to do, if he found her. He sometimes pictured it being as simple as giving her a hug—the hug he should have given her in Amsterdam: They'd hug, she'd feel better about whatever it was she'd been crying about, and then, well, mission accomplished. He now recognized the naïveté of this—the arrogance of this whole endeavor. Her life, her needs, had all the complexity that his did—that anyone's did. What did he expect to offer her?

"It's all right, Jonah," she said, as if guessing his thoughts. "I absolve you of everything. And you'll be fine, too. You'll get together with some new girl, you'll be able to figure out a life for yourself that feels meaningful. And a year from now," she added, smiling crookedly, "I'll attend the groundbreaking of the Babylon Center." She lifted her purse up on her shoulder.

He knew there probably wasn't anything he could do for her. Most likely, one way or another, he'd misunderstood everything again. But to just give up, to not try at all—would be wrong. "What if it were true?" he said.

"Please, Jonah . . ."

"I mean—what if you could believe it?"

She was already shaking her head. "You honestly think you can convince me of that? God sent you?"

"I mean, I know how it sounds, but—hasn't there ever been a time when you just felt—when you just—knew?"

She thought abruptly of the creek, the night before she'd gone to college. There had seemed to be so much in the world then—so much more than she could ever feel, touch, know—and she'd wanted to submerge herself in it—drown in it. But it had turned out—there was so much less—

"Please don't do this to me, Jonah," she said. But wasn't there something here she still wanted? she asked herself. Why else would she have come?

"All I'm saying is, there's a reason we're in this room. Us, and no one else. That has to be proof of something, doesn't it? Judith," he said. "Here I am. We could leave—right now. It's not too late."

And all at once some new form of possibility broke across her mind. So much had been lost—so much of the hope, of the promise of the girl in the Polaroid. But what if it could be regained? Or what if it had never been lost at all? Was she not still that girl? She saw an image of the two of them sitting at a kitchen table somewhere, each doing a copy of the Sunday crossword puzzle. Was it possible—that after everything—?

No, she thought. No. It was too hard. It had been too long. And in the next moment she was angry—furious. Who did he think he was—to do this to her again, with the arrogance of his unearned faith? And her anger resolved into a very clear intention, a familiar need: to prove that she was right—about everything. She would show him exactly what the two of them being in that room amounted to. Revenge, Judith thought.

She moved over to the switch by the door and turned it on. A single circular fluorescent on the ceiling buzzed to life, cast an unnaturally blank light into every corner of the room. He stood watching her uncertainly from beside the bed. No, she thought, without the beard, he was not bad-looking. They would do what came naturally.

Now she did take off her coat, dropped it to the floor. Beneath it, she was wearing a knee-length cotton dress, its blue almost neon in the stark light. She took off her high heels, and Jonah watched her shrink three inches in height, one foot at a time. Then she sat down on the bed, tucked her knees to her chest, hugged herself—like *une pauvre petite orpheline*, she thought. After a moment, he sat down beside her—because, she thought, they were all the same—and this was what was natural. In the sudden illumination, she could see the fine lines at the corners of his brown eyes, the jutting angle at the tip of his nose. "You've waited a long time for this," she said. Then she put her left hand on his neck, pulled his head toward her, and kissed him.

He kissed her back for a few moments, but as she opened her lips wider he pulled away. "I don't think this is . . ." he began.

"What else could it be?" She pulled his head toward her again, but he moved her hand away.

"What are you doing?" he asked.

"You came here to save me. So let me feel you saving me." She moved in to kiss him again, but he sat back. He searched her face in confusion, but in the fluorescent glow it seemed to be only surface: makeup-tinted skin, sheer black eyes. "Is this really what . . ."

"What did you think, that I would leave with you?" she said. "Give up my life, because that's what God wanted? Don't be stupid, Jonah. That isn't the way the world works. The way it works is, we make each other feel good for a couple hours, and then we never see each other again." She reached down and intertwined her fingers with his, lifted his hand to her face. "That is the only thing you can do for me." She moved his hand down to her breast. "Wouldn't you like to fuck me senseless, and then never have to think about me again?" She had expected to be so turned on, doing this—but all she felt was sadness. But then, as she felt his hand gripping her breast—his eyes now pained, angry—there was the arousal. And they began to kiss—frantically, mindlessly, their tongues making riot in each other's mouths. She shoved the contracts off the side of the bed as they lay down, pushed themselves up with their feet.

Maybe she had been right all along, Jonah thought—this was the most it was ever going to be. He could do this—and he could go home.

"I do everything," Judith said. "You have no idea how sexually adroit I am."

"You would use a word like 'adroit' at a time like this," he said with disdain—and admitting this disdain only seemed to turn them both on more. He reached under her dress between her thighs, pulled down her panties.

She gripped his head again, as if forcing him to stare at her. "It's not your fault you got stuck with such a conceited, ungrateful bitch. Do you know whose fault it is? Whose plan it was? And don't you want revenge?"

"Shut up," he said—grabbed her hands away by the wrists, pulled her dress down to her waist. She lifted her hips and he pulled the dress down off her legs, yanked apart the clasp of her bra and tossed it away, so she was now completely naked. He stared at her body: her arms thrown back above her head, a line at her throat where the makeup gave way to pale white skin, the deep concave of her belly moving up and down between ribs he could count as she breathed, her skinny legs tapering to her ankles, her body entirely hairless.

She said, somewhat self-conscious, "I've been skipping lunches, I'm not. . . ." But then she understood his look a little better. She should have kept the lights off, she thought.

"I really thought—I really thought it would be more . . ." he said.

She felt sorry for him again—for both of them—because she realized this had been her last chance at something, too. But she hadn't been brave enough—or he hadn't—or they'd fallen one miracle short. It was very sad to her that even now, she was hoping for something miraculous. She ought to know better.

She touched his face, gently this time. "It's not our fault. We're only bodies." And she began to undress him—taking off his shirt, his pants, his boxer shorts. "We're only bodies . . ."

They started to kiss again, both naked. In a similar moment, with Zoey, his body had betrayed him, or maybe rescued him, but as he moved on top of Judith, he could tell there would be no such divergence this time. And all he did want, was to fuck her senseless—fuck away the entire last few months. Yes, it was hard to let it go, when you'd seen what he'd seen. But it was hard to hold on to it, too.

"Hey," she said, just as he was about to start. "You'll be okay, right?" Her eyes had a tearful look. "I mean, we both will. In the end. Don't you think?" He saw she had taken handfuls of the bedspread— as though holding on to it—to the room, to this moment—for dear life.

He stopped. He didn't know what would become of either of them after they left this room—after they'd consigned whatever this might have been to a brief remembered fuck. He didn't know if she finally could be called worthy of divine intervention, if she was drowning, or melting, or unalterably vulnerable and naked—whether this was true of him, or of anyone, or of everyone. It was God or it wasn't. The visions had been real or they hadn't. But he knew that whatever he did, wherever he went—whether he became a partner in a law firm in San Francisco, or sold malarial drugs in Africa, whether he convinced Zoey or Sylvia to take him back, or got together with someone new, for love or nothing like it—he would never be able to forget the look on her face, or the question she'd just asked. In the end, it wasn't God or the visions or the Hasid you couldn't escape. It was yourself.

But where naked human bodies are concerned, deciding you shouldn't do something and not doing it are, of course, very different matters. And he wanted her to know he was sure. Well, he thought—it was time to suffer what his faith demanded. He stood, and then went over to the dresser. He opened the top drawer and leaned over so his nose was in the gap between the drawer and the top of the dresser's frame. "What are you—" she said as he slammed the drawer shut.

The cracking sound and the caterwaul of pain he let out and the realization of what he had done and the sight of him jerking onto his back as though the force had knocked him over all reached Judith at the same time. She scrambled to the edge of the bed. Blood was gushing from both his nostrils. A feeling of wrenching awareness and terrified awe came over her. She leapt to the dresser and pulled open the drawer—was leaning over when he realized what she intended. He tried to speak but could only spit out a few disordered syllables, grabbed her around the waist and she tumbled over on top of him—and they lay there, naked on the carpet, their legs entangled, both panting.

And then she began to laugh—her clear, mezzo-soprano laugh. "Okay, I admit it," she said, laughing harder now. "That was more than I expected."

They were up all night. It was hard to get the bleeding to stop; they went through most of Jonah's T-shirts, using them as bandages, Judith made four separate trips to the one working ice machine in the Aces High, on the ground floor on the opposite side of the building. Eventually, though, it slowed to a trickle, finally petered out altogether—and

Judith wiped the caked blood off Jonah's chin and his chest with one of his socks, which she wet in the sink.

Neither of them had eaten since the afternoon before, but all she found in the kitchenette were cereal and ground coffee. Apparently he didn't cook much, either. But he insisted that she at least have something, and she indulged him: sat cross-legged at the end of the bed, eating a bowl of dry cereal, while he sat at the pillows, his head tilted back against the wall. She told him about where she'd grown up, about what she'd done after her parents died, about the Colonel, her work in Las Vegas—all the blanks he hadn't been able to fill in for himself. He told her about his own upbringing, about his law career, his life prior to the visions. There were certain symmetries in their lives, she noted: differences, too, but perhaps more fundamental similarities.

At last, as a tentative morning light filled the window, Jonah fell asleep. But Judith wasn't tired at all. As he slept with his head still back, his mouth open, snoring dully—as though he were trying to communicate with a water stain on the ceiling in a sonorous, whalelike drone—she stood up and opened the door to the room, went outside.

It was a desert morning in November; she wore only one of his last clean T-shirts and a pair of basketball shorts she'd taken from one of his drawers, but she didn't mind the cold—even took pleasure in the sensation of goose bumps forming on her arms as she stepped from the doorway out onto the concrete of the corridor. She'd left her shoes inside—ones the Colonel had given her on an occasion when he'd elected to give her a gift—but she decided she didn't care. She liked the sensation of the concrete against her feet, too. Her toes were painted a burgundy color—and as she looked down at them, she had the urge to remove this: remove the matching polish from her fingernails, the makeup from her face, the product and dye from her hair. But it could wait an hour or two.

In bare feet she padded along the corridor, then down the stairs inside the building and out into the parking lot. The early-morning traffic was still thin—only a few cars and delivery trucks passed by. Soon, though, the commuters would be heading to work; the offices of the Downtown Las Vegas Development Group would begin to fill up.

Jerry Steadman would be knocking on her door, wanting to know about the contracts. All of them would want to know. Those hoping for her failure (and that was more or less everyone) would probably take the fact that they hadn't heard anything yet as a positive omen. Let them have it, she thought: She renounced all rights and privileges to the Colonel, to his works. In light of the last hours, there seemed a fundamental smallness to him now.

She traced a route around to the back of the Aces High, where she guessed, correctly, she would have a view of the strip. The vacant lot behind the building was littered with broken glass, splinters of concrete—everything sharp or filthy or both. But again, she didn't care: She walked onto the lot, taking little inhalations of breath with each spike of pain on the soles of her feet—welcoming every prod, every prick.

The sky had a towering quality in the West that you didn't find in the Northeast—and its blue was so fine at this hour it was almost indistinguishable from white. Set beneath this sky, the mammoth hotels of the strip looked even quaint—mismatched tchotchkes on a mantel: a black pyramid, a cream cylinder, a green toothpick. From here, all of it conformed to a lovely morning.

And Judith realized she was smiling.

Because she found—it was all still here. She could sense, not her parents exactly—but something of the joy of them, what might be called the best of them: their way of seeing the world—the richness they identified in it—the hope they had for it. It was all still here.

She asked herself: Could it have been God? It seemed a lot to believe—but she could not deny the thrilling strangeness of it all. If nothing else, it had to be called uncanny: everything he had seen, and all he had done on account of it; how he had followed the path of faith and coincidence to find her here—he, someone who had been raised as she had, someone who could speak to her in her own language, as it were. It was the two of them who'd ended up in that room, as he'd said—the two of them and no one else. Yes, it was uncanny—but perhaps it had no more and no less than the uncanniness present in any moment.

She took another step toward the sky, the horizon. She knew it was a stupid, clichéd thing to feel, but she let herself feel it anyway: She felt free. From the moment she had heard the cracking sound of Jonah's nose, she felt she had woken up—thrown off the self she had been only the day before: a parody of the person she might have become; a martyr to the injustice of her own life; or nothing at all, really—one more subject of a false king. Somehow, when Jonah had done that, he had proven something to her—something she had stopped believing a long time ago. And now she stood before this morning—liberated.

But then, she thought, hadn't she seen herself as liberated at times in working for the Colonel? Had she not merely traded one man and his faith for Jonah, and his?

It was, she had to admit, a good question—she had always been perspicacious. But it was a question she was not interested in answering. What she wanted was this feeling: this morning, this sky, this faith, this renewal—and she took another step forward, as though to push herself more fully within it. Then she felt a sudden piercing pain as a shard of glass burrowed into her foot.

She let out a yowl, lifting up the wounded foot. She balanced unsteadily for a few seconds, finally started to hop across the lot to the thin strip of concrete tracing the back of the Aces High—this, of course, sending fresh stabs of pain into the uninjured foot. And as she hopped her way across the lot, she could not help thinking—that this was all so familiar.

Reaching the building, she sat back against it—lifted the damaged foot over her opposite knee. The arrowhead of glass was embedded just beneath her second toe. She tucked her lips into her mouth and with two fingers slowly drew it out—moaning as it finally came free. Then she held the glass before her eyes: dark green, and with a single drop of her blood at its tip. And Judith began to cry.

She didn't cry because of the pain. She cried for all the mistakes she had made, over and over—for the excesses of her zeal, for what she had done to Claudette, for all she had lost and given up and failed to do because of what had happened to her parents—to try to be dead, like them. Eventually her crying subsided—its sound seeming to have sunk into the morning sky.

She was such a strange person, she thought, now with a heavy sort of sorrow—and there would be no escaping that into a new self. She would always be the same, stumblingly fanatical woman she had always been—since the day she brought home her first piece of homework in kindergarten and did it with such delight at the dining room table. The fanaticism would always be there, as much as the perspicacity, as much as the grief, as much as the aloofness that seemed inextricable from the academic mind-set with which she'd been brought up—her zealotry always impelling her to take one step, or a thousand, too many. No one would ever appear to rescue her from that. She glanced once more at the horizon—then began hopping around to the front of the building.

She made it to Jonah's door; as she was about to open it, the door beside it swung open and a skinny, dark-skinned man in a blue cap and an oversize pink polo shirt walked out, carrying a broom. He stared at her, aghast.

She couldn't imagine what he made of her: in a billowing T-shirt and basketball shorts, barefoot and bleeding, having stayed up all night. "I'm a friend of Jonah's," she began, lowering the toes of the wounded foot to the ground. "I was just . . . visiting . . ."

He nodded his way through this information—and then he broke into a startlingly happy smile. "You are the woman!" he declared.

"Oh," she said. "Yes, I suppose that's right."

This, apparently, was hilarious: He nearly doubled over with laughter, clapping his hands in delight. "I said to him, I said today," he laughed. "Oh, I told him, sister, I told him."

Judith was touched that Jonah had told other people about his search for her—was touched, too, by how genuinely pleased this man seemed that it had been a success.

"Now you must tell me, sister," he said, when his laughter finally abated. "Where were you hiding?"

She hadn't thought of herself as hiding—though she understood that from a certain point of view, she had been. "It's . . . difficult to explain," she answered.

"I always keep my eye on him, sister," the man went on, tapping his eye. "Now you keep an eye on him, too."

She couldn't identify his accent as anything but African, and this ignorance bothered her. "Where are you from?" she asked him.

"From Mozambique," he replied. "In Africa."

"You speak Portuguese, then?"

He answered in what she could recognize as the language, but she didn't understand it. She was fluent in French, conversant in German and Italian, and if there had been a copy of the *Aeneid* lying around, she could probably have translated a good deal of it. But she didn't speak Portuguese—and it struck her, you could spend your whole life, and never know what you'd need to learn.

"What's Mozambique like?"

He considered for a few seconds, as though the answer was complicated—which, she reasoned, it must be. "Mozambique is beautiful. Not like here. Oceans, mountains, people. Everything in Mozambique is very beautiful. But too much . . ." And he made his face elaborately sinister and performed a gesture of plucking something from his pocket.

"Graft?" Judith offered.

"Here is better. Work, work, work, you get a little money, yes, only a little money, but then more and more. My brothers come soon," he said. And then he added with pride, "Later, I will marry." He reached into his back pocket, took out a Velcro wallet—handed her a three-by-three photograph: a heavy-set woman with dark black skin and a somber expression on her face, her hair elaborately braided, seated before a screen painted with blue sky and gauzy white clouds.

Judith thought of the portrait of her great-grandfather that had hung in her childhood living room. She thought of her family: the Kleins, her mother's side, murdered en masse in Europe, her grandmother the only survivor, arriving in Philadelphia at sixteen; the Bulbrooks, her father's side, immigrants from Austria to New Jersey sometime in the first decade of the previous century, for forty years owning a shoe store on Bloomfield Avenue in Caldwell. They had left Europe, as this man had left Africa, survivors of everything—and built a new home, a new family, from out of nothing. Those were her forebears.

"It's too bad there's only one America," she said to him. "It's too bad there's nowhere else to go to start all over from here."

He didn't answer, just smiled at her—and after a moment she realized he hadn't understood. And why should he? she thought. His English was better than her Portuguese. Besides, he was in the midst of playing the central role in a great story: the migration across continents—the genesis of a new way of life for his descendants for generations to come. Maybe one day his portrait would hang in the living room of his great-granddaughter—and she would grow up to be one of those hypereducated overachievers who goes on to change the world, or doesn't: like Judith Klein Bulbrook.

No, there was no other America. There was no other place where this man's story would have been possible, where hers would have been possible. And as the Colonel often said, there wasn't much of it left. For the first time it occurred to her that she owed something to the stories that had preceded hers; that she had to have a certain faith in those stories, and in her own story, as well. Only she could be the hero of her own life. It was the way she'd been raised.

She went back into the room. Jonah had gotten up, was gathering his things from out of the drawers—packing. "Wait," she told him. "There's something I have to do first."

5. AND GOD SAW THEIR WORKS

The sun rose higher in the azure sky above Las Vegas, illuminating fully the city below, the mountains across the horizon appearing like spectators in an amphitheater, gathered there to see what the day held: whatever feats, whatever failures. Pastor Keith had gotten out of bed, was stirring the sugar into his coffee as he sat at the table in his kitchen, the radio on, the spoon clinking against the side of the mug as he stared at the wall and tried to imagine how he would explain what he'd decided. By then the Colonel had been at his desk for hours. He had before him the latest blueprints for the lobby of the central tower

of the Babylon Center—he was deciding where to end a line that
indicated how far the concierge desk would extend to the east in front
of the windows before the lake. He made the line, he erased it; he
made the line again, he erased it again. A thousand feet below him, on
the casino floor, convention-goers were lined up for coffee, their
badges in plastic sleeves around their necks. Only a few of the table
games were open, but every row of slots had a player or two—trying
their luck. In Summerlin, to the west, neighbors were walking from
identical doorways down identical drives for the newspaper. In the
shelters on Foremaster, to the north, all the beds were being cleared
for the day, and everyone going out was informed to come at least an
hour early if they wanted to be sure of a bed when the doors opened
again that night. How they would fill the intervening time was up to
them: It was, after all, a city like any other. In Istanbul, Lindsey and
Bonnie were standing in their matching North Face jackets in front of
the Blue Mosque. In Amsterdam, Max and Rafik were playing chess
on the houseboat—joints burning in the ashtray between them as they
talked. In New York it was already well into the morning. The traffic
on the bridges and tunnels had cleared a little, the dog walkers and
food trucks appeared on the sidewalks. Milim Oh, now a resident at
Cornell, was seeing patients as part of her oncology rotation. In the
offices of Cunningham Wolf LLP, lawyers were busily preparing the
final settlement between BBEC and Dyomax. On Spring Street, Brett
was showing a one-bedroom apartment to a middle-aged divorcé,
warming him up to give him the card for Guru Phil. Becky and Danny
were talking on the phone for the second time that morning: It was
part of a long, painful reconciliation or a further prolonging of a tor-
turous breakup. Who could know? Sylvia was at her desk, reviewing
the org announcement of her promotion to vice president at Ellis–
Michaels. It was what she'd wanted; she felt happy. And Zoey was
avoiding working on the *Glossified* article she needed to write by
updating her résumé, and was procrastinating from that by scrutiniz-
ing the JDate profile of the man she was seeing for the first time that
night. He was a lawyer, but on the other hand, he did yoga.

Here we go again, Zoey thought.

And Judith and Jonah were buzzed through the gate of the Greater Love Hath No Man Church. They weren't expected, but Fernanda told them the pastor would see them, and escorted them past the semicircle of chairs in the basement that had been set up for the weekly ESL class. In his tiny office with the purple JESUS SAVES! banner, which Judith had never seen before, Pastor Keith greeted them both with his customary assurance that they were welcome there. He seemed only mildly surprised to see them together. By the questions he asked, Jonah thought he expected them to ask him to marry them. But that was not why they had come.

Judith returned the contracts he'd signed the previous day—a little worse for wear in their plastic folder. She explained to him who owned the Downtown Las Vegas Development Group, and what its purpose was, and what the Babylon Center would be, and where it would be. And then she placed on his desk a check for $876,000. She listened to his objections serenely, just as she had listened to Jonah's. It was the least that she owed, she said when the Pastor was done. Trying to buy the church as she had was wrong—and she'd known it was wrong, which was why she'd tried to do it. This, she told him, was what her parents would have wanted.

Pastor Keith stared at the check on the pile of papers on his desk for a long time. "This is a miracle," he finally declared—though to Jonah he sounded uncertain. "Miracles happen every day." He finally took the check and put it into the pocket of his sweater vest—a little wearily, Jonah thought.

As they came outside, the day had become only more glorious—the sun only brighter, the oceanic blue of the sky only deeper. And Jonah saw that already dozens of people had lined up for the soup kitchen.

They returned to the Aces High. They had stopped by Judith's apartment before going to the church. She sat with the duffel bag of her things beside her on the bed as Jonah began to pack the clothes from the dresser into the suitcase he'd come with. As he opened the last drawer, the man in the next room was shouting again: "Oh my God, fuck you! Jesus Christ, you fucking bitch! Fuck you! God damn it, fuck you!"

Jonah shut the drawer. "I don't understand."

"What?" she asked.

He turned around to look at her—her long, thin legs folded before her as she sat on the bed. "What will happen to that church?" he asked.

"It will stay open."

"Yeah, but for how long? I mean, it's not like they won't go ahead with the casino, right? It's not like we stopped anything, is it?"

She recognized the desperate look on his face. "Do you want to stay and try to stop it?" It seemed an unlikely choice—but she found she was in the opposite place from him: After today, she was eager for anything.

"But what would be the point of stopping it?" he said, flinging his arms in the air. "What would we be saving? Pawnshops, and abandoned buildings, and"—he kicked the dresser—"and, and, a church no one even goes to . . ."

"There are things worth saving there," she told him. "There are things worth saving anywhere."

"But it's all over now—and it's all still there. What was the point—of any of it?"

"I'm here, aren't I?" she answered. "It's not all over."

"Oh? So what happens now?"

"I don't know," she said. And then she added, hopefully, "We'll see."

He looked at her: blond hair frizzing, face pale without its makeup, black eyes, lanky frame, surgically perfect nose—brilliant, introverted mind—all her baggage. Did she really think it was so simple? That the two of them would just go off together? And what did she imagine they would be? A couple? He hadn't been looking for a new relationship—was that what she wanted? Would that be enough, after all of this? And how would it work between them? What if he disappointed her? What would that represent? What if it ended the way all his other relationships had? Or what if his visions made a life together impossible? And would there be more visions? And if there weren't, would that mean success or failure? That he had fulfilled God's plans or not? And how could you ever be certain God had a plan? When did it stop?

When did you know?

V. THE DESERT, THE OCEAN

Jonah walked from the room in the Aces High, through the parking lot—past the motels and bus stops and vacant lots—across a final strip of highway—and into the desert. He walked until the last of the road sank into the heat shimmer of the horizon behind—and Jonah saw in every direction the unbounded desert—the scrub clinging to its face giving its tracts the look of a vast, sealike rolling. And he lay down with his back on the scorched sand and with his face toward the sun, relentless and colorless—and he unfurled for the Lord his sorrow: "I never knew what it meant to be a man of God. I don't know what I've done, and whether it was according to your will or not. I don't know what the world is, and when I see you in it, it's only in glimpses. And there is so much more in the world I know is not you. How can I live in a world I can't comprehend? How can I serve a God whose will I can't understand? It would be better for me to die than to live." And as a cloud moved across the dome of the sky, a shadow was cast across Jonah's face—and in the cool of this shadow Jonah felt a final mercy—felt all that was best in life—all that was good, and all that was holy—and in a few moments the sun had climbed higher and the cloud drifted away and the shadow was gone—and God said to Jonah, Is there not so much more under heaven than shadow?

And Jonah rejoined our vast and mysterious world.

ACKNOWLEDGMENTS

It's a privilege to have the opportunity to thank a few of the many people without whose assistance *The Book of Jonah* would not have been possible. I am forever indebted to Susan Golomb for seeing something in my writing and for supporting it in innumerable ways, as well as to Terra Chalberg, Eliza Rothstein, Soumeya Bendimerad, and Krista Ingebretson. Gillian Blake, my tireless and extraordinary editor, Stephen Rubin, Maggie Richards, Kenn Russell, Kathy Lord, Caroline Zancan, and the rest of the team at Henry Holt were fantastic partners in the creation of this book.

Michael Ellis and Lauren Popper Ellis provided valuable early feedback, and Sheila Dvorak Galione's insights were essential, as they've been for as long as I've known her. Caroline "Rolls" Hailey, Leslie Geddes, and Michael Geier helped ensure the characters could speak, and swear, correctly in a variety of languages. I am also grateful to everyone at the Catholic Charities of Southern Nevada for opening a window on the admirable work they do every day.

I was extremely fortunate to have had teachers—in the public schools of Amherst, Massachusetts, at Columbia University, and at Oxford University—who made it their business to give me a good education. This book is a testament to their hard work. I'm even more fortunate to have the family I do—people who supported and encouraged me in my writing when the rest of the world didn't even know I was doing it. Mom, Dad, Jon, Sarah, Aleigh, Jeff, Grandma, my aunts, uncles, cousins, niece and nephews, and in-laws—thank you for being there. The memories of my aunt Ruth, my aunt Franny, and my grandpa Harry were inspirations in completing this book. I also want to express my gratitude to my friends, all of whom are brothers and sisters to me, too.

Finally, the greatest good luck I ever had was at the old Yankee Stadium in August 2004, when I sat down beside a woman who has filled my life with joy and adventure ever since. Julie, without your generosity of spirit, your faith, your intelligence, this book could not have been written. I don't know if I can ever find a way to thank you for that—but I'm grateful I have a lifetime to try.

ABOUT THE AUTHOR

JOSHUA MAX FELDMAN is a writer of fiction and plays. Born and raised in Amherst, Massachusetts, he graduated from Columbia University, and has lived in England, Switzerland, and New York City. This is his first novel.